What Do You Fear?
Book 2: Evil Lives

Thank you Alex
I hope you enjoy the
stories

What Do You Fear?
Book 2: Evil Lives

E. L. Jefferson

ACKNOWLEDGEMENTS

Thank you to my friends for all your support

DEDICATION PAGE

This book goes out to everybody out there that's still fuckin' up.

One meets destiny often on the road taken to avoid it.
French Proverb.

TABLE OF CONTENTS

Is it really, never too late to ask for forgiveness? If you feel you need to, do not let fear hold you back.

A STRANGER CALLS

Asister desperately needs to talk to her brother; it has been months since they have last spoken or seen each other. Starting with their mother, Elana has called everyone she could think of who might know the whereabouts of her brother Eric. She does not care that they have not spoken, or seen each other in a while. She loves him dearly, and now frantically searches for him. She knows her time is running out.

It is only a matter of days before it will be too late. On the third day of her search, her mother gave Elana a number to call. It is for an old female acquaintance of her brothers; that their mother recently ran into. Elana calls the number that this friend gave her, it is the last number she had for her brother Eric. When she calls the number, she is pleased and relieved to hear his voice.

"Hello Eric speaking."

"Eric this is Elana, how have you been big brother? I've been trying for days to contact you. Why haven't you called me, Eric?" she says excitedly

"Hey sis how have you been? It's good to hear your voice. I've been doing ok; I just started a new job at a warehouse in Forestville. So I've been busy with that."

"Eric, you need to call me. I've missed you". She smiles as she says those words.

"I've missed you too baby girl, my friend told me she saw Ma. You of all people know how my life has been. I'm really trying to get my life together this time Lana. I am forty-eight and too old for the dumb shit I use to get myself into. I've got my own place now, and I'm working a good job."

"Eric that's wonderful and I'm glad to hear it, but you know if you ever needed help with anything I'm always here for you."

"I know Lana, but when do I stop leaning on my baby sister and her husband? I appreciate everything you've ever done for me Lana. I really do, and I'm man enough to admit that. I do plan to pay you back for everything you've done to help me. This new job is working out really well for me."

"You know it's not about that. I don't care about you paying me back anything. You're my brother and I love you. There are only two of us now, and we need to stick together."

"I know Lana; I just didn't want to come around you, until I was sure I had everything where it needs to be. I want you and Ma to be proud of me, as a brother and a son. I just want to clean up my act, because I don't see too many more chances coming for me."

"We've always been proud of you Eric, none of us had it easy growing up. It would have been a hell of a lot harder if we didn't have you to protect us. Even in the hardest times we never forgot or stopped loving you."

"Thank you Lana, that really means a lot to me. Now I feel bad for not having called you or Ma before now."

"Please don't feel that way Eric, I understand and it's not a problem. I know you've spoken to Ma on occasion, but you're a hard man to find when you don't want to be found, even for her."

"I never could keep much from you, not even when we were kids. You always knew when something was up with me. I knew it wasn't much, but I would call Ma every now and then. Just to talk for a minute, I'd ask her not to tell you we'd spoken, until I was ready to call you. I wanted it to be a surprise when we did hook up. Now that we have, I want to take you and Ma to dinner this weekend." Eric feels great joy now as he speaks with his little sister.

"That would be great Eric, I know Ma would love that, and so would I. Eric, now that we have re-connected let me tell you why it was so urgent for me to find you."

"Sure Lana; whatever you need just say the word; and I'll take care of it."

"Good Eric, because what I have to say may be difficult for you to hear."

"Go right ahead Lana, I'm all ears."

"Eric, Sherman is dying, and he wants to see you before it's too late, before he dies." There is a long pause between the siblings. For a long while, Eric says nothing. He heard what his sister said, but he does not know exactly what his response should be. He lets her words

2

sink in as he considers his response to her inquiry. "Eric are you still there? Did you hear what I said?"

"Yeah, Lana I heard what you said; I honestly don't know what to say to that. You know exactly how I feel about that motherfucker." His temporary joy turns to anger.

"I know Eric but he's dying and in a lot of pain. He's been asking to see you for days. It seems he can't stop asking about you."

"Fuck him! His pain is nothing compared to what we went through. Lana you know I love you, and I'd do anything in the world for you, you know that. But as far as I'm concerned we never had a father, and I don't give a fuck if that sorry piece of shit nigga dies today or tomorrow!"

"Eric please, hear me out. I know hearing that must have been hard for you. But can't we let the past go. I used to feel the same way you do, but over the years, I've learned to let those feelings go. I don't forgive him anything; there was a time when I hated him as you do. There was a time when I would have liked to hurt him for leaving us too. But I can't live with hate in my heart for the rest of my life. The man is dying Eric, can't we put our bad feelings aside in this case."

"Have you gone to see him already?" Her brother asks.

"Yes, I've been to the hospital two times. I've even met three of his other children."

"He has other children! That motherfucker has at least three other kids? Hell, I don't know why I'm surprised. To be honest with you Lana, I really don't want to hear any more about his ass or his other kids."

"I know I'm asking you a lot Eric, but can you find it in your heart to go see him. Eric, just go see him one time, for only a few minutes?"

"Lana, I really can't understand why this is so important to you. Has that bastard ever tried to contact any of us? What the fuck did he ever do for any of us including Ma? So what he's dying, and now he wants to see his kids. What the fuck kind of bullshit is that? When he could have been with us our whole damn lives, he chose not to be. Now the motherfucker is dying and daddy wants to see his kids."

"Eric trust me. I do know how you feel, and I can't make you do this. Just hear me out one last time, don't do it for him, Ma, or yourself. Like you said, the hell with him, I do understand that. Eric I have always depended on you our whole lives. You have always been my hero of a big brother. You have always come to my rescue when I needed you. Even when you're not around, we are always connected. We have always been close after everything that's happened in our lives, and I cherish that. Please do this one thing for me, and for the family that we've lost. You're the oldest, and you represent us, so for Paul, Deborah, and Dolores please do this and I will never ask you for anything again."

"Lana this is that important to you?"

"Yes Eric it is, because I have accepted things the way they are, and I can forgive the past."

"Lana you always had a way of getting to me like no one else could. I guess you always will sis. If this means so much to you, I'll go see his dying ass, not for me, but for our family."

"Thank you Eric, this means a lot to me, I love you Eric."

"I love you too Lana."

"Do you want me to take you where he is?"

"No just tell me where he's at, and give me the room number. I'll make my way there tomorrow."

"Ok, call me at home if you want to talk afterwards. Even if you don't want to talk about him please call me."

"I will Lana. Talk to you later."

Elana gives her brother the name of the hospital, and his room number. She also tells him the hospital enforces visiting hours, because there are many terminal patients in the ward he will be visiting.

That night as he lies in bed, Eric thinks long and hard about the conversation he had with his sister. He cannot sleep even though he has been drinking since he hung up with her hours ago. Eric swore he would never touch alcohol again after the last incident he was involved in, but the news his sister gave him has taken a toll on him. In spite of all he has been through and all the shit, he knows he has put her through. She loves him without condition. He has conflicting feelings about what she asked him to do. Although he hates it, he knows he will do as she asked, only because he loves her. He eventually goes to sleep, once he justifies in his own mind, a more personal reason for paying Sherman a visit.

The next evening at 8:00 p.m., Eric finds himself standing outside the hospital where his father is dying. A friend at the warehouse gave him a ride after work. He decides to walk in before he changes his mind. He intentionally chose to come late in the evening just before visiting hours terminate at 9:00 p.m. He doesn't want to be in that man's presence any longer than he has to be. Eric tells himself that no matter how long he stays, he kept the promise that he made to his sister. He walks in without checking in at the front desk, and goes straight to the elevator. He takes it up to the eighth floor, and follows the numbered signs to room 821. Eric approaches the hall leading to his father's room. It is located at the end of the corridor. He notices four people leaving that same room. He sits down in a chair across from the empty nurse's station. Eric discreetly watches the four individuals as they approach him, sign out on the visitor's log, and quietly pass him on their way to the elevator. The four do not speak to each other, as they walk together, holding hands, but Eric notices the profound sadness they each show on their faces. Tears falling from both the women's eyes as they try to control the sadness they feel. The men with them try to appear stoic, but the sadness easily shows through.

After they get on the elevator, and the doors close, Eric walks over to the visitor's log, and reads the names of the four people who just left Sherman's room. He notes that all four signed the log as Sherman's children, and they didn't stay very long according to the log times. Walking down the corridor, Eric notices that there is an unnerving smell in the air on this floor. For some reason a voice in his mind tells him it's the smell of death. That thought does not bother him; in fact, it almost gives him a sense of comfort. That maybe Sherman is dead, and he won't have to deal with him.

What the fuck, Eric thinks to himself. The motherfucker got to see his other kids before he died. Eric stops at the closed door, not sure, if he wants to walk in or not. His heart is beating slightly faster than it should, and he even feels himself tremble a little. He closes his eyes, takes a deep breath, opens his eyes, and walks in the room. The first thing he notices in the dimly lit room is the smell; a sickly combination of antiseptic and the death smell he noticed earlier. He looks past the empty bed closest to him, and stares at the occupied bed. Eric stares at the sleeping figure, and decides that at one time he was a good-sized man in his youth. The man now appears quite frail, IVs and monitors hooked up to his body. The monitors make no sound, but

Eric can see the electronic pulses and other activity on the screens that monitor the man's vital signs. Indicating that he is not dead yet. Eric looks from one monitor to the next; one in particular catches his attention. It says Morphine Drip Control Unit. All three monitors though show some signs of life in the now frail man lying in the bed. He stares at the old man lying there and thinks, he himself, looks nothing like that old bastard. Eric thinks that their only similarity is their height and size. Eric slowly walks over to the bed, takes away one of the two chairs on the right side and sits down. Eric stares at the two remaining chairs on the far side of the bed. No doubt, his other children sat in a circle around him as they visited him. Eric sits beside the bed and stares at the man lying there. Hundreds of questions race through his mind. Years of questions, he needs answers to. He wonders if even a fraction of them can be answered here tonight, before this motherfucker checks out. He decides that it doesn't really matter. Nothing this old man can say to him is going to matter or change a damn thing. He decides to leave after only a few seconds of looking at the dying old man. Having kept his promise to his sister, Eric wants to leave. He tells himself he saw the motherfucker before he checked out. Conversation is neither desired nor required. Eric stands, turns toward the door, and begins to walk away when his father speaks.

"Son, is that you? Eric, is that you son? Please sit down." Eric turns toward the man's voice, looks at him, and slowly returns to his seat. The elder man holds out both his hands, and begins to open his arms as if he wants to hug Eric. Eric sits down and does not move he is repulsed by the thought of touching him, and the smell that lingers over him. Ignoring the gesture, he simply stares at the man in the bed. "Son can you please give me a hug? I miss you son."

Eric notices Sherman's voice is still rather strong for a man in his condition, not broken or soft, but it seems to hurt him to speak louder than he is. As if, there is a problem with his throat. Then Eric notices the small bandage just below his Adams Apple. "I don't want to hug you." Eric says, as he looks in his father's eyes. Sherman puts his arms down, obviously hurt that his son does not want to touch him. He continues speaking to his son.

"Son, you're my oldest, there is so much I want to tell you, and talk to you about before it's too late. Your sister was here a few days ago. We had a good visit, she really grew up into a good woman, and I only wish she had a grandson for me to hug as well."

Sherman looks at his son, and continues speaking in a strained voice due to his pain.

"You see son, I'm dying of renal failure, and the doctors say I'm too old for a kidney transplant, so I can't get on any of the donor lists. The best they can do for me is managing my pain. I only have one kidney with partial function, and son you wouldn't believe the pain I have. Sometimes it's so bad I can't take it anymore. Son, I have a big favor to ask of you. Would you agree to be tested, to see if we would be a match for a kidney transplant? I need a kidney son, and the only way that's gonna happen is if one of my male children donates a kidney to me. I don't want to die son. Would you please help me, would you do this for your father?"

Eric stares at Sherman dumb founded, not sure what to say to him, if anything. Then Eric notices something in the old man's aged eyes as he speaks; something that is very familiar. A look Eric has seen all his life but could never give it a name. It stirs very negative feelings in him, and it pisses him off. Looking at Sherman and listening to the bullshit he just ran down on him, Eric decides he will have the conversation with him he has always wanted to have.

"Old man just who the fuck do you think you are! My head is all kind of fucked up listening to you. What the fuck makes you think I give a damn about you dying of anything. I haven't seen or heard from you in how long? My whole fuckin' life and you have the balls to ask me for a fuckin' kidney. I'm your oldest; there is so much you want to talk to me about, so much you need to say to me. Because you're dying, you think that gives you that right, after all these fuckin' years, to claim fatherhood for a son you abandoned years ago. After all this damn time, I'm supposed to embrace you as my father and help you. Give you one of my kidneys. Old man you must be delusional, or that shit they have you on has you tripping. To think I would be stupid enough, to agree to some shit like that, and believe me, I'm far from stupid. Now I totally understand why you wanted to see me so damn desperately. I know you didn't tell Lana that bullshit about you needing me to donate a kidney to your ass. She would have told you to go straight to hell. I don't know how long your ass has been here dying, but I would probably be right in guessing all your other male children, and who the fuck knows how many that is, told you to go straight to hell too. Otherwise, I wouldn't be here, well you can add my name to the list too motherfucker, fuck you! Before I leave here though, I have a hell of a lot to say to you." Eric feels the anger within reaching the boiling point. "First of all, what the fuck do you know about my sister or me for that matter? Hell, what about the three of us who are gone, my brother and two sisters who aren't here anymore? And don't call me son again, I'm not your fuckin' son and I never have been," Eric responds.

Sherman starts to call Eric son again but catches himself. "Eric, please there is so much I want to tell you about my past. I know your upset with me and you have a right to be, but there are things you don't know. I'm still your father whether you like it or not, and we need to talk. So would you please give me a chance and listen to me, please? I'm begging you son."

"Hold the fuck up! You're still my what? Did you say you're my father, so I have to listen to you! Old man who the fuck do you think you're talking to an idiot? Motherfucker you haven't been shit to me, or any of my sisters or my brother in over forty years! The only reason I'm here is because now, after all these decades you need something from me." Eric responds angrily. Eric at this moment is trying with all his might to contain the fury he feels. He now knows the only way to get rid of what he is feeling is to tell this man, who calls himself his father, exactly what's on his mind, and what he feels in his heart.

"You know, I honestly don't know where to start with you. Let me tell you something off the break. Before you get shit twisted, and all fucked up, you need to know that I feel exactly nothing for you old man. The only reason I brought my black ass here is because I promised my sister Lana I would. I love her with all I have in me, and I promised her I would come see your dying old ass." Eric pauses briefly to allow himself to calm down.

"If that is how you feel then please leave Eric, I see we have nothing to talk about, and you're not going to help me no matter what I say," Sherman says as he looks away from Eric.

Eric stands and points at Sherman, then holds his fist inches away from Sherman's face. "Oh hell nah, Old man! You don't get rid of me that easy. I'm gonna be here now for a while. Everything in me that's fucked up is about to be released on your dying ass tonight goddamnit!

And you're right. You can forget about the kidney thing." Eric says to Sherman in a menacing voice. Sherman looks up at his son standing over him and speaks.

"I'm dying Eric, can't we make peace, can we do that please." Sherman pleads.

"Fuck no! I have a lifetime of fucked up experiences to tell you about old man, and you're gonna listen if it takes all night."

Sherman reaches for the intercom on his bed to call the duty nurse. He wants Eric removed from his room. Eric stops him and whispers something in Sherman's ear. Sherman looks into his son's eyes and puts the intercom down. At that moment a very young looking nurse making her rounds enters the room. She informs Eric that visiting hours are over, and that all visitors are required to leave now. Eric walks to the foot of Sherman's bed, stands there, and stares at him.

"Nurse this is a friend of my family, I haven't seen him in a while, there is no one else in the room but us. Is there any way he can stay with me a while, my youngest daughter was allowed to stay overnight with me a few days ago. Please nurse, I don't have much time?" asks Sherman.

"That would be ok as long as you feel up to it Mr. Sherman. I'm going off duty now so I tell you what; I just won't let the duty nurse know you have a late visitor. Good night Mr. Sherman, I'll see you in the morning." Responds the nurse as she turns to walk away. Sherman replies that he will be fine and the nurse leaves the room. Eric returns to the seat he was in after the nurse leaves the room.

"Now old man, before we get this going, what exactly is it you want to say to me?" asks Eric

"Eric, I just want you to know that I love all my children. I'm sorry for not being there for you when you were growing up. Eric back then things were different. I was different, and I was young, and didn't understand what it was to be a father. For that mistake I have felt shame all my life. Can you understand what I'm saying son, can you find it in your heart to forgive me?"

Eric says nothing at first as he stands and approaches the bed. He takes the beds control and raises the bed to almost ninety degrees, and he sits at the foot of the bed, looking at his father.

"That's the best you can do, can I forgive you, and you're sorry. I have a better question, why should I forgive your sorry ass? I don't know, or even remember you, but I know this. I sure as hell remember every moment of my life without a father being there with us. I remember every night my mother went to bed crying, because it was such a struggle for her to take care of us on her own. I remember her not abandoning us when she could have done the same shit you did. I remember the pain she felt each time one of her children died. I remember her getting beat by a sorry ass boyfriend, and I was powerless to help her. She hung in there and sacrificed her whole life for us. So to ask me to forgive your ass for abandoning us is one more slap in the face to me, and my family. Before you die, I want you to know what it was like for us growing up. I'd like to be here when you breathe your last useless breath. I want the satisfaction of watching you die helpless and useless. The way vulnerable children are helpless, when they have no one there to protect and guide them. Before that happens though you need to know what our lives were like. I honestly don't know where to begin old man, so we'll start with my first memories of grade school. I'll tell you this too old man; you will listen to every goddamn word I have to say to you, even if it takes all fuckin' night."

Sherman can say nothing, he can do nothing, and he is totally helpless. His son talks and his life sign monitors quietly track his vital functions. His heart monitor reacts occasionally, as he listens to his son. He simply sits in his bed; sitting up in the position his son put him in. The pain he feels in his back he keeps to himself. He wishes now that he had never asked to see his oldest child. He had not anticipated there would be so much fury, in the man who now sits at the foot of his bed. Sherman had hoped all his children would embrace him in his final hours, he was wrong. He has never been in any of their lives for any significant amount of time. He wanted to die knowing that they had forgiven him, and that they had some degree of love for him. He wanted so badly to be acknowledged as their father; to share some small part of lives he had nothing to do with cultivating, before death takes him. He also realizes that most, if not all, of the hatred directed at him now is partly his own fault. So he decides with his last bit of strength to listen to the story this man, who he cannot embrace as his son, has to tell.

"Do you have any idea what it's like to sit in a classroom full of kids your age? Kids that are not related to you, at a new school, say around six years old. The teacher asks each child to stand, and say their name. Then to tell the class What their father does for a living. Before the teacher got to me all the kids proudly talked about what they knew of their fathers work. I remember it even being a little funny. Six year olds trying to describe an adult's job they know nothing about, and the teacher playfully helping them along.

Well there wasn't a damn thing funny about what I had to say when it was my turn to speak. I remember every word I said, and how I said it. Being six years old, I proudly stood up; put my hands at my side. Looked around the class as I said my name smiling, and said with a child's innocence. I don't know what my daddy do. He don't live wit us, my mommy say he ain't shit. All the children put their hands over their mouths and ears, and I didn't know what to think. The teacher immediately stood up and shouted 'Eric! Go to the back of the room and stand in the corner!' That came with a smack across the ass, as the bitch escorted me to the corner. Where I was made to stand until lunch hour, and I had no idea what I had done to be punished, and humiliated like that. Then I had to eat by myself because the teacher wouldn't let any of the other kids sit with me. Now, I don't know how many babies you have in the world, or how many of them you actually had a hand in raising. But kids can be extremely cruel to each other. That's something else I learned quickly after I started going to school. I remember telling my mother about that day in school after I got home; she hugged me and told me I had done nothing wrong. I clearly remember her saying to me. Baby it's not your fault, I don't want you to be ashamed of anything. Your daddy didn't want to stay with us, but it's ok, because we have each other, and I will take care of our family. I do remember her taking me to school the next day and going to that teacher's ass. Ma didn't go at her physically, but with words. I learned two very important lessons that day, that my mother was my protector, and never to talk about your sorry ass in public, if it could be avoided. You see old man, I learned at an early age how fucked up it was to not have a father around. There were other kids in my situation, and we learned to keep certain shit to ourselves. The strange thing about that is, we could look at each other, and somehow we knew that we were the fatherless children. We were the kids who were not good enough to be friends with children who had both parents. We were the fuckin' outcasts, even in our own schools and neighborhoods."

Sherman says nothing. He simply listens to his son, sadness showing all over his face, and the pain in his back growing more intense, and moving down his legs.

"Then motherfucker there were the times the school would have activities. Like fathers coming to lunch day. Father son activities day, bring your father to school day, father son dress alike day, father son field trips and shit that I wasn't allowed to go on because of you. Back then schools incorporated a lot of activities around the family. All that father son shit, and you're sorry fuckin' ass was nowhere to be found. We had to carry that shame. Now mom did her best to be with all of us when she could, for school functions, but she had to work. Since we lived with our grandparents, on occasion grandfather would come to a function, if he could. It was nice being with him. I'd walk next to him proudly holding his hand. My little chest full of pride, and it felt good because I had a man with me too, like everybody else, a real life grown man. But I would always see that fuckin' look in every body's eyes. The kids, the fathers, and the fuckin' teachers all had that look in their eyes. That look that says you don't have a father and I do. That look that said to me your old grandfather is not your real daddy. That your one of those fatherless kids, and I'm not, and I'm better than you. I learned to spot that arrogant, conceited look in people's eyes, that look that says I'm better than you and your nothing. But you know something; my grandfather gave me the key to get over all that bullshit. He explained to me in very simple terms, I didn't have to try so hard to make people like me, or except me. Either they would, or they wouldn't, so to hell with them. You just find something your good at, and be the best at it, and when you make real friends you'll know, because they'll always be there for you and you for them. It broke my little heart when grandfather died a year later. I remember thinking another man, my grandfather left us all alone again, and it hurt like hell. But at least he was there for us my whole life up to that time. Shortly after he died though other things changed for us, and I didn't know why until years later, but I'll come back to that. But before grandfather died I made him proud, because I quickly learned what it was I was good at, fighting and academics. Grandfather and I would spend hours watching boxing matches. I'd listen to him talk about the great fighters of his day. He would even show me a lot of different moves, and explain to me why they worked or didn't. We would go to the local gym, and watch the fighters train. We would be there for hours on the weekends. I started training and working with the fighters and I loved it. I took that shit and I learned to fight the hard way, in the streets. After taking a few ass kicking's I got good at it real fast. For every beating I took, I learned from the guys at the gym what I did wrong, and corrected it. This would cause me no end of trouble later in my life. But in time I became the defender of my family because we had no one else to protect us. I also learned quickly that grandfather was right about something else. After I learned I really had a talent for my schoolwork, I soon became a star pupil. And in time nobody cared, I didn't have a father like they did, because I had something they didn't. I could hold my head up high because I was smarter than them. I took great pride in the fact that many kids hated that about me, and my brother and sisters, but because I could also kick the shit out of many of them nobody fucked with us. Mom was always so proud of the grades we brought home, our papers and report cards always made her smile. But you know another thing we, the fatherless children learned. We were always among the smartest kids in any class throughout school. I never could figure that one out, my brother and sisters included were very talented students. As were most of the other fatherless children, I've ever met growing up. Many of us fucked up royally later in life. We did lack a serious component in our lives though, any fuckin' idea what that could be old man? Eric directs that question at Sherman and he says nothing, only the deep sadness in his eye responds for him. Eric continues. Another thing that I've always had is one hell of a memory, which allows me to relive this shit over and over again. For instance, like how the holiday gatherings were occasions we use to look forward to. Suddenly all that shit changed after Grandfather died. You still with me old man? You need to listen to this shit, I'm about to tell you some real shit." Eric states. Sherman responds by nodding his head, the pain in his back and legs getting worse.

"Eric would you please lower the bed just a little, my back is starting to hurt." He pleads.

"Fuck you and your back; I'm not going to let your ass go to sleep on me. And the pain in your back is nothing compared to the pain we've suffered, so your just gonna have to man the fuck up and deal with the shit. The same way we were forced to deal with our pain.

Hit that damn morphine drip button, you'll be alright." Eric tells his father. "As I was saying family gatherings used to be fun at first, because it gave us a sense of belonging within the family, that my family was accepted for who we were. I started out truly loving all the grown-ups as only a child could. I looked up to every adult in the family who would come to picnics, cookouts, and holiday dinners, until some shit kicked off at one particular Christmas dinner that I would never forget. I really thought those bastards cared about us, then after grandfather died I learned that the only reason we were tolerated was because of him. Can you imagine what it's like when a child enters a room full of his aunts, uncles, and adult cousins? And he is referred to as one of Donnas Little Bastards. The adults would smile and laugh when they'd say that shit, so I thought it was a good thing at first. Do you know what it's like when you're told to leave a room your other little cousins can enter? They are welcomed and not talked about like animals, especially when your mother is not there to see it or hear it? Of course the child doesn't know at first, their talking about him, and his family in a fucked up way. Then you realize that you're treated differently than other kids in the family, and you don't know why. You're given different foods from the other kids when your mother is not around. Certain family members don't want you around their own kids. The presents we got at Christmas, if any, from those fuckers were a joke compared to other kids in the family. I remember one specific year; I was ten years old. It was time for the children to open gifts from family members. All the other children got really nice toys, and other presents. My mother gave very expensive toys and gifts to her sister's and cousins children. Among the adults, it had been pre-planned who was going to buy what for whom. Now Ma only ever got one or two nice toys and clothes for each of us. That was fine. There were five of us. Well on this particular fuckin' Christmas day. I clearly remember my family sitting at our mother's feet, at my aunt's house after we ate dinner. We watched as gifts were exchanged back and forth among all the adults, and kids in the family. There were a lot of children. I remember the excited looks, and smiles on all the kid's faces as they opened their gifts, and screamed out with joy. I remember the gifts from my mother to those other little motherfuckers, and at that time those were damn nice toys and other gifts. I remember my brother and sisters sitting there waiting patiently for our gifts from the family. Waiting for our presents to come around, we watched for damn near an hour. As the pile of wrapped gifts got smaller and smaller, not one of our names was called to get one. My mother bought all that shit for other motherfuckers, and not one of them even got her a gift. I remember Uncle Butch had to go back to Grandmother's house just to pick that shit up. Uncle Butch himself gave out four new bikes. We looked at Ma, and none of us could hold back the tears. My mother jumped up and said, 'What the hell is going on here! Where are the things for my kids?' Eric smiles as he recalls his mother saying that. You know what those rotten motherfuckers said to her. Her sisters, aunts, uncles, and cousins, all them motherfuckers had the nerve to tell her that they were gonna take care of us later. My grandmother was in tears, and so were we. I watched my mother turn into the Incredible Hulk on those motherfuckers. Close your eyes old man while I describe what happened next. Picture my mother in action, defending her family, against a bunch of sorry ass no good no fuckers, who would purposely treat children that way. To do what you're sorry ass wasn't around to do. My mother stood there for a second, taking in what her own sister said about taking care of us later, and the look on her face turned menacing. When Ma spoke she was pissed. Oh, hell no!, you niggers must be out of your goddamn minds, if you think I'm gonna take this kind of shit from any of you motherfuckers. I do what we all agreed to do, and you motherfuckers think I'm gonna let you get away with this shit. I could have spent my money on my own kids if I had known you fuckers were gonna pull this shit. I'll be damned if I let any of you treat my kids this way. She called the names of everyone she bought a gift or toy for. Ma told those little bastards, and the older teenagers to give her shit back. Those who didn't respond she went to them; the fury in her eyes was like fire. No one said shit, or tried to stop her. Throughout the house she went and took her gifts back. She cursed every adult in that motherfucker out along the way. All except my Grandmother and Uncle Butch, who himself was disgusted by what they had done to us. I learned something else about my mother that day. How strong she could be, and that they were afraid of her. I had never heard my mother really curse, or even seen her angry, but when she went off on those fuckers, not one of them made a move to stop her, or even said shit back. Now uncle butch had her back because they were always

15

close, and he was like a surrogate father to us. I don't think that is what really kept their asses from getting stupid though. They realized how ugly they really were, and how fucked up it was to pull that shit on my mother and us. My grandmother told everyone there, that if grandfather were here they never would have pulled that stunt on Ma. The old dude was really feared and respected by everybody in the family. I later learned that growing up Grandfather favored my mother since she was the youngest of his daughters; I guess many in the family always resented that, so they took the shit out on us. My mother gathered us up; we got our coats, and got the fuck out of there. Uncle Butch walked Grandmother to the car, loaded all those toys, and shit in the car. Then when we were ready to go, he started, then turned off the car, and went back inside my aunt's house. About five minutes later he came out that motherfucker with two of the bikes he had brought over there. He tied them to the hood of his car and we got the fuck away from there. Did you know that the family predicted that we would all end up in jail, as prostitutes, or derelicts living on the streets? That's what they thought of us, my own fuckin' family. That was one of the last family functions we ever went to, our relationships with the entire sorry ass family changed after that. It would be years before I would even speak to any of those bastards again. Hey! old man open your eyes, did you see that, was my description vivid enough for you to picture that shit? Did that give you even a small idea of the kind of shit we had to deal with growing up?"

Sherman looks at Eric and he has no idea what to say to him. He knows there is nothing that he can say that will erase away the pain of those early experiences. He looks at Eric, and then turns his head away in shame as he speaks.

"I don't know what to say Eric, what would you have me do? I can't change the past, and I can't say I'm sorry enough about what you all went through."

"Your right about that old man but let me ask you a question, because what I told you is just the tip of the fuckin' iceberg. I want you to answer me this, if you could change your life from what it was, and instead been with us our whole lives as a father should be, would you?"

Sherman closes his eyes and opens them; he looks at Eric and gives him his answer.

"I'm too old to lie to you Eric, and in too much pain. I had a good life, and I've made many mistakes, as much as it hurts me to say this to you, I wouldn't change my life as it has been. Not even to be the father that you needed me to be. Or to the sixteen other children I have out in the world. Eric you don't understand how things where back then, you don't know how it was."

"Motherfucker then make me understand why you abandoned us. Tell me why you'd have kids, and then just say the hell with them. We needed your sorry ass, and now death is knocking on your fuckin' door. You show up now, and you need us for body parts. I can't believe this, to top it all off, you want us to forgive you. Is the answer the same for all your other children motherfucker or just us? Have any or all of them forgiven you for abandoning them? Besides the four people I saw leave this room, how many of your other children have forgiven your sorry ass? Did any of them feel sorry enough for your ass to give you a kidney, because you're dying?" There is a long pause between the two.

"Since you don't have an answer for me, it must have been hell no." Sherman says nothing and refuses to answer Eric's questions; the shame he feels prevents him from even looking at Eric. Eric looks at Sherman, and he feels a rage build within him that he has felt many times in his life. There is an internal struggle building within him, and he tries with all his might to control the thoughts and feelings he is experiencing.

"You lay your sorry ass there and you ask me to forgive you, how the fuck can you possibly think that I would ever do that. You know something old man, even if you would have lied about changing your life. I wouldn't have believed you. Obviously, your idea of being a man was to live your life as you pleased. Have goddamn babies everywhere, with absolutely no intention of taking care of them what so ever. Did you even know that two of my sisters and my baby brother are dead? Do you know how they died or when? I know you're sorry ass wasn't at their Funerals. Do you have any idea of the toll that took on Ma and the years it took her to get over their deaths? She had to watch three of her children die, no mother should have to deal with that, where the fuck were you when our lives unraveled? Let me tell you how they died, kids with so much potential trying their hardest to do the right thing. Living in the hood in Southeast D.C. Left to the mercy of the streets took a serious toll on all of us. I tried to protect us from a lot of that. I tried as hard as I could, but I wasn't able to protect us the way we needed. And in some cases the wrong way, I ended up causing my family a lot of pain going to jail, trying to do what I thought was right. Paul died when he was 17. He and two friends were going out to celebrate their High School Graduation. Paul was always a good kid, not getting into trouble like his older brother. The Air Force recruited him as a Communications Specialist; he was looking forward to starting his military career. Paul also planned on going to college while serving in the Air Force. He and his friends went to a movie to celebrate, and where heading to a pizza place afterwards. A truck hit the car they were riding in head on, while they were stopped at a fucking traffic light. Paul and the driver where killed instantly they told us. The young man who was riding in the back seat is now crippled for life due to his injuries. Did you even know that my brother is dead? Paul had so much to live for, and he was taken from us like that. The driver of the truck that hit their car wasn't even scratched. The fucker was a repeat offender with multiple drunken driving convictions. He had no insurance, and no compassion for the three young lives he ruined. In court, that bastard showed no remorse or regret, his lawyer portrayed the innocent victims as the guilty parties. They portrayed it like it was my brothers, and his friend's fault they were stopped at a fuckin' light when he smashed into them. That motherfucker got off with a slap on the wrist again, I said fuck that, I eventually caught up to him. I dealt with his ass my way. I made sure he'd never kill another young person because he got off on getting fucked up drunk, and getting behind the wheel of a car."

Sherman looks at Eric and asks him what he did to the other driver.

Eric tells Sherman it's none of his fuckin' business. Like the number of children he has out in the world that he never cared about, but needs now. When Eric speaks, it is with a fury that sends Sherman's heart into overdrive.

"What happened to the driver that killed my baby brother is none of your fuckin' business." Eric tells Sherman to shut up and listen to how his two younger sisters died.

"Deborah and Delores were crushed by Paul's death, and so was I. We did our best to move forward with our lives the way Paul would have wanted. The girls were doing much better than me, for a while it looked like they would be fine. But it seemed that bad luck always found a way to fuck with us. Years later Deborah was diagnosed with, and died from ovarian cancer; she was a nurse and engaged to be married to a good man.

She was on a fast track to get her career going and start her own family. Then by the time we learned she had cancer, it had spread to the point that there was nothing that could be done for her. We were with her when she died; she went peacefully in her sleep at 27. Delores never really recovered from Deborah's death, as much as we tried our best to help her. They were very close, and when Deborah died, it's like a part of Delores died as well. What we didn't know at the time was Delores had turned to drugs big time. I suspected it, but by the time we found out what really happened she died of a drug overdose at twenty-nine. I was in jail at the time, for beating her sorry ass boyfriend nearly to death, for beating on her. I always suspected him of turning her on to the shit that killed her. I was allowed to go to her funeral, and then I spent the next two years in jail for assaulting the man who beat my sister. When I got out that motherfucker he was the first person I went to go see. Let's just say he'll never put his hands on anyone else's sister or daughter." Eric looks at his father and smiles, but the smile doesn't convey anything close to happiness.

Sherman looks at Eric and wishes that a nurse or a doctor would come into his room. This man who now sits at the foot of his bed terrifies him. There is a certain menace about him that is both frightening and foreboding. Sherman does not want to hear any more of these stories. These very tragic stories about people he never knew. Even if they are his kids, he can't change what happened, and he can do nothing about their lives or deaths. This is not the reason he wanted to see his oldest son. He wishes that he would just leave and let him die in peace. All Sherman wanted before he died, was to hear his kids say that they loved him, even if it wasn't true he just wanted to hear the words. Just maybe one of them would help him live a little longer. He sees something else in Eric's eyes now, and it terrifies him. It has nothing to do with love.

"What do you think so far old man? Do you have anything to say? I use to always wonder what our lives may have been like if our father was with us. Not anymore, but that thought would creep into my mind from time to time. Now I will grant you this, I have met people who hated their father, and the motherfucker lived with the family. He was usually an alcoholic, a deadbeat who wouldn't work. A junkie or women beater, because he wasn't man enough to do, what he needed to as a man or father. Motherfuckers like that did nothing but bring shame to their families. In many cases when a sorry fucker like that up and left, died, or got locked up, it was a cause for celebration. I already told you a little about how our lives have been; let me tell you a little about the woman you left behind with her five children. My mother is kind, loving, and generous, just as my Grandmother was. She did the best she could with us, and I give her all the credit in the world. She protected us, fed us, clothed us, kept a roof over our heads, and sacrificed for us. I can't say enough about her or praise her enough for the things she did for us. But I guess to someone like you that doesn't mean Jack-shit right. She didn't do anything more than what a mother is supposed to do for her children, right old man. Was that the secret to your plan? You would choose to fuck women who in your estimate would be fine raising children without your sorry ass, if they got pregnant? My mother got us all to adulthood and did a good job; fate is what fucked us over. Obviously, at least one of your other baby mama's did the same thing since I saw four more of your grown children earlier. Did you ask one of the men in that group for a kidney as well? I would have loved to have been here, and seen the look on your face when one or both of them told you to go to hell. I'm happy as hell my mother is still here, after all the shit she had to go through, but it damn sure wasn't easy. Old man my head is still fucked up about something though, I need to ask you a question, but first let me help you out with your lines."

Eric walks over to where Sherman's IVs are set up; he traces the power cords for the morphine drip, and the nurse station intercom and unplugs them. Sherman's eyes go wide, and he opens his mouth to say something then stops. He knows his words would have no effect on this man; Eric sits back in his seat.

"I noticed you pushing that damn morphine button a little too much, that shit must knockout the pain fast, but it doesn't last long does it. How does your back feel old man? I hope your pain won't become too unbearable, we still have a long way to go. Now the question I want the answer to is, where does a sperm donor get off calling himself a father? Can you please answer that for me?" Do that and I promise I'll get the fuck outta here, and let your old ass die in peace?" Sherman does not want to speak; the pain in his back is so intense now. He wants to scream out for someone to help him, any one, but he is afraid. He feels himself lose control of his bowels and he shits himself.

"Goddamn! Old man, did you shit on yourself? Damn you stink, but I'll be leaving soon, and someone will come clean your sorry ass up. Being helpless is a fucked up feeling isn't it old man? We still have more talking to do so deal with it."

Sherman understands Eric wants him to suffer, to humiliate him, but he can't understand what good his suffering will do to change anything; I'm dying Sherman thinks to himself

"Alright Eric I'll try to answer your question, but first, could you please plug my pain medication back in, and let me call a nurse to help me?" Sherman pleads in a painful voice, his eyes starting to water, and the feel of sitting in excrement is beyond humiliating.

"This is not a negotiation old man, and after you shitted on yourself I don't want to come anywhere near you. Answer my question, what makes a sperm donor think he's a father?"

"Eric I know I made some awful mistakes in my life, and I have many regrets. Like most men I've come to realize that while I can't make my mistakes go away. I can at least be man enough to say I was wrong. I know it doesn't make much sense to think that any of my kids would have feelings for me. Or to expect that any of the children I fathered over the years would want anything to do with me now. I held out hope that at least one of them would care a little, none of them did. Of the ones who chose to come you were the last to come see me. I held out some small hope that because you're my oldest son, that a bond would exist between us. That I at least would still feel it, and I did, I knew it was you as soon as you came in. You see Eric; dying makes a man take a long hard look at himself. The life he's lived and the mistakes he's made, I'm afraid son; I just don't want to die alone." Sherman pleads.

"Bullshit! Old man, you don't want to die period. You keep saying the same shit over and over again, and I'm glad your old ass is scared. And for the last damn time, there is no bond of any kind between us. You said to me earlier that you wouldn't change your life even if you could. You selfish motherfucker you don't regret one minute of not being with us. You want to use me, and you're other children for spare parts, like we're some kind of human parts store you can tap into when you need it. You not only have a lot of fuckin' nerve, it takes real balls for a motherfucker who no one has seen in decades, to come around now, and ask for help of any kind. That speaks volumes about just how arrogant and selfish you are, and probably always have been. So I'm not buying your explanation about your regrets, but you know who I would give all my organs to if it meant saving them?"

Sherman says nothing in response to Eric's question, but now tears of pain and humiliation start to fall down his face.

Eric looks at Sherman as the tears fall down his face; he feels absolutely nothing for him. "You disgust me old man, I don't give a fuck about you crying dude, and did you hear what I said."

"Yes Eric I heard you, but my back hurts so bad son. Please give me back my medicine and let me get cleaned up." Sherman pleads.

"I'll make your pain go away before I leave, but I'm not done with you yet old man. As I was saying; I'd give all my organs, and my life for my mother and sister, you on the other hand can kiss my ass. Which leads me now to tell you a little about how my life turned out; it wasn't very good at all. As smart as I am, I have accomplished only one real goal I set for myself. That goal was to watch over my family as much as I could, and to keep people from hurting them. If I couldn't stop it from happening, I damn sure took care of motherfuckers who did harm to us afterwards. Hey! Old man, would you like to know how that impulse became so deeply ingrained in me? Of course you do. Eric answers for Sherman and continues talking. Whether you want to hear it or not I'm gonna keep saying it because it's true, I did what you were not around to do. Shortly before we moved away from the safety of my Grandmother's house in Northeast D.C., an area we were all comfortable with. My mother met a man whose name I can't bring myself to say anymore. We moved to Southeast D.C., a neighborhood called Barry Farms, a part of the city that was for me, an eye opening experience from day one.

We were surrounded by violence and violent people everywhere. One of the most violent people I'd ever encountered, was the asshole my mother moved us in with. Of course it didn't start out that way. He was nice to all of us, at first, maybe three or four months in is when shit would change for the worst. And I would be changed forever. My Grandmother never liked that motherfucker, and she loved everybody, she had good reason to hate his bitch ass. That motherfucker use to beat my mother on a regular basis. I remember the first time I actually came face to face with that kind of violence. It scared the shit out of me. One night we were all in bed, but I couldn't sleep. That bastard had different times for each of us to go to bed; since Lana and I were older, we could stay up till 7:30 p.m. The younger kids had to be bathed and in bed by 7:00 p.m. That was his rule and even Ma couldn't change it, anyway on this one particular Sunday night I was wide-awake. I heard them come in from wherever it was they had gone that evening. They were arguing down stairs. It was then that I heard a sound I would never forget, the sound of my mother crying as he smacked and punched her. I instinctively jumped out the bed and ran downstairs. This motherfucker was standing over her, and she was pinned in a chair. His fist pulled back getting ready to hit her again, as he cursed her. Her mouth was bleeding and her eye was swollen. She was holding her arms up in a defensive position to ward off his blows. I shouted, don't hit her again!, I ran toward him crying tears of fury. I went right at his ass, he stopped me and pushed me down, and ordered me back to bed. My mother jumped out the chair and ran for me to protect me with her body. All the while she was telling that bastard not to hit me. He did anyway, and I fought back as hard as I could; which only made him hit me harder. He was a grown man. I was only a boy, I could do nothing much against him, and of course he knew it. After he got tired of hitting us he left the house after Lana came down stairs. She saw what was happening and she started crying. Lana shouted at him to stop. Lana and me went to Ma who was still crying, she hugged us and said everything was gonna be ok. She put us in the bed and I could hear her cry all night. That kind of shit went on for years, sometimes it got so bad we all would hide in our closets. We would stay there until he stopped hitting on her and the house went silent. Then one day when I was about fourteen and a little bigger, but nowhere near his size yet. I left my brother and sisters in the closet, and I said fuck this shit. You see Ma told us to hide their when he would go off on her. We'd sit their helpless and crying. But with each ass whooping I took from him it made me a little bolder, and a little harder. I told my brother and sisters to stay in the closet. I grabbed my baseball bat. Lana tried to stop me, but I pulled away and ran to their room. I could hear him smacking her. I ran in the room and right to his ass, it caught him off guard because he never expected that. I swung

23

my bat with everything I had in me, and caught his ass on the thigh; he screamed and went down like a fuckin tree. I was gonna bash his goddamn head in, but Ma grabbed the bat from me, I remember saying, I'm sick of you hitting her, but before she could get between us he caught me in the chest with a punch. Needless to say I went down from the blow, but I stopped him from beating her that night. You know years later I would see a movie called 'What's Love Got To Do With It' starring my boy Lawrence Fishburne, about the life of Ike and Tina Turner. The way Ike use to go off on Tina is the way that bastard would go at my mother. I actually had to walk out on the movie, because it brought back so many bad memories about that part of my life. As time went on Lana and me grew to hate that motherfucker with everything we had in us. I made no attempt to hide how I felt about him. He actually cared a great deal about Delores, Deborah, and Paul he never spanked them. If he had to punish them, it was extremely mild and involved no violence. While he'd kick the shit out of me, I wouldn't let him touch Lana; if she defied him, and he went to hit her I was right there fighting his bitch ass. You see every time he whooped my ass I would find a reason to fight in school. He didn't mind that so much as long as I won, and my grades stayed good. If my mother got called to the school about me fighting, when that bastard got home I'd be in trouble. I didn't care because every day I formed a plan to one day get his ass back. I also remember all the summer trips and vacations that motherfucker would take my younger brother and sister's on. Lana and me never went on any of them; we didn't want to do shit with him. Because he cared about my brother and sister's I knew they'd be ok with him and Ma. When they went out of town I'd ask Ma to take me to my grandmother's house. One day I came home from school and I saw Ma's face with a black eye. I was furious. She made me calm down, and said she would deal with it. She asked me to not go at him, for fear he'd actually hurt me. Also, that day I saw something in her face when she spoke to me that said she wasn't taking his shit anymore. That night I saw Uncle Butch's car parked in the alley by our house. I assumed he was visiting with Ma. After some time had passed, I heard a commotion outside, I got up to look out the window, and Uncle Butch was kicking that motherfucker's ass. It wasn't even close, he was either no match for my Uncle, or he was only good at beating on women and kids. My uncle beat his ass bloody, that bitch motherfucker got in his car and hauled ass. You see old man; my mother actually had love for that motherfucker. She paid a terrible price for it. She also got tired of him beating on her, and forcing sex on her. As I was becoming bolder and growing less afraid of him every day, it would only have been a matter of time before he did real damage to me, Lana, or Ma. So whenever that bastard even looked like he was about to get stupid I did what my Uncle Butch told me to do, call him. You see that pussy wouldn't fight a real man back, and every time I called my uncle he'd run like the bitch he was. That also taught me a lesson. Over the next few months, he moved out of our house, after taking a few more ass kicking's from my uncle. But he'd pay Ma visits when we were at school, because she'd have new bruises on her sometimes when we'd get home. The last time I saw her like that was the last fuckin' straw for me. A few weeks had gone by after his last visit, and nobody had seen his sorry ass. We assumed he was gone for good. He had taken all his shit, and I was fine with that. On one particular Saturday afternoon we were out back playing basketball, and that motherfucker's car pulls up. My two best friends and me were there, and when I saw him, I promised myself that he would never step foot in my house again. My mother and our neighbors were out back talking, and having a good time enjoying the summer day. When she saw him, her whole demeanor changed. I could see the fear on her face, and I said to myself, hell no! goddamnit, this shit ends today. I called my boys over and said that's the motherfucker right there I told yall about. Now we were all about the same age and size, but we were all fighters and a little crazy. They too had grown up to similar violent shit at home, but we were coming to an age and size where we didn't have to take it anymore. My call to battle was all it took, we just started grabbing shit, baseball bats, iron pipes, my boy had his nun-chucks, and we blocked that bastard's way. He told me to go get my mother for him, like we were bullshitin'. I said fuck you, your bullshit stops today you sorry piece of shit. My boys stood by my side. We were gonna T-off in his ass. He actually stood there for a minute looking at us trying to decide if we were serious. Then one of the adult men in the crowd that gathered said to him. 'I suggest you get in your car, and carry your punk ass away from here. Because if you're still standing after they go to your ass, your gonna have to deal with me.' That motherfucker looked at the man who said that, then at us again, and my mother. I saw real fear in his eyes for the first time, that look I never forgot. That bastard looked at me, and I said to him in a low voice that only we could hear. Don't worry motherfucker, we'll meet each other again, I owe you big time. He turned away, got in his car, and drove off. That day that motherfucker left us for good; it was the happiest day of my life. You can't imagine the power I felt when I was finally able to stand up to that piece of shit, and years later, we did meet again. We had it good for a long time after that. I vowed that I would never let another man get away with putting their hands on anyone in my family. As the years went by I gained a serious reputation as a fighter, and something of a problem solver. Which meant that violence was always involved? I made damn sure that anyone my sisters dated knew what time it was. That if any of them were stupid enough to hurt them, that I would fuck them up with a quickness. I tried not to interfere too much in their affairs, but sometimes my over protectiveness did get in the way. When it would get too bad Ma had a way of reeling me in, and I always listened to her. A few of those punks tried me, and paid the price, it also cost me as well. In the form of assault charges, and some lock up time, but I didn't care. You see old man I was doing my job as I saw it."

Sherman looks at Eric and his pain now is so great he actually starts to sob out loud like a baby. He hears every word Eric says to him, but his pain is so bad he finds it difficult to concentrate. The growing pain in his lower back and legs is unbearable, but he can do nothing. Eric notices the old man crying, and wonders if he should give him back his morphine. He quickly dismisses that idea, and decides to lower the bed until the old man feels some relief if any. Whether he does or not, Eric decides he will not get the drugs back.

"Look old man why the hell are you crying, the shit can't be that bad. I tell you what, I'll lower the bed a little how's that?"

"No Eric, I need my medicine, please let me have my medicine." Sherman begs Eric.

"I don't think so, you can handle a little pain, and it's nothing like the pain I had to deal with. Like the pain of losing sisters and a brother. Like the pain of seeing your mother hurt. Like the pain of going to jail for protecting your family. Like the pain of not being able to keep a girlfriend, or get a decent job. Like the pain of hopelessness, and squandered potential. Is this the kind of pain you feel old man? Because if it is let me know, and you can have all your shit back."

Sherman turns his head away and continues sobbing like a baby.

"Ok goddamnit! I'll lower the bed just a little, let me plug the shit back in first."

Eric plugs the bed in and slightly lowers it, knowing that what he's doing isn't helping Sherman's pain.

"Now getting back to what I was saying earlier, I graduated high school, but because I had a record for fighting I couldn't join the military. I was not gonna leave my family in the hood alone. My grades were good enough to get me academic scholarships, but again I had a police record for crimes of violence. So it didn't matter how smart I was, I couldn't use the money to go to school. I found jobs though, but they never lasted because I always thought I was meant to do something better, and honestly I didn't apply myself. I tried Job Corp for a while, but that didn't go anywhere. I tried to find work in the security field and in the Federal Government, none of that shit panned out because of my record. Then I became depressed and turned to the streets, and drugs to ease my pain. Nothing hard, just weed and sometimes booze, and with that came the fights and jail. Every time I thought shit couldn't get any worse for me, Lana was there helping me any way she could. Trying to find me work or giving me money when she got paid to keep me going. I almost never had a steady girlfriend. I found it hard to establish that kind of relationship with women. Oh I got my share of pussy, but every time in my life, when the right one would come along, it just wouldn't work for me. Sometimes because I'd put my family before them; and other times they felt I didn't have enough to offer them in the relationship. But you know what old man; I had no problem accepting that. I refused to be the kind of nigga that used and manipulated women. I damn sure never hit a woman, and I was gonna get mine on my own. I needed to prove to myself that I could be successful on my own. I had the intellectual ability so I knew I had a chance. You know a lesson I learned old man. From two of the sorriest fuckin' men ever to be in my life. You and the fucker we lived with. You two pieces of shit taught me two very important lessons, without really ever teaching me anything. One: how not to treat a woman, and two: that nothing is as important to me as my family. I sure as fuck won't thank you. Mom and Lana stuck by me though, and they continued to encourage me. I figured at one time, I'm still young so things can turn around for me at any time. You know what old man for a while they started to, I got a decent job working at McDonalds that had promotion potential. I decided I'd take one class a semester at a Community College. Academically it would have been a breeze for me, and it would have kept me off the streets and close to my family. But like I told you old man, fate had a way of fucking with us, and it was almost never for the better."

Eric stands up and moves toward Sherman. He stands at the side of the bed looking down on him as he speaks, he makes Sherman turn his head to face him, and tells Sherman to stop fucking crying.

"This you need to hear, and understand old man. One night I was returning home from work. On that day, I was promoted to Swing Manager, after only six months on the job. I was feeling quite proud of myself, and then guess who I had the fortune of running into? It was downtown Washington D.C., I was headed for my bus stop very late on a Sunday night. I turned a corner on Fourteenth Street where the old Towne Theater use to be. Then I ran into the motherfucker I most hated in the entire world besides you; the bastard that use to beat my mother and me. The one who I swore to pay back for all that hurt. Do you want to know what kicked off next old man?" Eric asks Sherman.

Sherman shakes his head as he speaks.

"Please, Eric you don't need to tell me, I don't want to know." Eric looks at Sherman and smiles.

"When that piece of shit and I came face to face we both froze. One thought ran through my mind, fuck him up, and that is exactly what I was going to do. I dropped my small tote bag to the ground, and stood right in front of him. It had been almost six years since I last saw him and in that time, I grew much taller, bigger, and stronger than him.

He was six-feet tall and I easily looked down on his bitch ass. Our eyes locked for only seconds, like two fighters in the ring staring each other down. I saw a look in his eyes that I had seen only once before. That look of fear I'd seen when my boys and I were gonna kick his ass. This time there was also panic in him, as if he wanted to run but something was forcing him to hold his ground. He should have run, because I wouldn't have chased him. Seeing him turn rabbit would have been satisfaction enough for me. He even had the nerve to try to talk to me, as if anything he would have said to me would have made any difference."

Eric tells Sherman what happens next.

"Hey Eric, how have you been?"

"Why do you give a fuck how I've been?" Eric responds, as he squares off on him.

"Look Eric you take it easy, I have to be somewhere, so I need to get going." He says with fear in his voice.

"Motherfucker you must be out of your mind. If you think, I'm letting you walk away from me. Remember, I owe you bitch."

At that moment Eric steps slightly to his left and throws a left hook at his face, Eric's full weight is behind the blow when it lands. Eric feels extreme satisfaction when he hears the sound of his jaw breaking, and he goes down to his knees. Eric brings his right foot back, and kicks him full force in the ribs with the tip of his boot. The force of the blow is such that it almost lifts him off his hands and knees; he gasps for air and falls on his back. There is no one around to witness the beating so Eric taunts him to get to his feet, and fight him back now that he's grown. He tries, knowing he must now defend himself or suffer a horrible beating. Eric continues to taunt him as his adversary forces himself to stand on shaky legs, while holding his burning ribs. He looks at Eric now with a fire in his eyes, and tries to attack, throwing, and missing a left jab he tries to follow-up with a right, but he doesn't have the strength, and the pain in his chest prevents him from executing the punch effectively. Eric easily avoids his clumsy attack, squares off in front of him, and lands a perfect left hook to the liver, followed with a right uppercut; he goes down again. This time he does not attempt to stand. Blood pouring from his mouth and nose Eric grabs him by the collar, pulls him to his feet, and throws another right hand to his face. He holds him up and hits him repeatedly. After many blows, he lets the limp body fall to ground. Eric walks over to where he fell and looks down on the helpless figure now bleeding at his feet. Eric remembers the beatings he suffered at this man's hands, the beatings his mother took at this man's hands, and the helplessness he felt for all those years. He looks at the piece of shit lying at his feet, and almost feels sorry for him now. But years of horrible memories, and mistreatment over power any compassion he would feel for this animal. Eric begins to stomp him mercilessly in his chest and abdomen, bringing down his foot with all the force he can muster. The man on the ground is gasping for air. Vomiting blood and other fluids, he is totally helpless. Eric stomps him to the body and face with both feet. When Eric stops his attack the man at his feet is barely breathing and cannot move. Eric looks down on him, and thinks to himself that he has vindicated his mother and his family by punishing this bastard for what he'd done to them. Leaving the man on the sidewalk to suffer in pain Eric retrieves his tote bag, and begins to walk away when a thought makes him stop. What if he tells the police, or comes back one day to seek revenge against your mother. Eric starts to panic but quickly recovers his senses, he realizes that there is no one around, and no one saw him beat this man into unconsciousness. The bus stop, cars, and trucks parked along the street hide the body from passing traffic. Nevertheless, Eric knows now he has to do something before someone finds his barely alive body on the sidewalk. Eric has an idea; just sit his ass in the bus stop on the bench. It's only about two feet away, and just leave him there. He grabs the man by the collar again, easily drags him to the bus stop bench, and sits him there. The man's body falls sideways on the bench, still un-conscience, and bleeding profusely from the nose and mouth. Eric also notices a pink fluid coming out of his ears and that makes him smile.

Eric starts to panic again knowing that this will not solve his problem, until he looks down the street and realizes that express buses travel very fast on this road at night and they don't stop at this location. They pass right by. All he has to do is wait for one and he can solve this problem. He can get rid of this bastard for good. Eric sits him up on the bench and waits. He sees a bus approaching from blocks away at a high rate of speed with only one headlight on, and he realizes this is a one-way street. The bus is coming fast as he gets himself ready, if he can time it just right he can throw this bastard under the bus just before it passes. Eric looks quickly down both ends of the sidewalk, it is dimly lit, but no one is walking toward him, and he sees no one across the street. He once again grabs the man by the collar, pulls him to his feet, and stands with him on the side of the bus stop that hides them from oncoming traffic. Eric is grateful that the bus stop is covered in movie posters, so he is all but invisible to the approaching bus.

He prepares to throw him in the street just before the bus passes. Eric thinks he must time this right; the bus is at the corner coming to his location fast. He knows it's going too fast to make a stop at his location. He readies himself. Eric pulls the man's body toward his chest preparing to throw it with all his might in the street. As the bus approaches his stop, he throws the body to the street headfirst, goes around the bus stop the opposite way, picks up his tote, and walks quickly away from the scene. Eric smiles as he hears the buses tires crush his head.

The look on Sherman's face and in his eyes convey disbelief, shock, and horror. Even through his pain, what his son has just told him is monstrous. Sherman looks at Eric and asks him a question.

"Eric, did you really kill that man, wasn't beating him enough?"

"Hell no it wasn't enough, I wanted to make that bastard suffer the way we suffered. When I realized he might come back at us later I had to finish his ass off. The story doesn't end there old man, after I saw the bus run that fucker over, I felt a profound sense of satisfaction. Knowing that he would never hurt my family again or any other women. I was scared though, because the possibility existed that I would get caught for killing his ass. I walked home across the Douglas Bridge because I was way too full of nervous energy. I crossed the bridge throwing away my shirt, boots, and jacket in the Anacostia River. After I wiped his blood off my hands with the shirt, I was wearing. I had an extra shirt, and sneakers in my bag that I put on. I was scared that the cops would be at the house waiting for me all the way home. When I got home there were no cops waiting for me, and no helicopters overhead. Ma and Lana were there downstairs in the kitchen. I spoke real quick, and hauled ass up stairs to the shower, I found myself sitting outside at 1:00 a.m. thinking about what I had done. I had actually killed him. Lana came outside and we talked, I didn't tell her I killed him, but I told her that I beat the hell out of him, and that it was easy. But damn it, she had a way of getting things out of me. I told her that I did more than just kick his ass. I stopped short of telling her about the bus thing. She looked at me, and didn't press for more information; she simply said he got what he deserved. Whatever you did to him is fine by me. We never spoke about his ass again. You see old man, after no one came to lock my ass up for killing that piece of shit. I realized that while what I did was fucked up. When it came to my family, I was justified in doing what I had to, and I did get away with it."

Eric sits back down at the side of Sherman's bed

"Earlier you made a comment about wishing Lana had a son, well motherfucker she was pregnant at one time, years ago when she was in her late twenty's. She was seeing this guy named Shawn for a couple of years before she moved in with him. He lived in Baltimore, he was a paralegal, and she was in the Federal Government. As far as I knew, they were cool. He begged her to move to that dirty ass city with him and eventually she did. A few months after she moved in with him she got pregnant. Well as things turned out he wasn't happy at all about her being pregnant. He tried to convince her to abort the pregnancy. Lana wasn't going to do that so dude fucked up royally. She was five and a half weeks pregnant and he decides he's going to make her have an abortion. Lana found out from her doctor that she was carrying a boy, she had already named him Paul, remember old man, Paul died when he was seventeen in 1980. Lana was in her late twenties, and she was ready to have a baby. They got into an argument which led to things getting physical. That weak piece of shit beat a pregnant woman as if she was a man in the fuckin' street. I guess hoping she'd loose the baby. By the time, Ma and me got to Baltimore, and to the hospital Lana had lost the baby due to internal hemorrhaging. She was able to let the doctors know that that pussy boyfriend of hers had been drinking before he came home, and attacked her. She almost died herself, it's a good thing Shawn didn't have the balls to come to the hospital. He would have died right there, and I would have gladly gone back to jail. Lana was damn near in a coma and Ma was freaking out, eventually after Uncle Butch got there I left the hospital. I went to her, and Shawn's place to confront that bastard. Oh he was going to die; there was no doubt in my mind about that. When I got to his apartment building, I went upstairs, knocked on his door, there was no one at home. So I sat on the steps in front of his door, and waited for him to bring his punk ass home. He eventually came home around 3:00 a.m., sloppy drunk, I watched him stagger up one flight of steps and vomit, by that time he hadn't seen me, and he was fucked up. I guess he was sorry for what he'd done, and tried to wash his sorrows away with booze. I didn't give a fuck, he was gonna pay for what he'd done to my sister, and for killing my nephew. Seeing him stagger up those steps gave me the perfect plan. He had already thrown up coming up one flight of stairs so I was gonna make sure he had himself a nice explainable accident. When that pussy saw me he didn't even recognize me at first. When he got closer, all he could do was talk in slurred words. Vomiting as he got closer. What he said to me pissed me off even more.

Eric, I didn't want to have no damn baby, why Lana have to have damn baby, I sorry for hittin' her, I didn't mean to hurt her. He sat two steps from me and passed out right there. I thought to myself that if a man could do what he did to my sister after drinking, I'll never touch alcohol again. That pissed me off even more, that the bastard had to get drunk to attack her in her condition. I grabbed his little ass by the seat of his pants and shirt, brought him to the top of the stairs, and tossed him head first down that flight of stairs. I watch as his head made contact with the wall full force, but I didn't hear anything break. I went down, got his ass again and threw him down the next set of stairs. This time after his body came to a stop I saw his head was turned at a real fucked up angle so I knew his neck was broken. I left that motherfucker right there, and as it turned out when the police investigated. It was determined that he fell down the steps after vomiting everywhere, breaking his own damn neck after having come in from drinking. He was filled with sorrow, for almost killing his pregnant girlfriend. His death was ruled an accident by the police and no one questioned it. When Lana was released from the hospital two weeks later, it took several months for her to physically recover from that experience; she was also able to sue that bastard's estate, and eventually was paid quite a bit of money from his insurance company. It took time, but eventually she was able to recover and move on with her life. Sometime later Lana met a good man, and got married. But unfortunately, because of the damage done to her body during, and after the attack she was never able to have children."

Sherman looks at his son and wishes that he would just leave. He doesn't want to hear any more of these tragic stories. He doesn't care about any of this. He just wants this lunatic out of his room so that he can die in peace. He knows he better not give voice to that thought because the man in front of him horrifies him.

"In case you're wondering old man, Lana and I did eventually talk about Shawn. Wondering if I got my hands on his ass, before he had that unfortunate accident, I told her I was the accident. She looked at me and I told her, that fucker killed my nephew, and almost killed you, and I wasn't gonna let him get away with that. She hugged me, told me she loved me, and said he deserved to die for what he did to our family. She knew what I'd done, and nothing between us changed, she has always stuck by me, and I will always be there for her. Now I don't think I need to go into any more of Lana's or Ma's life with you. I think you get the point, but suffice it to say they eventually made it, and are doing fine now. Especially after the settlement money, Lana got. So what do you think about how your children's lives turned out old man?" Eric asks Sherman.

"I'm glad your mother and your sister are doing well now." Sherman manages to say through his pain.

"Ok you're glad they're doing ok, what about me motherfucker? What do you have to say about me and the things I've done!" Eric shouts at Sherman.

"Eric I'm sorry that you feel you had to kill those men, Eric the things you've done are horrible, what have you become." Sherman asks Eric.

"I became what you and that bastard we used to live with made me old man; I became the person I needed to be to protect my family. I wasn't always there to prevent bad things happening, but when they did I was there for my family. Unlike your sorry ass, and you have the nerve to ask me what I've become as if you're my fuckin' judge. Oh just so you know, the motherfucker that killed my baby brother was dealt with as well, let's just say he won't be running over any more kids and getting away with it." Eric tells Sherman.

The pain in Sherman's back is unbearable now, he thinks that maybe if he screams with all the strength he has left someone will hear him, and come to the room. He looks at Eric with bloodshot eyes, and wonders what it will take to make this thing leave his room. Sherman will no longer bare the pain in his back; he looks at Eric and decides he is going to demand that he give back his medicine and leave. In a voice strained with pain, Sherman makes his demand.

"Eric I don't know why you'd come here and do this to me, there is nothing to be gained by causing me any more pain, and trying to hurt and humiliate me now, I'm dying anyway. Eric why don't you give me back my medicine and leave me alone to die?"

"Well old man to be honest with you, when I first walked through that door my only intention was to tell you exactly what I thought of you and leave. I rehearsed that speech all day; I was gonna say my peace, and get the fuck out of here. You fucked that up when you had the nerve to ask me to be an organ donor, and for you of all people. You see old man, remember I said to you, all my life I've always been able to spot certain looks in people's eyes. Those looks that speak volumes about how they really feel. Be they looks of arrogance, hate, fear, contempt, or conceit. Well you had that look of arrogance in your eyes the first time we made eye contact. Your ass is dying of renal failure, and you still feel like you're entitled by some supreme right of Fatherhood. Some twisted sense of ownership to children you don't know, and have never given a damn about. But you're so full of yourself that you knew somebody was gonna save your dying old ass with a kidney. When you had the balls to ask me for a kidney, and then brought up the fact that Lana didn't have a grandson for you, it all clicked in my head. Chances are if Paul had survived you would have been arrogant enough to make the same request of him, you made to your other male children. That thought really pissed me off old man. That you could be that selfish and egotistical. But what the hell, you've been that way all your life right, so maybe yours is a fitting end that you die alone and in pain."

Sherman has no response to what Eric just said to him. He simply closes his eyes and cries. His entire back is numb now, he cannot feel his legs, and the smell of shit in the room is overpowering. Something deep inside him tells him to speak his mind, to fight back and he gets angry. When he opens his eyes again he feels something different now, anger at this man who would condemn him and his life, anger at this admitted murderer who would pass judgment on him. He decides it is time to act like the man he is, and not some pitiful shadow of what he once was. Sherman looks at Eric, and what Eric see's is communicated by his eyes. Eric easily picks up on the look in the old man's eyes.

"Oh, are we feeling defiant old man, is there something you need to say to me."

"Yes there is, you need to get the hell out of here, and leave me the hell alone. I don't know you, and I don't want your ass here. As soon as anyone comes in here, I'm going to tell them what you've done to me, and have your murdering ass arrested. You don't scare me boy." Sherman says in a strained but defiant voice.

Eric's response is laughter, but there is no joy in the sound, he looks at the helpless old man and laughs for at least twenty seconds. All the while staring at Sherman. When Eric calms himself, Sherman knows his bluff of bravado has been called.

Eric gets up, and walks to the window. He turns the handle at the base of the window until the doublewide window opens out all the way. He stands in front of the open window and breaths in the fresh night air. Breathing the air at the window reminds Eric of that other smell he detected earlier. The smell his mind told him was the smell of death. Eric decides that it is time to get the hell out of this hospital; he said what he came to say to the old man. Eric turns to look at the old man lying in the bed, their eyes meet once more, and unspoken words pass between them, Eric walks over to the bed and stares down at him, Keeping his eyes locked on Sherman Eric picks up the TV's remote and turns out the lights in the room. Without warning, Eric grabs the old man by the throat with his left hand and squeezes, he rips off the old man's nasal cannula, and then he rips out every IV line from his arms and the electrodes from his chest. Still holding the old man by the throat he pulls out the power cord for the cardiac monitor that was plugged into the beds head board. Holding the old man by the throat with his left hand, he uses his right hand to take hold of the old man's left arm. Eric then forcefully snatches the old man out of his bed, and forces him to the window. Eric is surprised at how light Sherman is. Eric thinks to himself I could throw him across the room. The old man can barely stand, he has no strength in his legs, but Eric keeps him from falling down. Once Eric gets him by the window, he holds him up against the wall. The old man's eyes get wide as Eric increases the pressure on his throat, then Eric forces Sherman's face against the screen in the window, Sherman can't see his face but Eric whispers in his ear. Sherman is so frightened he pisses down his legs; he can only concentrate on the voice whispering to him.

"I promised I'd come see your ass, I never said anything about not killing you."

Sherman can barely speak, the only words that make it through are "no, no, no, don't," as he tries to beg Eric to not hurt him. Eric continues to whisper in Sherman's ear.

"Like I said to you earlier when the nurse was here, I'm the last motherfucker you should have asked to see, but I'm here now, and I owe you motherfucker. Don't do or say anything stupid. You know old man, this could have been avoided any number of ways. But what's done is done right, isn't that the way you see shit. Well I'm gonna do to you what you did to us. You threw us out the window when we were young, now I'm gonna do the same shit to you, now that you're old and useless. Any last words motherfucker?"

Words cannot describe the fright that Sherman feels now, he knows Eric intends to do what he said he is going to do. Sherman's heart is beating so fast now he can't talk, tears won't stop running down his face, and he can't stop his old body from trembling. Sherman can only pray that someone comes to help him. Eric continues to whisper in Sherman's ear.

"OK then, no last words, that's cool. They say when you die your life flashes before your eyes old man. When I get to hell let me know what you saw."

With that, still holding the old man by the arm and throat Eric moves Sherman back just enough to give himself some forward momentum, with all the strength in his body he brings Sherman's body forward toward the open window, and throws his body against the thin screen, actually lifting Sherman off the floor. The screen rips instantly and Sherman plummets eighty feet to the pavement below. He doesn't make a sound on the way down. Eric takes a hat out of his jacket pocket, puts it on, and exits the room. Eric takes the stairs down to the lobby and walks out of the hospital.

That same evening Lana has a very interesting phone conversation with her mother, who she called to inform that she had gotten Eric to go see Sherman.

"Hey Ma, I talked to Eric and he agreed to go see Sherman." She tells her mother with excitement in her voice.

"That's good baby, but I need to tell you both something about him that I've been keeping to myself for a long time."

"What Ma?"

"Sherman is not yours and Eric's father."

The only thought that goes through Lana's mind is for her brother. Oh! My dear God.

Sometimes our hearts desires find us. When it happens for you don't let fear ruin it for you.

CRUISE CONTROL

American Café, Friday 5:00 p.m. Gaylord Hotel, Fort Washington Maryland.

Jared pulls his car into the huge parking lot of the Gaylord Hotel Complex, puts it in park and sits there for a while. He lets the day's events run through his mind and smiles when he repeats his new job title to himself. I am now the Chief Design Engineer for the NASA 2020 Lunar Mission. Jared thinks back to the feeling he had when his supervisor called him into his office this morning, at 11: 00 a.m. He had been running his design calculations through his computer thinking he had made a mistake, or forgotten something that was critical in his designs.

He knew the project needed a chief designer, and he'd been working on his designs for three years. If he'd missed something, he knew he would not be considered for the promotion. When he got to his supervisor's office and saw the entire mission staff. He didn't know what to think. His supervisor asked him to have a seat.

"Jared, I want to be the first person to tell you that all the mission managers went over your designs, for the new Lunar Lander. We think they are fantastic!" Jared felt his heart beat so fast it seemed that it was going to beat through his chest. His supervisor continued.

"Not only are your designs innovative, we think your engine designs may be revolutionary, and the cost projections are well within the project's budget." His Project Manager stood and offered his hand as he said, "I would like to introduce you to your team as Chief Design Engineer of the 2020 Lunar Lander Mission. Congratulations!"

Jared stood, shook his supervisors hand, and all the members present. He still couldn't believe he got the promotion two hours later. He spent the rest of his day being congratulated by everyone in his department. Now that he'd left work he needed to relax. He realizes he hadn't even told his wife the good news. The excitement of the day was so overwhelming. Jared decides he will call her from the bar. He gets out of his car, and walks to the hotel. He enters the beautifully decorated Atrium of The Gaylord, and proceeds to the escalator to go down to his favorite bar. Jared walks into the bar, and notices that it is already crowded and it's not even 6:00 p.m. yet. There are seats at the bar so he decides he better get one before they're all gone. He sits down, and waits for the bartender to come over.

"Hello Jared. The usual?"

"Yeah Stan, that would be fine." "One Scotch and soda coming up." As Stan makes his drink, he asks Jared how his day went.

"Jared, how's the big moon project coming?" Jared looks at Stan as his drink is placed in front of him.

"You're looking at the Chief Design Engineer of the project as of today," Stan's eyes get wide, and he yells.

"Man are you joking? You got the promotion! That's terrific, congratulations!"

He extends his hand to Jared as he speaks.

"Jared I'm happy for you. You've been working on that project for years. You deserve the promotion. Oh, this drink is on me."

"Thanks." Jared says.

"Have you told Janet yet?" Stan asks.

"No, and while I'm thinking about it let me call her now." Jared replies.

"Ok, and tell her I said hello." Jared gives a nod, and takes out his phone to call his wife. Stan goes to take care of his other customers.

Jared dials his wife's cell phone number, and waits for her to pick up.

"Hey baby, how are you doing?" Janet says.

"Baby you won't believe what happened to me today." Jared says as he tries to hide the excitement in his voice.

"What baby? How did your design meeting go?"

"Janet, I got the promotion to Chief Project Designer." Janet screams as she hears the news.

"I was going over my designs this morning when I got called to my supervisor's office. Janet, I walked in, and the whole management staff was there. I really didn't know what to think. I was told they loved my designs, and I got the promotion. The first black Design Engineer on a major NASA Project." He tells his wife excitedly.

"Baby I got it."

"Oh Baby! I knew it was gonna work out, you've worked hard as hell on this project. There was no one else who could have done the work you did. Baby I'm so proud of you. Are you at the café baby?" She asks.

"Yeah, after today I needed to celebrate. Hey you want to come down after work and join me?" Jared asks his wife.

"No baby. I have a better idea." She continues. "I can't leave the hospital before 8:00 p.m., but you stay there. Relax and enjoy yourself. I'll go home when I get off, and have a nice romantic dinner waiting for you. When we finish dinner we can celebrate till the sun rises." She giggles. That thought sets Jared's mind into overdrive.

"Baby why don't I leave now, and wait for you at home?" Jared feels the excitement in his pants.

"No baby, you stay there, and I'll have everything waiting for you when you get home. So don't come home before nine." She laughs.

"All right I guess I can wait, but when I get there I expect to be treated like a Chief Engineer." Jared laughs.

"I got you baby. You'll get service fit for a king. I gotta go baby, I'll see you at home at nine." She says with emphasis.

"Ok baby, that's a date." He replies and hangs up.

Janet goes to her office, and makes plans to leave early, she has a lot to do, and she wants to make this evening one Jared will never forget. She thinks to herself how much she loves Jared. The pride she feels for her husband swells in her chest.

Jared clips his phone to his belt, and returns his attention to his drink. He takes a drink, and as he does so, he turns his head slightly to the right. He notices a very beautiful woman sitting next to him. In fact he thinks to himself that she is stunningly beautiful. Stan walks up and asks Jared how Janet is doing. He tells him she's fine and that he can't wait to get home.

"Big night planned?" Stan asks.

"You know it. She has a surprise for me when I get home." He tells Stan smiling. Jared holds his now empty glass up gesturing to Stan for a refill.

"One more Scotch and soda coming up." Stan says.

Jared turns his head to the right just as the woman sitting next to him turns to face him.

"Hello." Jared says.

"Hi." she responds. "My name is Gabrielle." She smiles and extends her hand toward Jared.

"My name is Jared." He responds, and takes her hand. She turns toward him and asks does he come here often.

Jared tells her he is a regular but when he does come to the café he doesn't stay long, and always leaves early on Friday evenings.

"Why is that? It seems such a waste to come to such a beautiful bar, and leave early." She replies.

"It's just that I'm not a big drinker, and while the café is nice, it gets crowded and stays that way till it closes."

"That's true." Responds Gabrielle. Stan brings Jared's drink over just as Gabrielle finishes her response.

"Hey beautiful, what can I bring you?" Stan asks her.

"I'll have a White Zen." She responds.

Jared notices she speaks with a slight accent and wonders where she's from. He cannot place the accent. With her long jet-black hair and fair completion, Jared thinks she must be of Hispanic origin. He also takes note of the way she's dressed. Very stylish, he thinks to himself. The color black suits her. The black form fitting designer jeans, and grey, low cut top calls attention to her large breasts. The short black jacket sets her outfit off; accented by the silver bracelets and necklace. She's definitely out to have a good time. After placing her order, she returns her attention to Jared.

"Well, Jared, what is it you do for a living if you don't mind me asking?" She says with a smile, flashing a mouth full of perfect white teeth.

"I'm a Design Engineer with NASA." "What does a Design Engineer do, although I probably wouldn't understand it anyway?" She says with a smile.

Jared finds himself getting excited, as he begins to explain to Gabrielle what he does for NASA.

"What I do is design and build propulsion systems for space probes.

The project I'm working on now is a spacecraft that will be going to the moon in 2020. I've been working on the designs for years; this probe will be able to independently search, and explore the lunar surface. It will search for water, and future landing sites, for the permanent base that will eventually be built on the surface of the moon." Jared continues.

"The machine you're building will be able to do all that?" She asks.

"No, you see the part of the project I'm responsible for is the propulsion system.

Think about it like a car's engine, only much more sophisticated. I designed propulsion systems that will enable the craft to make it to the moon, from high earth orbit. However, it will use only a fraction of the fuel it took for the first Lunar Landers. And my systems will enable the craft to launch from the moon's surface, and make it back to Earth orbit without needing to be refueled."

"My systems will eventually enable us to explore the solar system like never before." Jared explains.

"I can tell how excited you are; just by the way you explain what you do."

"Yes this is an exciting time for me, and today I was promoted to Chief Design Engineer of the project."

"Congratulations! Jared, I'm happy for you. That sounds like a reason to stay out late and celebrate." Gabrielle tells him with a smile.

Stan comes over to check on the two new friends. Just as Gabrielle, and Jared raise their glass to toast Jared's promotion.

"Our local NASA Engineer tell you his good news beautiful?" Stan asks Gabrielle.

"Yes he did, and we have to celebrate his good news, and hard work."

"All right Jared, another round?" Stan asks. "No I don't think so." Jared responds.

"No Jared, we have to celebrate your promotion, and have a little fun. It's Friday." She says as she puts her hand on Jared's arm, and moves a little closer to him. Jared notices her hand on his arm but doesn't react. Stan also takes note of where her hand is.

"So what'll it be my man, another round?"

"Why not, I'll have another drink."

"What will the lady have?" Stan asks.

Before she could answer, Jared puts up his hand, and says just the Scotch. For an instant, she looked at Jared as if he had insulted her. She quickly recovers, and tells Stan to bring her another White Zen on her tab.

"Coming right up" Stan says as he walks away.

"Gabrielle, please understand something. I am married, and I don't buy drinks for women other than my wife, or friends I've known for a while. I just don't want to give you the wrong impression." Jared explains.

"I'm not offended." She replies. "I would like for us to become friends though, I find you very attractive, and interesting. Don't you think I'm pretty?" She asks as she places her hand on top of his again. At that moment, Stan brings their drinks over, and places them on the bar. Jared quickly removes his hand from under hers and holds his glass.

"Gabrielle, in response to your question I think you're a very attractive woman. But I will not fool around on my wife. Now I don't mean to presuppose here, but I'm not interested in any woman but my wife. Do you understand what I'm saying?" Jared asks.

"What do you mean when you say presuppose?" Gabrielle asks.

"What I'm saying is I thought you might be hitting on me. I don't want to give you the impression that that's what I want." She picks up her glass, and looks deeply into his eyes as she takes a drink.

"So you're saying you don't find me attractive at all?"

"I already told you I do. I think you're very beautiful."

"Jared, what is the harm in us getting to know each other. Having a little fun in the time we have? I think you're a fine man. We could do whatever you want. We could go upstairs, or get a room somewhere else and celebrate. Let's see where the night takes us. I'm not trying to take you from your wife. I think that we could have a lot of fun, and it would feel so good." She says smiling.

Jared takes a drink of his Scotch, looks at Gabrielle, and wonders what it is she sees in him. Of all the guys in the bar. Especially the single men, why try to pick up a married man?

"Gabrielle can I ask you a question?"

"Yes you can handsome, anything you like." She says with a slight smile on her face.

"I'm just curious … As obviously beautiful as you know you are, why me? Or better still, why would you want to waste your time with a guy who's married?" For emphasis, Jared holds up his left hand to display his wedding band.

"I find you attractive. I saw the wedding band on your finger when I sat next to you. It's a lot less complicated with a guy who already has someone. I don't want you to leave home. I find you very interesting, and I am sexually attracted to you. Is a little extra sex gonna kill you?" She says laughing softly.

"Many things can kill you, and ruin your life at the same time. I'm sure you're aware of that. I'm very happy, and satisfied with my wife. I'm very flattered that such a young, beautiful, woman finds me attractive, but I only have eyes for one woman." Jared tells her.

"So you've never played around on your wife? Not even once? You never even thought about it before?" She asks, again getting close to Jared and touching his arm.

"If we acted on every impulse we have, the world would be a far more dangerous place than it is now." Jared reaches into his inside coat pocket, and takes his wallet out. He then reaches inside, and pulls out a picture of his wife and hands it to Gabrielle. She takes the picture, looks at it, and tells him his wife is very pretty. He takes the picture back and puts his wallet away.

"I've been married for eleven years, and I plan to stay that way." He says with a smile.

"Jared what does she do?" Gabrielle asks.

"She's a doctor. But Gabrielle I don't want to discuss my wife with you, if that's ok."

"Sure I didn't mean to get personal, I'm sorry."

"No it's ok, but why don't you have a boyfriend? I'm sure there has to be a thousand guys, who would love to call you their girl." Jared asks.

"Well when it comes to men, I haven't had the best luck. Even looking the way I do. She says laughing. Many of the men I meet are intimidated by my looks. When I'm involved with someone, no matter how much I'd tell him that I'm not seeing anyone else, I get accused constantly, of not being faithful. I just got sick of dealing with insecure guys. Sometimes, on the occasion, I'd meet a nice man who was married. If we became involved, I wouldn't be accused of cheating, because he had a wife at home he had to go to. I have needs as well, and a very healthy sex drive. But even those situations got crazy sometimes. Men want to own you, even when they can't have it that way." She says with a distant look in her eyes.

"Gabrielle I would never have thought that a woman as attractive as you, would have those kinds of problems. I can say with some confidence that you would be irresistible to just about any man on the planet, married or otherwise." Jared takes another sip of his drink, and puts the glass down.

"Just not to you though." She says laughing.

"Gabrielle, I know I'm old enough to be your father, or close to it, and you know the other reason." Jared says laughing.

"Age is not the most important thing though. Jared you are not even close to being old." She says.

He finishes his drink, and puts the glass on the bar.

"Gabrielle, it's unfortunate that you've had to deal with the kinds of men you described. But, look, you're young and you will find the one for you. But can I just say one thing, and I hope it helps a little?" She nods her head.

"A married man would tell you anything he thought you wanted to hear. Men that are married do not often leave home for the mistress. She is just his play thing. She fills a void that for whatever reason can't be satisfied for him at home. Ultimately the other woman is the one who is left alone, and hurt. The reason for this is those married men who have girlfriends, or that do leave their wives for the other woman never forget how they met her, or what they did to the woman that was his wife. Someone he supposedly loved at one time. What the two of them did behind the wife's back is always on his mind. She had no problem being involved with another woman's husband. She helped him destroy his marriage, and tear his family apart. She would damn sure leave him the same way for the next man. He never truly trusts her, and he even begins to resent her in time. The man who appears to be happy with the other woman Gabrielle is always constantly worried about losing her to another man. He has to worry about what it is she's doing, when they aren't together, and whom she's doing. Because he knows he can never truly trust her for as long as they are together. Gabrielle, I hope you never find yourself in a horrible situation like that. Now, I didn't speak from personal experience. That is what I've been told by far older and wiser men than myself who did go through situations like that." Jared stands and calls Stan over to pay his tab. He again extends his hand to Gabrielle, and tells her goodnight.

"Jared, goodnight, and it was nice meeting you. And your wife is lucky to have you." Gabrielle says.

"No Gabrielle, I'm lucky to have her."

"Goodnight again, and you be good." Jared says with a smile as he walks away.

Gabrielle watches Jared walk away, and thinks he's taller than she had first thought. She lifts her drink and says in a voice only she can hear "fuck that space geek." She calls Stan over and orders a glass of ice water.

"You got it beautiful. How'd you like meeting my man Jared?" Stan asks.

"He's ok, but not my type, and he's married." She tells Stan as he gives her the water she ordered.

"Excuse me, is this seat taken?" The man says who just walked up to the empty seat next to Gabrielle.

"No, the guy who was sitting there is gone. Wifey called him, and told him to bring his ass home. He said his curfew was nine." Gabrielle says laughing.

"That's why I don't have one of those. Damned if I wouldn't have cut my phone off if we were talking. Fine as you are. She would have had to come drag my ass out of here." They both laugh. "My name is Chris." He tells her.

"Hi Chris, my name is Gabrielle."

"So you don't have one of those, meaning you're not married?" She says smiling.

"Hell no, and I don't ever plan on it. I like the fact that I don't have to answer to anyone, and I set my own curfews. I like my freedom to come and go as I please. I can do whatever I want with whomever I want."

She turns to face him. "So you're out to play tonight? No girlfriend to answer to either?"

"Not the same thing baby, I can do what I want. If I had a girl, she could have her space too. That's how I roll baby."

"Do you come here often, Chris?" She asks.

"Every now and then. I usually hit a few spots on Friday. If I come here first I stay about an hour, and roll somewhere else. What about you?" Chris asks.

"I like this bar. It has great atmosphere, and the people are cool. Not a bunch of young thugs, hotheads, and low life's."

"Yeah I heard that. But since this place is new, it's expensive as hell." Says Chris.

"Well look at the crowd, and how people are dressed. This bar is always full, and it's barely past nine. I think the people who come here, are a more upscale crowd than at some other places. That's why they get away with the prices. Is money an object for you Chris? It's hard to play when you're worried about your wallet."

"Nah baby, money isn't an issue, but I can do the same thing someplace else for less." Chris says laughing.

"As in picking up women among other things?"

"That's not all I'm about. I'm not cheap, but I don't believe in spending a lot of time, or money in one place. That includes bars, and on women. See, women think that a man is supposed to do that. I say why can't they spend some on me too? But the atmosphere here is nice. I just don't think that it's necessary to spend a fortune for me to enjoy myself."

"Ok. But like they say, you get what you pay for. And as long as you have to pay for anything, you might as well get the best for your money right." She states.

"Well what did you have in mind sexy?" He asks.

"Chris baby, you probably couldn't afford me. Not that I'm for sale, but my tastes are a bit expensive."

"I'm not trying to buy you, I just want to talk and enjoy your company."

"That would be fine, and that doesn't cost a thing." She says laughing.

Stan walks over to Chris, and asks him what he would like to drink. While he gives Stan his drink order, Gabrielle is sizing Chris up. Gabrielle wonders if he is even worth the trouble of her talking to him. *Cheap motherfucker* she thinks to herself.

"So when you're not out bar hopping, what do you do for work?" She asks with a smile.

"I've been a bus driver for metro for six years now. My goal is to transfer to subway train operator." He tells her.

"That sounds interesting. I'm sure you'll make it. I'd bet you're good at what you do." She says. Stan returns with a Rum and Coke for Chris. He offers to buy Gabrielle a drink, and she orders a White Zen.

"Thank you for the wine." She says.

"What about you? What do you do for work? If I had to guess, I'd say you're a model."

"No, I did try that for a while, when I was in New York. It didn't work out."

"That is hard to believe, you must be one of the finest woman in here. What happened?" He asks.

Gabrielle explains, during her time as a model the people she worked with, both men, and women constantly hit on her sexually. On one shoot for a make-up ad, the photographer tried to force himself on her after a location shoot. Gabrielle tells Chris that experience scared her so bad she was ready to leave New York. After a few more close calls, she tells him, she decided that modeling, and New York was not for her. She decided to move to D.C. to be with her sister. Until she could find a job, and move out on her own.

"Eventually, I plan to go back to school. But for now, I just want to have a good time." She says.

"Cool, I can understand that. One day I'm gonna carry my butt back to school, and finish my Associates Degree to qualify for the train operator position."

As Chris takes a drink, Gabrielle thinks to herself, the whole time she was talking, Chris could barely take his eyes off her breasts. She thinks to herself that he probably didn't hear a word of the bullshit she was telling him. One more drink, and it's time to get rid of little man. That thought almost makes her laugh out loud.

"Gabrielle you have an accent. Can I ask where you're from? Don't get me wrong, I like the way you sound. I just can't place the accent."

"Oh it's ok; I was born in the Dominican Republic. My family moved to the states when I was young."

"The Dominican Republic … That's cool. Do you get home often, and do all the women look like you?" He asks.

"To answer your questions Chris No, I don't go home often, because my parents are here. And yes, all the women look like me." She says laughing. "You would like it there trust me."

"Damn, I have to make it a point to go there one day. Would you be my guide?"

"Why would you need me, you're going to meet women?"

"Well I don't know the country."

"If you go you'll find your way." She says laughing.

Chris moves a little closer to Gabrielle, and as he does so he realizes that the perfume she is wearing smells as good as she looks.

He thinks to himself, I would love to get a piece of that fine pussy. I'm damn sure going to give it a shot.

"So Gabrielle, how long do you think you might be here this evening?"

"I usually don't leave before midnight, If I'm enjoying myself."

"Well if it's ok with you, I'll try my best to see that you do, while I'm here."

"Oh. Well tell me; what would you do Chris, to make sure I enjoy myself here with you?" She says smiling.

"We can sit here, have a few more drinks, talk, and see where the night takes us. Do you always come out by yourself? Where are your girlfriends?" He asks.

"I have a few friends, and we do hangout together sometimes. I'm alone tonight. Why, what did you have in mind?" she asks. Gabrielle takes a drink of her wine, and looks over her right shoulder, as if she is searching the crowd. She finishes her drink before returning her attention to Chris.

"Let me get you another drink." He calls Stan over, and orders her another glass of wine.

"Thank you, Chris."

"No, what I meant was, if you planned on meeting your girls, or whatever here tonight. I could call some of my boys, and we could all hook up here. Any of my boys, would be happy as hell to meet your partners. Especially if they look anything like you." Gabrielle smiles at that last statement.

"Maybe some other time. I'm all alone tonight. Don't tell me a big handsome man like you needs a chaperone." They both laugh.

"No it's just that I understand sometimes women feel safer in groups, and you are just meeting me for the first time. I just want you to feel comfortable with me, that's all."

"I do Chris, and I'm a big girl who can take care of herself."

The bar is now completely full and very busy, so Chris asks Stan to bring her another glass of wine in a few minutes.

"Chris are you trying to get me drunk, so you can take advantage of me?" she says smiling as she gently squeezes his arm.

"No, I just want you to enjoy yourself, and I don't mind buying a fine woman a drink."

"If I weren't so fine would you be here talking to me? What if I was plain and fat? No, baby you want to fuck me and you know it." She says. That statement mildly shocks him and makes Chris laugh out loud.

"Well I'd be lying my ass off if I said I didn't want to. I know we just met, but what man in his right mind wouldn't want you?"

"Well baby, I have to tell you, if I knew you longer maybe, but I'm not that easy."

"I didn't say you were. I'm just out to have a good time like you. You brought up fuckin' not me." He states

"Yeah, but it's on your mind, I bet your dick is hard right now, just thinking about giving it to me." She says as she takes a drink.

"You want to feel it?" He asks. Gabrielle laughs out loud, She thinks to herself, *now it's time to get rid of him. He's starting to irritate me, and I have absolutely no intention of letting this loser even smell my pussy.*

"You're a bad boy, Chris. Maybe one day, if I get to know you better, I'll do more than that." She says as she touches his arm. He turns to face her.

"We are adults, and if that's where things go then I'm down."

"I know, but it can't go there now, you know what I'm saying?" She states.

"I understand, but since we are on the subject. Is there anything I can do that would change your mind about that?" He says smiling.

"Not today, handsome. Besides, you don't look like the kind of man that needs to beg. You get what you want, if not now, then later."

"True that, but I'd beg your fine ass if that's what it took." He laughs.

"Well there are a few reasons why it can't happen. Besides what I already told you, I don't think you want it bloody. It's that time of the month, so she's on lock down." Gabrielle laughs.

"Damn! girl you put it out there. But hell, fine as you are that wouldn't stop me."

"Maybe so, but it's not happening today." Gabrielle takes a drink and thinks to herself that he's totally disgusting. *This motherfucker wants to fuck me so bad, even telling him I'm on my period wouldn't discourage his nasty ass.*

Chris waves Stan over, and asks for his tab. He decides that he's pretty much done at this particular bar. He is not going to waste any more time, or money on Gabrielle. As fine as this bitch is, it's time to roll out to some place a little less expensive. Find a ho who may not be as fine, but isn't bleeding. He gets his tab and thinks, fuck this, sixty-five damn dollars for a few drinks? Yeah it's time to roll the fuck out.

"Gabrielle, do you think I could get your number? I would love to keep in contact with you."

"Sure, so would I. Call my cell, and we will stay in touch." She gives Chris her number. They both save the new numbers in their phones. Chris pays his tab, stands to give Gabrielle a hug, and tells her he'll be calling. He says good night, and leaves the bar.

Gabrielle turns back toward the bar, and is relieved that Chris is gone. *Cheap ass bastard.* She thinks to herself. There was no way in hell I'd let a loser like him touch me, even though he is cute. I feel sorry for all the stupid bitches out there that would though. Knowing that somewhere there's a woman that would be desperate enough, to allow herself to be fucked by someone like him, makes me angry. Stupid bitches like that deserve what they get.

Gabrielle waves Stan over, and lets him know she is going to the ladies room, and that she'll be right back. After a few minutes, a customer walks up to her empty seat. He waits for the bartender to come back. When he does, the customer asks for a Long Island and inquires if the woman who just left the seat was coming back. He is pleased when he is told yes. After a few minutes Gabrielle returns to her seat at the bar, looks at the man standing next to her seat, and gives him a wink as she sits down. The man standing next to her seat says to himself, goddamn this motherfucker is fine. He stands there waiting for his drink, and prays that the guy sitting at the next stool finishes his beer, and gets the fuck up so he can sit next to her.

"One Long Island Iced Tea."

Do you want to start a tab?" Stan asks.

"Yeah that'll be ok." Stan gives the customer his drink, gets his name, and leaves. He takes his drink, and stands next to Gabrielle's seat.

"That's a strong drink. Just one of those would have me tipsy all night." Gabrielle says as she looks up at the man standing next to her.

"If that's the case then as soon as the bartender comes back I'll have to order you one." He says.

"Hi, my name is Gabrielle."

"I'm Lamont. Gabrielle, nice to meet you."

"That name fits you. If you don't mind my saying, you are a beautiful woman." She smiles, touches his hand, and thanks him for the compliment.

"So will you let me buy you a drink?"

"Sure, but what you're drinking is way too strong for me. A glass of wine would be fine."

"I'll buy you anything you want." Now, Gabrielle I have to ask. As fine as you are why are you out by yourself tonight?"

"Well, Lamont, sometimes you just want to be by yourself. I'm not the kind to hang out with a lot of people." She states.

"Well I was referring to your man. I could hang out with you all night. I just don't need dude walkin' up on me."

"You don't have to worry about that, because I don't have a boyfriend."

"That's hard to believe as pretty as you are. But, what the hell. That just means I don't have to worry about some ass attacking me over you."

"No, Lamont that's not going to be a problem for you."

"But I have to ask again out of curiosity, why don't you have a man? You must be one of those fine crazy motherfuckers." They both laugh.

"No, Lamont. I'm not crazy, or mean. At this point in my life I'd rather not be bothered. Sometimes, it's ok to be alone, don't you think?" She says smiling.

"If that's what you want, sure."

"Now, Lamont, you have a ring on your finger, so where's your wife?"

"Her ass is right where she wants to be. At home." He says laughing.

"How long have you been married?"

"It'll be fifteen long years in January."

"You make it sound like that's a bad thing. I think its sweet you've been able to be with someone that long. Hell, I can't keep a man more than a few months, before he starts tripping." She says.

"Gabrielle, that might sound sweet from your perspective, but from mine it hasn't been that way for a long time. Hell, I can't do shit with her. She won't even go out with me. Not to a movie, a bar, dinner, nothing anymore. I stopped offering to take her ass out with me years ago. But even on the rare occasion I do ask her, she always tells me no. She tells me to go on, and enjoy myself. Look how nice this place is, full of people having a good time. I always have to come here alone. I've gotten used to it, so it doesn't bother me anymore. Now, she does like to do holiday, and family shit. We don't have kids, so we took care of the nieces and nephews when they were little. But as far as us hanging out together, on dates and shit; that hasn't happened in a long time. And you know what's really crazy about the whole family get together thing? Other than the kids who are mostly grown now, I can't stand most of her family." Lamont says laughing.

"That's too bad; you're a good looking man. What's her problem?" Gabrielle asks. Before Lamont can answer, Stan comes over, and Lamont buys her a glass of wine, and himself another Long Island.

"I honestly stopped trying to figure that shit out years ago baby. It's not like I didn't try. I didn't wake up one day, and just say, fuck her. But when I finally realized, I wasn't getting anywhere with her I said to myself, fuck it. I'll do me, and I won't worry about her anymore. Gabrielle to someone as young as you, that might sound fucked up, considering how long I've been married. Any married man will tell you, a lot of shit changes when you say those two words, I do. After that, you start getting old. Hell, I take care of the house, the bills, shopping, and most of the cleaning, because I enjoy doing it. She doesn't have to do any of that stuff. Just take care of me. Hell, she can't even do that. I get tired of jerking off."

"Damn Lamont baby, I'm sorry to hear that. Does she work?"

"Yeah she's worked for the State Department for the last twenty years. She has a damn good job, but it's like when she comes home from work, all she wants to do is watch TV, and sleep. She never wants to go out, and it's not like she has much house work to do. We don't have kids, or anything to take care of. It's been that way for years.

Hell, I've been with the Post Office for as long as she's been on her job. I went from being a mail carrier to a supervisor. I work long hours sometimes. I would still want to come home, and chill with my wife. I would get told shit like, I'm tired, or I'm not in the mood. A man can only take so much of that shit. Lamont tells her.

"Do you think that she might be seeing someone else?" Gabrielle asks.

"To be honest, that has never really crossed my mind. I don't think she would fuck around on me, but you never know. Hey, and at this point, I really don't care if she is. As long as she keeps that shit in the street the hell with it." Lamont says.

Lamont takes a long sip of his Long Island, and thinks to himself how he can keep Gabrielle's pretty ass focused on him. He thinks to himself how much he'd enjoy fucking her.

"Do you fuck around on your wife Lamont?" She asks.

"Hell, I have. It's not like I'm fuckin' everything that walks, but I have."

"Well let me ask you a question? Do you and your wife still fuck?"

The question does not startle him but it does excite him. He thinks that for her to ask him a question like that, she must be open to giving him some pussy. He thinks all he needs to do is play it cool, and guide her to where she wants to go with this. The man sitting next to Gabrielle gets up and leaves. Lamont quickly takes the empty seat, and moves very close to Gabrielle.

"It goes back to the same thing I said earlier. She's always complaining about being tired, or not in the mood. We don't fuck nearly as much as we used to. I can't lie, when it's there, its good. But those times are few and far between."

"That is truly sad. That is the reason many women can't keep a good man, because they do dumb shit like that. They get him, and forget what it takes to keep him, or they stop caring. You hear women bitching all the time about what their men don't do anymore. Married woman act as if they don't know why their men fuck around. If lazy bitches, like your wife handled their business at home, they wouldn't have to worry about their men fuckin' up in the street. Oh, Lamont, I'm sorry. I didn't mean to call your wife that. It's just that in my opinion it's wrong to treat you that way."

"It's ok baby. It's not like I haven't felt the same way for a long time."

Lamont takes a drink, and smiles to himself. He asks Gabrielle if she wants another drink. She tells him yes, and he orders her another glass of wine when the bartender comes back.

"Thank you again for the wine Lamont. I hope you don't mind the way I voice my opinion. Sometimes I get carried away, and my language does get a little spicy." She says laughing softly.

"Hey baby I'm forty-eight years old. That doesn't bother me at all. I get a little raw at times. Especially when I get fucked up. Everything about you is sexy, and when you curse it turns me on."

"Oh, so I turn you on do I?"

"Hell yeah, you just don't know!" He says.

"Why don't you try telling me? But I have to warn you Lamont … You better be able to back up any shit you talk, or I will be very disappointed."

"Baby you don't have to worry about that. I won't say shit I can't back up."

Gabrielle leans close to his ear and whispers. "Something you said earlier I want to correct. You are not old and I think you're a damn sexy man."

"Thank you. I try to keep myself in good shape." He says.

"Good, then let me ask you. If I let you, how you would satisfy me in bed?" Lamont's heart jumps in his chest when he hears that question.

"Baby I'd much rather show you. Talk is cheap. Performance is what matters. I could sit here, and talk bullshit all night about what I'd like to do."

"That's true. She says. So you're a doer not a talker. Ok, but give me just enough to make my pussy tingle."

Lamont leans to the side and their shoulders touch. He turns his head toward her ear and whispers, "It's been weeks since I had some pussy. I'll suck those big, pretty tits until your nipples get sore. I'll feast on your pussy, and fuck you for hours anywhere you want to be fucked."

Gabrielle whispers in his ear that she wants to feel his dick. She puts her hand on his leg, and moves it toward his crotch. She feels a bulge, and gently squeezes it. Lamont feels her hand on his dick, and even through his slacks, he feels the warmth of her touch. She feels him get bigger under her hand. She makes a barely audible moaning sound. Gently squeezing his dick, she brings her glass to her lips and takes a drink. They are sitting with their thighs touching, and Gabrielle's head is resting slightly on Lamont's shoulder.

"Damn girl your hand is warm. Don't make me cum in my damn pants." He says laughing.

"You better not. I want you to cum in my mouth." She says just loud enough for Stan to hear as he walks up.

"Sounds like everything is fine here, can I bring you two another drink?" Stan laughs.

"You want another drink baby?"

"Sure."

"Two more drinks coming up."

Gabrielle takes her hand off his dick, places them on her lap, and leans over to him.

"Yeah baby, we're gonna have a good night. I can't wait to ride that big dick. I have to go to the ladies room cause you got me all hot, and wet now. I'll be right back so don't you run off." She says.

"I ain't going no damn where." Lamont says. In his mind, Lamont is jumping for joy. I'm about to fuck one of the finest women I have ever laid eyes on. I'm so damn glad I came out tonight; I was in the right place at the right time. I don't have to worry about the wife. She's not going to call, and she'll be sleep when I get home. It's cool as long as I'm home by 3:00 a.m. At least I show that much respect for her, he thinks to himself.

When she comes back they will finish these drinks, decide on where to go, and get the fuck out of here. He feels like a kid in a candy store, and he's gonna feed her all the dick she can take. The Gaylord Complex has several hotels, so all they have to do is pick one. They can walk from the bar to any one they choose. He is ready to take all his sexual frustrations out on Gabrielle's pussy. Lamont can hardly wait for them to finish their drinks, and leave. He can still feel her warm hand on his dick, he thinks to himself. He is gonna hit that pussy for all he's worth, then some. That thought almost makes him laugh out loud.

"Lamont, here are your drinks. Can I bring you anything else?" Stan asks.

"No my man close me out." Lamont replies as he gives Stan a credit card, and ten dollars in cash as a tip.

"Thanks, I'll be right back with your card." About ten minutes after she left Gabrielle returns to her seat.

"You miss me baby?"

"You know I did sexy." "Hey I ordered us one more drink. I figured we knock these last two out, go get a room, get our freak on, and order some room service."

"That sounds great to me. Lamont I have another question for you. What would you say if I told you that I could hook up a three way for you? You, me and my girlfriend Margaret. She is very pretty. I'm sure you'll like her. Would you like that baby? You have a lot of dick in those pants. I might need some help." She says smiling rubbing his leg.

Lamont thinks to himself she must be bullshitin'. This can't be happening to me. Can a motherfucker be this damn lucky in one night? I get to fuck two bitches at the same time. Hell yeah I'm down for that. Gabrielle squeezes his thigh.

"Baby, you ok with that? If not don't worry about it, I'm still gonna fuck your brains out. I just thought you might enjoy something like that."

"Is your friend here now?" He asks.

"She will be in a few minutes. In fact she just called to see where I am. Her name is Margaret."

"How do you know she'll be down with this?" He asks.

"Trust me, if I ask her she'll be down. She's as big a freak as I am. I'm sure she'll like you because I do." Gabrielle says laughing. Gabrielle's phone rings, and she sees that it's her girlfriend. She looks at Lamont, and holds up her finger to let him know she is going to take the call.

"Hey girl where are you?" "Ok, I'll be right there." She says and hangs up. "Baby I'm gonna go meet her upstairs. Order her a Cosmopolitan on me, and I'll be right back."

"No I got her drink, you go get her, and I'll be here waiting.

Lamont again thinks to himself, this is too damn good to be true. He runs scenario after scenario through his mind. What is it going be like to experience sex with two very young, beautiful, women at the same time? He knows he can handle the sex, but he does not want to find himself in a situation where he can't get it up. The Long Islands he has been drinking have him a little fucked up now. So he decides to take a little insurance. He reaches into his inside coat pocket, and feels around for the little blue pill that's there. Lamont holds the pill between his thumb and forefinger. He quickly pops it into his mouth when he thinks no one is watching, and takes a drink of his Long Island. Now he is ready for some serious fucking, he says to himself. Stan comes over with his receipt and credit card and thanks him again.

"Hey Stan, a friend is going to join us, so can I order another drink?" Lamont asks.

"Sure. What will it be?"

"Make it a Cosmopolitan. I'll pay cash for this one."

"One Cosmo coming up." Stan says.

A few more minutes go by before Gabrielle walks up with Margaret. When they get to the bar Gabrielle taps Lamont on the shoulder.

"Hey baby, I want you to meet my friend Margaret." Lamont turns around, stands up and takes Margaret's hand, and says hello. He can't believe how pretty she is. He thinks to himself, both these bitches are off the chain. Margaret is wearing dark colored blue jeans, a white top, and a thin black leather jacket. She is just as fine as Gabrielle. Lamont notices they are about the same build, fine, and thick as hell in all the right places. Margaret might be slightly taller, but not by much. Lamont knows that if the men here knew what was about to go down with him, and these women he'd have the envy of every man in this bar. All he can say to himself is, *thank you Jesus, I'm in heaven*

After introductions are made, they sit at the bar with Lamont in the middle.

"Hello Lamont. Gabrielle tells me you're looking to have a little fun tonight. I sure hope you can handle it, because we're gonna put it on you tonight." Margaret tells him.

"You are a good looking man." She says as she takes a drink of her Cosmopolitan, and feels his thigh.

"Yeah baby, I'm more than ready. Like I said to Gabrielle I'll give you all the dick you can handle."

"So Lamont, what do you think of my friend? Gabrielle asks.

"Shit she's fine as hell. You both are." Lamont says.

Both women smile, and get as close to him as possible without sitting in his lap at the bar. Lamont feels the warmth of their bodies next to him, and the sensation is almost too much to bear. He feels himself growing more excited by the second. He can barely control himself. His dick is so hard it hurts, and he can't wait to get busy. Margaret leans next to Lamont's ear and says,

"So Lamont my girl tells me you have a really big dick. Can I feel it?"

After Lamont took his pill, he adjusted himself so that his dick rested on his thigh. He feels its length against his leg. Lamont is good and fucked up now. He can't wait to feel her hand on his dick.

"Do what you need to baby my shit is rock hard." He tells her. Margaret puts her hand on his thigh, and immediately feels his dick. She moans as she feels the large long bulge under her hand. She gently squeezes as she strokes his dick, taking in his full measure. She moves her hand toward his zipper and tells him she wants it, and then she looks at Gabrielle.

"I told you he has a big one." Gabrielle states.

Stan comes over, and Lamont closes out his tab, tipping Stan a few more dollars.

"Thanks Lamont, you have a good evening." Stan says as he takes his money and walks away.

"Baby where do you want to go? We're almost finished our drinks. I'm horny as hell." Gabrielle says.

"Let's leave here and go to the Marriott across the street. I'll go and order some food, drinks, and pay for everything." Lamont says.

"No baby we'll pay for the food and drinks. We're gonna have to keep your strength, and your dick up." Gabrielle says laughing.

"That works for me." Lamont say.

The three get up and walk toward the escalator. Lamont holds Gabrielle's left hand as they walk, and holds Margaret around the waist with his left arm. He thinks to himself that tonight he has got to be the luckiest motherfucker on the planet. The three walk toward the lobby talking, laughing, and enjoying the moment. Lamont thinks to himself that he's fucked up, but not so much so that he won't be able to enjoy the fuck of his life. That thought makes him smile because he knows he's going to enjoy every second of what is to come. The air is calm and cool. It is the perfect night to be in bed. With two very fine women who want to fuck his brains out. The anticipation for him is incredible as they head toward the Marriott. In just a few minutes he's going to realize the fantasy of men the world over. They cross the street and head to the hotel. It too, is a beautiful hotel, but not quite on the scale of the Gaylord. Lamont doesn't care about the cost of the room. He got paid today, and even if he hadn't, money wouldn't come between him and these fine bitches. No way in hell He thinks to himself.

Lamont walks up to the front desk to check in. Gabrielle tells him they are going to the rest room. He is told that the hotel only has suites available. He tells the clerk a suite would be fine. He also orders a bottle of champagne. Lamont is told the champagne will be brought up to his room in a few minutes. He charges everything on his credit card, signs the invoice, and waits near the Atrium for the girls to come out of the rest room.

Gabrielle and Margaret walk up to Lamont. They each grab one of his hands and walk to the elevators.

"Lamont what floor are we on baby?" Asks Gabrielle.

"We're on lucky number seven." He says.

When they get to the elevator, Gabrielle presses the button. When the elevator arrives they get on, and Margaret pushes Lamont into the left corner, unzips his pants as the elevator door closes and pulls his dick out. She then turns, and places her back against his chest, while holding his dick with her right hand behind her back. Gabrielle stands to their left blocking any view of his exposed dick. Lamont's dick is rock hard as Margaret strokes it. She holds his dick up and against her back. He has his hands on her waist holding her from behind as he enjoys the feel of her hand. The elevator stops on the third floor, and two people get on. Margaret continues to slowly stroke his dick. Lamont looks at the two people who just got on the elevator and nods hello to the couple. He does not want to speak because he's enjoying her hand, and doesn't want to give it away by talking. The couple gets off on the next floor and the door closes. Gabrielle says she wants to taste that big dick. Gabrielle leans in to take the head of his dick in her mouth. While at the same time feeling Margaret's breast, she moans as she uses her tongue to tease the head of his dick. The elevator comes to a stop on the seventh floor, and the doors open. Waiting to get on the elevator are two middle aged black woman. They freeze in place as Gabrielle's head slowly comes up from between Margaret and Lamont's bodies. Her hand still on Margaret's breast. Gabrielle smiles at the women, and walks off the elevator followed by Margaret and Lamont, his dick still in her hand.

The two women stare in amazement as Margaret leads Lamont out of the elevator. She is still holding his dick in her hand against her back. When the trio gets around the corner, the two stunned women talk to each other.

"Girl! did she just lead that nigga out of the elevator, and down the hall holding his dick?" One friend says to the other.

"Ah, yeah, and that nigga had a big dick too. It looked like his dick was attached to that bitches back." Her friend replies laughing.

"Hey, I ain't mad at her. I guess they about to get their freak on big time. I wonder if they need some help with all that dick?" Asks one of the women.

"Nah, they look like pros. I bet he paid big money for those bitches." Both women laugh hard and get on the elevator.

The three get to the room door. Lamont gives Gabrielle the key. She opens the door and they walk in. Gabrielle takes off her jacket and puts it on the sofa. Margaret let's go of Lamont's dick, and puts her purse and bag on a table. Lamont struggles to put his dick back in his pants. All three walk around the suite, and Margaret opens the curtains to the balcony and walks outside.

"Baby, when will they bring the champagne to the room? We should probably wait until it gets here before we start fuckin'." Margaret asks.

"That's cool with me. I'll call room service and check on it now." Lamont replies.

"Hey baby, while I'm on the phone with room service should I order up some food?" Lamont asks. Gabrielle walks over to Lamont and sits next to him.

"Well I guess you could, but wouldn't it be better to wait until we're done? We'll probably be hungry as hell afterwards." She says.

"Yeah baby let's do the food afterwards. We can drink the Champagne. I want to pour it on your dick, and lick it off." Margaret says.

"We also have a bar here in the room. So we can get our drink on here as well. Would you like me to fix you one now baby?" Gabrielle asks.

"Sure, make it a vodka and orange juice." Lamont says.

He sits on the sofa in front of the Flat Screen TV. Lamont watches as his drink is fixed. Lamont's only thoughts are about the good time he is going to have. Margaret takes her bags into the bedroom, and asks for a glass of wine. When she returns, Lamont is relaxing on the couch and both women drink their wine at the bar counter. A few minutes later the Champagne, and fruit bowl arrives at the room. Gabrielle and Margaret walk over to the kitchen area. Give a knowing look to each other, put their glasses down on the counter, and walk over to Lamont.

"Lamont baby, we need to get in the shower, but before we do that, we're gonna put on a little show for you. So you just sit back and enjoy while we get undressed." Gabrielle tells him.

Before they get started both women remove their shoes. The women move the long table in the middle of the seating area to the side to give themselves more room.

They stand a few feet from Lamont, face each other and begin to undress. Gabrielle holds Margaret by her waist, and gives her a long passionate kiss. Margaret puts her arms around Gabrielle's neck and the two women are frozen in their embrace. Their lips are locked in passion. Lamont is so turned on by what he's seeing he can't wait to join in. He feels his dick getting rock hard, but for now, he just wants to enjoy the show. The women break their embrace; Margaret takes off Gabrielle's belt, and lets it drop to the floor. Her top is removed next then her bra. As Lamont watches, he can't wait to suck those big, beautiful, firm tits. Gabrielle's nipples are hard and Lamont is almost salivating.

He finishes his drink, as he watches the women freak each other. He knows the alcohol has him fucked up, but the girl on girl action has him totally alert.

Gabrielle unbuttons Margaret's top, takes it off, and throws it to Lamont. He catches it and smiles. Her bra is removed and thrown on the sofa. Gabrielle teases Margaret's nipples with her tongue as she removes her jeans, kissing Margaret's navel as she slides her pants down her legs. Margaret steps out of her pants while Gabrielle holds them at the ankles. Shit this is driving me crazy, my dick is so hard it hurts. Lamont tells himself. He gets up to fix another drink, and stands watching the women while Gabrielle's pants come off next. Lamont takes in the beauty of both women now. They have on only their panties now. They embrace for another kiss. Their breasts firm and touching, skin beautiful, and wrinkle free, hips and ass perfectly rounded. Lamont can't take anymore. As he starts to get undressed, the women now have their hands in each other's panties. Their fingers tease each other's pussy. Their kissing and moaning getting louder with every touch. The women look at Lamont and stop him.

"No baby, we're gonna undress you now." Says Gabrielle as the women break their embrace. They gesture for Lamont to come to them. He rushes to get between them. Lamont holds Gabrielle by her waist and bends down to kiss her. He figures they are both around five-six or seven.

Margaret reaches around his waist from behind, unbuckles his belt, and unzips his pants. Her breasts feel good against his back he thinks to himself.

"How tall are you Lamont?" Margaret asks.

"Six feet pretty lady."

Gabrielle unbuttons his shirt, and Margaret takes it off. The women remove his pants next, and his underwear. His dick is at attention and Margaret takes it in her hand and begins to stroke it.

"Damn baby you have a big dick and it's nice and warm." She says. Lamont thinks to himself *Thank you Viagra.* Standing in front of him, Margaret takes the head of his dick in her mouth. She sucks it slowly for a few seconds.

"Come on let's get in the shower cause I'm ready to fuck." Says Gabrielle as she walks toward the master bedroom. Margaret slides her lips off his dick and they follow her.

"Hey let's get in, and get out so we can get busy." Gabrielle says.

Gabrielle turns on the water and gets in, soon followed by Lamont and Margaret. He's surprised that they all fit in the shower stall so comfortably. He watches the water as it flows over Gabrielle's hair and body. He thinks she is even more beautiful with her eyes closed. She looks almost angelic to him, as she washes her body. With her eyes closed Gabrielle gives Margaret the soap, and turns around so she can wash her back. When Margaret finishes she turns to wash Lamont's body. Starting with his dick she lathers him, gently stroking his dick with her soapy hands. The warm water and her hands feel good to him. She moves from his dick to his stomach, and chest. They both soon rinse off. Gabrielle gets out and closes the door. She tells Lamont she's going to have another drink ready for him in the bedroom when they get out. Lamont wants to fuck. The hell with another drink he tells himself. He knows he is already fucked up, he does not really want to drink anymore, but fuck it, he tells himself.

One more drink won't hurt. Soon he is gonna have both these fine motherfuckers sucking his dick. That thought drives him wild. A little longer, and he'll be in heaven he thinks to himself. They rinse off again and Margaret grabs a towel, wraps it around herself and gives Lamont one.

"You ready to have some big fun baby?" Margaret asks him.

"Hell yeah, this is gonna be awesome." Lamont says slightly slurring his words.

She leaves Lamont to dry off and goes to the bedroom. Lamont quickly dries off, and he starts to walk out of the bathroom naked but stops. He liked the way they undressed him. He wraps the towel around his waist so the girls can take it off. He thinks they can unwrap him again and their present will be his Viagra assisted hard-on. He then walks into the bedroom. He sees Margaret lying on the bed on her stomach. Her head is facing the foot of the bed, and her perfect naked ass is calling to him. All he can think of is fucking her doggy style. While her girl watches. His dick is bulging under the towel as he walks toward the bed. Gabrielle walks in the bedroom with his drink.

"Here's your drink baby." She says as she hands Lamont the drink, and removes his towel. She holds his dick in one hand and puts the other around his shoulder as she reaches up to kiss him.

"Baby I like it up the ass."

Margaret says as she smacks her ass. Gabrielle, still holding Lamont's dick leads him to the bed and Lamont slams his drink back. Lamont kneels on the bed and positions himself behind Margaret. Gabrielle goes to the dresser. Lamont holds Margaret's hip with his left hand and guides her ass to his dick. Margaret quickly puts a pillow under her chest and raises her hips, waiting for his dick to enter her ass.

"Wait baby, lube that big dick up with some KY first. Use a lot and pour some on her asshole too." Gabrielle says as she gives Lamont the lubricant.

While he lubricates his dick Gabrielle asks him a question.

"Baby do you trust me?" Lamont does not respond, he only sees that ass in front of him.

Gabrielle thinks to herself that he probably can't concentrate on anything but that big red ass in front of him. Gabrielle asks him the same question standing in front of Margaret, and waving her hand. As

Gabrielle speaks, Margaret rubs the back of Gabrielle's legs and pulls her closer so that she can kiss Gabrielle's pussy. Gabrielle cups Margaret's face in her hands, and continues to speak as Margaret licks her pussy.

"Baby you want to tie her to the bed, before you fuck her in the ass?"

"Hell yeah, I never done that before." Lamont slurs.

"Ok baby we're all gonna take turns being tied to the bed, you ok with that?"

"Yeah I'm down for whatever, just do it so I can start fuckin." I'm gonna tear this pretty ass up." He says.

With cum dripping on her back, Margaret tells Gabrielle to hurry so she can get this big dick up her ass. She fingers her pussy, and brushes her ass against Lamont's dick. The lubricant makes his dick slide easily against her cheeks and Lamont enjoys the sensation. While Lamont is rubbing Margaret's back, and ass with his hands and dick, Gabrielle quickly goes to the large bag that Margaret brought with her to the room. She removes two sets of shackles from the bag. She goes over to Margaret, bends down, kisses her, and tells her she's about to be tied to the bed. Margaret reaches behind her, feeling for Lamont's dick. Gabrielle kisses Lamont, and tells him she's gonna tie him to the bed also. He says nothing as Margaret forcefully strokes his dick, and at the same time tells him she wants him to cum in her ass. Gabrielle attaches leather ankle straps to both of Lamont's ankles, buckles them, and quickly attaches, and locks the chains to the lower front bedposts. She pulls tight on the chains until Lamont's feet are almost touching the headboard. Lamont has to hold Margaret around her waist, with both hands to keep his balance while kneeling on the bed. He's finding it difficult, because his legs feel like they are almost straight, and he can't bend them easily. He thinks to himself fuck it, I'll find a way to run up in this ass. He pulls Margaret closer to him.

"Come on Gabrielle hurry up! Shit!" Lamont screams.

"Hold on baby, you can fuck her as soon as I tie her ass to the bed." Gabrielle says.

Gabrielle attaches a Velcro wrist strap to Margaret's wrist. Gabrielle attaches it to the bed. She also attaches a leather wrist strap to Lamont's left wrist, and pulls out the slack until Lamont's left side is pinned against her body. She secures the chain to the leg of the bed.

"Damn baby this shit's a little tight." He says.

"No baby, wait till you put your dick in her ass. She won't be able to do shit but lie there, and take it." Gabrielle says. That thought excites him even more. Margaret folds her left arm against her chest, and raises her ass up, preparing herself to receive his dick in her ass.

"Ok baby go to work. Fuck her in the ass." Gabrielle says as she moves away to watch.

Lamont tries to use his right hand to guide his dick to her asshole. But since he can't move his left leg or his left hand he's finding it difficult to get in position. After a few attempts he finds himself getting frustrated. Every time she moves her ass, his dick slides between her cheeks. She can move her legs, and ass to help him but she's not. He thinks all she has to do is stay still, and he can get it in. He tries again to get his dick in Margaret's asshole, but as soon as he gets close she wiggles her hips, and his dick slips between her cheeks again. After a few attempts, Margaret voices her frustrations.

"What the fuck! Come on baby, put the dick in my ass, and go to work." Margaret demands.

"This is what you want right? Well take it motherfucka don't make me wait. Fuck my ass!" Margaret orders.

"Hold still baby I almost got it in, just move under me a little more." Lamont says breathing heavier with frustration and anticipation. Gabrielle walks over to the right side of the bed, and kneels next to Margaret.

"Come on baby put it in her ass. You're in the right position, and your dick is hard so just put it in." Gabrielle says.

"I'm trying baby, shit! I can't move the way I need to. Lamont slurs.

"You need me to help you put it in her ass baby? I know you're not used to being tied up, but you need to work this shit out. How bad do you want this ass?" Gabrielle asks.

Gabrielle puts one hand on Margaret's hip, and guides her into position. Lamont cannot raise his left side off the bed very much. He tries to raise the right side of his body as high as he can. The awkward position is starting to cause pain in his side but he tries anyway.

Gabrielle uses her free hand to guide his dick to Margaret's ass. While Lamont steadies himself with his free hand by holding Margaret by her waist. He tries again, but he can't pull back far enough so he still can't penetrate.

"Bitch, will you stop moving your ass, and let me get it in!" Lamont says in frustration. Margaret voices her own frustrations.

"Motherfucker are you blind, or too fuckin' drunk to get it in? Don't blame me because you don't know what the fuck you're doing." She complains.

The positioning feels awkward to him, and he is starting to get angry, both with himself and for allowing himself to be tied down. Lamont no longer wants to be restrained in this way. He tells Gabrielle to remove his restraints. Gabrielle moves off the bed and stands up. Lamont is breathing heavy, and is so frustrated he just lies on top of Margaret's back for a minute.

"Take this shit off my goddamn feet and hand." He demands.

"Ok baby we can do this without being tied down, but it would have been so much more fun." Gabrielle says.

"Let me take Margaret's off first and we can start again." She says. Gabrielle goes around the bed to release Margaret.

She unclips the fastener that secured the chain to the bed. Lamont rises off her back, and Margaret pushes away from him with both hands as Gabrielle helps her off the bed.

"Ok, now get this shit the fuck off of me." Lamont demands as Margaret removes the strap from her wrist, and lets the chain fall to the floor.

"Ok baby, we still have all night to have our fun." Gabrielle says as she knells on the bed, and lays on Lamont's back. She wraps her arms around his chest, then finds his dick with her right hand, and gently strokes it.

"Lamont, baby you can hit this pussy doggy style. I don't take it up the ass."

Gabrielle tells him. He lays on the bed with his eyes closed, enjoying the feel of her hand. He waits for Margaret to release him so they can do what he came here to do.

Watching the two on the bed, Margaret reaches under the bed. She quickly pulls out a long chained handcuff, attached to the leg of the bed, and closes it around his right wrist. The feel of the cold metal and the clicking sound of its closing immediately alerts him.

"Bitch I said take this shit off me." Lamont demands. Gabrielle quickly releases his dick, moves off his back, and stands. Struggling against the restraints, Lamont is now furious, and demands that he be let go.

"Bitch get this shit the fuck off me now!" He demands again.

Both Gabrielle, and Margaret check the restraints at both ends of the bed. Margaret goes to her bag, and takes out a handful of thick police style flex cuffs. She gives Gabrielle half, and they move to the bed posts, and quickly secure the chains of the restraints to the legs of the bed using the flex cuffs. Lamont pulls against the restraints with all of his might. He's frantically trying to free both his hands and legs. In a mad frenzy, he tries to pull his knees toward his chest, while at the same time pulling in his arms. Tied to the bed spread eagle makes his attempt to break free impossible, because he cannot get any leverage. He realizes after a few minutes he doesn't have the strength to break away. He is beyond furious now as he shakes, and struggles to free himself. The women stand there watching and laughing.

"You bitches better let me go or I'll kill your fuckin' asses!"

"Oh poor baby. You can't get your dumbass off the bed? That's what you get for letting us tie your drunk, stupid ass to the bed. How you gonna kill us if you can't touch us?" Gabrielle asks as she laughs.

Margaret walks over to Lamont, stands in front of him, and rubs him on the head.

"You wanted some of this good tight ass and pussy didn't you baby? Too bad you couldn't find the hole, because I was gonna let you fuck me." She says laughing as she stands in front of him rubbing her pussy.

Gabrielle takes something out of Margaret's bag, and walks over to the bed. She sits on Lamont's back, her ass against his. Lamont shakes and struggles like a bucking horse trying to shake her off. Her breasts bounce as he struggles.

"This is a fun ride baby. I bet it's not the one you had planned." Gabrielle says laughing.

"Bitch get the fuck off me. I'm gonna put my foot in both you bitches' asses."

Lamont says as he continues to struggle. He thinks he heard a door close in the next room. He quickly turns his head left and right. Doing his best to take in his surroundings, trying to see what is going on behind him.

"Motherfucker you can't do shit. Your drunk ass can't do nothing except shout like a little girl. I'm tired of hearing that bullshit come out of your mouth, about what your gonna do to us. You couldn't even fuck my girl in the ass, and it was right in front of you." Gabrielle says, and they both laugh.

"Fuck you, you skank ass bitch!" Lamont shouts.

At that moment, Margaret walks over, and slaps Lamont as hard as she can across his face. The slap not only startles, but scares him. He tries to look up at her, but he is in an awkward position laying on his stomach, and tied down. He also realizes for the first time that they really mean to hurt him. He believes someone else is in the room, besides the three of them and that frightens him.

"We're not gonna keep being bitches motherfucker. If we're bitches then, what the fuck are you? You know, don't answer. I'm tired of hearing your shit anyway. Gag this stupid asshole, girl." Margaret says.

Gabrielle takes the object she took out of Margaret's bag, and dangles it in front of Lamont. She explains to him that it is called a ball gag, and how it is used. She swings it back and forth in front of him like a pendulum. She watches with satisfaction as he curses louder, and struggles harder against his restraints. He watches helplessly as the red ball goes back and forth in front of his face. Now he knows he is in serious trouble, and that cause his heart to race.

"Ok babe, it's time to make you shut the fuck up."

Gabrielle says still sitting on his back. She takes the gag by both straps, and positions the ball in front of Lamont's mouth. She tells him to open his mouth.

"Open your filthy mouth please, Lamont. It doesn't matter whether you do or not. It'll just make things easier, and less painful for you. No, have it your way, motherfucker. You can struggle all you want cause you're going nowhere."

Holding the ball tight against his mouth, she pulls back as hard as she can. She bends his neck back, and forces the ball to wedge open his lips. Margaret comes over, and holds his head in place. Gabrielle quickly and expertly inserts one end into the buckle, pulls the strap and locks it in place. Both women let him go.

"I wish you could see yourself. You look really stupid tied to the bed with a red rubber ball strapped to your mouth." Gabrielle goes on as Lamont continues to struggle. "What's that you're saying baby? I can't make it out. It's that ball in your mouth, stupid. That's why it's called a gag. It'll muffle your bad mouthing us, and any other sounds you might make." Lamont continues to struggle to no avail. "Oh, you can make as much noise as you want. It won't matter."

At that moment, Margaret comes over to Gabrielle, and holds up a small digital camera. Gabrielle walks over to the bed, sits on Lamont's back, and pulls the straps attached to Lamont's head toward her, jerking his head back again. She holds the position, and Margaret takes pictures from several angles. Lamont struggles and tries his best to break free, but he can do nothing. Margaret gives the camera to Gabrielle. She takes more shots of Lamont on the bed.

"Let me get into a different position." Margaret says.

She stands in front of his face. She puts one of her legs on the bed, moves closer to Lamont's face, grabs his head with both of her hands, and rubs her pussy against the ball in his mouth. Then she gets on the bed, and pulls a blanket over the both of them up to the shoulders, and lays there while Gabrielle takes more pictures. She gets up and stands in front of him in her previous position.

"Oh baby, is it good for you? Does mama's pussy taste good?" Margaret asks as she rubs her pussy against the ball gag in his mouth again.

"Margaret let him have a very special drink of something warm and wet."

Gabrielle says laughing. Margaret stands in front of Lamont, puts her left leg on the bed; then with both hands on his neck she positions her pussy at his forehead, and pisses in Lamont's face, as Gabrielle takes more photos. Gabrielle continues to take pictures for several minutes from all angles around the bed. Lamont's smothered cries of rage are barely audible. Gabrielle moves in to take close-up shots now, and notices Lamont's eyes, and where he is looking. Gabrielle looks to her left and smiles. Margaret is enjoying herself. Her eyes are closed, hips are in motion, and the feel of the ball against her wet pussy has her moaning with pleasure. Her humiliation of Lamont heightens her sensations. She continues slowly rubbing her pussy against the ball in his mouth. Margaret's hips swaying in slow motion close to his face. As if she is dancing to a song, only she can hear. He lays on the bed totally helpless and more frightened than he's ever been in his life. Lamont wonders why this is happening to him. He's hoping this has got to be an alcohol induced nightmare. Praying that he is gonna wake up from this nightmare any minute. He can't understand why these women are doing this to him. He was nice to those bitches he thinks to himself. He wonders why they would treat him like this, and what are they going to do next. A serious panic runs through his mind and body, as he gets a look at the person who just entered the room. The hell with this he thinks. He screams in his mind for help to get out of this room, out of this nightmare, but no one can hear his thoughts. Tired and drunk but aware of what's happening, he lays motionless on the bed. All he wants is to get out of this room and run home.

Gabrielle walks over to the person that just entered the bedroom, and gives her a hug.

"Chantel, where have you been? We almost had to let this bastard ass fuck Margaret."

At the mention of Chantel's name, Margaret opens her eyes. She steps away from Lamont and goes over to the other women. Chantel embraces Margaret, and asks her if she's ok.

"Yeah, girl I'm fine, but I almost had to take it up the ass from that bastard. Good thing he had a little trouble getting it in, and way too much to drink." Margaret laughs.

"What kept you?" She asks.

"We'll talk about that later. Who do we have here, Gabrielle?" Chantel asks.

"His name is Lamont." "Well I think it's time we give Lamont what was promised."

Chantel removes her coat and then removes the rest of her clothing, and goes over to the bed. She stands in front of Lamont, with her hands on her beautifully rounded hips so that he can see her. As scared as he is now, he can't help but notice that Chantel is slightly taller than both Gabrielle and Margaret, and just as beautiful. She sits down, and calls Gabrielle over to take more pictures of her in provocative poses with Lamont on the bed.

"Have we done a piss shot yet Gabrielle." Asks Chantel.

"Yeah Margaret took care of that." Chantel calls Margaret over and tells her to lie on the bed as well. Gabrielle takes more pictures of both women with Lamont. They take pictures kissing and touching his body, each other, feeling under him and holding his dick. Chantel instructs Margaret to crawl under his body, and position herself as if he's fucking her from behind. She gets under him, and faces the camera; contorting her face with closed eyes, as if he's fucking her, while Gabrielle takes the pictures. For a fraction of a second, Lamont thinks this is all part of some twisted game. When Margaret gets under him, he actually thinks after everything that has happened that he is still going to fuck her. Another thought quickly comes to his mind when the camera stopped flashing. Why are these bitches taking pictures? Just as that thought comes to him, Chantel comes back over to the bed and sits down.

"Bring me his wallet Gabrielle." Chantel requests. A few seconds later the wallet is handed to her, and she opens it.

"Let's see what we have here. A nice stack of cash. Let's see how much." Chantel counts three-hundred-sixty dollars.

"Lamont were you gonna pay my girl for letting you fuck her in the ass, or was that supposed to be part of your fun too?" Chantel takes the money out of the wallet, and puts it on the nightstand. "What else do we have here?" Chantel asks.

She empties the contents of his wallet, Credit cards, debit cards, and various insurance cards. She stops when she comes to the pictures and his driver's license. Lamont doesn't know what to think at this point. He thinks to himself if the pictures they've taken get out, it could ruin him at work, and at home. He wonders if all this is about money. I'll give them the fuckin money if that's it. What do these bitches want? He says to himself. He continues to struggle against his bonds, and make unintelligible noises. Gabrielle and Margaret are sitting across from the bed on the sofa drinking wine, and smoking cigarettes as Chantel speaks to Lamont.

"Lamont is this picture of your wife?" She turns the picture toward his face so that he can see it. He simply continues to struggle, and make noises as he looks away.

"Look at the picture Lamont. What do you think your wife would say, if she could see your dumb ass now? I bet she thinks you're a loyal husband doesn't she Lamont? Does your wife know you fuck around? Oh, I keep forgetting it's hard to talk with that gag in your mouth. I still can't help wondering. What would this pretty lady in the picture say, if she could see her husband now." Chantel states as she looks at the picture, and walks over to Lamont. What would be her reaction if she saw you tied to a bed, naked, in a room with three very gorgeous and naked women? What do you think would go through her mind Lamont?" Chantel asks again as she smacks his ass. He can only mumble his response. "Gabrielle, if this was your man, and you saw him like this in photos what would you say?"

"I don't know. I would be some kind of fucked up though." Gabrielle responds as she takes a sip of wine looking at Lamont.

"Well, I would first say this has to be a joke. No way is that my man. But looking at the pictures we took, I'd be crushed, hurt, crying, and all kinds of shit." Responds Margaret as she smokes her cigarette.

"Chantel I want to hear what he has to say." Gabrielle asks.

"Yeah, let's find out what it's worth to him for these pictures to not find their way to his wife and job." Margaret adds.

"Ok, let's find out. Take off his gag Margaret, and let's hear what he has to say for himself." Chantel says.

Margaret walks over to the bed, sits on Lamont's back, and removes the ball gag from his mouth. As she does that, Chantel takes more pictures.

"Before you say something stupid, just listen. You heard what we were saying. Answer the question." Margaret tells him before she releases the straps.

Tired, drunk, and now frightened Lamont tries to maintain some kind of composure once the gag is removed. He figures if he can keep his cool they will let him go.

"Shit, why y'all doing this to me? The fuck did I do to y'all? I thought we was friends Gabrielle. Let me go, and I'll just walk away. You can keep the damn money. Just untie me from this goddamn bed." Lamont says in a slurred angry voice. Chantel stands up and tells him that's not the question she asked.

"Answer the goddamn question I asked you! You will leave when we say your ass can leave!" Chantel shouts. Lamont turns to look at Chantel and responds.

"What fuckin' question bitch? I don't know who the fuck you are. If you want money, I can get you a lot more. Untie me and let me go to the goddamn ATM. I can get you more money. Just turn me the fuck loose." Lamont says.

"Put the gag back in this motherfuckers mouth Margaret. He doesn't want to cooperate with us." Lamont renews his struggle, and curses the women as the gag is placed back in his mouth.

"All you had to do was answer my very easy question. It wasn't that hard Lamont but you fucked that up too." "Margaret go get ready so we can get this over with." Chantel says, as all three women leave the bedroom.

Lamont looks at the women frantically wondering what she meant by get this over. He doesn't want to find out, so he again tries to break free of his restraints. He is now terrified because he is convinced that these women mean to seriously hurt him in some way. Chantel returns a few seconds later. She places the bag she brought back with her in a chair by the bed. Gabrielle, now wearing a robe comes into the room, and sits on the sofa. She is followed by Margaret who is also wearing a robe. She sits on the bed with Lamont.

"Lamont does your wife let you give it to her up the ass? I bet you can't even ask her that question. I bet you're afraid to ask her that. Why is it that married men always want to do shit with other women that they can't, or won't do with their wives?" Chantel asks.

"Because men like him, want to think that their wives are good girls. Men like him don't want to treat their wives like freaks. They don't want to abused their wives assholes like that, even when they want it. Men like him are afraid that if the real woman comes out, they'll lose respect for her, or they can't handle what they ask her for." Gabrielle responds.

"Does she give you head when you want it, Lamont? Do you eat her pussy? Can you even satisfy your wife in bed Lamont? How big a freak are you with her at home? You ever ask her to do a threesome? I bet you're too much of a pussy to explore that shit with your wife, aren't you Lamont? But you couldn't wait to fuck my girl in the ass could you?" Chantel continues talking as she gets out of the chair in front of Lamont, and walks over to the sofa. Gabrielle opens her robe and takes her place in the chair.

What Lamont sees sends him into a mad frenzy. Gabrielle is wearing a dildo, as she sits; she strokes it, and smiles as she looks in Lamont's eyes. The sight is horribly freakish as thoughts of escape at any cost go through his mind. Lamont goes berserk as he pulls and struggles like a trapped animal. He tells himself that he will break away from this bed. His anger is so great. He wants nothing more than to kill these women. His muscles strain as he twists, and he turns his body as best he can to break his restraints. He struggles with all the strength left in his body. He succeeds only in exhausting himself. All his screams of protest are muffled by the gag in his mouth.

"All you motherfuckers care about is yourselves. As long as you get yours, that's all that matters. You rotten bastards never get enough, and you don't care who, or where you get it from, or who gets hurt. Just so that you're not confused baby I'm talking about men like you. As long as you get your rocks off, you're good to go." Chantel says.

Chantel looks at Margaret as if she's giving her a silent command. Margaret stands, removes her robe completely, gets back on the bed and positions herself between Lamont's out-stretched legs. Chantel hands her a bottle and sits back on the couch.

"Well baby you get to experience firsthand what it's like to be abused the way we were. You ever wonder what it's like to have something forced in your ass baby." Chantel asks Lamont.

As Chantel speaks, Lamont feels cold liquid dripping on his legs and ass. He feels something cold touch both cheeks of his ass, and the object finds its way between them. He looks at Gabrielle in blind terror. His eyes focused on her crotch, she smiles an evil seductive smile at him. Lamont is in a sheer panic that he's never experienced, and can't control. His body involuntarily recoils from the object touching him. He tries to speak but can't. He attempts to scream out in protest but his words make no sense. He feels the object slowly, forcefully penetrate his ass hole. His head and chest comes off the bed as he tries to pull his arms into his body, but the restraints he's attached to won't allow him to. The gag muffles his screams, but they are strong and agonizing as the object is forced into his rectum. Margaret works the dildo she's wearing in Lamont's ass slowly, and repeatedly. She strokes his asshole easily at first, applying more lubricant as she goes. After a while her thrusts become more forceful. Lamont's only thought is pain. It's the pain of having what he now knows is a dildo forced in his rectum. His mind can't comprehend what is happening to him. He has no words to describe his pain, and humiliation. His mind only registers agony. Margaret is not gentle as she strokes him in the ass. Her thrusts become harder, and more forceful as the lubricant does its job. Lamont screams with each trust, and the tears he cries come in torrents. Margaret holds him by the waist. and continues thrusting harder and harder. Her sweat drips on his back. She pauses on the down stroke, leaving the entire dildo in his ass so she can catch her breath. As she does so, she lays on Lamont's back, and holds her sweat covered breasts against his body. She asks Lamont a question that does not register. She compounds his torment and humiliation by gently rubbing his arms as if that will make his pain go away.

"How does this feel baby? Isn't this what you wanted to do to me? Didn't you want to put your dick in my ass?" She says as she applies downward pressure. Lamont reacts by moaning louder, and jerking his body as if trying to get the dildo out of his ass.

I think you said you were gonna tear my asshole up, didn't you baby? You wanted to put that huge dick of yours in my ass, and fuck me till it hurt didn't you baby. Well motherfucker this is what it feels like!" Margaret says as she resumes thrusting it faster, and harder in his rectum. Every humiliating second is captured digitally by the camera the women brought with them.

Chantel takes photos from every possible angle around the bed. She captures the inhuman look of pain on Lamont's face. She captures the agony, and tears in his eyes with each flash of the camera. She captures the helplessness on his face, as he is unable to give voice to his torment, or to free himself. Margaret finally stops, and slowly withdraws the mass of plastic, and rubber out of his ass. It is wet with lubricant and blood.

She kneels between his outstretched legs sweating from her exertions.

"How did that feel baby? It was only seven inches in your ass. You'll get used to it. The bigger ones feel better right? Isn't that what you motherfuckers tell us? Doesn't every man brag about how big his dick is, even if it isn't? I got a big dick baby. You're gonna love this dick in your pussy. Well baby all you have to do is just relax when you feel it go in." Margaret says as she laughs, and gets off the bed. She then sits in front of Lamont, and shows him again what just came out of his ass.

Lamont knows that each one of the women plan to fuck him, and once again he reacts violently, trying to summon what strength he can to try and free himself. But like his earlier attempts, the result is the same. He can go nowhere. He wants to beg the women to let him go, but he can't. The gag and now the saliva he is drooling around the gag block his words. He cries and screams in his mind. Lamont asks God to give him the strength to get out of this room, and away from these monstrosities.

"Hey baby we're just getting started. I went easy on you. Gabrielle has a bigger dick that's about the size of yours. Let me know how you like it. I need to take a shower." Margaret says as she gets up, and heads for the shower.

Gabrielle approaches the bed slowly, lubricating the dildo she's wearing by stroking it with KY as she gets closer. She tells Lamont to look at her, but he refuses so she gets on the bed as he continues to struggle with everything he has left. Even through his pain, he struggles. He does so even more when Gabrielle starts to force the fake dick she is wearing in his ass. The gag muffles Lamont's screams, but he screams anyway as another fake dick is forced in his ass. Chantel sits in the chair watching as Gabrielle goes to work fucking Lamont in his ass. She is merciless to him, and enjoys hearing his muffled screams of pain, and the contorted movements of his body. Every time she strokes him she pulls the fake dick out almost completely, leaving in only the head, and rams it all in him again. She makes a grunting sound every time she strokes him. It's not the passionate sound a woman would make when she's getting fucked. It's more the sound a man would make when he knows his dick his hurting her. The sound she makes is one of payback and pain. She does this repeatedly. Lamont is in so much pain now, that his high-pitched screams of agony are almost heard through the gag. Chantel watches as her girl goes to work on Lamont's ass. She knows that Gabrielle is enjoying herself as she long dicks Lamont. Chantel thinks to herself Gabrielle really is a beauty. She's enjoying herself so much as she fucks this idiot it's almost sickening. She looks like a beautiful demon. Her eyes seem to change every time she pulls out of his ass. Her head's back and eyes closed as she comes up. On the down stroke, she lets the weight of her body push the dick in his ass, as if she's almost falling on his back. But it's those beautiful eyes that captivate Chantel. Gabrielle opens her eyes as she fucks him, and looks down as she continues fucking him. She wants to see that blood stained dick forced in his ass. All Lamont can do is scream and cry. Gabrielle begins to talk to him.

"You like this baby? You like this big dick in your ass don't you bitch? Say you like it bitch! Tell big daddy you like this dick in your ass you dirty fuckin' whore! I can't wait to put all this dick in your pussy bitch, and then I'll let you swallow the whole dick, and cum again down your fuckin' throat. I'm gonna tear this ass to shreds before I let my boys fuck you too. Tell me how much you love this dick bitch!"

Gabrielle speaks as she's fucking him but is talking to no one. The words come out of her mouth, but they seem to flow from somewhere deeper inside of her. It is as if she's recalling memories of a very painful past, and is lost in time. Her heart is pounding, and her body is drenched in sweat. Her hair is wet and there is blood on the sheets. Still those beautiful dark eyes lock onto those of Chantel, and they both smile. Lamont is so exhausted and in such pain that all he can do is lay there and cry, as Gabrielle slowly withdraws the fake dick out of his ass. Gabrielle gets off the bed and walks away. She turns to look at Chantel and heads for the shower.

"You want to know what she was talking about when she was fucking you Lamont?"

The only thought going through his mind is of escape. He wants to beg them to leave him alone, to stop the torture of his body. He wants them to stop what they are doing to him, and to ask why they would hurt him this way. As he cries and lies on the bed, he asks himself what the fuck he did to deserve what's happening to him. His mind, and body are in such torment that when Chantel speaks, nothing she says registers with him.

"Do you have any idea what it's like, to be raised in a country where the only thing a woman has to look forward to, is being raped, and sexually abused? Where the more beautiful you are the more desirable, so the abuse starts even earlier. A place where you are kept ignorant, and the only thing you're good for is to be passed around to be some man's sex slave. Where we come from young girls are taught, at an early age that they can get what they want, if they are willing to fuck for it. That could be for food, clothes, for somewhere to sleep. Education isn't even on the list of priorities, Lamont. So by the time most of us are in our early teens, we've already been through countless men. Most women in my country can't read, or write, but we are experts at fucking by the time we're in our early-teens. We're kept as sex slaves in filthy shacks to have someplace to sleep. We fuck for food in order to eat. We're kept waiting for the next man to come along, and when he does we don't get a dime of the money we got fucked for. Guess where that goes? To the pimp we work for.

Sometimes we are even sold by our parents, to pay their bills or debts. In my case that's what happened to me. My father sold me to pay a fucking gambling debt. We are gang raped at parties, and passed around like old shoes. We grow up accepting that this is the life we are supposed to live, and that this is the way it is because we've never been taught anything different. That's the life many women have in the Dominican Republic. Men from all over the states, and the world come there on vacation, and weekend trips just to fuck us. My country is known for ours women's beauty, and our pussy. Sometimes we are treated like human beings, but for the most part we are abused and treated like trash. If a young girl is lucky enough, to get through what you call grade school she's doing well. That doesn't happen often, but in my case I was one of the lucky ones. I was able to get out of that life, and leave that shit hole. You want to know how Lamont?"

Lamont hears her talking, but none of her words register in his mind. He is cold and shaking uncontrollably. Lamont's only thought is getting away from these demons, and getting out of this situation alive. So when she asks him another question he can says nothing.

"Oh baby you're shivering. Let me get a blanket for you." Chantel says.

She goes to the top of the bed, and pulls a blanket over his naked body. She takes note of the blood on the sheet and on Lamont. Chantel sits back in her chair and continues.

"When I was seventeen a man bought me from my pimp, and made arrangements to bring me to the states. You can guess why, but I was happy anyway. I was leaving for a better place. Well when we got to the states it quickly turned into a nightmare. I found myself on the streets of Houston working as a prostitute. One night me, and three other girls were working a roach infested motel. The girl in the room next to mine was fucked, and killed by the man she was with. When I heard her scream, and the gunshot I jumped out the back window and never looked back. I made a promise to myself that that would never happen to me. A woman I met soon after took me in, and helped me to get away from all that shit. She used to be in the life, and so she knew what I'd been through."

At that moment, Gabrielle and Margaret walk into the bedroom dressed in the clothes they were wearing earlier. They pour themselves each a glass of wine and light cigarettes. Chantel continues talking to Lamont.

"Years later after I got my shit together, I vowed that no one would ever use me that way again. I eventually went back to that hellhole I call home, and I was determined to help other women who were growing up the way I did, but not having the resources to accomplish what I wanted to was difficult. I soon learned that things weren't quite going the way I planned, so I decided to go another route. Soon after that, I formed a new plan, than I met Gabrielle and Margaret, and they decided to join me."

Lamont looks at Chantel and turns his head away. Tears continue to flow from his eyes. He can't respond and nothing that he would say would stop her. He knows this, so he closes his eyes and waits for whatever is to come.

"Well, I think I've talked enough. It's time to get this over with." Chantel walks to the side of the bed Lamont is facing, and orders him to look at her. He does what he is told, and she removes her robe and lets it fall to the floor. Lamont cries like a baby. Then his screams get progressively louder. Unable to get away from what is to come, and knowing that there is no one to help him, he struggles against his restraints. All he can think about is escape. Chantel pulls the blanket off him, and asks Gabrielle to bring her a towel so that she can wipe away some of the blood flowing from his ass. Chantel takes the KY bottle from the dresser, and lubes her fake dick as she prepares to fuck Lamont with it.

"Which one is that Chantel? It looks like the twelve." Gabrielle says.

"It is." She responds. "Oh Lamont stop acting like a baby. No one ever died from being fucked in the ass." Chantel says laughing. "You just had nine inches in your ass so this won't be that bad." She says.

Before Chantel starts, Lamont's cries get louder and louder. He begs in his mind for someone to stop this. He's begging for someone to help him. He wishes with all his might that this night is just a horrible nightmare; that he will soon wake up from. When he feels the dildo go in his ass, he knows it's not a dream, and he screams both physically and in his mind. Chantel pushes it in slowly and methodically, easing the obscenely long dildo in his ass. Gabrielle and Margaret look on while smoking and drinking wine. Chantel works the entire length of it in his rectum. When she can push no further, she slowly and methodically strokes him in the ass until she gets tired of fucking him.

Her head is back as she arches her body backward and holds onto Lamont's legs. Her breast bounce as she rhythmically thrusts forward. Like the two previous times, Lamont can do nothing but take what the women are doing to him. As Chantel fucks him, his eyes bulge so large he thinks they may burst in his head. He can only make noises now. Lamont no longer has the strength to scream, and the gag now has his mouth numb. He just wants this torture to stop. Tired now after her exertions, she finally stops and pulls the fake dick out of his ass. Its' entire length is covered in his blood. Lamont feels the relief of its' withdrawal, but the damage is done. The burning pain screaming in his mind is so intense; he feels it might drive him insane. He lies on the bed not moving, not thinking, and only cry's tears of pain. He breathes heavily, as he feels the blood flow freely from his rectum.

"There that wasn't so bad was it Lamont? Was it good to you baby? It was damn good for me. I'm going to take a shower. Take the gag out of his mouth." Chantel says as she walks away and heads to the shower.

Gabrielle and Margaret sit there looking at Lamont's shaking body on the bed. They finish their wine, giving Lamont's pain not a single thought. Margaret walks over to the bed and removes the gag from his mouth. Lamont lies still on the bed with his eyes closed. He doesn't want to see these demons that have ruined his life, and destroyed all that he was. He doesn't want to remember what they look like, or their names or anything else about them. He wills himself to remain silent. His breathing is heavy and labored because he is in a state of indescribable fear, and great pain. He lays tied to the bed. Every muscle in his body screams in pain from cramping, due to his attempts to free himself. His pain tells him he is still alive, and of the damage, the demons have inflicted on his body. The bleeding and painful throbbing of his rectum reminds him of his now shattered manhood, and his broken psyche. He feels sickness in his stomach now from all the alcohol he drank, and wants to throw-up, but for now he is too frightened to move or even think much. He can smell the odor of their cigarettes, and his own blood. He can hear their talking and footsteps. Lamont can hear every other sound in the room, but he can't bring himself to react to anything. He has prepared himself for death. He tells himself that they are now going to shoot him in the head, or plunge a knife in his back. He no longer cares what they do to him, or what happens to his body. He has decided that after what has just happened to him he wants to die. When Chantel comes back into the room, she is also dressed as she was earlier. She tells Gabrielle and Margaret to make sure they gather everything they brought with them. The women are told to wait for her in the living room area of the suite.

"I don't think he's gonna need that cash, so I'll take that with me." Margaret says as she picks up the money, and walks out of the room. Gabrielle walks over to the bed, puts both her hands on his head, bends down, and whispers in his ear

"It's been fun, now go home to your wife." Gabrielle takes one last look at Lamont, and leave the room.

Chantel sits in the seat facing the bed. Lamont remains still and quiet.

"Well Lamont this is where we part company. I know exactly how you're feeling. You came here thinking you were gonna get your freak on. Instead, the only one that got fucked was you. Remember what I said earlier about the fucked up lives we had growing up. This kind of shit happened to us on a regular basis. Now you know what we went through and how that shit made us feel. But don't worry baby, in time you'll get over it, and you'll learn to live with it. Trust me. Sometimes you find support in the strangest places. Before I leave you Lamont, I'm gonna untie one of your hands so that you can leave when you're ready. Don't forget checkout time is noon." She says laughing.

Chantel takes one last look around the room. She wants to make sure that they don't leave anything behind. She spots the camera on the counter. She walks over to the bed, pulls the blanket over Lamont's body, picks up the camera, and takes one last photo of him. Chantel takes a key out of her pocket, and unlocks the handcuff on his wrist. As she leaves the bedroom she closes the door behind her. All three women leave the suite, and head for the elevator. They take the elevator to parking level three, walk to Chantal's car, and leave the building. Gabrielle opens the Champagne as they pull away. They drink the entire bottle on the highway. Lamont is not sure how long he lay on the bed without moving, or uttering a sound. It seems like days to him even though he knows it's been hours. Hours since the monsters left him lying on the bed bleeding, and in pain. His right arm is free, and it's taken him over an hour to free himself completely. His every movement is accompanied with varying degrees of pain. When he does finally free his limbs he curls into a fetal position, and lies on the bed.

He wants to get up, and clean himself but the pain in his rectum is still with him. He looks at the window, and sees it's still dark outside. Lamont knows it will soon be morning. He thinks to himself how the hell can he live with what was done to him. How could any man live with what was just forced upon him. He doesn't have the answer, and there is no one he can turn to for that kind of counsel. He simply wants to lay here and cry. There is no one in the room with him now to see his tears. He lets the pain of this humiliating experience manifest itself, in the form of tears that will not stop. Not wanting to think about what happened to him, but unable to hold back the memories. He realizes that those bitches could come back, or something worse could come in. So he wills himself to get off the bed, so that he can check the door to the room. He slowly, and painfully throws his legs off the bed, and he feels the pain of his damaged rectum scream to him to stay still. He stands on uneasy legs, and the pain in his ass sends him back to the bed. He cries out loud as the throbbing pain intensifies. It's as if the things used to abuse his body are still in him. The thought forces him to get up, and head for the suite's door.

He stops in the threshold of the bedroom door, turns, and looks at the bed and sees his blood on the sheets. He staggers to the front door of the suite, and frantically applies the locks on the door. He double-checks all three locks. When he's satisfied no one can enter his room he relaxes. Lamont tells himself he needs to clean himself. Standing at the door naked he realizes that he's cold, and wants to take a hot shower to wash away what was done to him. He walks to the bathroom and freezes as he enters. Lying on the floor he sees one of the objects that were used to abuse his ass. A large fake dick attached to what looks like some kind of harness covered in his blood. Having seen it, he now knows why his pain is so great. His anger makes him kick the object to the side, and he gets in the shower. He braces his hands against the shower wall, and lets the water flow over his head and face. The waters sooth his aching body, but the pain in his ass compounds when the hot water makes contact. He endures the pain, washes his body as best he can, and gets out of the shower. Lamont slowly walks into the living room area and gathers his clothes. He walks back to the bedroom, puts his clothes in a chair, and snatches the sheets off the bed. The site of his blood on them reminds him of his pain, but he decides he needs to lie down for a while. He lies on his side not knowing what he should do next. The hours go by without Lamont getting any sleep or rest at all. He finds himself replaying repeatedly in his mind the things that were done to him. He just lies on the bed wondering how he got himself in the position he did. He wonders how he will explain to his wife his coming home in the morning. He seriously contemplates not going home at all. He thinks to himself, how do I face my life now period. Those bitches did take pictures of what they did to me, and who knows where or when those pictures might show up. They got my driver's license so they know where I live. That thought causes his heart to beat faster, and frightens him to the core of his being. What if my wife finds out?

Not only what I've been doing, but what was done to me. Lamont thinks to himself he does not want to lose his wife, or his marriage, but how can he face her with what he's just been through. How can his not coming home be explained away

Realizing he doesn't want to explain anything he reaches for his wallet. Seeing that its content has been removed he looks around the room. He sees his things on the nightstand, and puts everything back into his wallet. Lamont is relieved to see his credit cards and license still here. He reaches for the phone, calls the front desk, and asks if he can keep the room another day. After talking to reservations, he is told he can keep the room Saturday, but he has to check out Sunday at noon. He is not ready to go home, or face his wife. He decides he needs time, to himself to think about his life; or even if he still has a life. Eventually relief comes to him in the form of much needed sleep. His tortured mind and body had to shut down for him to hold onto his sanity. He awakens mid-evening the next day. Daylight is fading as the sun starts to set. Lamont simply lays there with his eyes open, but with no will to move. He knows he can't stay here, and has to call his wife to at least let her know he's alive. He gets off the bed, and notices that the pain in his ass has not gotten any better, but it's bearable. It's more his broken psyche, and shattered manhood that is more troubling to him. He wonders, how he will still be able to call himself a man, after being violated the way that he has been. It crushes Lamont a little more that he must acknowledge such thoughts to himself. What happened, happened and nothing he can do will ever change that. Finally, he reaches for his cell phone, and dials his wife's number. He lets it ring several times. and is almost relieved when she doesn't answer. Eventually the voice mail picks up, and he lies about why he didn't come home last night, and why he won't be home tonight. Lamont no longer cares what happens to him, or what his wife may think or say to him. She now knows he is ok, and is out with friends. He thinks she will forgive him for this latest transgression in time; just as she has in the past. He loves her, and knows he does not want to lose her. She has always been a good woman, and he knows she loves him. He lies back down and wonders now, what kind of husband she will get back after last night. He thinks that maybe it would be best for her, if he simply left home, and never returned. He contemplates suicide many times during the course of the night; as he lays there unable to sleep. It seems to him that even time is his enemy. Time for him seems to have stopped, allowing his own thoughts to torture him without end. When he can't lie still any longer he paces the room slowly, trying to walk off the throbbing in his rectum. He doesn't want to eat or drink. He needs the safety of his home, and the feel of his wife's arms, but he is afraid. Afraid that if she touches him she'll know what happened to him, and she'll find out all the other rotten shit he's done during the course of their marriage. After many more hours of useless contemplation Lamont is tired now. He's tired of thinking about what was done to him. He's tired of thinking about ending his own life. He's tired of thinking about life without his wife. He just wants to go to sleep, and wake up in his own home. He thinks to himself he will simply take things step by step, one day at a time, and if he's very lucky he'll somehow survive this tragedy. After a few hours more of torturous thoughts, the mercy of sleep takes him. Lamont rises with the sun and gets dressed. He looks around the room to make sure he doesn't leave any evidence that he was ever there. He is thirsty, but he refuses to touch anything in the room. He leaves the hotel and vows to never step foot on this complex's goddamned property again. He is still in a deep depression, but all he can think of is the safety of his home. He needs to feel the comfort of his own bed, and the security of the walls of his home. He doesn't know what he's going to say to his wife, but he doesn't care. His main concern is getting home. He thinks that maybe next week he'll go to church with her. That would be nice he thinks. Lamont pulls up to his house, and sees his wife's car is not in the driveway. He is pleased about that. He thinks she must be at the early Sunday Service. He slowly makes his way into his house, locks the door behind him, and heads to the shower. His ass is still very sore, but he doesn't care because he needs to wash his body. After he gets out of the shower, he takes the clothes he was wearing, puts them in a trash bag, and throws them in the garbage. Lamont's only thought now is to get to the safety of his own bed, and go to sleep. He slowly climbs the stairs, goes to his bedroom, and gets in bed. He curls into a fetal position and is fast asleep. A few hours later a car pulls into the driveway of Lamont's home. The driver is relieved to see that her husband has finally returned home. She parks, gets out of the car, and goes up stairs.

"Lamont, baby it's Cheryl I'm home."

He does not answer her so she climbs the stairs, and goes to the bedroom thinking he might be lying down. She gets to the master bedroom, opens the door and she sees him lying on the bed asleep. She does not want to disturb him so she quietly exits the room, and goes downstairs.

She feels her cell phone vibrate, but she pays it no mind. She goes down to the living room, walks into her home office, and closes the door. Cheryl sits at her desk. Thinking to herself, she is tired of being frustrated, and humiliated by Lamont. She will not put up with his cheating, and him treating her as if she's a goddamn idiot any longer. She doesn't know what more to do to save her marriage. She knows they have grown apart instead of closer, and she would do anything to fix that. She remembers happier times when they were inseparable. There was a time when they did everything together, and enjoying each other's company, the way couples should. Now, Lamont barely spends time with her, and he never wants to do anything with her. She has done everything she could think of; over the years to get back what they once had, but nothing has worked for her, and Cheryl has even considered leaving him. It's Lamont who has changed, and who finds what he needs in the streets, with other women. Cheryl sits in her quiet office, and thinks to herself. I love that man with all my heart, but I promised myself I would no longer put up with his shit. I just want him to come back to me, and be the husband I know he can be; so we can be happy again. She takes a package out of her purse, and is almost terrified to open it. She opens it anyway, and takes out a letter, reads it, and then pulls out a packet of photos. She flips through photo after photo, of Lamont with different women in varying sexual positions. She wants to cry out in rage as she looks at the photos, but she wills herself to be strong. She imagines that this is the kind of shit; that that sorry bastard has been doing all these years with other woman. The thought makes her so angry that her blood feels as if it's boiling. He damn sure needed a serious lesson, and she feels some satisfaction now, as she looks through the photos. If her plan does not work, she doesn't know what will. Looking at each photo repeatedly, she knew what was going to happen, and what they were going to do to him. This is what she paid those women a lot of money to do to him. It took her a long time to decide to go forward, with this last act of desperation to save her marriage. Cheryl knew exactly what was going to happen, and how. She thinks to herself, that it is way too late for regrets at this point. They did what they were supposed to do, and now she must do her part.

She comes to the photos of the women using dildos to fuck her husband; while he is tied to the bed. She thinks to herself if she could have found another way, this would have been unnecessary. Cheryl thinks back to when she first learned about a service called Cruise Control on the Internet. A supposedly guaranteed program designed to make cheating husbands change their ways. After viewing the photos, she realizes just how brutally he was treated. Maybe this is what was necessary for him to realize what he has at home. That he needs to keep his dick in his pants, and at home, where it belongs. This should teach him. That strange pussy can be a very dangerous thing, in more ways than one. Cheryl hopes with all her heart that she did the right thing.

After viewing all the material, Cheryl gathers everything, and walks out to her fireplace, turns on the gas burner, and puts the letter and the photos in the flames. She watches everything burn to ashes, takes out her cell phone, and sees a new text message that reads, is he there? Be supportive, he is going to need all the love you can give him, to find himself again. She responds to the message. Yes, he is home, and sleeping. Only time will tell if he changes, and I will be very supportive of him. Thank you Chantel, I truly hope this solves my problem. She hits the send button, waits for the message to be transmitted, and per the instructions in the letter, she breaks the throwaway flip phone in half, and puts it in the garbage outside. Cheryl tells herself, she did what she had to do, because she loves her husband.

Manipulation is a skill only the fearless should practice.

THE IN-LAWS

Carol had a long talk with her only son this morning. He stopped by to see her on his way to work, like he does most mornings. Their conversation mostly concerned his wife, and that makes Carol furious. In her heart Carol knew, it was a bad idea for Daren to marry someone like Heather, but it was his decision to do so not hers, but that thought still pisses Carol off. Carol knew when she met Heather that she didn't like her. She was wrong for Daren. Her son has been married to that woman for barely two years, and as it turns out, she was right all along. She knew her son marrying that blue-eyed little bitch was a colossal mistake. It is not just the fact that in her opinion Heather seemed shallow and conceited. It is just that she seemed more like, the kind of girl that you have fun with, and forget about. Especially when you consider Heather and her family are dirt poor. Some women just aren't marriage material, and in Carol's opinion Heather falls into that category. These are things a mother knows. Besides, they both were too young to get married in the first place. Carol tried to convince her son he should wait until someone better came into his life, but he was convinced she was the one. Daren, like his father, tends to rely on feelings rather than facts sometimes, and Carol knows that that always bites you in the ass eventually. Aside from her looks, the blond hair, and the blue eyes Daren loves so much, that woman really has nothing much to offer him. Carol decides it's a mothers' job, to look out for her son's best interests, and it's time for her to have a conversation with that little bitch, before things get worse. Carol walks to the living room, picks up the phone, and dials her son's home phone number, as she tries to maintain her composure. After the first three rings, Heather answers the phone.

"Hello Heather speaking." She says in a pleasant voice

"Heather, this is Carol. We need to talk right now"

"Sure Carol, can you give me a second? I was just finishing breakfast, and the sink is full of dishes." After a short pause, Heather quickly returns to the phone.

"Why would your sink be full of dishes? Don't you know how to use a dishwasher? I'm almost certain those are standard pieces of equipment in restaurants, and they come with all new homes." Carols tells her condescendingly.

"Of course I know how to use a dishwasher. It's just a force of habit for me leaving dishes in the sink. My mom would always take care of that kind of stuff in the morning."

"Well dear, you're a grown woman now, or at least you're supposed to be, and your mother doesn't live with you. You have a husband, and a house to take care of. I think it's time you break that disgusting little habit, don't you?"

"I'm not sure where you're going with this, and if my husband doesn't complain, what do you care? And how I take care of my house is none of your concern, Carol." Heather starts to feel defensive.

"That's the point my dear. I don't think you know how to take care of a home, or a husband." Carol can barely fight back the anger she is feeling.

"You mind telling what you are taking about." Heathers frustration starts to build.

"Daren has told me about your housekeeping practices, and your bedroom habits, or lack thereof. And I want to know what your problem is."

"Carol, I know I'm not the best housekeeper in the world. And what happens in my bedroom is none of your damn business." Heather is so angry now she starts to tremble.

"What I find hard to understand Heather is how you manage a restaurant, but you can't manage your own damn home. Daren shouldn't have to come home, and clean up your messes."

"When I get home in the evenings I'm tired Carol. It's not like I don't clean my house, and I don't see how what goes on here is any of your business damn business."

"Where my son is concerned it becomes my business. Daren runs a very successful physical therapy practice. He shouldn't have to come home to a filthy house every day, and a lazy woman who doesn't know what being a wife is!" Carol is now furious.

"I am his wife, not you. I'm sick, and tired of you lecturing me on what I am, and am not. This is my house, not yours, and I don't answer to you Carol."

"Correction dear, that's Daren's house, and when it comes to my son, dear, I am exactly who you answer to." Carol is seething with anger at this point.

"It's not like I don't work just as hard as Daren. I like what I do, and where I work. I know you think that I married Daren for his money, but that's not true, and he knows I love him. I could care less about your family's money. When I get home I'm tired and cleaning house is not my top priority. That's why I suggested that we hire someone to come in and clean for us."

"And you expect Daren to pick up the cost of a housekeeper when you're young and perfectly healthy? Exactly what are your priorities? Because taking care of Daren doesn't seem like it's high on your list."

"That's not true. I'd do anything for Daren, and he knows it. He also knows I love him."

"Well if that's true Heather why is it you're always too damn tired to take care of him in bed?" Carol smiles after she makes that statement.

"That is none of your goddamn business! What goes on in my bedroom has absolutely nothing to do with you!" Heather is now furious as she speaks to her mother-in-law.

"Apparently there isn't much of anything going on in your bedroom. Just how long do you think someone like you, can hold on to a man like Daren, if you can't be the woman he needs you to be?"

"Carol, Daren, and I have problems just like any other young couple. We can work it out, and we don't need your help or interference. I know you never liked me, and you didn't want Daren to marry me. I have tried to get along with you Carol. I'm to the point now where I don't care anymore. I know you and Daren are very close, but I am tired of you always interfering in our relationship."

"I'm not interfering in anything. If my son comes to me with a problem, I'm going to help him. I honestly don't care how you feel about it, and what you think means even less. I will not let you or anyone else ruin my son's life."

"Well Carol I'm not going to apologize for not being the perfect woman you envisioned your son marrying. I'm finished with trying to get along with you. I love Daren, and he wants to be with me. You're our problem. He's not your little mama's boy anymore. As far as I am concerned, the biggest problem we have is him running to you; like you can solve all the worlds' problems. If you'd just leave us alone and mind your own damn business bitch we'd be fine!"

"Who the fuck!, do you think you're talking to? I may not be able to solve the worlds' problems, but I can take care of my men in ways you couldn't understand. My son's happiness is my business, and if you were a mother, or a real woman, and not a selfish, ungrateful little girl you'd understand this. So until my son comes to his senses, I will do whatever I need to do, to ensure he doesn't ruin his life.

After Carol makes that last statement, she breaks the connection, throws the phone on the sofa, and walks to her very large kitchen. She pours a cup of black coffee, takes a cigarette from the pack on the counter, and goes outside. As Carol releases the fury she feels, a very interesting thought comes to her, and she smiles as she lights her cigarette. Heather however sits down and cries. She tells herself she doesn't know how much more of this she can take. She asks herself is being married to Daren worth the constant aggravation, of having to deal with his mother. He simply believes his mother can do absolutely no wrong. After the tears have stopped falling, Heather tells herself she needs to get ready to head to the restaurant.

At least there, she can find a little peace. She also thinks that now would be a good time to talk to David. Daren's father is a kind man. She has always enjoyed talking to him, even though they aren't as close as she would like. That too is because of Carol. Maybe he can help her with his wife before things fall apart.

Doctor David Erickson is in his office reviewing x-rays of a patient's teeth, before he begins a root canal to alleviate the patient's pain. After he begins working, he is informed by his office manager Diane that his wife is calling, and is holding on line one. Doctor Erickson tells Diane to inform his wife that he will call her back. Diane gives the Doctor a knowing look and closes the door.

"Mrs. Erickson, Dr. Erickson is with a patient right now. He said he would call you back when he gets a chance." Diane tells her.

"I don't care who he's with. You tell him I need to speak to him now!"

"Mrs. Erickson, he just started a root canal on a patient. He really can't come to the phone now. I will make sure he calls you when the procedure is over." Diane tries to explain.

"I don't think you heard me. I said put him on the goddamn phone now! I don't care what he's doing. I need to speak to him concerning his son. If you don't get him on this goddamn phone right now, you'll be looking for another job! Have I made myself clear?"

"Please hold Mrs. Erickson."

Diane tries her hardest to contain her anger as she puts the doctor's wife on hold and takes her time going back into his office. She thinks to herself that if Dr. Erickson wasn't such a good person to work for, she'd leave this job, and work somewhere else. How a nice man like him, ever got hooked up with someone like her is unbelievable. She's a real bitch, and everyone on staff knows it. Diane remembers the person she replaced warned her about his wife. Diane steps back into the doctor's office, and sees that he has indeed started the procedure. She discreetly gets the attention of his dental assistant Nicole. Nicole quickly walks to the door where Diane is waiting.

"What is it Diane?"

"I'm sorry to interrupt but could you tell David that bitch of his, is on the phone, and wants to talk to him now"

"I know you told her he just started a root canal." Nicole responds.

"Of course I did, but that bitch doesn't want to hear it. She even threatened my job if he doesn't answer." Diane replies.

"Oh God, that woman gets on my damn nerves. Leave her ass on hold, and I'll let him know."

As Nicole walks back to the doctor and patient she gets the doctor's attention, and gestures to him that he has a call by making a phone sign with her hand, and putting it to her ear. At the same time, she also silently mouths the words your wife.

Dr. Erickson acknowledges Nicole's gesture. He finishes suctioning the patient's mouth and stands. He removes his mask, and eye-protection, and stops at Nicole's chair at the patient's side.

"I just put him under so he's asleep. Give me a few minutes to take this call, and I'll be right back. Just monitor his breathing, and suction his mouth if needed." The doctor walks out of the workstation and into his reception area. Dr. Erickson walks past

Diane's desk, and tells her he will take his wife's call in his office. She thinks to herself. How the hell, does he put up with someone like her? I almost feel sorry for him, but he married that bitch. David gets to his office, and sits down. He really doesn't want to talk to his wife now; he stares at the flashing red light on the phones console, and decides he may as well get it over with, so he can get back to his patient.

"Carol, what is it that's so important I had to leave a patient in the middle of a procedure?" He says with frustration.

"Have you spoken to Daren today?"

"No I haven't. Why would I have, it's 10:00 a.m.?"

"Well we talked for a long while this morning, and he is worried that what's her name is going to leave him."

"Her name is Heather. Carol, why can't you let them work out their own problems? They are grown adults, not children."

"Did you hear what I said? That no good wife of his is talking about leaving him."

"Oh God Carol. Can we discuss this when I get home? I really don't have the time to deal with this right now."

"Well you're going to have to make time. I'm not going to stand for this. I knew it was a mistake for Daren to marry that ungrateful little bitch!" Carols rage building again.

"Ok they're having problems like most couples do. Let them work it out." David shakes his head as he speaks to his wife.

"Am I supposed to just sit around, and do nothing while that little bitch wrecks my son's life?"

"Carol please don't do anything. I have three patients to see this morning, and I'll come home so that we can discuss the situation."

"You do that. I will not let her ruin my son's future!" Carol hangs up without another word.

Carol abruptly hangs up the phone on her husband, leaving David sitting in his office, contemplating yet another confrontation, between his wife and daughter-in-law. He asks himself a question he's asked many times before. Why can't Carol stay out of our son's affairs? He is grown, and his mother refuses to allow him to be his own man. Every goddamn time he has the smallest problem, she runs to his rescue. David lets out a sigh of irritation, knowing what he has to look forward to when he gets home to Carol.

He also knows how ineffective he is, when it comes to issues concerning his wife, and son. He tells himself to put those thoughts aside, and go take care of his patient. As David leaves his office, he thinks to himself. As much as he loves Carol, he is almost at his wits end, about how to stop her from meddling in Daren's affairs. After David finishes with his morning patients, he informs his staff that he would be taking the rest of the day off. He instructs them to re-schedule his remaining patients, clean the office, the equipment, and take the rest of the day off. On his drive home, David wonders how long the argument will be, and how uncompromising his wife will be this time. He tells himself that maybe it's time he put his foot down with Carol. After all, Daren is a married man now, and Carol needs to let him act like one. Daren needs to deal with his own issues. Carol acts like he's a damn baby still sucking her tits. David also thinks to himself that maybe it shouldn't always be him that caves in. Maybe if he stood up to her more when it comes to Daren, he wouldn't need to go through this crap on a regular basis. David shakes his head, and continues driving. He just hopes Nicole and Diane enjoy their afternoon, compliments of his wife. As David pulls up to his house, he sees his son's new BMW in the driveway. It's the fourth car his mother has bought for him. The boy has his own money, and she still buys him toys. David figures his mother called him, and he came right over, to whine to her about his marriage, or whatever else is on his mind.

David tells himself that he's going to have a real, man to man talk with his son today. David pulls up to his garage and see's Daren come out of the house. Daren heads to his own car. He doesn't bother to speak to his father, as he gets in his car, starts it, and prepares to pull off when his father stops him.

"Son we need to talk. Do you have a minute?"

"I'm going home, and try to get my head together so that I can talk to Heather this evening dad. I just came back to get something I forgot this morning. I feel much better after talking to mom." Daren responds.

"How about we get together later for a drink son? I need to talk to you as well."

"Fine, dad. We can do that." Daren responds.

"Alright son, I'll call you this evening, and the drinks are on me. Say hello to Heather for me."

David waves goodbye to his son. As he watches his son drive away, he is a little disappointed with himself, for not insisting that the whole family discuss this current issue now. David walks to his front door, goes in, and calls out to his wife that he is home. She responds by telling him to come out to the pool. David thinks to himself that she sounds calm so maybe this won't be a full-blown argument. And even if it comes to that, he knows how to calm her down, after she lets off a little steam. When he sees Carol standing outside by the pool, he thinks to himself that she is still a truly ravishing woman. He also thinks to himself, maybe that's one of the main reasons he tolerates her behavior. That and the fact that he's never been a confrontational person. Watching his wife by the pool, David feels himself becoming sexually aroused; just by the sight of her. His wife is topless, wearing only black bikini bottoms, and a sheer see-through top. Her large round breasts call to him as he watches her approach him.

"Hello honey, I certainly hope you were wearing more than that when Daren was here." He says smiling.

"Of course I was, David. I changed when he left. I got so mad after talking to him earlier this morning, that I felt like I needed a swim to cool down." Carol responds.

"Do you want to take your swim before we talk? Maybe it will help calm your nerves."

"No, let's talk on the patio. What will calm my nerves is to see my son get rid of that useless wife of his."

After that comment, David and Carol move to the shade of the patio, and David wishes he'd stayed at work. He asks his wife if she'd like a drink. She tells him to get her a glass of white wine. David goes to the bar, pours her a glass of wine, and returns to her side.

"Carol, what's going on with Daren, and Heather now?"

"She's a poor excuse for a wife, and an ungrateful bitch. That's the problem."

"Carol, what has she done that you have so much animosity toward her? Why won't you give her a chance? They've only been married for two years, but I think Heather is a very nice person. They're young. Don't you think they should be allowed to work out their own problems?" Carol looks at her husband, and rolls her eyes before she starts to speak.

"Daren is not happy with her. He should never have married her in the first place. She has no education, no class, and she manages a goddamn fast food restaurant. Frankly, I never could see what it was he saw in her, other than a piece of ass. He deserves someone better than her. Someone who appreciates him, and all he has to offer."

"Carol, that's not fair, and what she does for a living should have no bearing on their relationship. You know not everyone is as wealthy as we are, and money is not everything. There are more important things in life than money, and material possessions. What is wrong with someone her age managing a restaurant? That's a significant accomplishment for a twenty-six year old. Hell, baby, in your opinion no one has ever been good enough for Daren. You're just being snobbish again, and you forget that she was his choice, not ours."

"How dare you call me that? I am not ashamed of our wealth or status." Carol says as she looks at David with fire in her eyes. Since you mention it, goddamnit, she was never good enough for him. She doesn't have a damn thing to offer him. He does everything he can for that ungrateful little bitch, and he can do much better than her. She probably only married him for his money. so if the little bitch wants to leave, let her."

"What makes you think it's about money? You and your lawyer insisted that Daren make her sign a pre-nup, so Heather walking away with his money is not an issue. Does Daren want out of the marriage? Did he tell you that?" David asks.

"He says he's not sure. That bitch is playing games with his head, he thinks he loves her."

"What do you mean he thinks he loves her, honey? If that's the way he feels, then I think the best thing we can do is let them work out whatever the problem is."

"You would say something like that David. If my son is in trouble, I'm going to help him, no matter what the situation is, or who it involves. I will not ignore my son's problems, and hope everything turns out for the best. If I can do anything to help, I will.

I know you're not going to sit there, and side with her over me, and your own son."

"Honey, I don't want to take anyone's side here. All I'm saying is that we should let them work this out on their own. Then, if they choose to part, we will support their decision; I still haven't heard what the issue is this time."

Carol turns toward David, lights a cigarette, and tells him the most recent problems his son is having with his wife.

"Daren tells me she gets lazier, and dirtier every week. She doesn't want to take care of the house he bought for them. Daren tells me she's a filthy housekeeper, who rarely lifts a finger to clean the house, or even pick up behind herself. So that leaves him having to come home every day after he leaves his office. To clean up her messes.

She even had the nerve to suggest that he hire a housekeeper, because she doesn't want to do housework. She thinks it should be no problem for him, because he can afford it. I don't have a housekeeper David, and our house is easily twice the size of theirs. Now you tell me why she should have a damn housekeeper. If she can't keep her own house in order, I'd hate to see what that restaurant she manages looks like. She hasn't cooked a meal for him in months. She throws her damn clothes, and shoes all over the house. Her junk stays where she leaves it, until he cleans it up. He tells me that is her way of rebelling against him. Daren believes not taking care of his house, is her way of showing him she's taking him for granted. On top of all this, she practically stopped paying her own bills, and she works. She relies on him to do everything. Now this ungrateful bitch has him thinking she's unhappy, and wants out of the marriage. After everything, he's done for her. She can go straight to hell. Now you tell me ... is that someone you want your son to spend the rest of his life with? What the hell kind of wife is she?" Carol asks David.

"Carol did Daren and you discuss his leaving Heather, or did you suggest that he leave? You know how he values your opinion about everything." Says David.

"That's the way it's supposed to be. I didn't suggest a goddamn thing! I'm his mother, and no woman will ever care about him the way I do. My son was hurting, and confused, so your damn right I listened to what my son had to say. I voiced my goddamned opinion. Now would you like to tell me, where the fuck you're going with this David?" Carol says angrily.

"All I'm saying, baby, is that Daren is twenty-seven, and maybe it's time you allow him to be his own man. He was smart enough to graduate college, and to start, and run his own physical therapy practice. I'm just saying that maybe it's time you cut the cord. Let Daren be his own man." As Carol turns toward her husband, David wishes he had kept that last statement to himself.

"You tell me how the hell have I ever prevented Daren from being a man, David? I love him with all my heart. I love him the way a mother should love her son, and I have never stopped him from pursuing any goal he ever wanted for himself. I never stopped him from playing sports in school, from dating whomever he wanted, or from choosing his own college. I didn't choose where he lives, or tell him he couldn't marry that woman. Daren is a good man, and I just want what is best for him, and his life. I need to know that my son is happy, and I will always do what I think is necessary to help him. From the moment he was born, I've been there for him, and I'll always be there for him. I don't care David if you like it, or not. Whether you agree with me or not. Don't you ever again dare tell me what my son is, or is not man enough do to! You may feel that he's out grown the need for your help, or advice. I don't. He will always need his mother!" Carol quickly gets up, and walks to the bar. She pours herself another glass of wine, and stands there for a moment trying to will herself to calm down.

She takes a drink of her wine, and David comes up to her, and puts his arms around her waist from behind. Carol resists his touch at first then she closes her eyes, and calms herself. She puts her hands on his wrists, and tries to pull his hands off her. David resists and holds her a little tighter as he presses against her back.

"Baby, I'm sorry. I didn't mean to upset you. I only want everyone to be happy, and I thought that if we could talk this thing through, we'd find solutions that would satisfy everyone. Carol it was not my intention to imply that Daren is less than a man. He's my son as well, and I'm concerned about is happiness just as you are."

David continues to hold his wife as he talks to her. He is doing his best to relax her. He knows how protective she is of their son, and he also realizes that he should have chosen his words much more carefully. Carol says nothing as he speaks. She opens her eyes, and takes another drink of her wine.

"Baby, come with me. I know what will help you to relax." David says.

David takes his wife by the hand, and leads her back to the lounge chair she was sitting in when he came out to the pool. Carol resists at first but decides to let him take her to the poolside. He holds her by the waist, and kisses her forehead. She closes her eyes as his lips find hers and they kiss passionately. David's hands find her ass and breasts, and he gently squeezes them as they continue to kiss. He lowers her to the lounge chair and kneels beside her. He puts a soft pillow under his knees and leans forward to suck her breasts. Carol begins to moan with pleasure as his lips, and tongue teases her nipples. Slowly, David's right hand caresses his wife's stomach and hips. His fingers find their way inside her bikini bottoms, and to the softness of her pussy. He very gently lets his fingers play until he feels the moistness of her, while at the same time stimulating her clit. Carol reacts to the feel of his fingers as two of them find their way inside her. Not moving his fingers, David kisses her breasts and stomach, tantalizing her skin with his lips, and tongue as he slides downward. David uses his free hand to slide off her bikini bottom, and repositions himself so that his head is between her legs. He parts Carol's legs, and his tongue goes to work on her clit. His tongue circles, and kisses it at the same time. Carol's moans of pleasure are intensified as David gently eats her pussy. She puts both her hands on David's head, holding his face stationary for a few seconds. She closes her eyes and moves her right hand to her breast, squeezing it, and teasing her nipple as she sucks on her left ring and index fingers. Her pleasure is total and intense. David finger fucks her. while eating her pussy for the next twenty minutes. Carol's moans get louder and louder as she feels herself about to climax. She puts both her hands on David's face, feeling the warmth of his skin. and holding his face in position as she reaches her climax. With her eyes still closed, she screams with pleasure, and passion, and thoughts of someone else. As Carol opens her eyes again to stare at the clear blue sky, a plan comes together, and she knows exactly what she needs to do.

"Oh baby, that felt so good. You always know how to relax me." Says Carol.

David, still kneeling by her side moves to lie on top of her. She accepts the weight of his body, and kisses him passionately. She puts her arms under his and holds him tightly. As David holds her with his head against her face, Carol stares at the blue skies overhead. Her body is still tingling from the orgasm David just gave her. When they break their embrace, David tells Carol he loves her, and that everything will work itself out.

David then gets up, and goes into the house. Carol thinks to herself, *Yes, I will most definitely work this out.*

Thirty minutes later, Carol goes into the house, and up to the master bedroom. Having deciding that the head is what she needed, and not a swim. David is in the shower when she walks in the room. For a second, she thinks of joining him, and then she hears the water turn off. She sits at her dresser combing her hair. When David walks out of the bathroom, she turns to face him opening her arms for him to come to her. She embraces him, while seated, her face pressed against his stomach. She opens his robe, takes his dick in her hand, and puts the head in her mouth. She teases the head of his dick with her tongue and slowly she sucks it until it gets hard. She lets the dick expand in her mouth until she can no longer contain it. She sucks him hard, and slow the way he likes it. As she takes him in her mouth, she pulls down hard on the dick and holds it. His dick more than fills her hand. David, standing over her and holding her ample breasts with both hands, feels himself about to explode, and he doesn't want to. He moans as he feels the contractions that signal he's about to cum. He thinks to himself, Carol's mouth feels so good and hot. He thinks of how he has never had a woman who gave head as good as her. With that thought, he explodes in her mouth. She swallows the first shot of cum, and lets the rest of his release shoot between her breasts. David almost screams as he watches his cum shoot out, and slides between her breasts and down her stomach. Still holding his dick in her hand, Carol rubs the head of his dick in the cum between her breasts. She takes the head of his dick in her mouth one more time, and kisses it before she releases him and stands up. They embrace and kiss. Carol breaks the hold and looks into his eyes.

"I guess I better take a shower now. That was good baby." She says and heads to the shower.

Carol walks into the bathroom and goes to her side of the room. She sees David has already cleaned his side of their bathroom. David comes into the bathroom, and tells Carol he is going to stop by his office to get some paperwork done. He also lets her know that he and Daren will be getting together later for a drink. They are going to have a father-son talk. She tells him that will be fine, because she has no plans. She will see him when he returns later in the evening. Carol gets out of the shower, puts on her robe, and goes downstairs to her office. She picks up the phone and dials her lawyer's office.

"Good morning. Law Office of Michaels, Stevens, and Myers, how may I help you?" Asks the receptionist.

"This is Carol Erickson; I need to speak with Chad Myers. Tell him it's urgent. Says Carol.

"Hold please."

"Hello Carol, how have you been, and how's the family?"

"Chad, please stop pretending like you care. However, since you asked, David and I are fine. I just sucked his dick. Now I have an issue I'd like to discuss with you."

"Would you like to discuss this issue over lunch? It's been a while since I've seen you and I'..." Carol cuts him off.

"No Chad, I wouldn't. And before you take this somewhere it doesn't need to go, I have no desire to have sex with you ever again. I thought I was clear after the first time. It wasn't that great."

Carol's comment bruises his manhood and cuts right through Chad's soul. He thinks to himself, why does she have to be such a cold-hearted bitch?

"I do need to come to your office to discuss a project I'm working on. You need to clear whatever it is you're doing. I'll be there in an hour."

"Sure Carol, for you that's not a problem. Can you clue me in on what you're working on?" He asks.

"We'll go into the details when I get there. But I'm thinking of investing in a new business venture, and I require your help."

"Well Carol, when you tell me what it is you want to invest in, I'm sure we can lay the proper ground work. It would be very helpful though, if you could clue me in on what the investment is. We wouldn't want you to invest your money unwisely." He says.

"Chad, how much am I worth?" Carol asks.

Chad holds the receiver to his ear, and punches commands on his keyboard to bring up the Erickson Account before he says anything to Carol.

"As of today, your account shows a balance of one-hundred-fifteen-million dollars." He tells her.

"Well that tells me I can do pretty much whatever I want. I don't need you or your firms' approval or consent to invest my money. Just be ready when I get there." She states and hangs up the phone.

Chad shakes his head, hangs up the phone, and begins preparing to meet with one of his firm's wealthiest clients. He reminds himself that Carol Erikson could have chosen any of the senior partners including his father to manage her account. She eventually chose me as her account manager based more on my background, and talents as an attorney rather than her lover, which in the end didn't go anywhere. Chad briefly thinks back to the first time he saw Carol. There was an aura about her that he found electrifying. After all, she is a beautiful woman. He was sexually attracted to her the instant he saw her. It became even stronger after he learned what she, and her husband were worth. He remembers how flattering he found it, that she requested a meeting shortly after I joined the firm, as a Corporate Financial Consultant a few years ago. She took me to dinner, and we talked all afternoon about finance. He remembers being impressed with her level of knowledge and understanding when it came to investing, and financial matters. This helped to make sense of why her husband allows her to handle their money, and not him. According to her, he could care less about their combined wealth. After talking with her that first evening, I knew she was a woman who knew exactly what she wanted, and no one was going to take advantage of her or her money. Chad remembers putting off his girlfriend whenever she wanted to see him. He even stood his girlfriend up on dates, whenever Carol needed him. I thought that this very wealthy, beautiful, middle-aged woman was my meal ticket if I played his cards right.

One evening in particular he recalls meeting Carol at The Crowne Plaza Hotel in Downtown DC. She insisted I meet her there. She didn't want to hear about the dinner plans I'd made with my girlfriend. We had a drink at the hotel bar, and she told me she wanted me to come upstairs with her. Once in the room, she let it be known exactly what she wanted from me. Chad thinks to himself, when they got in bed he thought he'd fuck her for all he was worth. He gave her everything she asked for then some. She rode my dick like a bucking bronco. She damn near had me screaming. When she was done she didn't say a word. She simply got up, took a shower and wouldn't let me get in with her. The bitch got dressed, told me the room was paid, and left without saying another word to me. Chad lets the disappointment of the memory go, and tells himself that it doesn't matter what she thinks of his love-making skills, he got his. As long as he keeps this bitch happy, and making money, he gets paid a great deal of money himself, and that gives him power in the firm. Although sometimes he wonders why she even bothered with the rendezvous at all. His ego tells him if he wasn't all that, then she wouldn't continue to allow him to manage her account. He smiles to himself, and gets back to work on his preparations. He still thinks to himself, he'd love to fuck her again if given the opportunity.

An hour later, Carol arrives at Chad's office. She is escorted into his conference room where he sits waiting. His secretary shows Carol to her seat at the large conference table, and leaves the room. At the meeting, Carol explains what her plan is, and what she intends to invest in. As Chad listens to her plan, he is not entirely stunned she wants to do something like this with her money. He knows how cold Carol can be. After she makes her initial proposal, he informs her of the best way to carry out her investment idea. The meeting between the two lasts two hours. At its conclusion, Chad informs Carol that he will contact her in a few days, to let her know of his progress. In addition, when her new goal has been achieved. She gets up, and leaves his office without saying another word to him. Carol returns home early in the evening to find her husband in the study reading.

"Hey babe I thought you, and Daren had planned on having drinks this evening." David turns to face his wife as he speaks.

"We were but Daren called to cancel because something had come up with Heather. I told him we could do it another time." David tells her. Carol walks up to him, and puts her hands on his shoulders as she speaks.

"I tell you what … I'll make us a nice romantic dinner for two. We can enjoy a nice quiet evening together. Would you like that dear?" She asks.

"That sounds wonderful Carol." He says as he puts his arms around her waist from his seated position.

Carol bends down to kiss him on his forehead, and whispers in his ear that she has the perfect dessert for him after dinner. She breaks away from him and heads to the kitchen to prepare their meal. David smiles as he watches her walk away, and thinks to himself how much he loves her, then returns to his book. David also has another thought. Maybe it would be a good idea if he talked to Heather. Maybe he can find the underlying cause of what's going on with her and Daren. At the same time talk with Heather about trying to improve her relationship with Carol. David thinks to himself how he has always had a good rapport with Heather. He would like it if his daughter-in-law and wife could work out their differences. Maybe it's time he tackled this on-going family crisis from a different perspective. Maybe it's time to try another approach. If he can get Heather to talk to him, about how she feels from her perspective, that just might give him what he needs to help everyone involved, and to finally bring this family together. David thinks to himself, God knows I've tried with my wife, and son and it gets me nowhere. David puts his book down, picks up the phone, and dials his son's home phone number.

After the phone rings a few times Heather answers.

"Hello Heather, this is David, how have you been?"

"Hi David, I'm good and you?" Heather smiles as she talks to Daren's father.

"I'm doing well."

"David, Daren isn't home right now, would you like to leave him a message?"

"I didn't call for him. I want to speak to my daughter-in-law. It's been a while since we got together, and I'd like to know if we could get together for a lunch date one day next week."

"Sure, that would be wonderful. I have a doctor's appointment next Wednesday morning at 8:30 a.m. and I'm free after that. Would that day work for you?"

"Next Wednesday it is then. Is everything all right?" There is a little concern in his voice.

"Yeah, this is just an annual check-up. I missed my last one, and my doctor told me to get my butt to her office this time." Heather says laughing.

"Good. I know you like seafood, so how does Pier 18 sound? Let's say around noon." David asks.

"That would be perfect. I'm really going to be looking forward to it." The joy in her voice is obvious."

"So will I. We have some catching up to do. I won't hold you up any longer. I'll see you next Wednesday. Enjoy the rest of your evening Heather."

"Ok, you do the same and I'll see you next week. Bye."

After David hangs up the phone, he starts to let himself hope, that maybe this was a very good idea. Maybe now he'll be able to take real steps to mend his family's relationships. David thinks to himself of how fond he is of Heather, and hopefully soon he can change his wife's mind about her too.

Tuesday morning of the following week, Carol gets a call from Chad Myers.

"Hello Carol, everything is in place. Your new partners would like to set up a meeting with you as soon as possible. I'm surprised it all went so smoothly."

"Have my terms been agreed to?"

"After you sign the partnership documents yes, and since your investment has been verified. You are a one-third owner; you can get rid of whomever you like. No questions asked."

"That would be fine then. Can you arrange something for today around noon at your office?"

"I'll get right on it. I don't foresee a problem with that so I'll see you at my office today at noon."

Wednesday

David arrives at the Pier 18 Seafood restaurant at 11:45 a.m. having taken the rest of the day off from his dental practice, to meet with his daughter-in-law for lunch. He is shown to his table, and shortly afterwards, Heather arrives and is shown to their table.

"Hello Heather, how are you doing?" David asks as he stands to hug Heather.

"I'm doing fine. I've been looking forward to this since we talked last week." She responds.

"How did your check-up go?" David asks.

"It went well. I'm in perfect health. Would you like to know what else the doctor told me?" Asks Heather.

"Of course I would. Since we are going to be here for a while, would you like to start off with a glass of wine before we order lunch?"

"Water would be fine. I don't think I should be drinking in my current condition." Heather says as she looks at David smiling.

It takes David only a second to run that statement through his mind, combined with her smile, and the glow he perceives around her face.

"Heather, are you trying to tell me you're pregnant with my grandchild?"

"Yes, six weeks pregnant." They both stand and David walks over to her. They embrace, and he congratulates her. After a long hug, and David saying again how happy he is for them, they sit down.

"Have you told Daren the news yet?" He asks.

"No, I wanted to wait until I see him at home this evening. I haven't even told my mother." She responds.

"Heather this is absolutely fantastic news. I think I'm more thrilled than you are. Since you haven't told Daren. I won't say a word to anyone, until you break the news to him yourself."

"Thanks David, I appreciate that. I feel really comfortable talking to you about this. How do you think Carol is going to feel when she finds out I'm pregnant?" Heather asks nervously.

"Heather, I think a grandchild is exactly what we need in this family at this moment."

"I can't see her being anything other than thrilled for both of you." David responds.

"I certainly hope so because to be honest with you, and please don't take this the wrong way. I have had it up to my eyebrows with Carol. Short of me leaving Daren, I don't know what I can do for her to accept me."

"Heather, believe me I'm not offended, and I understand how you feel. Carol can be a bitch when she wants to be, but I also know the sweet caring side of her as well. I also know it hasn't been easy for you to deal with her. Growing up an only child, she didn't learn to play well with others. Her father, who was wealthy, spoiled her to no end. When we met, eventually married, and had Daren she spoiled him as well. David continues. She and Daren have always been an extremely close mother and son. I sometimes feel that they lock me out of their lives. I'm busy with my dental practice, and my patients. Daren went off to college, and after graduation started his own therapy practice. We decided to sell our company. That left Carol with nothing to focus her attention on except Daren, and managing our accounts. I know Carol can be a bit of a snob and overbearing, but I don't want you to worry about that anymore. I think news of a baby will really change the way she feels about a lot of things. Believe me, you don't have to prove yourself to anyone, and having my son's baby tells me how much you love him. I also want you to know that I support you one hundred percent." David tells her.

The waiter comes to their table. They place their order, and continue with their conversation.

"David, hearing you say that really makes me feel good, and I want you to know how much I appreciate it. Carol and I have had some bitter conversations over the past few months. I just hope that she and I can work out our differences, for the sake of my marriage. I have my faults. I know I'm not the best housekeeper in the world, but I'm getting better, and I will learn to do things to our satisfaction. But the one thing that bothers me. She thinks that when it comes to sex, I'm not there for Daren. I know they talk all the time about everything, and that doesn't bother me. I'm happy they're so close, but that's just not true. Daren can have me whenever he wants, and it's usually him who's too tired to fool around. I hope this topic isn't making you feel uncomfortable."

"Not at all, Heather. What goes on in your home is no one's business. I know Daren is happy with you. You are my daughter-in-law, and the mother of my grandchild. There is nothing that we can't discuss. I'm also a doctor, and I know for a fact you can't get pregnant without having sex." They both laugh and continue talking until their lunch is brought to the table. For the next hour, they finish their meal, and continue their very pleasant conversation.

"Heather, I have an idea. How about we break the good news to Daren, and his mother at the same time."

"What do you have in mind?" She asks.

"I was thinking that we all meet at the house around 12 noon on Friday. You and I will act like everything's normal until then. When you two arrive I'll keep Carol occupied, and you take Daren out by the pool. I'll have a very special flower arrangement on the deck set up for you two. You'll know it when you see it, but it won't give anything away, and I'll make up a story to tell Carol if she asks about it. I'd like you two to sit close to the flowers when you give him the news. Then the four of us will make an evening of it."

"What's the story with the flowers, if you don't mind my asking?" Heather requests.

"If you don't mind, I'd like to set up a hidden video camera to record his reaction when you tell him the good news. I don't want to record your conversation, just his reaction to the news. It might be something nice for you two to share, and show to the baby one day." David tells her, his excitement obvious.

"I think that's a wonderful idea. Let's do it."

"Alright, I'll call you Friday morning to let you know everything is in place, and we'll go from there. This is going to be an awesome surprise for everyone. I'm so happy for you and Daren. I know everything is going to work out from here on." David tells her.

"David, I just want to let you know again how much I appreciate you, and everything you've done to help me over these last two years. You've been the father to me that I never had growing up, and I just want to say thank you."

"Don't give it a second thought. I'll do whatever I can to help you, and I hope you know that."

Heather and David leave the restaurant together. He walks her to her car, hugs her one more time, and watches as she drives out of the parking lot. He walks to his own car thinking that this is truly the turning point that will make everyone, including his wife, happy. We finally have a grandchild on the way. David finds himself smiling all the way home.

Thursday morning 9:00 a.m.

Heather reports to work at her usual time. She feels fantastic. She thinks back to just a few hours ago as she woke up in Daren's arms. She did not want to leave him. She thought about her lunch with David all night, and how good it made her feel. She feels joy in knowing that he cares about her, and how she feels. David fully accepts her as a member of his family. Furthermore, he's made the arrangements for her big announcement. She almost told her husband the news after they made love, and Daren told her how much he loved her. A voice calls her name, and snaps Heather's attention back to the present. She recognizes the voice as belonging to Mr. Snyder, one of the co-owners of the restaurant. He requests that she come to the office with him. Heather smiles and follows him to the office.

"Good Morning Heather. Please have a seat." Heather sits down in the chair across from his desk.

"Good morning Mr. Snyder. How can I help you today?" She asks.

"Heather, I have some bad news to tell you. The restaurant has been bought, and the new owners want to make major changes in staff and management. I am sorry to tell you that your position has been cut along with five other positions. I disagreed so strongly, with what the new owners want to do, I was bought out. So I'm gone as well."

Heather is stunned at the news of losing her job. For a split second it was as if an electric shock coursed through her body, and momentarily paralyzed her. She doesn't know whether to cry or curse, but she quickly recovers as Mr. Snyder continues speaking.

"Heather, please believe me. I tried my best to fight for you, and all my employees that have lost their positions due to these cuts. Nevertheless, in the end, there was nothing I could do. But I wanted to be the one to tell each of you face to face what happened."

"I understand Mr. Snyder, and I appreciate your telling me face to face. I understand this is not your fault. I just don't know what I'm going to do now. I haven't been without a job since I was sixteen. This just feels wrong to me somehow." Heather responds.

"I understand how you feel. I'm no longer a restaurant owner. This is what I love so I have to start over as well, and I will. I have been authorized to pay you four weeks of severance pay, and the new owner's group will mail all of your final documents to you. I want you to know that it was a pleasure working with you Heather. When I start another restaurant. I want you with me." Mr. Snyder tells her.

"I understand, sir. I've enjoyed working with you as well. I'll clean out my desk, and locker but first I just want to say goodbye to the crew."

When Heather stands up, Mr. Snyder approaches her, and gives her an envelope. They say their goodbyes with an embrace, and final words of mutual respect. Twenty minutes later, Heather is in her car heading home. When Heather pulls into her driveway she realizes something that she hadn't earlier. Something inside seems to be missing. A part of her is gone, and a thought and a feeling come to her out of nowhere, the thought that her job as a manager was a huge part of her life. Now it is gone. She feels as if she no longer has an identity, and that her self-worth is reduced to nothing. She remembers the happiness she left the house with, only a few hours earlier is gone now, because tears begin to fall down her cheeks, and she can't make them stop. Then, she thinks of her mother-in-law. The mean things Carol is going to say about her when she finds out she no longer has a job, and she cries harder. Heather sits in her car for another five minutes, and then wills herself to go in the house. She needs to talk to someone, and she knows exactly who to call. After Heather gets in the house and calms herself down, she realizes that the stress she feels is not good for her, especially being pregnant. She decides to call David and talk to him. She picks up the phone and dials his office number.

"Dental Office of David Erickson." The receptionist answers.

"Hello, may I speak to Dr. Erickson if he's available? Please let him know it's his daughter-in-law. Heather cannot hide the unhappiness in her voice.

"Hold please, while I transfer you to the doctor's office."

"Hello Heather, what can I do for the new mommy to be?"

"David, I hope I didn't catch you at a bad time. I really need to talk."

"Of course Heather, are you ok? You don't sound well at all."

"David, I'm not. I went into work this morning, and was told that new owners bought the restaurant and that my position has been eliminated. David I don't know what to do."

"I can tell by the sound of your voice that you're upset. I understand how you feel

Heather, the loss of a job can be devastating. But I don't want you to worry about your job now."

"How can I not, David? I've worked all my life, and now I feel lost and useless."

"Heather, I want you to understand something. While I do respect how you're feeling now, that simply is not true. Companies sometimes make changes when management changes, and that's no reflection on you. We can and will work this out." Heather hears genuine concern in his voice.

"How, David? I don't know what to do. I don't want to sit around doing nothing all day. That's not who I am, it never has been."

"Heather, after the baby is born I'll buy you a restaurant, if that's what you want. In the meantime, until you have to quit working due to your pregnancy how would you like to work for me?"

"David that sounds wonderful, but I don't want to impose on you like that. I'd never considered working with you or Daren. Daren has asked me on different occasions would I be interested in running his front office, and I've always said no. I want to contribute to our family on my own without relying on him or his family's money."

"I certainly respect that Heather, but don't look at it like that. We are all family. You're my daughter-in-law. Anything I can do to help you, I will, just as I would help Daren. I know you're a very competent manager, and that's why you'd be perfect for me."

"David, I don't want to just move in on somebody else's position in your office. Just because I'm related to you, and I certainly don't want to cause someone else to lose their job. Besides I'm a restaurant manager. I don't know anything about working in a doctor's office." The sadness in her voice returns.

"It's not all that different, Heather. Your management skills still apply. Heather, I understand your concern. I've had an office manager position open in my office for quite some time. My receptionist Diane has been doubling as both since my last office manager left."

"David, what is Carol going to say when she finds out I'm working with you? She already thinks I'm not good enough for Daren, and I'm not pulling my weight around here."

"I don't want you worrying about that. I can't see Daren having any objections with me temporarily using your management skills to assist me in my practice. Heather I truly believe that after Carol learns you're pregnant with her grandchild, everything is going to change for the better." His joy at the thought of a grandchild makes him smile.

"David, I appreciate your help so much. I was so upset before I called you. I really didn't know what to do."

"We can't have that. Anything I can do to help I will. I also meant what I said about the restaurant. After the baby is born we can look into finding you a new place of your own."

"Do you really think Carol would go along with something like that?"

"Carol is smart when it comes to money. If she got involved, you can bet it would be a wise and profitable investment. But let's say for the sake of argument that she didn't. I have my own money, and if it's a restaurant that you want then I'll see to it that that's what you get. Have you told Daren about your job yet?"

"No, I was gonna tell him when he gets home this evening."

"Heather, how does this sound? We have so much family business to discuss on Friday why not just hold off until tomorrow. After you make the announcement about your pregnancy, we can sit down as a family, and deal with the job issue. In fact, I'll suggest that now would be the perfect time for you to work with me, because of your condition. I truly believe Carol and Daren would have no objections after our news."

"Thank you so much for everything, David. I don't know what I'd do if I didn't have you to talk to."

"That's what I'm here for. So let's do this, why don't you come by my office today around noon? We can have lunch and talk some more. We can coordinate the time tomorrow for our rendezvous at the house."

"That would be great. I don't want to sit here thinking about what happened this morning anyway.

"Good. I also want to give you a key to the house, and I'll let Carol know just in case I'm running a little late tomorrow, and no one's home. I think Carol has some business to handle early in the day. I plan to finish up my morning patients before we all get together. Even though the office closes at noon on Fridays, I sometimes run a little late."

"Ok that sounds like a plan. I'll see you at 12:00 noon. Thank you again David you are the absolute best person I know.

"Thank you Heather, you're my only daughter-in-law, and I love you. I'll see you at noon.

Heather hangs up the phone, and she starts to feel relieved. The terrible burden of losing her job at the restaurant starts to fade from her mind. She tells herself that she will accept David's help, and that maybe things might start to get better after all. She thinks about what it's going to feel like to be a mother. That it's a chapter in her life that she, and Daren can look forward to, and experience together. She smiles, looks around her home and decides maybe it's time for a change. She gets up and decides to clean her home from top to bottom. After David gets off the phone with Heather, he calls his wife.

"Hey babe do you have any plans for tomorrow?"

"Not particularly. Why?"

"Good, I have a surprise for you, and it's going to blow you away."

"Now I'm curious. That sounds wonderful. You want to give me a clue or are you going to keep me in suspense until then?" Carol smiles.

"I'm sorry babe you're going to have to wait until tomorrow, but trust me it's going to change your life. I mean like nothing you can imagine." David can barely contain his joy.

"Wow! this must be some surprise. All right David I won't try to get it out of you. I'll wait until tomorrow. Are you going to be home early?"

"Yeah, I don't have anything special planned after work. Why don't we go out to dinner this evening?"

"That would be fine handsome. I'll wear something really sexy, but I promise I won't ask you anything about your surprise."

"All right, I'll see you this afternoon. Love you babe."

Love you, too.

Friday

Heather gets up in the morning feeling refreshed and happy. Even though Daren was too tired to make love to her last night, she decides it doesn't matter. She feels the excitement, and anticipation of breaking the news of her pregnancy to her husband. She decides to fix Daren breakfast, and vows to herself to not let the news slip out before the family gathering. After breakfast, Daren leaves for work after he kisses Heather, and tells her he loves her.

As Heather cleans the kitchen, a thought occurs to her. Thinking about what David said to her about the baby. Heather realizes that it is a life changing development. All their lives are about to change and so will their relationships. Heather starts to believe that Carol will indeed come around. David is certainly happy for her and Daren.

Heather thinks that maybe now would be a good time to try, and have a woman-to-woman talk with Carol. This really could be a turning point in their relationship.

So with newfound confidence, and a sense of purpose, Heather decides on a plan of action that she hopes will improve her relationship with her mother-in-law.

Heather leaves the house feeling alive, and full of confidence. She feels the joy that comes with knowing that new life is growing inside her. As she looks up, she feels as if the cloudless blue sky was ordered just for her. The air is cool, and the temperature is perfect. She gets in her car and heads to David and Carol's home. She thinks to herself that maybe before everyone gathers at the house. It would be icing on the cake if David and Daren walked in to see us both pleasantly talking. and really enjoying each other's company. Heather decides that she is going to make that happen today. Heather arrives at her destination at 11:25 a.m. feeling happy, and confident. She feels she can pull this off. She sees Carol's BMW in the driveway, and the double garage doors are closed so she knows Carol is home. In her mind, she decides that she will no longer refer to Carol as that bitch. She is determined to finally make things work between them.

She parks her car next to Carol's, gets out, and walks to the door. She starts to ring the doorbell, but then remembers she has the front door key. Heather uses her key to open the door, and goes inside. She looks around and calls Carol's name, announcing her presence.

"Hello Carol its Heather. David gave me a key. I wanted to come by and talk, Carol."

Heather thinks this damn house really is huge, and that Carol could be anywhere. Heather knows there is a pool and Jacuzzi outside so she walks through the house calling Carol's name until she makes it to the patio door. She stops, looks around, and doesn't see Carol so she turns around and heads back to the front of the house. She walks into the kitchen calling out Carol's name.

"Carol are you home? It's Heather."

As Heather walks into the kitchen, she sees the jacket Daren left the house wearing this morning hanging on the coat rack. Heather thinks maybe they stepped out for a minute. They are all supposed to gather here in a few minutes anyway. In a way, she is relieved to know that Daren is already here with his mother. It'll probably make things go a little easier, and that thought now makes her smile. She really needs to make things work between her and Carol. Heather decides to go back to the living room and wait for them to return. She sits down, and takes out her cell phone to call David, and let him know that she is already at his home. She dials his number, but before she hits the send key, she thinks she hears a sound coming from upstairs. She dismisses it, and then she hears it again. She puts her phone on the table, and walks toward the stairs thinking that maybe Carol is home, just watching television or something. Smiling as she walks up the stairs, the sound she thought she heard probably is the TV. Heather walks to the top of the stairs and turns right; trying to remember which of these huge rooms is the master bedroom. She walks down the hallway, and sees the double doors opened, and remembers that the back room is Carol's. Now she hears music, so she decides that is why Carol could not hear her calling out.

The back bedroom takes up the entire back section of the upper floor. Heather walks to the open door, and simultaneously starts to call out Carol's name when she sees a woman's naked back to her, and a man under her. The embarrassment of catching them in bed hits her like a wave. A split second after seeing the couple in bed, she realizes that it must be David and Carol. Carol is on top, riding him like there's no tomorrow.

She now realizes that the sounds she heard earlier were Carol's moaning, and the music. The last thing she needs, is for Carol to see her having sex, she turns to walk away. Heather see's the man's legs before she turns to walk away, and sees a tattoo on the man's ankle. It's a green and red Chinese Dragon that circles the man's right ankle.

Heather is silent and frozen in place. Her eyes focus on the ring on his right hand, a gold, and diamond dragon ring she had made for him. She watches as his hands move from her waist to her breasts. The realization of whom and what she's watching sends a shock through her body so forcefully that she almost faints. Carol's back is turned to Heather, and her head is down as she thrusts harder, and harder on the dick inside her. Heather is frozen as she watches Carol work her pussy on Daren's dick. Carols head sways with her body's movements, and her moans get louder, and louder as she feels herself Cumming.

As she throws her head back with her hands on his chest, she opens her eyes and looks into the mirror facing her. Carol doesn't take notice at first, but she then sees a figure standing in the middle of the doorway. She slides her pussy all the way down on the dick and freezes in place. She turns her head toward the open door, and Carol's eyes meet with Heather's and she smiles. The ability to speak leaves Heather body. She wants to scream, but can't find her voice. She stands there, frozen by shock, and revulsion. Her heart pounds and her breathing comes in short bursts, as what she's seeing imprints itself on her mind for all time. She wills herself to run the fuck away from this horrendous scene. She turns, and as she does so, projectile vomit erupts from her mouth. Heather runs down the hallway needing to leave this place. She needs to wake up from this hellish nightmare that she walked into. She screams in her mind to wake up, and she continues to vomit. Heather makes it down the stairs, to the freedom that the door will give her once opened. She makes it to the door, and as she does it opens. She sees David standing in the threshold. She doesn't notice the large bouquets of roses he's struggling to hold, Heather bolts out the door crying, and shaking hysterically. David is dumbfounded as he watches Heather get in her car, and back out so fast that she runs over the curb, and speeds away. David walks into the house, looks up, and sees Carol standing on the upper floor at the railing. She's naked under her open white robe, and smoking a cigarette. Daren follows Carol out of the room. He looks at his father, and walks down the corridor to the hallway bathroom. As David looks up at his wife he closes the front door.

"Carol. She didn't need to find out this way."

"You gave her a key; anyway, what's this big surprise you've been dying to tell me?" Carol says smiling

Man was once afraid of the darkness, then his own shadow. As his intelligence grew he found something else to fear.

Sunday July 31, 2011
Washington, D.C.
7:00 p.m.

Evening television broadcasts all over the Washington D.C. Metropolitan Area on every station, are interrupted to report a breaking news story of staggering proportions. In the next thirty minutes, the story is reported all over the country, and the world.

"This is Brian Williams coming to you from the NBC News room in New York. We interrupt your regularly scheduled program, to bring you breaking news of events that are occurring in the city of Dubai, the capital city of The United Arab Emirates. The local time in that part of the world is 4:00 a.m. Saturday morning. Dubai is nine hours ahead of us, on the east coast. NBC news has just confirmed reports that the Burj Dubai Tower, is on fire. This magnificent tower opened this past January, as the worlds' tallest man-made structure. The tower is eight-hundred-eighteen meters tall or, two-thousand-fifty-four feet. Now to put this in some kind of perspective for our viewing audience, this tower is almost half a mile tall, and it is burning. At this time, we don't know the source of the fire, and just how much of the structure is actually on fire. We also have no information on the extent of the damages, but the preliminary reports we have received suggest that this massive structure has suffered tremendous, maybe catastrophic damage."

The news anchor touches the microphone in his ear, looks at his teleprompter and for a second, looks into the camera, and says nothing. After another second he reports new developments.

"Ladies and Gentleman of our viewing audience, we have just received another report coming out of that region. That the Burj Al Arab is also burning, and that several tremendous explosions have been heard, and seen in, and around the city of Dubai. The Burj Al Arab, many of you may know is the sail shaped hotel, and the worlds' tallest hotel. At nine-hundred sixty-three feet, this hotel is frequented by celebrities from all over the world. From the Hollywood elite, to the giants of the sports world, some of the world's wealthiest people often vacation in Dubai, and often stay at this luxury hotel.

It is said to be one of the most photographed, and visited landmarks in Dubai. We have not been able to get any reports from the Islamic News Agency, Al Jazeera, at this time. If you look at your screen, we will put up both the Burj Al Arab, and the Dubai Tower. We will leave them on the lower right corner of you screen. NBC news has just received confirmed reports, that the Dubai Tower is indeed on fire, and that the local authorities do not have the resources, manpower, or know-how to combat, or contain fires on such a massive scale. I've just been informed, that we have video taken from a cell phone that's just come into the news room. We'll bring you that video as soon as we can."

"As reported earlier, it is Saturday morning there, and the time in Dubai is now approximately 4:20 a.m., Saturday morning. We have just been informed that today, August 1, 2011 starts the religious observance of Ramadan in the Islamic World. I would imagine most, if not all, of its residents are asleep at this time, but with events of this magnitude taking place around the city that will definitely change."

The reporter again touches his earpiece, briefly pauses, and continues with his report.

"I've just been informed, that we are ready to bring you live footage, of the Dubai Tower in flames. As I understand it, a British citizen out on a morning jog shot this fifteen-minute video, just after the fire started. Bear in mind that we do not know how the fires started. We only know that they are burning out of control. We go now to the video of the Dubai Tower."

The cameras switch to the video, and it is broadcast live, Viewers across the region witness an incredible sight. From what is seen on the video, it appears that the Dubai Tower's entire ground level, facing the camera is completely engulfed in flames; the sight is both horrifying, and magnificent, that such a large area of this massive structure is completely engulfed in flames. It looks like a rocket that has fired its engines, and is unable to blast off. The tower's construction appears to be a system of alternating, semi-circular, glass encased columns, of different heights that reach into the sky. The first columns of the structure at ground level are hundreds of feet tall. The flickering light of fire can be seen on the interior of the structure through the windows, at least half way up the first two columns of the structure. From the video, it also appears that, immense holes are visible in the structure. Viewing the video from ground level, it looks like tremendous explosions, had ripped gigantic sections of the lower portion out of the building. Thick black columns of smoke engulf the tower as it burns, obscuring the rest of the tower, as the smoke stretches into the sky. The flames not only ravage the interior of the tower, but walls of flame light up the twilight sky as they race up the tower's exterior, and find their way through some of the tower's windows. It looks like something out of a science fiction movie. The lower outer shell of the tower looks like a giant metal sparkler, as the flames slowly rise. The entire ground level of the tower seems to be lit from the inside, as the fire rages without pause further up into the tower's great height. Flames appear to encircle the massive tower at ground level. The exterior glass windows, of the lower portion of the structure appear melted, and many appear to have been blown out from the inside. From the video, it is impossible to tell exactly how high the flames have traveled, into the tower's interior, but bright flashes seen on many of the upper floors suggest the fire is rising. The news station plays the video from start to finish twice, while reporter Brian Williams describes what he is seeing. He then continues his report on events as they come into the news room.

"We have confirmed reports of several more massive fires, and explosions in, and around Dubai. We have also confirmed that one of these explosions took place near the Dubai Tower. Because of the magnitude of these happenings, we will not be re-joining your regularly scheduled program, and we are going to stay with this developing story.

Before we went to the video of the Dubai Tower fire, we reported that the Burj Al Arab was also at the time reported to be burning. We have confirmed that to be true and we will bring you the latest news as it comes in to the newsroom. We do know..." Brian Williams stops as new updates flash across his screen.

"Excuse me. NBC news has positively confirmed that there are, at least five, massive fires burning out of control, in the city of Dubai.

Tremendous explosions are still being heard all around the city. We now have a live video only fed of the Burj Al Arab. This is being sent to us via a link with a French news agency."

What the live video shows the world is a scene out of a nightmare. Burned human bodies, and pieces of bodies, have been thrown all over the grounds of the complex. The French camera crew taping, and transmitting the footage, make a point to show the viewers every bit of gore surrounding them. Human arms, legs, burned torsos, and other burned and dismembered body parts are shown, no matter how upsetting these images are. Finally, turning from the gory scene of the bodies that litter the grounds around the massive hotel, they again focus on the burning hotel itself. It appears that the hotel has been gutted from some kind of massive blast. Viewers can see that a few of the bottom floors, of the hotel appear to have been blown away, and utterly destroyed. The entire lower half of the massive structure engulfed in flames on both the interior, and exterior of the hotel. If this were a scene from a movie, the special effects would be spectacular. It is made even more horrifying, because this is not a scene from a Hollywood movie, but a real structure, and it is full of helpless and trapped guests. As with the Dubai Tower, huge plumes of black smoke and flames engulf the hotel turning its beautiful white exterior black. The flames race through the lower sections, and into its interior. The video plays while Brian Williams gives voice to what he is seeing.

"Ladies and gentleman of our viewing audience: I have to tell you, that in all my years of reporting the news, I have never seen a site like this. Nor have I ever seen flames burn as intensely as the fires we are witnessing now. The fires appear to incinerate everything in their path. We have just learned that the Burj Al Arab, was booked to capacity with guests. My producer tells me, that the hotel could easily accommodate a thousand, or more guests. We will try to get an exact number later in our broadcast. The video feed we are receiving from the French news agency is now focusing in on the top floors of the burning hotel. I can't believe what I'm seeing. We need to warn our audience that what you are seeing is real, and that we are not in control of this footage. Again, the footage we are watching is sent to NBC News via a link with a French news agency. We are receiving a video link only, and fortunately, there is no audio feed. What we are seeing now are dozens of hotel guests on every floor visible to the camera, trapped in their rooms on one side of the huge tower.

They are using what appear to be chairs, and tables to break out the huge floor to ceiling windows to escape the flames, and smoke. It is a desperate and probably futile attempt to escape the burning hotel. It is now impossible to escape the fire through normal escape routes, due to the damaged interior, and the massive walls of flame we are now seeing on the lower floors. This is absolutely horrifying, and inconceivable that these people are trapped in what is now effectively a burning death trap. We have seen no firefighting response to assist those trapped. So far we have not seen a single emergency response vehicle in any of the video we've seen. Dubai's Fire and Rescue response to this crisis appear to be either non-existent, or they are so overwhelmed with emergencies in other parts of the city, that they cannot mount any kind of effective response to what we are seeing. This is simply unbelievable that these people could have these towering structures built, and have no emergency plan in place to deal with massive fires that occur in them." The anchor continues, disgust apparent in his voice.

"The world is watching as hundreds of people are apparently about to die in these fires. I would highly recommend that if you have young children at home, that you not allow them to view this footage. The video shows floors not engulfed in smoke, and flame has people at the windows. The people are using whatever they can to attempt to break out the massive windows of their rooms. It may be extremely difficult for any of these people to manage breaking the windows of this hotel. We have to assume that windows of the sizes used in this hotels' construction are manufactured to be very strong. As far as we have seen, there is still absolutely no way the guests can be rescued except by air, and we have seen no indication that those kinds of complex operations are underway to help those trapped. Quite frankly, there is no indication that the government of Dubai is even capable of mounting such efforts. I have to ask, where is the Dubai Governments' response to this crisis? It simply boggles the mind that this government, has yet to make any official statement concerning these events, or attempt to help those who have become trapped in this burning hotel."

"We reported just a few minutes ago about another massive explosion occurring near the Dubai Tower. We have learned that now the Dubai Mall is burning out of control. This is just simply unimaginable. The City of Dubai is being attacked, as if they were at war. The Dubai Mall is a complex spread over 12 million square feet. That makes it the largest mall in the world, and now, it too is burning." The news anchor again looks off camera for a second, then back again, and continues with his report. "My producer informs me that we now have confirmed reports that the Dubai International Airport has also suffered massive explosions. This is incredible. We have confirmed reports of three massive fires burning out of control in the city of Dubai. The Dubai Tower: The World's Tallest Building, The Burj Al Arab: The World's Tallest Hotel, and the Dubai Mall: The World's Largest Mall. Now we are getting reports of explosions happening at the Dubai International Airport. As unbelievable as this may be, it appears forces somewhere have indeed declared war on The United Arab Emirates, and is on a campaign to destroy this beautiful city in the desert. These events are simply unprecedented in non-war times, Not since 9-11 have we seen anything close to what's happening now in Dubai. Before we bring you the most recent footage we have, let me explain what you are about to see. We have just learned that a fuel tanker exploded, near the Dubai Airport. At this time that's all we know, but we may be closing in on the source of these horrific fires."

"We are now ready to bring you footage from an unknown source, of what appears to be a large truck of some kind approaching the airports' main terminal, and then a massive explosion occurring shortly afterwards."

"From the video we are receiving, it is difficult to determine the size of the vehicle, but I would hazard a guess that it was a fuel tanker of some kind. Again, it's difficult to determine just how large that truck was, as the video was shot from a distance, and it is still dark in Dubai. What is apparent is that there were dozens of taxis, and people in that area when the tanker exploded, and all incinerated by that blast. The tanker appeared to be moving at a very fast speed, as it approached the terminal, and then the vehicle seemed to turn directly toward the building. This airport is open twenty-four hours a day so there are dozens, if not hundreds of people at the airport working, and catching flights even at this hour. You can see many people running away from the scene, as those closest to the main entrance realize that this vehicle is about to intentionally crash into, and through the airports' main entrance."

A few seconds later, the video records a massive explosion.

"The blast reminds you of a mini-nuclear explosion, as a giant mushroom cloud of fire erupts from the top of the structure for a few seconds. The blast destroys the roof of the main terminal building, spreading deadly flames everywhere. Seconds later another tremendous fireball blows through the roof of the terminal. The blast is so powerful that flames shoot out through every visible door and window the entire length of the terminal at ground level. The destruction that blast must have caused is unimaginable. Not since we witnessed the devastation and utter horror of airliners crashing into the World Trade Center Towers, have we seen anything of this magnitude."

The anchor looks into the camera and continues reporting.

"The devastation that is occurring in Dubai now is simply beyond belief. We have no numbers on the loss of life at this time, but it has to be a horrific number, I wouldn't even speculate as to how many are injured, or have been killed at this time. We still are receiving no reports from the Islamic News Agency Al Jazeera. Now this news agency strikes like lighting, when it comes to reporting tragedies happening around the world, and spreading unfavorable news about the U.S. throughout the Middle Eastern region. But as of now, they are reporting nothing concerning the explosions, and fires in Dubai, nor have we heard from the Government of Dubai. At this time we have received word from our own government officials at the White House, and the State Department concerning these events. They will be issuing statements shortly. We will be standing by for any news that comes from either the State Department, or the White House, and will bring you that information as quickly as possible. We will pause now for a short break."

The news of the devastation taking place in Dubai is now being broadcast by every news agency, and cable channel in the country. It quickly races across the Internet. We re-join NBC News.

"For those of you who have just joined us, we are broadcasting the devastation that is taking place in the City of Dubai. The Capitol of the United Arab Emirates, where today begins the Islamic Holy

Observance of Ramadan, What we know so far, is that around 4:00 a.m. Saturday morning in Dubai, a series of massive explosions occurred in, and around the city." "We have confirmed that The Burj Dubai Tower, The Burj Al Arab, The Dubai Mall, and The Dubai International Airport have all suffered major explosions. These structures are burning out of control at this hour. NBC News has obtained video footage from several sources in that capital city, which we have been airing to show our viewers. NBC news has no personnel on the ground in that region at this hour, but we have received numerous reports from other sources from within the city of what's been taking place."

Brain Williams is again given an update on his teleprompter.

"NBC News has just been informed, that in a matter of minutes we will be taken to the scene of the Burj Al Arab hotel fire live. A German news team that was on scene covering another story in the region earlier today is now on scene, and broadcasting to our German counterparts. We will stay with this report for as long as we can. When we return from break we will be broadcasting to you live, the events that are taking place in the desert city of Dubai, which is being devastated by explosions and fires."

When the news broadcast resumes, the caption for the story reads, "Devastation in the Desert, Dubai Burns." News anchor Brian Williams's returns, and the news broadcast continues.

"Good evening, I'm Brian Williams, and this is a special late report of NBC News coverage of the devastating series of events taking place in the City of Dubai. It is now 5:30 a.m. Saturday morning in Dubai. In addition to events we reported only ninety minutes earlier, NBC news has confirmed reports of other major structures, in that city that are either on fire, or have been utterly destroyed by explosions of an unknown nature."

Brain Williams touches his earpiece, and responds to instructions. Looking in the camera he continues... "We take you live to Dubai to the scene of the Burj Al Arab hotel fire. Again, this is the sail shaped hotel, in the lower right corner of your screen. This footage is being sent to us by a German news team that is on scene."

What the live video shows is the massive once beautiful hotel, now a charred, and burning ruin. The black clouds of smoke rising into the air obscure the famous sail shape of the hotel. Fire rages ever higher into the interior, ravaging anyone still alive, and lighting the hotel from the inside with bright flickering light that can be seen in the twilight for miles around, as the hotel on the beach burns.

The heat, flames, and smoke burn to death and suffocate hundreds of terrified and helpless guests. Men, women, children, and staff who could not escape, or were not killed in the initial blasts, are now dying. The thick billowing clouds of smoke that have filled every corner of its interior choke the life out of anyone still left clinging to life in the tower. The Hotel is built on a small man-made island, and the fires can be seen all around the grounds of the building. Massive sections of the structure now fall to the ground, as the hotel burns without pause. With no firefighting equipment, and no firefighters to combat the fires engulfing the hotel, it burns unabated. The world watches as human beings are consumed by fire, as they press against their rooms' window hoping for a rescue that never comes. Their rooms fill with fire, and poisonous smoke. Those fortunate enough to have broken through the inches thick glass of their rooms are not even greeted with fresh air. The warm dry air of this desert nation feeds the fires as smoke now covers the hotel. The victims have nowhere to go, hundreds of feet off the ground. They are as helpless as their fellow guest, many of whom have already perished in the flames. A few can be seen jumping to their deaths not wanting to die by fire, but many simply stand in the windows screaming, and crying for help. The world watches a terrified woman who managed to break out her window standing outside on the ledge. Smoke pours from her rooms interior, she holds two small children in her arms crying and screaming for help. As smoke pours out her window, flames can be seen at the woman's back. She jumps to her death taking her babies with her. The world watches this horror live on high definition television, and wonders why this rich Arab Nation isn't doing anything to save these people. The hotel has been burning intensely for over three hours, and its badly damaged structure can no longer support itself. As gracefully as it once stood, now it feels the pull of gravity. Slowly, almost with a certain grace, it tilts sideways as if its sail-shaped structure caught a blowing wind. It starts to crumble under its own weight, and then crashes to the ground. Much of the structure breaks up on impact, and lands in the sea. All the hundreds who may have been alive in the burning hotel are now dead.

The video is replaced with Brian Williams again reporting.

"It is extremely difficult to find the words to accurately describe the scenes we have just witnessed. A fabulous hotel that stood nearly a thousand feet tall has come crashing to the ground, and fallen in the sea, killing all inside. It is difficult to find the words to describe a mother jumping to her death, and taking her children with her. I can't imagine the utter helplessness and terror she must have felt. Our estimates are that over one thousand people were just killed. If you noticed in the video there where bright, lights flashing in the distance, almost as if the water were burning. We are now told that structure is the Palm Jumeirah, a man-made island. Much of it engulfed in flames, and is now a ring of fire burning on the sea. And still we have received no word from the Government of Dubai or its' rulers concerning these events. The people of that country have to be terrified. Wondering the same thing, where are our leaders in this time of extreme crisis? I can only imagine the helplessness that the people of that region must be feeling, as they awake to their landmark structures burning, destroyed, and no one from their government has made any kind of public statement concerning events taking place in the region."

Brian Williams continues his report with more updates that have just come in.

"New video has just come in to the NBC news room, again shows an exploding fuel tanker that utterly obliterated another famous structure in that city. We cannot confirm the source of this video at this time. We will bring you all available information concerning this new development as we receive it here. Because of the events now taking place in Dubai, we have in our studio two experts from the U.S. Army Corp. of Engineers. who will attempt to answer some of our questions concerning the events now taking place in Dubai. First, we have Colonel Andrew Mitchell who is an expert on explosives and demolition, and Major Arthur Macready whose specialty is structural engineering. Thank you gentleman, for joining us this evening. Let us begin with Colonel Mitchell. You are an expert on explosives and demolition. Based on what we now know, that apparently fuel tankers are being used to attack these structures, can you give our viewing audience an idea of just how powerful such an explosion would be, and the damage it would cause?"

"I'll try to answer to the best of my ability. Brian, as you and your viewers know fuel is highly flammable. Now I don't know if the fuel in those tankers is gasoline, kerosene or some other flammable liquid, or even a flammable solid. But understand, any fuel source that burns can be made to explode with devastating effect, if you have the knowledge to detonate the substance used for maximum destruction. If we assume the flammable substance is gasoline, we have to take into account the amount of fuel a tanker can carry. Typically the fuel tankers we see in the U.S. can carry anywhere between eight, and ten thousand gallons, or sixty thousand pounds of fuel. To look at it another way, if the tanker is loaded to capacity, that's thirty tons of potentially explosive material."

Anchor Brian Williams interrupts the Colonel, to cut to the latest video of another explosion.

"We have to interrupt Colonel Mitchell, to broadcast the latest in a string of horrific explosions that have taken place in the desert City of Dubai, in the last few hours. My producer informs me the video you are about to see, is an explosion that occurred just outside a mosque in Dubai. It's The Jumeirah Mosque to be specific. This is the best-known mosque in Dubai, and it's the only such Mosque where non-Muslims are allowed to even enter. This video was sent to NBC via a Russian news agency. We are told a Russian couple vacationing in Dubai shot this footage, and this video is time stamped so it will show the time of the explosion. We turn now to the video, and we must warn you of the graphic nature of the video you are about to see."

The video shows a large tanker approaching the mosque from a side street, at 4:45 a.m. Dubai time. The tanker is grey in color, and has no visible lights on, or markings on the side visible to the camera. There is someone behind the wheel who can be seen as the tanker approaches the camera. The camera zooms in on the drivers' compartment, and a woman is driving the tanker.

It is moving fast toward the mosque, but slows as it jumps a curb directly in front of the glowing Mosque, and then accelerates down the beautifully decorated and lit walkway leading to the Grand Mosque itself. The time on the video is 4:50 a.m. Again, no lights are visible from the rear of the tanker. It continues to pick up speed, and there are no stairs leading up to the Mosque so the tanker rams full force into the front entrance of the structure at 4:53 a.m. The entire tanker is now inside the Mosque. At 4:54 a.m., the only image recorded is a blinding flash of light, and then a huge fireball erupts out of the structure, completely blowing apart the great dome of the mosque. Only a fraction of a second later, the blast is spectacular. At the same instant, the great towers of the structure are blown off the mosque, and crumble to the ground. At 4:59 a.m., the entire structure has been obliterated, and a huge burning hole now blazes with fire where once a magnificent house of worship stood. The video abruptly stops. The video switches back to Anchor Williams as he continues his report.

"This is utterly shocking, and almost beyond belief. We have just watched a female suicide bomber drive what appeared to be a fuel tanker into the Jumeirah Grand Mosque, detonate the tankers content, and annihilate the structure. We will get back to this shocking new development momentarily. Let us now return to our military experts."

"Colonel Mitchell, having just witnessed that devastating explosion, can you continue with your analysis now that we have positive confirmation, that fuel tankers are indeed being used as weapons of mass destruction against these structures?"

"Certainly, Brian. As I was saying earlier, if you know how to detonate a substance such as a large quantity of a flammable like gasoline you can create a truly devastating, and destructive explosion on the order of what we've just seen. Although having witnessed that blast, I'm not confident in assuming now it was strictly an explosion, caused by an exploding flammable. They may be dealing with much more powerful substances than fuel alone. However, when dealing with flammables, the key is to detonate the fuel, and not just burn it. The explosion of that tanker obliterated that mosque, and that was a huge complex." States the Colonel.

"Is it possible for you to explain, to our viewers just how someone might rig a loaded fuel tanker to explode with the kind of force we've seen, and not just burn the fuel? And can you give us an idea of the magnitude of such an explosion?"

"I will not go into specifics, on how to accomplish something that destructive, but it is very possible if you know how to detonate the fuel. It would be irresponsible of me to divulge information like that, and to do so could jeopardize countless lives in our own country. I will not discuss systematically how to accomplish something like that. But I will tell you, thirty tons of an exploding liquid like gasoline, would easily dwarf the destructive power of the van sized fertilizer bomb we know was used to destroy The Alfred P. Murrah Building in 1995," the Colonel continues.

"At ground level a detonation of that much material, could easily destroy many structures, and multiple detonations on a single target would be nothing short of catastrophic. If the target survived such a blast, or a series of blasts, it would be damaged beyond repair."

"Thank you, Colonel Mitchell for your insight. We now turn to Structural Engineer Major Macready. Major Macready based on what we have just seen, and what Colonel Mitchell has told us, is there any structure that could survive explosions of this magnitude?"

"That's a difficult question to answer. There are certain structures that are designed to survive explosive blasts. Underground bunkers for example, can be designed to withstand explosions within certain parameters. Civilian structures such as office buildings, malls and hotels however, are not, nor where they ever intended to survive under these conditions. There are many factors to consider when trying to determine a structures survivability when subjected to these conditions. The size of the structure, the materials it's made of, and its internal support structures and so on. Buildings of such size and complexity, as the hotel and tower in Dubai I'm sure have modern and elaborate fire suppression systems, because fire is probably the biggest foreseeable threat facing structures of this size. The hotel stood nearly a thousand feet tall, and the tower over twice that height. But as we saw on 9-11, fire suppression systems can be overwhelmed, and even destroyed in massive explosions rendering them useless. Ground level explosions are particularly dangerous because they can destroy many key structures that support the buildings weight, thus weakening its foundation. If you recall, there was an explosion that took place inside the World Trade Center some years ago. It might have destroyed the tower, and killed thousands had it been more powerful, or placed better to destroy or damage key support structures. But even that blast caused massive internal damage. We've seen the Burj Al Arab hotel collapse due to the damage it sustained in the tanker blast. Much of the lower levels destroyed, weakening the structure so that it could not support its upper level, so they collapsed. Just as the World Trade Center towers collapsed when the levels above the fires collapsed onto the lower ones. The Dubai Tower is such a massive structure, that it could possibly survive if the fires are extinguished in time. The ground level of the building is currently burning, and we know from the video footage that we have been able to see, that great holes have been blasted into the structures lower section. If this building sustained multiple blasts which we now think it did, it too may soon collapse. Taking into account what Colonel Mitchell has told us, we don't know exactly what the explosive was, what was used to detonate it, or the internal damage that has been caused by the blasts? If this were a smaller structure, say, approximately the size of the hotel, I would say that it would be only a matter of time before it too collapsed. Since the fires have not yet been addressed, they will continue to burn, and further weaken the structures internal supports. From an engineering stand point, buildings of this size are very complex, and the materials used in their construction have to be very strong to withstand a number of forces, that act against the building. Two of the major forces that can cause serious problems for skyscrapers are wind and earthquakes. These can be compensated for during the design and construction phase. Designers don't factor in surviving internal or external explosive blasts when it comes to designing and building these kinds of structures, because it just wouldn't be practical or cost effective."

"Thank you Major Macready for your insight, we'd like to ask both you gentleman, to stay with us in the studio to share your observations on this developing story."

The cameras return to Brian Williams.

"We are now receiving reports from Al Jazeera, the Islamic News Agency, and we will join that news feed live in just a second."

The cameras cut to the news desk of the Al Jazeera newsroom and a male reporter. The reporter is visibly disturbed by the events he's reporting, and nervousness can be heard in his voice. The report is joined in progress. (Translated from Arabic)

"At this time we can only speculate about the cause of the fires, and the explosions that have been heard, and seen in the downtown area of Dubai. We do know that the Dubai Airport is burning, and that several prominent locations are on fire at this time. The government is asking all citizens to stay indoors, and to avoid the areas that are now burning in and around the downtown area. The government is also asking that all foreign news agencies currently sending broadcasts outside of Dubai, to cease these operations at once. Any and all foreign news teams found to be sending news feeds to their respective agencies, will have their equipment confiscated, and could face penalties up to and including imprisonment. The Government of Dubai has the current crisis under control. In addition, has just issued orders that all citizens are to stay indoors until further notice. All visitors to the country are to maintain their current locations, and not attempt to leave Dubai. A new development has just come in. The country of Dubai is now in a state of emergency and effective immediately, the borders are closed. All law enforcement and firefighting personal have been called to duty, and all citizens should know that the Government of Dubai is responding to the emergencies now taking place. We will return with further updates shortly."

The video feed switches back to Brian Williams and NBC News as he addresses viewers.

"What I find curious is that the government of Dubai wants to silence all news feeds coming out of that country. As if, any nation on the planet could suppress news of events of this magnitude, in a time when everyone has a cell phone and internet access. Why would they want to hide these developments from the world? Now Al Jazeera reports, that Dubai has now been placed in a state of Martial Law. They've closed their borders, and are allowing no one to enter, or leave the country. Dubai is in lockdown. The country is burning, and still we have heard nothing from their leaders. NBC news has been following this breaking story for the past five hours, so we will now sign off the air, and return Sunday morning at 6:00 a.m. with another Special Edition of NBC News coverage. We will bring you all the latest news concerning the incredible events happening in Dubai. So for now, this is Brian Williams saying good night, we will return Sunday Morning at 6:00 a.m. Good Night."

By 6:30 a. m. the next morning every news agency in the country is reporting on the events that have taken place in Dubai. Developments on the internet however, have been streaming non-stop, on every tragedy that has occurred since the fires started ravaging the country. The most watched video in the history of the internet has been showing for hours. It has received millions of hits in the last two hours alone. Major sites carrying the story have crashed due to the amount of traffic on the net. People all over the world are posting their thoughts about what they have seen, and news agencies around the world are reporting the story.

NBC News is now back on the air, with continuing coverage of the events taking place in Dubai, and the sensational story that has the world talking. We join the broadcast with Anchor Brian Williams already in progress.

"The British Broadcasting Center (BBC) has just reported that a rouge cell of the terrorist organization Al Qaeda, has just claimed responsibility for the attacks on Dubai, and they are promising even more attacks in that region. This terrorist cell calling itself The Dagger of Allah is promising to cut out, and destroy all western influences in the Middle East starting with the City of Dubai. In just a few moments the BBC will broadcast a recorded video of the leader of this terrorist cell. We have been told here at NBC news that the leader of this terrorist cell has been identified as Muhammad El Tariq. If you recall, this man was thought to have been killed in 2005 during a raid in Afghanistan, at a camp where Osama Bin Laden was supposed to have been in hiding. It is also believed that Al Qaeda leader Osama Bin Laden, had El Tariq thrown out of that group. Prior to the raid in Afghanistan, for his radical beliefs, and the extreme violence El Tariq preached even against other Muslims and Islamic nations. Especially Islamic Nations who have adopted western ways, and strong financial ties to the west."

Brian Williams informs his viewers that the video is ready to be shown.

"We switch you now to the BBC video feed of the Terrorist Muhammad El Tariq."

Before the video is played, a still picture of El Tariq is put on the screen. He is sitting down and is wearing the traditional long white dress of the Middle Eastern people, and the traditional headgear. He appears to be in his mid to early fifties. His facial hair is black, eyes brown, and his completion is the dark brown of a Middle Eastern native. However, El Tariq has a long facial scar under his right eye that extends to his right ear lobe. The video begins to play.

"I am Muhammad El Tariq. As the world is now aware, the city of Dubai with all its western filth and influence is now burning in the desert. This mecca of decadence, and disease with all of its evil, that has been spreading across the Middle East like an unstoppable cancer will now be purified by the fires of Islam. The faithful of Islam will no longer tolerate the west's influence on our culture, our people, and our sacred beliefs.

We will destroy all such western influences in our cities in every nation in the Middle East. Starting with Dubai, the world has witnessed our power and our righteous wraith. The leaders of this fallen city of filth have misled their people, and have become nothing more than evil corrupt western capitalists. The leaders of this nation bathe in the filth that is the United States and Europe. They have lost their way, and have turned their backs on Allah and their people. We will not let the evil of the west and the foulness that is the United States continues to pollute our nations. Dubai has become a city of evil and foulness where the laws of our God no longer mean anything. Its people are as those in the west, greedy, unclean infidels. Just as in the United States, whores over run the streets degrading our way of life, and spreading evil everywhere. We will cut out this cancer and return our people back to the ways of the one true master of the universe, Allah. The so-called leaders of this fallen nation have for years allowed themselves to be corrupted by the west. They bed western whores in one of the filthiest cities on the planet, London, England, and swear they are our righteous leaders. I will prove to the good people of Islam and the faithful of Allah just how corrupt these so-called leaders have become. The video you are about to see will prove that these are not men of our God. These men are not followers of our faith, but evil, treacherous men who should be destroyed like the rabid dogs they have become. The false Sheik Muhammad is supposedly in London on states business, faithful of Islam and Allah judge for yourselves."

The video of El Tariq speaking is replaced by a new video. This video shows the ruling family of Dubai, including Sheik Muhammad, his brothers, and many of his top government officials. In what appear to be very large, and lavishly decorated lounges of some sort, each man is sitting on a sofa, and many white women can be seen coming into the lounge. These women are obviously of European descent. They're scantily dressed, wearing see-through, full-length negligees. After the women enter the room, at least two women sit with each man. Sheik Muhammad clearly seen here, stands to greet one of the women who approach him. He holds her by the waist with both hands, and kisses her as his hands fondle her breasts. The other woman who goes to him sits at his side and watches as he kisses her companion. The men are seen in the lounge with the women drinking large quantities of alcohol. The women keep their glasses full as the men drink. Slowly the Emirian Officials leave the room with the women. At this point most of the women are either topless or completely naked. The video switches to a suite now occupied by Sheik Muhammad, and the women who were with him in the lounge. Both women are completely naked as is the Sheik. He is seen sitting on the bed, with one woman sitting on his lap facing him while the other kneels on the bed behind him, the woman behind him rubbing his neck and shoulders. Her large breasts against his back, while she kisses the woman on the Sheiks lap. He sucks the breasts of the woman on his lap, and she strokes his dick. The woman sitting on the Sheik now is seen sliding off his lap, while holding his dick in one hand she goes to her knees, and takes the head of his dick in her mouth. The woman at the Sheiks back can be seen lowering him to the bed on his back as she positions herself on top of his face, putting her pussy on his opened mouth. After a few minutes, she moves herself off his face and starts to passionately kiss him.

The Sheiks legs are hanging over the bed now, and both woman are now sucking his dick wildly. They take turns swallowing his full five inch dick. This is shown for a few minutes, and then a naked blonde haired man walks in the room, the young man putting a large pillow under the Sheiks feet. The women look at the naked man and invite him to suck the Sheiks dick, as the woman holding the Sheiks dick points it in his direction. Each woman gestures with one out stretched arm for him to join them.

As the young man moves between the Sheiks legs, his arms outstretched on the sides of the Sheiks hips, he bends down, and takes the head of the Sheiks dick in his mouth and vigorously sucks it. The women watch for a while and put pillows under the Sheiks head so that he can watch as the blond haired man sucks his dick, while they rub the Sheiks chest and put their breasts in his mouth. The women then move to the younger man, taking turns stroking and sucking his dick as he re-positions himself at the Sheiks side while still sucking his dick. No audio accompanies the video the world watched. Shown censored on TV in the U.S., but seen uncut on the internet everywhere. From the expression on the Sheik's face as he raises his head, he appears to scream with pleasure as he cums in the young man's mouth. He pulls one of the woman to him and begins to sucks her breasts. All four are now laying on the bed freely kissing, woman on woman, man on man and combinations of each. The Sheik then lays on top of one of the woman and puts his dick in her pussy. He doesn't stroke her; he just lays on top of her. The young man positions himself behind the Sheik. Holding his dick in his hand, he puts what must be lubricant on his dick, and pushes his dick in the Sheiks ass. The Sheiks face can be seen clearly as the woman he is laying on holds his head in her arms as the young man fucks him in the ass. The sex video ends and returns to the Terrorist El Tariq.

"I have just shown the people of Dubai, and all those faithful to Allah the true and foul nature of this evil corrupt western puppet. The good Muslims of the world now know the kind of degradation, and evil that live in the heart of this false prince. You saw with your own eyes how he laid with English whores, and allowed himself to be sodomized by a gay man. I call on all Muslims faithful to Allah, to not only condemn the dog Sheik Muhammad, but all those in his family to a sentence of death. Kill him! Kill All Americans, and all Europeans on sight. Death for the corruption, and shame these dogs have brought to our people. This vile and false leader of the righteous people of Allah must not be allowed to set foot on our holy lands ever again, lest he infests our lands with further corruption, and the filth that is the west. We will cleanse our lands of everything that reminds us of western corruption. Dubai was first to fall, and we will spread our righteous fires all over the Middle East, and the world until we destroy Europe and the Devil's lands known as the United States. You will never see my followers coming since you perceive us as weak, until it is too late. The West will burn along with its presence in our lands, and all those here who have turned away from our beliefs. We are nowhere and everywhere. We are the cleansing flame of Islam, we are the Dagger of Allah."

The video ends and the NBC News broadcast continues with Brian Williams.

"These developments are absolutely unbelievable. The world has just seen footage released by the BBC of terrorist Muhammad El Tariq claiming responsibility for the horrendous attacks on Dubai, and revealing to the world a sex scandal involving the ruling family of Dubai. Sheik Muhammad's sex scandal, and the released footage, which by the way, could not be seen in its entirety on American

Television, is now the most talked about story on the internet, and around the world. It's eclipsing the destruction of some of the monuments that are attributed to that royal family's leadership. The BBC also reports that just after the airing of that footage on British Television; Sheik Muhammad was taken to a studio where he was going to address his people, and the world concerning the disasters in his homeland. When he got to the microphone on live British Television, he was just about to begin his address, when an aid rushed up to him, whispered something in his ear, and escorted him off stage. At this time the Sheik's exact whereabouts are unknown, but he is still in London."

"All of our viewers now know, at 12:00 Noon Dubai time. The Burj Dubai, until that time was the world's tallest man-made structure. That massive tower has fallen to the ground. With its destruction came the annihilation of another Dubai landmark. As the tower fell it didn't simply collapse straight down as we saw happen with the World Trade Centers. The massive Dubai Tower fell without warning at an angle, and came crashing down on top of the Dubai Mall, which is located just beneath it killing hundreds of people who had gathered at the site despite warnings to stay away. We understand hundreds of people descended on the scene, to help in any way they could to combat the fires at both structures. As the tower fell at the angle it did, there was nowhere for would-be rescuers to retreat to. Hundreds, maybe thousands crushed as the tower fell onto the Dubai Mall with such force it was registered on the Richter scale. The mall too had been burning for hours when the tower fell. We do know that there are a large number of businesses, hotels, apartment complexes, and various government agencies located all around the vicinity of the fallen tower complex. Because the tower was a half-mile high, how many were affected by its collapse, and the number of people injured, or killed on the ground, no one can say at this time. Last night we saw the destruction of three of Dubai's world famous landmarks. We also know that their International Airport is still burning at this time, which is cutting off any aid that could reach the country anytime soon by air. Now the world's tallest structure has fallen, destroying property, and human life on a scale never before seen. We do know that at least one of the tankers used, to destroy the Grand Mosque was driven by a female suicide bomber. So we now know that these horrifying attacks are the work of suicide bombers, and can be attributed to a terrorist leader who was once an Al Qaeda member and a confidant of Osama Bin Laden."

"There are now a multitude of questions that the world wants the answers to. While we don't yet have many answers, we can report to our viewers that NBC news has learned that there is a White House press conference scheduled for noon today, where President Barack Obama will address the nation on the events taking place in Dubai. As many of you are aware, the President is hosting a meeting of world leaders at the White House on global warming, and the effects of greenhouse gas emissions on the planet. It will be interesting to hear what the other world leaders have to say concerning the events taking place in Dubai, and what, if any aid they are prepared to render to that country."

"We turn now to NBC's Chief Terrorism Expert and Professor of Middle Eastern studies at Georgetown University. Professor Frederick Bonn, thank you for being here with us this morning. Professor Bonn, you are fully aware of the events that have occurred in Dubai over the past few hours. What do you make of what is happening there?"

"Thank you for having me, Brian. As you are aware, that region of the world is always in turmoil of some sort. It is however interesting to note that Sheik Muhammad was indeed a good friend of the British Governments. Many of the massive structures that Dubai has become known for were indeed contracted through British, French, and German firms. Sheik Muhammad had a very good working relationship with those three European Nations, as did the leaders who came before him. Those relationships with the west had often been a point of contention, with many other so-called leaders in the Middle East, especially those governments, and terrorist factions who see the west as corrupt and evil. Many in that region spoke out against the modern mecca that Sheik Muhammad, and his ruling council wanted to create for its people. Those opposing his ideas in country often are met with censure, or other very unpleasant consequences.

The government of Dubai saw itself as apart in many ways from its neighboring Islamic Nations; especially how they conducted their business affairs with other countries, In particular the way in which they handle foreign affairs, and commerce policies. The luxuries this government has provided for its people were paramount, but it reminded many in that region too much of the west's indulgence, in what they see as decadence, and the deterioration of their own culture. The ruling family in Dubai has over the years made many silent enemies in that region. However, the vast majority of Emirians do remain faithful to their Islamic heritage. Still many in the Middle East side with El Tariq, and feel that Dubai has become lost and has strayed away from the traditions of Islamic culture and heritage. The ruling family's vision for Dubai has always been a problem for Sheik Muhammad, his brother who ruled before him, and their father." States the Professor.

"Professor Bonn, knowing many in that region are unhappy about the westernization of Dubai, why then would its rulers continue on that course knowing that they were making enemies, of others in the region? Can you give us your thoughts on that topic?" asks the anchor.

"Well Brian, to stay in line with other Middle Eastern powers, Sheik Muhammad, and his family have always publically supported radical violent groups such as the Taliban and Al Qaeda. They have even provided financial backing for these groups, and we know that to be a fact. If you recall after the 9-11 attacks on New York and Washington D.C., Sheik Muhammad, and other leaders of the Middle East came to the U.S. They did not publically condemn the attacks. On the contrary, they all offered token financial aid to the U.S., and immediately blamed the U.S. for the attacks it suffered. Upon their return to the Middle East they applauded the terrorist attacks."

"We also know that peace in that region is a fragile thing at best, even among neighboring Middle Eastern countries. In addition, what unites them is their shared hatred for the U.S., but to have a Taliban or Al Qaeda faction directly, and brutally attack another Islamic Nation is unprecedented. How this will ultimately play out, at this point no one can say."

"Professor Bon, in light of the sex scandal involving Sheik Muhammad, and many of his top officials in London, can he return to Dubai and rule effectively?" Asks the anchor.

"I would say that Sheik Muhammad and his family's days as the rulers of that nation are over. After having seen the video in its entirety, as I'm sure most of the world has. I would say he would be killed shortly after he set foot on Dubai soil. Family members at his palace may already be dead, or at the very least facing violent protests. Exposing this scandal to the world was done to discredit not only the

Sheik, but the ruling family, and his government. There is no doubt that there will be mass chaos there for years to come unless other world leaders step in to stabilize that region."

"Professor Bonn, what do we know of El Tariq himself?" Asks the anchor.

"El Tariq is one of the most violent and radical individual's active in any of the known terrorist groups currently operating in the Middle East. We know that he is of Emirian decent, but much of his early years are unknown to us at this time. Many in power in these groups openly opposed his views on how best to deal with the west, and specifically on punishing Middle Eastern nations, and their people for having ties to the west. El Tariq advocated a total cessation of relations with the west, and total Jihad on the U.S., and British governments, after the early wars in the Middle East. This was especially so after the Soviets failed in Afghanistan. We do know that El Tariq was once a member of the Taliban and Al Qaeda. He was subsequently removed from both organizations, and he was targeted for assassination at one time by both groups. He briefly resurfaced following the bombing of an Al Qaeda training camp in 2005, where Osama Bin Laden was believed to be in hiding as you reported earlier."

"Professor Bonn, is it possible that this man El Tariq, and his organization could have coordinated, and carried out this series of devastating attacks on Dubai?" Asks Brian Williams

"Yes, this is exactly the kind of destruction El Tariq has always advocated. Direct and devastating destruction on intended targets, to include civilian populations. El Tariq was educated at a university in Saudi Arabia, and trained as a chemical engineer so he has the education, and the training to construct devices of mass destruction. And he obviously has acquired the financial backing which wouldn't surprise me to learn was another Middle Eastern government."

"Professor, can we attribute any other acts of terrorism to El Tariq?"

"Yes, mostly his attacks centered on small U.S. Military targets, and soft targets such as crowds of people. His most notable attack prior to the events in Dubai was a popular outdoor market in Israel in 2006. In that incident, a lone female bomber drove a pick-up truck loaded with explosive into a busy outdoor market, detonated her bomb and killed roughly eighty people. Over half those killed were Palestinians. After that bombing, El Tariq was highly criticized by other terrorist factions, and no other terrorist leader wanted anything to do with him. Shortly afterwards he went underground, and hasn't surfaced until now."

"Professor, what do you make of his use of women to carry out these attacks, and is that something we'll see more of?" Asks the anchor.

"The use of female suicide bombers is not new, but we are seeing more of them. You recall in his address on the BBC, El Tariq warned that his people were everywhere and nowhere and that those he targeted would not see them coming. El Tariq has used female attackers almost exclusively since he first came on the scene, and the reason is simple. Many people still refuse to believe that a woman could be a suicide bomber or terrorist. Furthermore, the more attractive she is, the less likely people are to fear her in that way. In the early days of the suicide bomber, it came to be expected that a man would sacrifice himself, for whatever cause they were fighting. However, it was one of El Tariq's beliefs that if they sacrificed their men to carrying out these bombings, then they would too quickly deplete their ready supply of fighting soldiers. El Tariq saw women, and children as expendable assets so he wouldn't hesitate to strap bombs to children, and send them in the field. That was one of the many reasons El Tariq was expelled from other terrorist organizations. Now we see those same terrorist organizations using more female suicide bombers today, just as he advocated, and for the very same reasons. And it wouldn't surprise me if every explosion that occurred in Dubai had a woman driver behind the wheel of the tankers used to destroy those targets. In these cultures, woman are far more expendable than men or even young male children. This shows you what they think of their women, which is not very much at all. Muhammad El Tariq is someone the world had better take seriously. This man and his organization have devastated a major city, and killed untold thousands of his own people, so he wouldn't hesitate to do the same anywhere else in the world."

"Thank you for your insight Professor Bon."

"Thank you for having me." The professor replies.

The camera turns back to Brian Williams.

"That was Professor Frederick Bonn, our Chief Terrorism Expert. We will take a short break, when we return we will continue our coverage on this special edition of NBC news."

In Dubai at this moment.

Mass rioting is taking place in and around Dubai. Foreign tourist and non-Emirians caught on the streets, and trapped in the country due to boarder closures are attacked mercilessly. The police force in Dubai is powerless to control the population, and the violence taking place there is such that the officers who are charged to enforce what laws exists there join with their rioting countrymen. The Dubai International Airport has burned continuously since the tanker explosion, and the flames are slowly consuming every building of the complex as well as complete power failure. All workers have abandoned the airport leaving frightened, desperate passengers stranded on aircraft that have been waiting for hours for takeoff clearance. The thick clouds of smoke covering the airport, and much of the country's airspace would prove to be extremely hazard to any aircraft attempting to land, or take off, so all air traffic in and out of Dubai ceases. During the attacks that destroyed many of Dubai's major landmarks, their key electricity generating station is destroyed.

This has left much of the city without power or running water. The population goes into a state of panic and bedlam follows due to the attacks, and the recent developments concerning its rulers. In the frenzy that follows, hundreds of enraged people descend on the Sheiks Palace like packs of wild beasts. The armed guards who stand their ground, and refuse to run like many of their comrades manage to shoot, and kill a few of the intruders, but they are overwhelmed by the crowd, and are killed by the frenzied mob with their own weapons. The intruders storm the gates, and climb over the walls like roaches. They force their way into the majestic home of the Sheik looking for his family. Dozens of staff members have long abandoned the Sheik's home leaving his many family members to fend for themselves. Orders are shouted by an unseen man and the intruders fan out looking for any target, they can find to unleash their fury.

Doors are broken down throughout the palace, and every room is searched. Eventually the Sheiks wife, three daughters, and four young sons are drug from their hiding places,, and brought to the ground level of the palace before a cheering crowd of men and women. The Sheiks wife, and her daughters are thrown to the ground, held down and force to watch as her sons, and their brothers are stripped naked, held down and castrated. The boys look at their mother crying and screaming as their penises and testicles are cut off. One by one, each dismembered organ is then thrown in the mothers face. Each cut off dick is then forced head first inside the mouth of one of her daughters, and the woman's' mouths are taped shut. As the crowd cheers for more blood, the boys are then dragged up a long spiral staircase screaming and bleeding profusely as the blood shoots from between their legs. The end of a rope is tied to the railing, and the other end around their necks. One by one, each boy is thrown over the railing. Their mother screams, and vomits every time she hears the neck of a son break.

The daughters are then dragged up the same staircase. Their brothers' slippery, sticky blood is everywhere. The women are unable to scream due to the way in which they are gagged, but vomit and blood can be seen pouring out of their noses and around the tape on their mouths. One by one, ropes are tied to their necks, and they are thrown over the railing. In the crowd both men and women, young and old, cheer as each woman is thrown over the side. Chants of "Allah is great", Allah is good", "Allah is just" erupts from the crowd as each woman's' body flies over the rail, and her neck snaps. A sister's body bumps a brother's lifeless body, and they all swing side to side, back and forth in a dance of death as their mother is forced to look up, and screams with all her heart.

Her screaming only excites the crowd now as the mob's attention turns toward her. Orders are given in Arabic, and the people move to the sound of the commander's voice. Expensive furnishings, rugs, tables, and other assorted furniture is placed in the middle of the room under the dead bodies. The mother of the dead children is tied to a chair, and placed in the middle of the stacked furniture. She is doused with a liquid. Her screams, and cries become louder as she looks up at her dead children still swinging by their broken necks, and there blood rains down on her. More orders are shouted, and everyone parts as the mob commander approaches the bound woman. He says a few words to her then he spits on her. He strikes a match, steps back, and throws it on her. As the flames consume her body, and destroy her flesh, her screams are soul shattering. For a second, everyone in the crowd freezes as they watch the mother of the seven murdered children burn. Slowly, as they watch her burn and scream they disperse throughout the palace, stealing everything that can be carried out before it burns to the ground. News reports reach the world media of attacks on Sheik Muhammad's family, which cannot be confirmed. It will be days before the world learns what really happened.

Islamic news agency Al Jazeera is reporting of mass riots, and violence in the city of Dubai throughout the day. There are also reports of massive power outages, and fires burning out of control in oil fields. Officials left alive in Dubai are reported on Al Jazeera asking for support from both the Islamic and international communities. Aid to restore order in the region. The Dubai Minister of Public Affairs goes on air in London, and asks that the United States and Great Britain send aide to the region in the form of Peace Keeping Troops. The Minister also requests other assets to assist the Dubai government to restore power, and stability to the region. The Minister tells the world The Dubai Government is on the brink of collapse, and all order breaking down. The news agency reports the people of Dubai are in a state of revolt, and are vowing to kill all those who associate with Al Qaeda and the Taliban.

Later in the their broadcast, Al Jazeera reports that spokesmen for both Al Qaeda and the Taliban condemn the attacks on Dubai by El Tariq's group, and have vowed to bring this mad dog to justice. Both terrorist groups disavow any, and all ties to El Tariq, and his people. Al Jazeera goes on to report that Al Qaeda will use its network of contacts, and spies in the region to hunt down and kill El Tariq and all his followers. An Al Qaeda spokesman pleads for Muslims in the surrounding regions to assist them in this task.

Looting and riots go on in the city non-stop. Huge numbers of people are beaten, and killed in the streets. Fires burn beyond all control. All order is soon replaced with total chaos. As these reports continue to be broadcast around the world, the President of the United States is about to start his press conference in Washington D.C.

At Twelve noon in Washington D.C. NBC news switches from Brian William's report to the live news conference of President Barack Obama at The White House Conference Room.

The President is shown walking down the corridor to the podium and is followed by several other men, all leaders of nations. As President Obama takes his place behind the podium to begin his address to the nation, the other leaders join him on the stage.

The President looks into the camera and begins his address to the American people.

"Good Afternoon my fellow Americans. Before I begin, I would like to acknowledge the other national leaders who you see standing with me today. To my left, Russian Prime Minister Vladimir Putin, German Chancellor Angela Merkel, Japan's Prime Minister Naoto Kan. To my right, England's Former Prime Minister Gordon Brown, French President Nichols Sarkosy and Spain's President Jose Luis Zapatero.

These distinguished leaders have left their respective nations so that we could come together, and discuss a problem that is threatening the entire planet, Greenhouse Gas Emissions, and Global Warming. Our discussions will last for the next four days here in our Nation's Capital. This topic is one that I, along with my fellow heads of state can no longer ignore. For the benefit of all people living today, and for future generations, we must find and implement solutions that will work for all nations to limit, or eliminate the production of greenhouse gasses, and other emissions that will one day cause havoc on our planet. If we ignore this problem, and do nothing, it is our entire world, and all its' people that will suffer. However, the world in which we all live is a dynamic and ever changing place. At any moment in time something could happen that changes the life of an individual or a nation. I am sure all of you are aware of the situation that has taken place in the United Arab Emirates in the City of Dubai. Terrorist attacks in a city, on a scale the world has never seen before. Not since the terrorist attacks our country suffered on 9-11 has the world seen a major metropolitan area devastated by acts of terrorism.

In Dubai, we have seen the destruction of multiple national landmarks in a single city, using weapons of mass destruction. We have seen countless people injured and killed. We also know of the scandal that will make regaining order in that nation a difficult task.

Terrorist organizations such as the Taliban and Al Qaeda, who the United States, and other nations have been fighting for years, now would like us to believe that they had nothing to do with these recent attacks in Dubai. The terrorist who we know as Muhammad El Tariq has taken responsibility for the attacks, and was once a member of both terrorist organizations, and is a UAE citizen."

"For so many decades now, the Middle East has been a war zone of fighting, and hatred that seems to go on without end. Now one of its own nations, has been brutally attacked by one of its own citizens, in the same manner Middle Eastern terrorists have attacked other countries around the world. Now those factions in the Middle East who have sponsored, and condoned terrorist acts over the years have come to know what it's like when they themselves are attacked in that manner. These countries now understand what it's like to live in fear and the uncertainty of not knowing who is a friend, or an enemy, or from what direction the next attack will come. The people of the Middle East, who have in the past sponsored terrorism around the world, now know what it's like for a country to suffer the horror, and devastation of such an attack. They realize, and understand now what every nation that has had to deal with terrorism goes through.

These countries now understand that this is no way to live, and that to continue to support and condone this kind of violence can lead only to destruction. They now know that the hatred they have for many decades directed at The United States, and its allies was wasteful, wrong, and counter-productive as they are now asking for our help.

In this time of crisis, requests for help have come from many Middle Eastern governments to The United States and to all the heads of state here with us now. As you all know we have removed all U.S. forces from the Middle East, and at this time I have no intention of re-deploying our troops to that region. Let me be clear. I have no intention on ordering our troops back to the Middle East. I will however discuss this current world crisis with my fellow Heads of State and we will decide together on the best course of action to take in dealing with this crisis. Thank you all."

President Obama leaves the podium followed by the other leaders, and they disappear from the view of the cameras. President Obama leads the men and their personal aides through the White House to a Presidential Situation Room. Before entering the room, each leader including Obama gives a personal aid his cell phone, and every electronic device on his person. The men walk into the room, and the door seals behind them. The men go into the room, and take a seat at a round conference table. Before the men begin their talks, Obama goes to his Presidential Desk, picks up a computer pad, and begins to enter commands into the device. The computer electronically seals the room, and all electronic, mechanical, and chemical emissions are blocked from coming into or leaving the room.

President Obama then joins the other leaders. President Obama quickly looks at each man and they begin their discussions.

Obama: Well gentlemen, so far everything is moving according to plan. The UAE is in total chaos.

Brown: It didn't take long for those arrogant fuckers to start begging for our help. Our Foreign Affairs Department has been getting requests all night for aid. Brown says laughing.

Putin: Obama, how many prominent citizens did your country lose, and how many of your political rivals? The Russian Prime Minister asks, and lights a cigarette.

Obama: No one the country can't live without. I was able to get rid of Hillary Clinton. It's unfortunate her daughter was with her. That bitch Sarah Palin, her mentor John McCain, and the Senate Majority Leader. Amazing how they all decided to vacation in Dubai at the same time. What about the rest of you?

Putin: Political rivals, and a few people who were becoming a nuisance.

Brown: Our newly elected Prime Minister. That old hag of a queen, who backed him against me, and most of her Royal Fucking Family. Parliament will hold a special session next week in which I will be reinstated as Prime Minister pending a special election which I will win.

Obama: Of course you will. We will see to that. Obama laughs and lights a Salem cigarette.

Kan: A few leaders of opposition parties and trouble makers like Kim Jon Ill and his son. We were supposed to meet in Dubai he and I, but state business held me up. I called him to let him know I would be joining him later in the week. Kan laughs.

Obama: Good. Their off the table now, so we won't have to deal with them or North Korea.

Merkel: No one of any importance to my position. Only a few troublesome politicians.

Zapatero: My wife just happened to be on vacation in Dubai during this incident. She was greatly loved by the Spanish people. Her death insures my re-election.

Sarkosy: My vice president, and chief political rival. They were to meet with Secretary Clinton while they were in Dubai. To hell with them all.

Putin: Have we confirmed these problems taken care of?

Kan: Yes, all confirmed dead. We knew every move they made, what they ate, when they went to sleep, and even who they fucked. Our best spies were all over that hotel. Everything they ate or drank that night at the hotel was laced with drugs to insure they didn't leave.

Obama: Where are we with El Tariq? Is that asshole dead?

Putin: After we recorded the last twenty-four hours of him making various statements for the press condemning his own people, and the west, he was killed after he watched the first tanker explosion in his homeland via satellite. He was placed in a gas chamber, and suffocated slowly. But at least before he died he got to meet the one man he most admired in the world. The look on his face was priceless. We have more than enough video of him to feed to the world press. Reports we are getting now confirm that those so-called terrorists over there are running like rats. Those that have been caught are being killed by their own people, and former supporters.

Kan: Now are we certain that the explosives used cannot be traced?

Brown: That's not possible. All our spotters reported that nothing survived of the tankers, and the explosives used are new, so no one will be looking for them. In addition, even if anything were found, those idiots don't have the capability to analyze what they'd find. We had strict control of all twenty-five tankers at our ship yards in Dubai, and the suicide drivers weren't even in country until a day before the operation. Their conditioning was perfect. All the tankers were loaded in London before they hit Dubai soil. The combination of Semtex, Petrol and TX-112 ensures we won't have to worry about anything being traced.

Obama: I loved watching those buildings fall. That TX-112 is some awesome shit. How many more suicide bombers do we have left?

Putin: We have fifty female bombers at our disposal at our training facility in Kiev. If in the next two operations we don't use them all, we will simply dispose of them. This number should be sufficient for the next phase of the operation.

Zapatero: Financing won't be a problem. We have wired the Sheiks entire personal fortune of 5.8 billion dollars to an account only we can access. We can funnel millions or even billions of dollars to our various political campaigns, or fund further operations. Payments have already been made to our assassins who were not disposed of.

Sarkosy: We have over four billion dollars of his government's assets in our central bank which has been moved to hidden accounts.

Obama: Where is that raghead fucker Sheik Muhammad now?

Brown: He and over half of his so-called government administrators, are quivering in their rooms at the Waldorf

Astoria under guard until it gets dark, then they will board a plane to Japan.

Kan: Where we will welcome them with open arms, until it's time to make them disappear.

Putin: Where are the rest of his people?

Brown: Some tried to abandon him after we leaked the video. They were caught, and killed.

Brown: It was amazing how they quickly westernized their dress. They got rid of those man dresses they wear, and shaved those ridiculous beards to hide their identities in an attempt to go un-noticed. It was quite amusing.

Putin: We want them to think they are inching their way home, and that they are safe until we decide when to get rid of them.

Obama; What happened to the woman they got caught on tape fucking?

Brown: All dead including the young man. We couldn't have any of them running around loose to tell that tale.

Putin: Good.

Obama: Have all our spotters been picked up?

Merkel: Yes, our people got all our spotters, and news crews. They too met with unfortunate circumstances. Something happened to the transport that was to carry them to the ship. I'm afraid we lost them all.

Merkel: What of Sheik Muhammad's family?

Zapatero: All dead, and his palace looted. We had our people incite the riots that brought a mob to his front door. These religious zealots are hard to stop once they get started.

They killed in the name of their God. They brutally tortured the wife, and murdered all his children.

Obama: Fuck it. How long shall we let them kill each other?

Sarkosy: Why should we interfere now? Let them destroy themselves to the last man. That'll make it all the more easy for us to carry out our plans.

Kan: I agree let the world see how these barbarians behave. Then when we do eventually intervene no one will question us.

Obama: Then are we all agreed we stall for time, taking no action to intervene for the next few weeks?

All the leaders agree.

Kan: And when we do, the first things we are going to take control of are the oil reserves those idiots didn't know they had. We've identified vast oil reserves in parts of that country they hadn't even begun to explore. Our estimates are those idiots were sitting on tens of billions, of barrels of oil.

Putin: Yes, our satellite scanners have confirmed this. There is enough oil there to power all our nations into the next century.

Kan: And we will annex that supply for ourselves to feed our people's energy needs.

Obama: Well gentlemen, are we ready to implement stage two of the plan? The timing will never be better. It is now time to fuck the Saudis, the way they've fucked all of us for years. Vladimir, how's Bin Laden holding up?

Putin: He's doing just fine. After we initiate our plan against the Saudis he will very suddenly and publically turn up dead.

Putin: Obama your predecessor would not have had the nerve to take this kind of action. He thought he could do it all alone with no planning, and with just his military strength. We needed a man like you in the circle. I salute you.

Brown: It's about fucking time we nuclear powers started acting like it.

Obama: Bush was a pussy, and a weak stupid man. Everyone here knows that.

All the leaders laugh and light various cigars and cigarettes. President Obama pours each man a drink, and they all stand. Each man raises his glass and Obama speaks.

"Let the real war on terror continue. Now we take Daystar to phase two." They toast each other, and continue discussions on implementation of phase two of plan Daystar.

Life is supposed to be an adventure, one that fear shouldn't control.

"**B**aby can I ask you a question; I have wanted to talk to you about this for a while. So before they bring our dinner out we need to talk, and please don't take this the wrong way."

"Crystal you can ask me anything you want; I'll always be honest with you." Derek responds.

"I think you know that I have very strong feelings for you, and the past two months have been absolutely wonderful. I need to know why you haven't taken me to your place yet. I mean you know where I live, what I do for work, you've met my mom, my best friend everything. It worries me a little that I haven't been to your place yet."

"Ok let me…" he starts to say, but she squeezes his hand, and cuts him off.

"No let me finish, she continues. I know you're not married, but I need to know is there anyone else in your life, something that you need to tell me. If so just let me know what's going on."

"Baby you have every right to feel that way. It's just that with me, I want to be absolutely sure that we are going to make it before I open myself up like that. He holds both her hands on top of the dinner table as he speaks. In the past, I have had really bad relationships, that started out strong, but didn't work out, and I just didn't want to rush things with us. And I didn't want to scare you away by moving too fast."

"Baby I'm not going anywhere, and I understand because I have had relationships that didn't work. I want us to work because I don't want to be with anyone but you. I'm in love with you Derek, and if that's a problem please let me know now." Crystal tells him.

Derek looks into her eyes, and he can see that she means every word of what she just said; he thinks to himself she just may be the one he can't let go. Still holding her hands, and looking into those beautiful brown eyes, he tells her that he loves her too.

Still holding hands they both lean forward over the table and kiss.

"Baby you make me feel so good, I just want to make you happy, especially now I know how you really feel about me." She says.

"Well baby I tell you what; after we finish our dinner I'll take you to my place. I don't want to lose you, and if that has been a concern for you I need to take care of that." Derek tells her.

Crystal's joy overwhelms her, she can't remember the last time she's felt this way, and she believes that the man sitting across from her is the man she could love for the rest of her life.

"Baby can I stay with you tonight?"

"Of course you can beautiful, you can do whatever you like, and I wouldn't want to let you go home anyway." Derek says.

"Ok, since I'm spending the night with you, would you take me to the station in the morning."

"I can do that, even though I don't have to be at the office till 9:00 a.m." He says laughing.

"Baby you know I'll make it worth you having to get up so early." She responds.

"It's all good baby, I will be well protected tonight, I have my own personal police officer to protect me."

"You don't need that baby, but I'd turn into a pit-bull on somebody's ass if they tried to hurt my baby." They both laugh at Crystal's remark.

The couple continues their very intimate conversation, enjoying the feelings they both share, and have admitted to each other. When their main course of steak and vegetables is brought to the table the food tastes that much better, and both look forward to the end of the night. The anticipated end of the evening is even greater for Crystal because she at last gets to see her man's home. When they finish Derek pays for the meal, and the couple leave the restaurant. They walk to the car holding hands, and enjoying the evening's warm breeze. Crystal asks Derek can they ride home with the top down. She explains she's always wanted a convertible, and Derek drives a new BMW, he tells her that he will do whatever she likes. They pull off, and drive toward the highway, and continue their conversation.

"Baby why won't you let me pay for anything when we go out. I don't believe that the man has to pay all the time for everything."

"That's the way I was raised Crystal, the man is supposed to pay when he's out with his lady."

"I understand, and don't get me wrong I appreciate the fact that you are the perfect gentleman, and have been since the day we met. But I don't have a problem with taking care of you too, which includes not letting my man pay for everything." She responds.

"Baby you do take care of me, tell you what, we'll work on that ok, I can compromise too." They both laugh as they drive down the highway to Derek's house listening to jazz music.

"Baby who is this you're playing?"

"This is Soul Ballet, my favorite Jazz Artist, this is from his new CD 2099." Derek explains.

"You can dance to this music, and this is considered Jazz?" She asks.

"Yeah baby, I have to turn you on to more of his music if you like this." Derek responds.

They arrive at his house about forty minutes later, and Crystal is impressed with what she sees. They pull up to his driveway, and he activates the garage door opener, she takes note of the outside of his two-story brick home, they wait for the door to fully open, and drive in. They get out of the car, and enter the house through the door in the garage.

"Well baby here we are, welcome to my home. Take your time, and look around." Derek takes her jacket and handbag and hangs them up in the living room.

"Baby I love your Kitchen, lots of room to work."

Crystal takes note of the size of the kitchen, and then walks to the adjoining rooms. She walks through the living room, his downstairs office, and Atrium. She notices how neat, his place is, and how nice his furnishings are.

"Baby come check out the family room." She follows the sound of his voice, and comes to the very large family room as Derek is turning on the gas fireplace.

"Baby you have very good taste in furniture, I would have been disappointed if you didn't, or your place looked like a pig pin." She says laughing.

Derek responds to her comment by snapping to attention and popping her a salute. "Yes Ma'am, Gunnery Sergeant Ma'am, or is that Sir?" He says laughing.

"Ma'am will do soldier." She says laughing.

"Baby you have a beautiful place, this house is a lot bigger than mine."

"How many rooms do you have?"

"All together thirteen not including the bathrooms. I got a pretty good deal on this, that's the advantage of being a real estate agent."

She walks over to him, and he takes her in his arms, and kisses her.

"Your place is nice, and only a little smaller than this. Your house is about eighteen hundred square feet, and this one is twenty-two-hundred. When you're ready to upgrade you have the hottest agent in the county working for you baby." They both laugh, and kiss again, only more passionately, both anticipating the love making that is about to follow.

They sit by the fireplace, talk a while longer in it's warm glow drinking wine, and after about twenty minutes they go up to the master bedroom. They get undressed, and take a hot shower, the heat of the water is nothing compared to the passion of their kissing. The lovers quickly exit the shower, and get in bed still dripping wet. He leads her to the bed, and lays her down. He caresses, and kisses her firm breasts, gently sucks her nipples while his hands find their way between her legs. Her body is still wet with water, but his fingers excite her pussy to get moist, and he starts to slid down her body until his tongue finds her other lips, and he goes to work on her clit. He expertly eats her until she can take no more, and screams in orgasmic pleasure.

"Oh, baby goddamn! Baby I want you so bad! Baby, I want it in my mouth; I want to suck your dick baby!"

They switch positions, and he lies on his back as she takes his hard dick in her mouth. She teases the head with her tongue, and swallows as much of his dick as she can take, working the shaft slowly, and methodically, her tongue constantly busy. Derek's moans of pleasure getting louder, and louder. She wants him to cum in her mouth, but not yet so she stops, and strokes him. She positions herself above his dick so that she can go for a ride. She gets on top of his dick, and lets it all slide in her, they both damn near scream with pleasure. They fuck for the next hour until they are exhausted, and satisfied, shortly afterwards they fall asleep arm in arm. The alarm goes off at 5:00 a.m., Crystal wakes up and goes to the bathroom to take a shower, before she wakes Derek to take her to work. She doesn't want to disturb him so she doesn't turn on any lights going to the bathroom. Crystal notices a fragrance in the bathroom that she didn't last night. It reminds her of a woman's perfume, but she can't quite place the scent. She decides it's not important, and disregards the thought, but she keeps telling herself it seems familiar. She takes her shower. Crystal lets her mind drift back to a few hours ago, and how good it felt to make love to her man, in his bed. She thinks he has finally let her in his life all the way, after their conversation, and that makes her happy. Crystal gets out of the shower, and quickly dries off. When she comes back into the bedroom Derek is awake, and watches her as she gathers her clothes.

"Good morning sexy, how did you sleep?" He asks.

"Like a baby, damn I didn't want to get up. I wish I could lie in your arms all day, but I have to be in court most of the damn morning." She responds.

"I know what you mean; I'll get myself together after I drop you off at the precinct. I do plan on getting a couple more hours of sleep before I go to the office though." He says.

"Ok baby rub it in, I'll be ready to leave in a few minutes."

Derek quickly gets out of bed, brushes his teeth, puts on a sweat suit and jacket, and is ready to go.

"Do you need me to pick you up when your shift is over." He asks.

"No, I'll get another officer to drop me off. Will I see my baby tonight?" She asks.

"Of course you will, I'll call you when I get home. You ready to roll baby." He asks.

"Yeah let's go, I'll change into uniform when I get to the station, and hopefully the day will go by quickly so I can be with my baby as soon as possible."

They leave Derek's house, and about thirty minutes later, they are at the station. He tells her to have a good day, she kisses him, and gets out of the car, and Derek watches her walk away. She has a very sexy walk for a cop he thinks to himself.

On his drive back home Derek thinks to himself that he has indeed hit the jackpot. Crystal is everything he could ask for in a woman. She is beautiful, smart, an excellent lover, and she has heart for a woman. He thinks to himself that makes since seeing how she's a Washington D.C. Cop. I really do love her, but I swear I didn't see that coming with us, I guess I'm getting old. He thinks to himself and smiles. Crystal is energized all day as she sits in court waiting for her last two cases to be called. She just wants to get the day over with, so that she can go home and relax. She is also excited about seeing Derek later. She can't wait to talk to her mother, and her best friend about how she, and Derek might be taking their relationship to the next level. That thought makes her smile, as she thinks back to the guys she dated before she met Derek. Most of them were intimidated by the fact that she is a cop, and of her independence. Crystal made her mind up a long time ago, that she wouldn't date another cop, no matter what agency he worked for. Her friends would always tell her that that would probably make dating easier for her. She didn't want the hassles that can come with dating someone in the same field as her, and in her case the potential dangers. To find a wonderful Guy like Derek is a blessing she tells herself. Those thoughts fill her with happiness, and the strength to get through her day. Crystal is excited when her last case is called, and disposed of quickly. She leaves the courthouse, drives back to the station, and catches a ride home with a fellow officer to her Fort Washington home. Crystal is relieved to be home after spending most of her day in court. Now she just wants to relax. She had an idea today for a surprise for Derek. She wants to take him on a cruise next month, but doesn't know what his schedule looks like. She soon came to the conclusion that she would just ask him, is that something he would be interested in doing with her.

That way she wouldn't waste her money if he couldn't go, or they have to choose another date. Having gone on cruises before, she knows what a hassle it would be to get her money back. The only thing that matters to her is that she wants to make him, as happy as he makes her. After Crystal gets home, and settles in, she decides to call her best friend Belinda, and share her good news.

"Hey Belinda, what's up girl?"

"Hi Crystal, not a lot tired as hell. I'm just trying to relax, after being on my feet all day at that damn salon, I swear sometimes I just want to sell that damn salon, and find something else to do."

"Girl please, after all the hard work you've put into that place, you know you'd never sell it. Besides if you did that where would I get my hair done." Crystal says laughing

"Yeah I guess, but it does cross my mind every now, and then. How are you, and the new man?" Belinda asks, curiosity in her voice is obvious.

"Girl, I think I'm really in love with Derek. I told him how I felt about him last night at dinner, and he told me he loved me too. Belinda my heart went crazy." Crystal tells her best friend.

"Crystal are you serious? He told you he loves you."

"Yeah, and I finally got to see his house. His place is laid out girl, I wouldn't have thought he'd have such good taste in furniture. Derek is a sharp dresser due to his job as a real estate agent. I didn't figure him for a slob, but I was pleasantly surprised to see he keeps his home just as sharp."

"I know what you mean girl, not all men are slobs though, just the ones I run into. Belinda continues laughing. It says a lot about a man who keeps a neat house. Hell, most guys take better care of their cars then their where they live."

"He makes me feel so good when we're together Belinda. I just want to make him happy."

"Do I hear wedding bells ringing? I like Derek too, I think he's really good people. I want to be the Maid of Honor Crystal."

"When that time comes of course your my Maid of Honor. No it's not quite there yet, but I really think he could be the one in time."

"Crystal you've known him now for how long? A month and a half." Belinda asks.

"Yeah, and we've spent almost every day together since we've met. I know it hasn't been very long but he is a great guy, and a perfect gentleman."

"No Crystal, it doesn't matter how long it's been, feelings can develop quickly in a relationship. Especially when you spend so much time together, and that's not a problem. As long as the feelings are mutual it's cool. I just don't want to see you get hurt, and I want you to be happy. If Derek's the one then go for it." Belinda says smiling.

"I know, and I appreciate your support, and concern, He told me there is no one else in his life, and I believe him. I know I still have to be cautious, and I will be. I'm not seeing anyone else and I don't want to. Even though Bobby is still trying to come back. He's a joke compared to Derek."

"Girl that fucking loser is still calling you?"

"Every now and then he'll send me a text, or an email, I don't respond to them so you'd think he'd get the message by now. It's not a problem though, he's not dumb enough to come around me. He knows I'd blow his damn brains out if he started any shit with me." Crystal replies.

"The hell with him, he's the one that fucked up. Trying to be a player, and played himself, stupid motherfucker, and that's the problem with some guys. Assholes don't know when they have a good thing." Crystal understands Belinda's contempt for her last boyfriend.

"I hate liars; it didn't bother me that he had other friends. Shit I did too, and our relationship was cool, but if you have to lie about unnecessary shit I have no use for you."

"Ok, enough about the loser girl I don't want to talk about his ass anymore." Crystal tells her.

"Crystal, you want to get together later for a drink?"

"You know I would like to, but Derek and I are supposed to hook up later."

"I understand, but I don't get to see my girl much anymore. At least not since, she met a certain someone." She says laughing.

"I hear you Belinda, but you know you're still my girl, I tell you what, let's do The Spot Friday after work."

"That'll work, Ok girl let me go, so I can get settled in for the evening. I'm probably not going to be up late anyway. You be good and tell Derek I said hello, love you. Belinda replies.

"I will, love you too."

After Belinda hangs up with her best friend, she relaxes on her sofa with a glass of wine. Thinking to herself Derek better not be playing games with her best friend, and that he means what he tells her. Crystal deserves to be happy, hell all she does is work, and study. The few guys that I have met that she has dated all turned out to be petty, and not worth a damn. She's not the type to fall in love easily, so Derek must be very special to her. I hope this relationship works for my girl. Belinda finishes her wine, and drifts off to sleep.

After her conversation with Belinda, Crystal takes her time going about her work around the house, and preparing dinner for herself, and her mother. She decides to get in the shower while their dinner is roasting in the oven. The feel of the warm water is relaxing as it flows over her body. She doesn't want to think about her hours spent in court. Her only thoughts are of Derek, and the feel of his hands caressing her body when they took a shower the other night. She can still feel his strong hands as they moved over her body, and the feel of being held and kissed by him in the shower. She moans with pleasure as she feels herself becoming aroused by her desire for Derek. She gently caresses her breasts as the warm waters run down her body. Her right hand rubbing her pussy and her fingers go to work stimulating her clit. Crystal imagines Derek's hands are touching her body. Crystal feels herself becoming more and more aroused, and her senses start to fire. She feels wonderful, and then she hears a knock on her bathroom door.

"Crystal, I'm home baby." She opens her eyes, and responds to her mother's voice.

"Hey ma, I'll be out in a minute."

"Take your time baby, I'll go check on dinner." Her mother says. Horrible timing ma, Crystal thinks to herself, and laughs out loud.

Fifteen minutes later Crystal comes down stairs, and joins her mother in the Kitchen, they hug, and go to the family room. Her mother had prepared appetizers of cheese, crackers, and wine and has it waiting for Crystal when she comes downstairs. Crystal's mother sits on the sofa, and gestures for her daughter to come join her.

"How'd your day go Crystal?"

"Fine, I had court most of the day, all my cases went well except for one. I had a DWI who failed to show so a warrant was issued for his arrest. So I guess I'll have to deal with that eventually. But as the life of a cop goes it wasn't that bad." Crystal tells her mother.

"How about you Principal Harris?"

"Baby please don't call me that, I must have heard Principal Harris this and that one-hundred times today. Her mother says laughing. I swear sometimes I want to just quit this damn job and retire."

"Ma, Belinda said the same thing when we talked earlier, everybody wants to quit their jobs today."

"After all the work that girl did to get that place started, she's not going anywhere. Besides they do damn good hair." Both women laugh. I saw your car in the driveway this morning, so what's going on with you and Derek." Her mother asks.

"Ma we had a serious talk last night at dinner and Derek told me he loved me. After dinner we went back to his house, and he drove me to work this morning."

"Hold on now Crystal, you left out a lot of info there baby, between dinner, and this morning." Her mother says laughing.

"Well if you really want to hear the details." Crystal says.

"No I think I can fill in the blanks." Responds her mother. "That's wonderful baby, now how do you feel about him."

"I love him ma, Derek is kind, and sweet, and treats me like a queen when we're together. You know I have dated some losers who weren't about a damn thing, but Derek is really not like them."

"Crystal I like Derek, and he seems like he has his act together. I was worried when you told me that you hadn't been to his place, after you'd been seeing him for a while. If a man can't take you to his place or if you can't call him at home there's a serious problem there."

"I agree with you one-hundred percent, which is why I needed to talk to him about that, he told me that there is no one else in his life, and I believe him. He said he just didn't want to rush into anything, and until he was sure about us. He wanted to take it slow. I know we haven't been together long ma, and I will guard my feelings, but he just makes me feel so good, and it feels right with him."

Her mother puts her wine down on the table, and places her hand on top of her daughters.

"I'm happy for you baby, just take it slow, one day at a time. Don't rush this or let it take you somewhere you don't want to go. I want you to be happy, but make sure it's right for you. You're not thinking about marriage or anything at this point are you?"

"No ma, I still want to go to Law School, and I've discussed this with Derek and he supports me all the way. He knows I've enrolled for fall classes, and I have no intention of quitting or not fulfilling my goals."

"Baby your father would be so proud of you if he were here with us, I just wish he could see the woman you turned out to be."

"I wish daddy were here too, I miss him so much." Crystal says.

"Me too baby, that damn cancer took him away from us far too soon."

They share the moment in silence, and give each other a heartfelt hug.

"Ok, enough of that Ma, how are you and Brian doing, is he coming over tonight? He wanted to, but I don't feel like being bothered tonight."

"What, is he not puttin' it down anymore? Crystal says laughing.

"No, he puts it down good alright, I'm just not in the mood today."

"Look ma I'm going to go to Derek's tonight, so go ahead, and call Brain and you two get your freak on." Both woman laugh.

While they eat dinner mother and daughter continue their conversations about the day's work, and the men now in their lives. After dinner Crystal's mother retires to her room and a hot bath. Crystal goes to get ready for her evening with Derek.

Derek calls Crystal at home at 8:00 p. m.

"Hey baby I was just thinking about you, I'm getting myself together now to come to your place."

"I know baby that's why I called. I'm gonna have to cancel tonight. I just got a call about the financing on a big project I'm working on, the sale may be in jeopardy. My Regional Manager wants to see all the docs tomorrow morning." Derek tells her.

"Is everything ok, are they trying to say you did something wrong?" Concern in Crystal's voice.

"No baby, nothing like that, the client wants to buy a home valued at 1.2 million, and the bank is hesitant to finance the loan. So I'm just going over all the documentation with our finance department, before we present them to the Regional Manager tomorrow."

"I understand baby, you take care of your paperwork. I'll hit the books myself; I may as well use the time to get some studying in."

"Thanks baby, I'll make it up to you tomorrow. There is something I want to show." Derek tells her.

"I love surprises; can you give me a clue?"

"No Crystal that would spoil it, I think you'll like it."

"Alright, I guess I can wait." She says smiling.

"I'll call you tomorrow afternoon."

"Goodnight baby, rest well." Derek tells her.

"You too baby."

After Crystal hangs up the phone, she feels a little let down by Derek's canceling their plans for the evening. She had waited all day to be with him, and now that wasn't going to happen. Oh well, she thinks, as she goes to the Den and turns on her desktop. I guess from time to time things will happen that forces us to change our plans. I may as well use the time wisely, and get some studying done. After about an hour her mother comes down stairs.

"Crystal I thought you were going out this evening."

"No Derek called to tell me that he had to cancel our plans. The project he's working on ran into some major problems that he had to deal with."

"Is Brian coming over to keep you company?" She asks her mother.

"Oh, I'm sorry to hear that, but there's always tomorrow. I'll leave you to study, and no he's not, I'm going to bed now alone." Her mother tells her with emphasis on alone, and they both laugh. It's ok; I'll see my baby tomorrow. Crystal thinks to herself. She studies until 11:00 a. m. and goes to bed.

The next day Derek calls Crystal at work, and asks can she meet him when she gets off. He tells her there is something he needs to show her. Crystal tells him that her shift is over at 3:00 p.m. and, of course, she'll meet him. He gives her a Maryland address in the Fort Washington area, and asks her to meet him there at 4:30 p.m. After her shift Crystal drives to the address Derek gave her, she's vaguely familiar with the area. She lives about thirty miles away from this location, but she has a few friends who lives within a few miles of this particular area. Following her GPS Navigation system, she drives into the Harborview Development Complex. She knows that this is probably the most exclusive housing in all of Prince Georges County. She wonders what Derek wants to show her here. She feels excitement anyway, she gets to see him, and whatever it is he wants to show her. She turns a corner, and sees Derek's BMW parked in the driveway of a very large home. She pulls up beside his car, gets out, and walks to the front door.

Before she can knock on the door, Derek opens it, and motions for her to come inside.

"Hey baby I'm happy you could make it, but why didn't you change out of uniform?" He asks.

"Well Derek you did say 4:30 p.m. I figured I'd just put on a jacket, and come right over after work. Anyway, I wanted to see my baby ASAP, even though we're going to dinner this evening I couldn't wait. She says laughing. Is this big ass mansion what you wanted to show me baby?" She asks as she walks away.

"Partly, but there is something else I want to show you as well. This is the damn reason that I missed spending time with you the other night. We just closed the deal on this house this afternoon, the owners move in next week. Derek walks up to Crystal, and holds her around the waist from behind as he continues to speak. I wanted you to see the reason I had to break our date, I don't want to disappoint you, and I know I did. So I just thought I owed my baby an explanation." He says. She turns around to face him, their bodies still pressed together.

"Baby if you have to work late, or if there is an emergency you need to deal with, and it causes us to alter our plans I understand. There will be many times when that will happen because of my job. We just have to accept that, and I do." She tells him.

He kisses her and tells her he loves her.

"Ok baby, now that we're here let me give you the grand tour before we leave." Derek tells her.

"Alright let's do it, can we start with the kitchen?" she asks.

"Of course, baby you have a thing for kitchens don't you?" He says laughing. Derek takes Crystal by the hand, and leads her to the kitchen.

"Baby this damn kitchen is three times the size of mine, one day I'm gonna have a place like this. This is impressive, when I become a lawyer, and start getting paid real money this is the kind of house I want." She says.

"Baby you might be in something like this before you know it." Derek says.

"Baby, you know something I don't?" She says smiling.

Derek walks up to Crystal, they hug and kiss passionately. His arms wrap around her waist, and he holds her tightly. She responds by matching her hold on him, and kissing him back with equal passion. His hands move to her hips, and then to her ass. He grips her cheeks firmly, and gently squeezes. Her moans let him know she is enjoying his touch. Derek backs her against the kitchens granite counter top, and his hands move to her breasts. She quickly removes her weapon from her belt, and throws it on the counter. Her body gets hotter with his every touch. As her moans of pleasure increase, she can no longer control her desires. She un-buckles her belt, and zips down her pants. Her hands find his crotch, and she gently squeezes his dick through his pants. Crystal unzips his pants, and her hand finds his hard dick, she pulls it out and turns around.

"Fuck me baby, I want your big dick in me now baby." She says passionately.

He slides her pants down to her knees, exposing her soft round ass. Derek holds her around the waist with his left arm, and uses his right hand to tease her pussy. He kisses her neck at the same time on just the right spot, and it drives her wild. He feels for the lips of her pussy, and uses his fingers to get her moist. She loves the feel of his fingers in her, and wants his dick to follow. Her juices flow steadily now, and she moves her ass against his hard dick, begging him to fuck her. Derek bends down to remove her right shoe, and pull off one of her pant legs. He kisses her ass cheeks as he stands up, takes his dick in his hand, and guides the head into her pussy. He works the head in slowly at first, but Crystal is so wet his dick slides in easily, and she helps him by pushing against it.

"Oh god baby you feel good." She says, and braces herself against the counter as Derek strokes her from behind harder, and faster. She can barely contain her screams of pleasure as his full measure is thrust in her pussy faster, and deeper. Crystal is now begging Derek to cum in her as he strokes her pussy in the kitchen, Crystal loves every minute of it.

"Oh God, Baby! I'm getting ready to cum, make me cum baby! Oh, shit! fuck me harder baby, you feel good, damn baby your dick feels so good. Ah, Shit! Baby I'm Cumming!"

Crystal screams as she reaches her climax, her entire body throbbing with pleasure. Seconds later Derek pushes his dick in her, and holds her against it as he starts to feel the involuntary contractions in his penis. He too lets out moans of passion, and heavy breathing as his cum pumps into her pussy. Crystal moans loudly as he cums in her, she can feel very pulsation of his dick as he releases his load. Her eyes closed, she lies on the counter top with her arms out-stretched, and moans with ecstasy. Derek slowly withdraws his dick from her pussy, and lays on her back, breathing heavily but calming himself he again kisses her neck, and rubs her waist and hips with both hands. She tells him how good he felt and that she loves him.

"Oh baby that felt so good, I needed that, but I want some more." Crystal tells him.

"Baby you can have as much of me as you want." He whispers in her ear. "I know the perfect place." He tells her. Derek completely removes his shoes, socks, and pants then hers. He picks her up in his arms, and carries her through the house, and down one flight of stairs to the homes theater room. The Theater room is beautifully decorated with dark blue wall-to-wall carpeting. It has twelve Burgundy, and black fully reclining lounge chairs with footrests, and cup holders set four to a row. As they enter the room Derek explains that the theater room is equipped with both a projector, and a seventy-five inch flat screen TV. Still holding her in his arms and standing in the doorway of the theater room Crystal kisses him, and tells him to take her to the top row. Derek puts her down, and she guides him to a chair in the middle of the top row. He sits down, and Crystal pushes the recline button. With his chair only slightly reclined she goes down on her knees, between his opened legs, and takes his dick in her mouth. She works his dick with both her hand and mouth until he is rock hard again. Crystal enjoys the taste of her pussy on him, and his cum. She does not cut his pleasure short, she sucks his dick until he cums in her mouth. Crystal swallows every drop, and quickly gets on top of him; she lets his long dick slide into her pussy. She holds the position applying downward pressure, Crystal moans, and shouts her passion aloud as the pleasure she feels is almost beyond her ability to describe in words. Her hands gripping his shoulders as she motions for him to remain still.

"Oh Baby don't move, please this feels so good, I feel you in my stomach."

Derek lets her ride is dick as he sucks her nipples, he feels the moisture of her pussy on his balls, and himself ready to cum again. Crystal reclines the chair back fully and, begins to ride his dick with more force. Derek squeezes her breasts, and sucks her nipples passionately as she slides up and down on his dick faster, and harder. Crystal feels the throbbing in his dick, and herself about to cum as she thrusts downward, and holds the position. Both lovers scream out loud as they cum together, they say nothing for the next several minutes. Each lost in their own thoughts. Lying on his chest Crystal breaks the silence.

"Baby, I have never experienced that before." She says to him.

"What baby?" He says.

"Cumming with my man at the same time, for me it was almost magical" she whispers her words. "Baby…She stops talking, and he feels her tears on his chest.

He says nothing, his response to her words is simply to hold her, and to comfort her as best he can until the moment, and the emotion passes. Many minutes pass before she says another word.

"Baby I know we need to get out of here, but I feels so comfortable lying on you like this, you make me so happy." She says still laying on top of him.

"I feel the same way Crystal, I do love you baby, and I don't want to lose you." He says.

"You don't have to worry about that baby; I told you I'm not going anywhere."

Crystal tries to rise off his chest, but finds it a little difficult. Derek tries to help her by pressing the button to reset the chair but it won't move.

"Oh! Derek, baby you broke it." Crystal says laughing.

Crystal stands up, and Derek gets off the recliner, and tries to reset the chair to it's up right position. He hears the motor running as if it's trying to operate, but the recliner will not respond.

"Baby I'm gonna go get my clothes, and use the bathroom while you fix the chair you broke." Crystal says laughing as she walks away.

"I think you had a little something to do with it too officer." He responds.

Derek stops pressing the buttons realizing that's not working, he stands behind the chair, and pulls up on the back, and head rest as hard as he can. Slowly the chair rises, and the footrest folds back into place.

"Ok, the hell with this, it's back in place, and no one will know we broke it, it's time to get the hell out of here."

Derek says as he leaves the theater room. Derek walks past the bathroom on that floor, and hears water running so he hurries up stairs, stops in another bathroom to quickly clean himself up, which only consists of washing off his dick, and washing his hands. He quickly rushes back to the kitchen. He wants to beat Crystal back there so that he can have the present he has for her ready when she comes back. He looks on the counter, and see's that her gun is gone, she must have come back up here first he tells himself. Derek opens a cabinet door under the counter, and pulls out a black box, and puts it on the counter. Then he quickly puts the rest of his clothes back on. He sits down to tie his shoes as Crystal walks into the kitchen. She walks over to him, bends down, and gives him a kiss.

"Baby I think we need to get out of here, but it was oh so much fun. I felt like a teenager in my parent's house getting a quickie before they came home, and caught us." She says. Derek stands up, and holds her by the waist and kisses her.

"Yeah that was fun wasn't it. Baby open the box on the counter." Crystal turns around and reaches for the box, she picks it up, and places it down on the counter with both hands resting on top. Derek again holds her from behind, and tells her to open it. She un-snaps the lock, and opens both doors of the box. When she sees its contents her mouth opens wide, and she brings both her hands to her face.

"Baby this is beautiful."

Crystal is frozen as she looks at the necklace in the box. It's a yellow gold double row pear cut link necklace.

"Thank you so much baby, I love it, this is really beautiful, I love you baby." She tells him. She turns to face him, and hugs him with all the tenderness within her.

"That's just a piece of jewelry, you make it beautiful baby." he responds.

They break their embrace; Derek turns her around, and puts the necklace on her. She wipes the tears from her face, and they kiss again.

As they prepare to leave Crystal thinks to herself that this man really does love me. I can't help touching the necklace he just gave me. He is proving to me how much he cares for me. The couple walks out of the house holding hands. Derek pauses briefly to ensure the front door is securely locked, and walks Crystal to her car.

"I'll call you tonight baby after I close out the file on this place." He tells her.

"Ok baby, you do what you have to, I understand, and we can do dinner another night, you've already made my day. I'll be home studying, so call me when you can." She responds. They kiss one more time, get into their cars and leave.

Crystal can't wait to get home so that she can call Belinda, and show her mother the gift that Derek gave her today. On the drive home every time she touches it she smiles. All she wants to think about is Derek, and how happy she is that the two of them met. She pulls into her driveway, and goes into the house.

"Ma I'm home, I have something to show you." She shouts as she puts her bags on the floor.

"I'm in the family room Crystal." Her mother responds.

Crystal goes to the family room, and her mother is there relaxing, watching TV. As soon as she turns toward her daughter she notices the gold necklace Crystal is wearing.

"Baby that is a beautiful necklace, Derek gave you that?" Crystal takes a seat on the sofa next to her mother.

"Yes today, he wanted to meet me after work, because he wanted to show me the reason he had to cancel our date the other night. He had me meet him at the house he just sold, and explained why our plans had to be changed."

"Well that was awful considerate of him, that man really is doing all he can to make you happy baby. Do you mind if I hold it?" Her mother asks. Crystal turns around, and lifts her hair so that her mother can unclasp the necklace. She holds it in her hands, feeling it's weight, and admiring it's workmanship. She is impressed by both its color and style.

"Baby I have a lot of jewelry, and I've never seen anything like this, this is a fine piece of gold. Do you want me to put it back on?"

"No I have to get undressed, and in the shower anyway." She takes the necklace, and puts it back in the case.

"Mom I really care for Derek more, and more every day. I just want it to last, but sometimes I'm afraid that this thing is too good, and it frightens me a little."

"Baby it's only natural to feel that way, don't let that bother you. What that tells me is that you're cautious about the relationship, and that's a good thing. Derek knows he has a good thing going with you, and it would be his loss if he did anything to mess it up." Her mother says.

"Like I said to you earlier baby, just take it one day at a time, and let the relationship play itself out naturally. In time you'll know what you want, and where you want to take things. I'll say this though, I think Derek is getting there, you don't give a woman a gift like that necklace if you're not serious about her. Her mother says. Hell, I may have to have Brian step up his game." They both laugh.

Crystal feels better after having talked to her mother; she decides that she will let her current relationship proceed full steam ahead. Crystal undresses, takes a long hot shower, and decides she'll call Belinda after she hits the books. After studying for two hours Crystal decides it's time to call it a night, and talk to her friend before she goes to bed. She gets her cell phone off her dresser, and dials Belinda's number.

"Hey girl are you busy?"

"No, not really, I just finished going over a little paperwork and now I'm watching some fucked up show on Lifetime. What's up Crystal?"

"I just wanted to catch up with you before I went to bed."

"Well there's not a lot going on over here. How have things been with you?"

"Girl, I don't know where to start. Derek and I are doing fine. He had me meet him at this house he sold in Harborview. He wanted to explain to me why he had to cancelled an earlier date. His apology consisted of fucking me like crazy, and a beautiful gold necklace." Crystal laughs.

"Girl you fucked him in somebody else's new house, a house at Harborview?"

"I sure did, one thing led to another, and before I knew it things got hot and heavy."

"How many rooms did you christen?" Belinda says laughing.

"The kitchen and the theater room."

"Damn! Girl you nasty." She says laughing.

"Belinda I have to show you the necklace he gave me. No one has ever given me anything like this before. It is so beautiful."

"Ok, why don't we get together after work, and go to The Spot for a drink." Belinda asks.

"We can do that, how about five O'clock." Replies Crystal.

"That's fine, hey was the dick good."

"Hell yeah girl, it always is. Hey Belinda I want to surprise him with a cruise. I want to go on. It's nothing fancy, just two days on the water. I was thinking of just booking it, and surprising him. What do you think?"

"That sounds like a nice weekend getaway. I'd say just make sure when you book it, that you get any insurance that covers cancellations, illness, and shit like that. That way you can apply the money you spend on another cruise. When were you planning on going?"

"I was looking at July 23rd, the ship leaves Friday from Norfolk, and returns Sunday the 25th."

"Hey, would you mind if me, and Phil joined you two?"

"No girl, that would make it even more fun. Let's talk about it tomorrow."

"Cool, goodnight nasty, I'll see you tomorrow." She says laughing.

"Nite Belinda."

The next day while at work Crystal decides that it might be best, if she asks Derek about the cruise she wants to take him on. So during her lunch break she calls him.

"Hey baby, you busy?"

"I'm never too busy for you Crystal."

"I have a question for you. Would you like to go on a cruise with me?"

"I'd go anywhere with you, but I have to tell you I've never been on a cruise before. Replies Derek.

"Well that's good, your first experience will be with me. It's not a long one, just two days on the water."

"That sounds like fun, if I can handle this one, we can try a longer one in the future. When did you want to go?" Derek asks.

"I was looking at July 23rdand 25th, we'd leave Friday, and come back Sunday. Belinda and her friend want to join us as well."

"Sounds like big fun, let me check my calendar. Baby I have a conference I have to attend in Charlotte on July 15th through the 19th, but that weekend is good."

"Charlotte, North Carolina? When did this happen?" Concern in Crystal's voice.

"I knew about this last week, I was hoping I wouldn't have to go. But I was told this morning that I'm going. Hey, why don't you come with me?"

"I won't be able to take that much leave on such short notice. I barely got the days off for the cruise. Baby when were you going to tell me about this? You leave in three days."

"I know Crystal, I was gonna tell you tonight. Hey let's not spoil things, remember what we talked about concerning our jobs. Let's just concentrate on our weekend getaway. That will give me something to look forward to."

"It's ok baby I understand, I just don't like you leaving me for almost a whole week."

"I love you too baby, now what do I need to put down on our get away?" Derek asks.

"Nothing baby, you already put it down. She says laughing. This is on me baby. I just wanted to make sure you were ok with the idea."

"Alright baby, whatever you want to do I'm there." Derek replies.

During their conversation, in the background Crystal hears a voice tell Derek he has an emergency call on line six.

"Baby I have to take a call, I'll call you this evening." Derek tells her, urgency in his voice.

"Ok babe, talk to you then."

Crystal hangs up her phone, and walks back to her desk, she's happy that Derek is cool with the cruise she wants to take him on. She also hopes everything is ok with Derek, and that emergency call he just got. She thinks to herself she is ok with him leaving town without her. It's just that her connection to him is getting stronger, and she likes the feeling it gives her. That same evening Crystal and Belinda meet as planned at their favorite place called The Spot, to have drinks, and to catch up on events that have been occurring in both their lives.

The two friends also finalize plans for the weekend getaway, that they both are looking forward to. Crystal however does not tell Belinda about how she feels concerning Derek's conference, and his being out of town, and away from her. The two friends leave the restaurant, and each heads home for the evening. Crystal is looking forward to talking to Derek before she goes to bed. Then she thinks to herself why not just drive to his house, and say goodnight in person, maybe even get some dick.

Before Crystal can turn around and head for Derek's house her cell phone rings. She looks at the display, and see's it's her home number. She thinks to herself her mother must know what she's planning. Just as I decide to go see Derek she needs something.

She picks up the phone, and greets her mother but a man's voice responds to her. She recognizes the voice as Brian's.

"Oh, hey Brian, I thought it was mom calling me. You call me to tell me to stay out so you two can get it on?" Crystal says laughing.

"Crystal I'm calling for your mother, she's not feeling well, and I'm about to drive her to Holy Cross Hospital." Crystal hears the seriousness in his voice.

"Brian what's wrong with her!" Crystal demands.

"Crystal I don't know, we were supposed to go to dinner. When I got here she was complaining about severe pains in her stomach. We called her health care provider, and explained what was happening, and they said get her to the hospital."

"I'm on my way home now." Crystal tells Brian.

"We'll be gone by the time you get here, why don't you just meet us at the hospital.

"Alright I'm headed there now."

Crystal puts her phone away, turns her car around, and heads for the Capital Beltway. She takes exit 495 north toward Baltimore. She knows Brian will take care of her mother until they reach the hospital, but Crystal is feeling very un-easy. The thought of something happening to her mother almost sends her into a panic. It takes great effort on her part to calm herself, and not let her imagination run wild. She focuses on getting to the hospital, she tells herself this could be nothing. That there is no need to panic, she calms herself and focuses on getting to her mother. Forty-five minutes later Crystal pulls into the visitor's lot of the hospital, parks, and rushes to the emergency room entrance. She walks in, and expects to see Brian but doesn't. She goes over to the reception desk, and gets in line to inquire about her mother. There are four people in front of her, and not knowing what her mother's condition is or even if they've gotten here, is now starting to get to her. Crystal wants to push these people out of her way. She doesn't care what their problems are, her mother may be in trouble. After about ten minutes Crystal gets to the receptionist, and asks if her mother has been admitted. After checking the computer, Crystal is told that her mother is in surgery. She is told her mother presented with an acute abdomen, possibly appendicitis. Crystal informs the receptionist that a man brought her in, and she would like to know if he can be paged. She is told to go to the fourth floor lobby. That's where Brian should be waiting. Crystal hurries to the elevator, she needs to find out what's going on. She gets off on the fourth floor, and follows the signs that guide her to the lobby. As soon as she gets there she sees Brian. She goes in, and takes a seat next to him.

"Crystal they took Jasmine right in, they think her appendix may have burst. But they aren't sure, the doctor just left, I told him you were coming."

"When will they find out, if her appendix burst, that can kill her?"

"Don't think like that Crystal, let's just wait until the doctor returns." Brian tells her. Crystal is extremely worried about her mother, but she feels better knowing she is now with the doctors. She and Brian wait for what seems like forever for the doctor to return. When he finally does come into the lobby he walks directly to Crystal and Brian, he extends his hand to Crystal.

"Hi I'm Doctor Williams, I'll be performing your mother's surgery."

"Are you Crystal?"

"Yes, I'm Jasmine's daughter."

"Your mother is being prepped for surgery, her appendix has not ruptured, but it does need to be removed. It's inflammation is what was causing her the extreme pain she was experiencing. Fortunately, for her we caught it in time. We are going to remove it, and she should be fine. I will need you to complete some paperwork authorizing us to do the surgery."

"Of course doctor whatever you need, is it possible for me to see her?"

"I'm afraid not at this time. The surgery won't take more than an hour barring any complications, and she's going to be out for the rest of the night. When she is in recovery you can sit with her, but it's very important that you do not disturb her."

The doctor directs Crystal where to go to fill out the paperwork, and returns to the surgical ward. After Crystal completes the paperwork she, and Brian return to the lobby.

"Crystal do you want to go home and change? I'll wait with her until you return."

"No Brian I'll leave when she comes out of surgery."

"Alright I'll wait here with you."

While they wait Crystal calls her office to request emergency leave, and is granted all the time she needs for this emergency. She then notifies her mother's office by leaving a voice mail message, and calling her assistant principal. Crystal also tries to call Derek several times but he doesn't answer his phone. He's not leaving for a few days, and she wonders why he's not answering his phone. She returns her attention back to the situation at hand. She and Brian sit, and talk then they both go to the cafeteria to get something to eat while they wait for her mother to come out of surgery. Almost two hours pass when Dr. Williams comes out to see them. Crystal is informed that her mother is doing fine, and that the surgery went well. After hearing the good news Brian and Crystal hug, Brian tells Crystal he will be back tomorrow after work. Crystal goes to recovery, and sees her mother on a bed sleeping. She touches her mother's hand and whispers she is going home now, but she'll be back first thing in the morning. She tells her mother she loves her, and leaves the hospital.

When Crystal gets home it is after 11:00 p.m. she undresses, and takes a hot shower. Before she goes to bed she calls Belinda to tell her what's happened. They make plans to meet at the hospital in the morning. Crystal also calls Derek, but again she gets no answer. So she leaves him a voice mail message asking him to call her as-soon-as-possible. She starts to tell him why in her message it's so important that he call her but decides against it. Crystal doesn't want to put her mother's business in the street, not even with Derek until she has a chance to talk to her first. Crystal is worried that she has been unable to reach Derek. She decides that she will deal with that when she does talk to him. She knows her main concern now has to be her mother. Crystal decides to go to bed, so that she can get to the hospital first thing in the morning. Belinda is going to meet her there at noon.

The next morning Crystal gets up, and prepares to go to the hospital. While she's dressing many thoughts go through her mind. Foremost of which is her mother's condition, she knows the surgery went well, but she can't help worrying. Crystal goes to her mother's room, gets her mother's gym bag, and fills it with various articles of clothing, shoes, undergarments, and various toiletries. Crystal calls her mother's office again to verify that her last message to them concerning her mother's condition was received. She also calls her squad sergeant again to inform him of her mother's status.

"May I speak to Sergeant Billings please?" Crystal is put on hold for a few seconds.

"Sergeant Billings speaking"

"Sarge, this is Crystal, I just wanted to verify you got my message last night concerning my mom. I spoke with the duty sergeant last night."

"Yes Crystal I got it. How's your mother doing? The Sergeant inquires.

"She had surgery last night to remove her appendix, they caught it before it ruptured."

"That's good news, look I have you on family leave for the next week. I'll take care of any court cases you have coming up, and your partner will take care of any paperwork you have due."

"Thanks Sarge."

"You take care of your mom, and let me know if you need any more time, you take care."

Thanks again sarge I appreciate it.

Ok, those bases are covered Crystal thinks to herself. She wonders if there is anything else her mother might need that she may have forgotten. She can't think of anything else to take her, but it doesn't matter she tells herself. She'll buy whatever her mother may need at the hospital. Before she leaves the house to go to the hospital, she decides to call Derek again. She puts the gym bag down in the living room, and dials his number, the phone rings three times before he answers.

"Hey baby, I've been trying to call you. I thought maybe something was wrong."

"No baby I just got tied up with work, and last night, I was in the office till late, closing out some files, when I got home I turned in early. I'm getting paperwork ready now to go to this damn conference."

"Ok I have something I have to deal with today as well, will I see you today?, I need to talk to you." Crystal tells him.

"Sure why don't you come by the house when you get off, or would you like me to come to you. I'll be in the office again late today."

"I'm not gonna be in any mood to go anywhere today so why don't you come here, you can stay with me tonight."

"OK baby that'll work, I'll be at the office at least until Six O'clock. So I'll stop by the house first, and come right over. Derek explains.

"That'll be fine, I'll be there waiting."

"Should I bring dinner or anything?" Derek asks.

"Yeah that'll work, just call before you come."

"Ok baby, I gotta run, but I'll see you this evening. Love you baby.

"Me too baby, see you this evening."

Crystal gets in her car, and heads for the hospital, in route she calls Brian to let him know she's headed there now. He tells her he'll be there around 1:00 p.m. She puts her phone away, and concentrates on getting to her mother's side. As she drives Crystal is aware that her service weapon is digging into her right side. She wishes she didn't have to carry the damn thing with her everywhere, but her department policy states she must carry it even off duty. Today she wished she had left it home, because she plans to sit with her mother most of the day. Her phone vibrates, and she sees it's a text from Belinda, Crystal reads the message. It says she'll be at the hospital around noon. I love that girl, I couldn't wish for a better friend then Belinda. Crystal thinks to herself. Crystal doesn't let her mind wander any more, she concentrates on getting to the hospital. She does however find herself constantly touching the necklace Derek recently gave her. After having to deal with the morning traffic, Crystal arrives at the hospital a little later than she would have liked but, it's still early. She looks at her watch and it's 10:00 a.m. She gathers her mother's gym bag, and two other bags in the car, and walks into the hospital. She goes to the reception desk, and asks what room her mother's been assigned to. Crystal is told her mother is in room 715, she stops by the gift shop before she gets on the elevator. As Crystal approaches her mother's room she hears voices coming from inside. She walks in, and her mother is discussing something with the woman in the next bed. Crystal is relieved to see her mother sitting up and talking.

"Hello Ma, I heard you when I was coming in so you must be fine."

"Hi baby!" Her mother says to her daughter as she extends her arms to hug her. Crystal puts the flowers on the table, and hugs her mother.

"I was worried about you last night, buy the time I got here Brian had already gotten you here, and they took you right to surgery. I waited until you were in recovery before I left." She tells her mother.

"How are you feeling Ma?"

"To be honest a little sore, but I'd leave now if they let me, other than that I feel fine. The doctor was just here, and he said it would at least be another day before I can get out of here." Jasmine explains.

"I spoke with Brian this morning, he's gonna be here around 1:00 p.m. he said. He told me what time you were coming this morning." Says her mother.

"Belinda is also coming around noon or so." Crystal responds.

"Thank you, baby for the flowers, and for calling my office for me." Crystal looks over to the next bed, and says good morning to the woman sitting there.

"Good morning, I'm Donna, I've been keeping your mother company. It seems we're both early risers. She came in last night about 2: a.m."

"Donna this is my daughter Crystal, you're gonna like Donna when she tells you what she does for a living." Jasmine explains.

"Nice to meet you Crystal, we were just commenting on some of these outrageous news stories."

"My mother and I do that every day at home."

"Crystal that's a very beautiful necklace you're wearing," Donna says.

"It was a gift from my boyfriend, I love it." Crystal says as she touches the jewelry she's wearing.

"Well Crystal now that you're here, you can join us for breakfast." Says her mother.

"That's fine with me, have you two ordered your food yet?" asks Crystal.

"Yes, it should be here anytime now, Donna and I decided to eat a little late to wait for you."

"OK, I am hungry, let me go to the cafeteria real quick, and I will join you."

Crystal leaves the room to go get her food, and it makes her happy to see her mother is in good spirits so soon after her surgery, and ready to come home. Then Crystal has another very pleasing thought, if her mother does come home within the next day or two, and since I'm off for the next week. I can go to Charlotte with Derek, at least for a few days. Brian will take care of mom, so I won't have to worry about that. I'll tell Derek the good news tonight when he comes to the house. When Crystal gets back to her mother's room with her breakfast, both women have had their meals delivered. Crystal sits at her mother's bedside, and the women eat their breakfast while watching the news. After they eat both women are taken at different times to have various tests performed, and brought back to the room. While Crystal's mother was gone Crystal learned that Donna is a paralegal working at the State Department, she's worked there for eight years, and is pursuing her law degree. The women make an instant connection with each other, as they talk about their careers. The different paths they each took, to accomplish the goal of getting their law degree. When Jasmine is brought back to the room, both Crystal and Donna are deep in conversation. To Crystal's mother they sound like two lawyers talking shop. Again, Jasmine feels great pride for her daughter; she knows that her daughter will make an excellent attorney.

"Well it's good to see you ladies getting along without me." Jasmine says laughing.

"It was hard ma, but we managed." Says Crystal.

"You were right Donna was just the person I needed to meet."

"I'll be happy to help you in any way I can Crystal."

"I was telling your mom before you came, I would have had my law degree by now. But working for the State Department, we are sometimes required to go to certain countries for various reasons. I've been to Mexico twice to assist with drug cartel case preparations. This last time two months ago, I must have eaten something or drank something that made me septic. I have been sick for months, and almost died. I haven't seen my house in over two months, or been with my husband. I will never go there again, so I can give you any help you need. We need more black female lawyers in the system." Says Donna

"I would appreciate any help, and guidance you can give me. Crystal replies.

"Hey, does anybody want to play cards?" I haven't played any since my last roommate a few weeks ago." Asks Donna.

"Sure, what's the game?" Replies Crystal.

"Whatever, doesn't matter to me." Replies Donna.

Donna gets a small tray with foldout legs, using it as a makeshift card table. Donna places it across Jasmine's thighs, so she doesn't have to get out of bed. With Crystal on her mother's left, Donna goes to her night stand to get her cards. When she turns toward Jasmines bed with the cards, a man opens the door, and walks in the room carrying a boutique of roses. Without thinking about it they look up, instantly smile. Both Crystal and Donna greet him simultaneously, with the same words spoken in unison, with almost the same volume, tone, and meaning. "Hey Baby."

Jasmine looks from one woman to the other, with the speed of thought, and then at the man frozen in time, mid-stride two paces beyond the doors threshold. The room's door silently closes behind him. Three words escape her as she brings her hands to her mouth, and she too looks at the man who just walked in, "oh my God" The words are barely audible, it is so eerily silent, death itself couldn't sneak in the room. Time stops for him, Derek doesn't know what to say, or do. His heart has gone from its normal beat, to the point where he can feel it pounding in his chest. He can actually hear his heartbeat; the sound is so loud it terrifies him. His hands sweat, and his mouth goes dry. He is trying to control himself by commanding his body to stop trembling, but control of his own body is temporarily not functioning. As he looks into the eyes of both his wife, and another woman he claimed to love, as well as her mother. Cruelly times resumes, and Derek doesn't have a clue what he's supposed to do in this situation. Donna and Crystal look at each other, than at Derek. A nanosecond after they spoke to him, and it clicks. Speaking in a shaky voice Donna asks Crystal a question.

"Crystal, where do you know Derek from?" Donna asks. Her eyes never leave Derek's, as she leans on Jasmine's bed.

"I met Derek two months ago at a club. He told me he wasn't married, and had no kids, that he lived alone, and had no girlfriend. Isn't that what you told me Derek!" Crystal shouts.

He says nothing.

"Are you going to answer her" Derek. Demands Jasmine. He wants to run, but can't, he tells himself to side with his wife, but he can't, his body won't cooperate with him, as he's never been this frightened in his entire life. His only response is to step further into the room on shaky legs, and wish he could run away. He looks at his wife and can say nothing; the look in his eyes is blank. The look in his wife's eyes filled with contempt for him. At that moment Crystal's best friend enters the room also carrying flowers, and is shocked because she knows something is very, very wrong.

"Crystal what's going on?" Belinda asks.

"You tell your WIFE! About us Derek? You sorry son of a bitch! Crystal says as she hurls a glass at him. It barely misses his head. Is the house you took me to hers, is the bed we fucked in hers, or were you using someone else's house like we did a few days ago. Did you fuck me in your wife's bed baby? The white canopy bed with the floral design, the bed made of Rosewood. Did you fuck me in your wife's bed? You sorry piece of shit!" Crystal shouts as tears pour down her face. Crystal doesn't notice, but tears are also flowing down her mother's face. Belinda wants to go to her friend, but something is stopping her, and she doesn't know why.

"What the fuck! is happening here Crystal?" Belinda implores. She gets no response.

Derek's only response is to drop the flowers on the floor, and sit in the open chair between the two beds. His shame won't allow him to look at any of the women in the room.

"I've been in this goddamn hospital for almost twelve weeks! sometimes not knowing if I was gonna die or not, and you've been out there fucking around on me. What? Derek you thought I was going to die, so you figured you'd go out, and have fun while you waited for that to happen? Is that what was going on all those times you couldn't stay with me more than thirty fuckin' minutes?" Donna can barely control her rage at this point. Is that what it was nigga!, you were out there screwing her during my surgeries, all those damn therapy sessions you said you'd be here for, but weren't."

Tears of betrayal flow down Donna's right cheek as she tries to control the rage she feels, and the nausea that is coming over her. Trying her hardest not to cry Donna asks Crystal to describe more of her house. Then she asks Crystal did Derek give her the necklace she's wearing. After Crystal describes Derek's house, and it's furnishings vividly, she answers the question concerning the necklace.

"Yes, He gave it to me after he fucked me in another house he supposedly sold to someone."

Crystal's mother is in shock. She lays on the bed, and says nothing. She is a very articulate woman, but the words that come so naturally escape her now as she listens, and tries to hold onto her daughter's hand. Crystal takes off the necklace, and gives it to her mother, who is now crying, who in turn gives it to Donna.

"Years ago I had four numbers engraved on this, 1 and 5 on two end links, and 0 and 5 on two of the middle links." Donna turns the necklace over and sees the numbers are there.

"That date mean anything to your sorry ass? I haven't worn this in years so you give it to another woman? Do you even remember when you gave me this necklace motherfucker? Donna screams. It was our fifth wedding anniversary, how could you do this type of shit to me, did you think I wouldn't notice. I've never seen another necklace like this one before today. Do you remember we had this made for our fifth anniversary? Donna now starts to scream louder at him. Motherfucker I hate you with all my heart! You filthy low-life piece of shit. I want you out of my goddamn life! Motherfucker! I wish you were dead, I hate you!"

Donna throws the necklace on the floor at his feet, and walks out of the room past a stunned Belinda. Derek never even tried to look up when she passed him. After thirty seconds he stands, and walks toward the door not even bothering to look at Crystal or anyone else in the room. In a motion too fast to see Crystal draws her weapon, points it at his face, and dares him to keep walking. Derek stops before he can put his hand on the door knob. Belinda looking at Crystal quickly moves away from Derek.

"Crystal baby, please don't do this, don't let this bastard make you ruin your life." Her mother begs her.

"Crystal, girl he's not worth it, please Crystal let this sorry ass motherfucker go."

A crying, and shaking Belinda begs her friend.

Crystal however doesn't hear a word her mother or Belinda is saying to her. Crystal has both hands on her weapon, and it's pointed at Derek's face. He leans against the door of the room too scared to try to run and pisses in his pants. He begs Crystal not to kill him, he can see the round in the barrel of her gun. The barrel seems as if it's ten feet around. Her every word to him brings more tears.

"You didn't have to lie to me, I asked you baby. I damn near begged you to be honest with me, I loved you honestly baby. No fuckin 'strings attached no baggage, no drama. All I ever wanted was to make you happy with me. Every word Crystal utters brings torrents of tears down her face, and pain to her heart. I fell in love with your sorry ass, and you said you loved me too. I would have done anything for you motherfucker! All I asked was that you not lie to me, you never had to lie to me, you're married, and gave me her jewelry. I'm so goddamn tired of being hurt, and treated like this, Fuck You Motherfucker!"

Holding the weapon firmly, it's pointed directly at Derek's face. The pain of her broken heart too much to bare, her finger slowly squeezes the trigger; Derek closes his eyes and sees his life flash before him. Belinda, and Jasmine realize what is about to happen in an instant before it does, all they can do is scream, as they are powerless to stop it, in an instant the weapon fires with a senses shattering report. Boom!

In her grief, she pulls the trigger. Her mother, and Belinda scream in unison, it is such a frightening sound everyone on the floor feels their pain. "No Baby! What have you done! Baby No! Dear God No!"

Her mother jumps out of the bed, and goes to her daughters limp body, she lifts her off the floor, and holds her still body in her arms. Blood running in torrents from the wound she inflicted on herself. Her mother tries to stop the blood, and gray matter from running out of her daughters head but she can't.

Belinda is on her knees at her friend's side crying, and screaming hysterically, she doesn't know what to do so she holds her beloved friends hand, and tells her everything will be all right. She looks to the door, and see's Derek is no longer there, the women's screams for help is quickly answered. Soon the room is filled with medical personnel. They try to save Crystal's life but it is no use. The bullets exit wound tore a hole in her head the size of a small orange, Crystal, and her broken heart died instantly.

Is it our own personal demons, which keep us from changing our perceptions? Maybe it's fear of self, or maybe it's something much deeper.

ONE OF MY OWN

Starbucks, at Tyson Corner's II Mall 4:00 p.m.

"Why are there so many niggers here today? I've never seen this many of them here before." Jessica says to her best friend Kim-Lei.

"Jessica, can you please give that a rest, and just enjoy your cappuccino? We came here to shop, hangout and have fun. Not to worry ourselves over black people, and where they should or shouldn't be. They do have the right to be here." Kim-Lei replies.

"Kim-Lei, don't act like you don't feel the same way as I do. Niggers make you nervous too. And you know most of them are thugs, and criminals anyway. Jessica continues. Don't stare, but look at the way that one in front of the GameStop is wearing his pants; showing his dirty boxers. That is so disgusting, and nasty. And you would allow that thing in your house, or place of business? I wonder if he really thinks that's attractive. I'd bet that nigger didn't even finish Jr. High School. So how does he get money to shop at a mall like this one? I'd bet he's nothing more than a damn thief, who steals for a living. We aren't in the hood where we both know all those people do is screw, and breed criminals."

"No, Jessica. I know that's not true. All blacks are not criminals. Hell, our President is black, so that says all blacks are not that way. Just as all whites and Asians are not the fine upstanding citizens you make them out to be."

"Well I didn't vote for Obama's black ass, and he's done nothing except destroy our economy." Jessica interjects.

"Blacks are different from us. We are not the same in the way we act, or think. Maybe that guy just likes the ghetto look like a lot of them do. Look, I don't know, and I don't care. To answer your earlier question, no I wouldn't allow that in my business, or anywhere else if it were up to me." Kim-Lei says to her friend.

"Kim-Lei, I just feel uncomfortable around so many of them. Its people who come out in public looking like that that causes us to feel this way. I feel like they're watching me, and just waiting to attack me because I'm better than them."

"Maybe that particular thug likes white girls like you, with long blond hair, and green eyes. Maybe I should invite him to have a cappuccino with us." Kim-Lei laughs.

"Kim-Lei, please don't make me throw-up. That nigger probably couldn't even pronounce cappuccino."

"Jessica, you need to stop being so paranoid. I don't care for blacks either, but this is the world we live in, and I accept that. We don't have to be friends with any of them, and I will agree, you have to watch yourself around most of them. But you can't stop living your life just because they sometimes show up where they're not wanted." Kim-Lei says to her friend.

"Why can't they all just go back to where they came from, and stay where they belong?" Jessica asks.

"I see you're not going to let this go. Why do we have to have this conversation all the time?"

"I'm not trying to spoil our day Kim-Lei. It's just that I'm not used to seeing so many niggers in our neighborhood. And when did you all of a sudden adopt this we are the world, and can't we all just get along attitude? What's next? You gonna start dating niggers now? You want to see if the rumors about them are true?" Jessica says laughing.

"Now Jessica you know full well, that that will never happen. I'd never let a black man touch me, and I don't care how big their dicks are. Besides, you know my family would never accept that. I'm just not as paranoid about the subject as you are. I've never had a bad experience with any of them." Kim-Lei says and finishes her cappuccino.

"Kim-Lei, you avoid being around them just like I do. Neither of us works with any of them, and neither of us have any nigger friends."

"That's true, but this is 2011, and even though I was raised in a household that taught me we are superior to them, and it is unacceptable to be with a black man, I'd like to think I've matured a little since college, and moved out on my own. Let me ask you a hypothetical question Jessica. You're my girl for life, and my best fucking friend. Let's just say for the sake of argument that one day I woke up, and in my travels I happen to meet a black man, that totally sweeps me off my feet. We fall in love, and I eventually marry him. What would you say to that?"

"Kim-Lei, you would hit me with something like that. We've been friends since grade school. You will always be my girl, but if that were to happen Kim-Lei, I honestly don't know how I'd feel. Since you brought that shit up, I'll tell you now, that I've always hated your damn hypothetical situations. You were always doing that crap in class. I'd be like sitting in class when you'd hit the teacher with something like that. I'd say to myself, God! she makes me sick when she does that. You'd always pull the whole class into those conversations." Jessica says laughing.

"You don't need to answer me anyway because it'll never happen, and besides I'd like to think that our friendship can survive anything."

"You know that's true Kim-Lei. But for the record, I outright can't stand any of them, and avoid them like the plague when I can, which is why I notice so many of them here today."

"Remember when I had to fly home from Chicago, and I had to sit next to a nigger on the plane?"

"Yeah, you told me they wouldn't let you change your seat, and he tried to talk to you." Kim-Lei starts laughing.

"Yeah, I was totally disgusted, and he was so dumb he couldn't see that I didn't want a damn thing to do with his black ass. He kept trying to talk to me, and put his filthy hands on me. So I said to myself I'll let you touch my hand if it means that much to you. I excused myself, went to the bathroom, pissed, wiped myself with my right hand, and went back to my seat. Then I gave him the hand covered in piss to properly introduce myself. Trying to be charming, he even kissed it. At that point, I told that nigger I was tired, and wanted to go sleep. I pulled a blanket over my head, and pretended to sleep but was really listening to my iPod. All the way home under that blanket I was laughing my ass off inside." Jessica laughs out loud after she re-tells the story.

"Girl you're nasty. Did you really do that, or are you just saying that's what you wished you'd have done?"

"I damn sure did, and whenever I think about it I laugh my ass off."

"I don't know if I could have done that, but that is funny as hell."

The friends laugh out loud at the shared story, and decide to go outside for a cigarette before they continue their day at the mall. After the friends finish their cigarettes, they go back inside, and visit many of the shops in the mall. Shopping for the next few hours, they then decide on a restaurant in the mall to have lunch. On the way to the food court, Kim-Lei takes Jessica by the hand, and leads her into Victoria's Secret.

She wants to pick out a sexy nighty to wear for her boyfriend. Kim-Lei wants a sexy new look when they get together this evening. As they go into the store, Jessica notices two black women at the counter, and one coming out of a dressing room. She finds herself not staring at the women, but paying attention to what they are doing, and the items of clothing they are buying. She thinks to herself that it's a good thing they only let you try on items after you pay for them. There are absolutely no exchanges, or returns allowed. It's a good thing because the thought of trying on under garments that have been on a nigger's body is repulsive to her. Jessica decides not to share this thought with her friend, and to act like she's not bothered by the women in the store. In the next thirty minutes, Jessica excitedly helps her friend pick out three nighties, and they lay them on a counter as they try to decide which one is the best of the three.

"Jessica, when it comes to this stuff you're better at choosing, so which one of these do you think I should get?"

"So you and Mark have a hot date tonight, huh?"

"Yeah, I want to wear something special. Something that'll make his mouth water." Says Kim-Lei.

"I'm sure one of these will do the trick. Do you wear lingerie a lot when you're with Mark?"

"Not really. He's like most men where naked is all he needs to get it going. I probably won't have it on five seconds before he rips it off." Laughs Kim-Lei.

"Well you're gonna have to make him savor the moment when he sees you in one of these. You want him to get rock hard the minute he sees you in it." Jessica says laughing.

"Ok, all three are two piece lace panties and bra. You definitely have the body for all three. Do we go with the white, red, or the black set? Personally I'd go with the red set. What do you think, Kim-Lei?"

"You think he'd like the red better Jessica?"

"Hell yeah, what man doesn't like a woman in red nighties. It's hot as hell."

Kim-Lei picks up the red set, and looks at it. She turns it around, and pictures herself wearing it. She smiles, and decides this is the one she'll go with. She tells Jessica she's going to go with the red set. As Kim-Lei makes her way to the register, Jessica returns the other two items back to where they got them. While Kim-Lei waits in line, one of the black women in line starts to talk with her.

"Hi, I bought that same red set a few weeks ago. I couldn't wear it after one wash because the color faded so badly, and the bra strap in the back wouldn't stay locked. The black set you, and your friend were looking at is a higher quality two piece. It's a little more expensive, but black would look better on you. It matches your hair, and will contrast great against your complexion. Red is ok, but black is much more appealing on a woman. I don't know if you saw the hidden feature on the bra. The black bra is made so your nipples can pop out, girl. Your man is gonna love that."

Both woman laugh, and after talking a little more, Kim-Lei decides she'll go with the black set. Jessica walks up to Kim-Lei, and Kim-Lei tells her she changed her mind, and that she wants to go with the black two-piece. Jessica tells her to stay in line. She takes the red set back, and goes to retrieve the black set. Jessica gets back to where her friend is in time to hear the young black woman say to Kim-Lei, 'goodbye and enjoy.'

"What was that all about? Why did you change your mind about the red set?"

"That woman I was talking to told me she bought the red set, and that it didn't hold up very well to washing and the black two-piece was a better quality set. It has a feature Mark is gonna love. Did you know this one has openings for the nipples to come out?" Kim-Lei laughs. Whispering in an angry tone, Jessica lets her friend know how she feels.

"Oh so your actually gonna take her word for it? You value that nigger's opinion over mine?"

"No, Jessica. I don't, but when she compared the two for me, the features she pointed out made a lot of sense to me. I think I'd look better in the black set, remember I want to try something different."

"Oh because she said so. I'll wait for you outside." Jessica tells her friend, and walks out of the store.

Kim-Lei watches her friend leave, and knows that she's going to have to smooth things over with her. Jessica can still be so immature, Kim-Lei thinks to herself. After Kim-Lei pays for her items, she walks out of the Victoria's Secret and looks around for her friend. After a few minutes, she spots Jessica standing by a Bank of America ATM talking to a guy. Kim-Lei thinks that that's the perfect distraction.

The guy she's talking to is tall, and very good-looking with blonde hair. He looks just the way Jessica likes them. Kim-Lei decides she'll let her friend have her fun talking to the guy, and she'll go outside, and smoke a cigarette. Kim-Lei gets just close enough to get Jessica's attention. When she does, she gives Jessica a sign to let her know she's going outside. Jessica acknowledges the gesture, and continues talking with her new friend. Kim-Lei walks over to the designated smoker's corner, and takes a seat under a tree. She lights a cigarette, and decides to call her boyfriend Mark.

"Hey babe, how are you doing?"

"Thinking about you sexy lady, what are you and Jessica up to? Mark asks."

"Jessica and I are at the Mall. We're gonna be here for a while. How's your day going babe?"

"Great! So far today, I've closed three finance deals on new Mazda CX-9's, and it's barely lunchtime."

"Excellent baby, we have to celebrate. I have something very special for you tonight." Kim-Lei smiles after she tells him that.

"That sounds interesting, I can't wait. We still on for dinner tonight babe?"

"We are, but would you mind if we skipped the club? I want to go straight home afterwards so we can spend some quality time together."

"That works for me. Hold on for a sec babe... Hey, I just got two more contracts, for financing on two more cars. Looks like I'm going to be tied up here with paperwork for a while. I probably won't feel like doing the club anyway. I'm red hot today babe." He tells her.

"You're hot anyway baby."

"You want to meet at my place this evening babe?"

"Why don't you pick me up at the mall around 5:00 p.m.? I rode here with Jessica. We can go to my place, and go to dinner from there."

"That's fine, but why are you going to be there so late?"

"We're probably going to see a movie after lunch. Besides, this is girl's day out. Don't worry; I'm going to take care of you tonight." Kim-Lei tells him with excitement.

"Sounds great to me baby. I probably won't be out of here before 4:30 p.m. I'll call you when I'm on my way. Have fun babe, and I'll see you later.

Kim-Lei says goodbye to her boyfriend, finishes her cigarette, and prepares to go back in the mall when Jessica comes outside, and walks over to her. Jessica sits by Kim-Lei, puts her bags down, and lights a cigarette.

"So who was the guy you were talking to?"

"His name is Elliot. He said he saw me earlier when we left the Starbucks, and wanted to say hello."

"Jessica, he's hot. Is that all he wanted?" Kim-Lei says laughing.

"He was sweet, and carried himself well. He didn't hit on me anymore, after I told him I had a boyfriend. He did give me his card, and asked if we could keep in touch." Jessica replies.

"Are you ready to go eat Jessica, because I'm starving? Jessica, please understand something, your opinion means everything to me. Please don't take what happened in Victoria's Secret the wrong way."

"It's ok Kim-Lei. I may have got a little upset at first, but I'm in no way angry with you. I realize that sometimes, especially in a clothing store those people are prone to give un-solicited advice. Anyway, let's just forget about it, and go eat." Jessica tells Kim-Lei

"Jessica, how about we see a movie after lunch?

"That sounds good to me. Jessica responds.

Mark is going to pick me up here later since he's going to be working late. What about your plans with Phil tonight?" Kim-Lei asks.

"The movie isn't going to interfere with anything. I'm not going to see him until later this evening. He knows I'm with you, and he knows today is our day."

"Alright let's do it then. Lunch first then a movie." Says Kim-Lei.

The friends walk to the food court, continuing their conversation about their plans for tonight with their boyfriends, and how good it is to just hang out with each other. As they make their way to the food court, they decide their going to have lunch at TGI Friday's.

The conversation then turns to which movie they are going to see afterwards. The friends have lunch, and decide they're going to see a romantic comedy. After two hours the movie is over, and they leave the theater discussing the film they just saw. They debate both the good and bad points about the movie like they've done dozens of times in the past. Kim-Lei feels her phone vibrate on her belt. She looks at her watch, and tells Jessica that Mark is on his way to pick her up. Jessica walks her friend to the front of the mall. When they get outside they hug, and say their goodbyes, wishing each other a fun night, and promise to talk in the morning.

Soon after they get outside, Mark pulls up to where they are waiting. As Kim-Lei gets in the car, Jessica tells her she has to go to one more store, to get her favorite scented candles, and then she's going home. Jessica waves goodbye as her friends pull away and she goes back into the mall. After Jessica leaves the store she notices that she stayed there longer than she had planned. She looks at her watch, and see's it's almost 5:45 p.m. and it's starting to get dark. She thinks to herself it's not that big a deal, as she heads out of the mall. She tells herself she still has plenty of time; to get herself together for her date with Phil. She decides to call Phil to let him know she's heading home. She reaches into her purse to get her phone, and as she pulls it out; Jessica's Bluetooth earpiece falls to the ground, and goes sliding across the floor. A couple walking toward her sees the small device come to a stop just in front of them. The young man bends down to pick it up for her. Jessica hurries to the device, and in an almost panicked voice tells the young man not to touch it. He seems puzzled when he hears her response to his trying to help. He recovers quickly, he and his lady friend continue on past Jessica, with curious looks on their faces. As they pass Jessica, they comment about her stopping him.

"Damn baby what was that all about?" The young woman states.

"I don't know. I only wanted to pick it up for her. Maybe she thought I was going to steal it or something. Crazy ass grey girl."

"I tell you baby, you just can't be kind to people anymore." Responds the young man, and the couple continue on their way quickly forgetting what just happened.

Jessica picks up her device, and hurries toward the door. As she walks outside she thinks to herself I didn't ask that nigger to pick anything up for me. I'm perfectly capable of doing that myself, and I sure as hell didn't want his black ass hands on anything of mine.

As Jessica steps out of the mall, she starts to feel the weight of her purse on her shoulder, and the three bags she is carrying. She tells herself it's no big deal though because her car is close. Before she gets to the curb, she sees a tall black man dressed in sharply pressed black BDU's. He is standing on the side walk, in the front of the parking lot. She feels a slight panic start to come over her. Jessica tells herself just walk past him, it's still light outside, and there are people around, so if he attacks me I will simply drop everything, and scream my lungs out. When she gets to where he's standing, she tightens her grip on her bags, and tells herself to quickly walk by him. As she does so, he turns toward her, and she begins to panic a little more as they make eye contact.

She tells herself he's a big nigger, and she wishes to God for him to just please leave her the fuck alone. The man nods in her direction, and speaks to her in a courteous manner as she literally runs by him.

"Ma'am would you like an escort to your car?" He asks.

"Fuck no! Leave me the hell alone." She says as she quickly walks past him.

He is taken back by her remark, and stares at her as she hurries away. A few seconds later she hears a familiar voice.

"Hey Jessica is everything ok? Do you need help with your bags?"

Jessica turns in the direction of the voice, and sees its Elliot. She stops, puts her bags down, and waits for him to get to her. When he does, she turns and looks at the black man still standing on the sidewalk. He is looking in her direction. She smiles at Elliot, touches his arm, and the panic she felt seconds ago starts to fade away. He smiles back at her, picks her bags up, and she leads him to her car.

"I thought that was you. Where is your girlfriend?" Elliot asks her.

"She left a while ago with her boyfriend. He picked her up here."

"Can I walk you to your car? You can never be too careful these days."

"Sure that would be nice; it's just a few rows down."

Elliot picks up her bags, and Jessica leads him to her car. She wraps her arm around Elliot's as they start to walk away. She turns toward the nigger on the sidewalk, looks in his direction, and smiles. He turns his gaze away from Jessica, and focuses his attention elsewhere. She is greatly relieved now that Elliot is with her. She thinks to herself she'd never be seen in the company of a nigger. The nerve of that fucker asking to escort me anywhere, she thinks to herself. I know damn well all he'd do is rob me, and steal my car. Those thoughts quickly pass as Jessica and Elliot approach her car. She uses her car's remote button to open the truck. Elliot places her bags inside, closes it, and prepares to walk away.

"Hey Elliot can I give you a ride to your car?" She asks.

"Sure, I'm parked just on the other side of the theater, by the Merchant Tire Dealership." He responds, and goes over to the passenger side door.

Jessica opens both doors, and they get inside. Jessica pulls out of her parking space, and take another quick look in the direction of the nigger. She is disgusted he had the nerve to ask could he walk her to her car. As she turns toward the right to drop Elliot off, they start to talk.

"Jessica, did that big guy on the corner say anything to you?" Asks Elliot.

"Yeah, he actually asked could he escort me to my car. I was like hell no! I don't trust any of those people. That's why I was so relieved to hear your voice. I thought he was going to follow me for a minute." She responds. Elliot looks at Jessica and smiles before he speaks.

"Oh, you didn't know that that guy is a cop?"

As Elliot makes that statement he reaches into his right jacket pocket, and pulls out a 9mm Beretta, and places it on his left thigh, his finger on the trigger, and the gun pointed in her direction. She looks at Elliot, and the smile he flashed her earlier, is replaced with an evil grimace that tells Jessica she is in grave danger. As Jessica looks at the weapon, her eyes grow wide, and her heart starts to pound in her chest. Elliot's last statement repeats over and over in her mind, "that guy was a cop." Her mind is frozen on those five words as they keep repeating in her mind. The horrifying feeling that comes over her intensifies with every passing second. She tries to remain calm as she forces herself to say something to Elliot.

"What are you doing with that Elliot, why do this to me. Elliot please tell me you're not going to hurt me?" Her voice trembling as she speaks.

"Bitch, I'm going to blow your fucking brains out unless you do exactly what I tell you. Just keep going toward the Merchants Tire place. Don't roll your fucking window down either, just keep driving and shut your fucking mouth."

As Jessica drives where she's told, the terror she feels is indescribable. She feels her breathing getting shorter and she finds it difficult to maintain even pressure on the gas petal due to the trembling in her legs. Every time she glances at the gun on Elliot's leg it appears to get bigger. As Jessica turns the next corner, Elliot's voice, and actions bring her attention back into focus. He rubs the gun against her thigh, and then pushes the barrel against her right side as he speaks. Jessica is so terrified all she can do is concentrate on what he is telling her, and hope the tears that won't stop falling down her face makes Elliot feel some sympathy for her.

"See that guy standing in the parking lot across from Burger King? Pull up beside him."

Jessica doesn't say anything; she does what she's told. She pulls her car next to the man standing in the parking lot as instructed, and puts the car in park. Her first thought is to bolt out of the car, and run as fast as she can. Elliott reaches for the car keys in the ignition, and turns the car off. He tells Jessica to not even think about trying to run. The man standing outside moves to the driver's door. Elliott gets out with her keys, and instructs Jessica to slide over to the passenger seat. At the same time, the guy who was standing outside gets in the back seat, and slides over behind Jessica's seat. Elliot quickly gets behind the wheel of the car, starts it, and they pull off. Jessica is so terrified she's trembling in her seat uncontrollably.

"Elliot, please. You guys can have my car, and there's money in my purse you can have. I swear I won't tell anyone about this. Please just let me go, and don't hurt me please." She begs.

Before she could finish what she was saying, the man in the back seat emptied the contents of her purse. Everything in the purse is now on the floor. He goes through her wallet, taking what he wants. The man in the back seat takes a knife, and puts it against Jessica's right side. He tells her to put her seatbelt on, and to un-buckle and unzip her pants. Jessica sits in her seat frozen, crying, and asking herself why is this happening.

"I suggest you do what he says, or he's going to put all five inches of that blade, in your pussy when we get to where we're going." Elliott tells her in a voice she doesn't recognize.

Trembling and crying, Jessica does what she is told. The man in the back seat reaches around her seat, and uses his knife to cut the waist strap of her panties then he violently yanks them off her body. Jessica screams as she reacts to her panties being ripped off of her ass. The man in the back seat holds them up for an instant, and throws them to the floor. He then reaches around the seat with his right hand, and starts to finger Jessica's pussy. Soon followed by his left fondling her breast.

"I told you Elliot, I knew this bitch was wearing red thong underwear, I won the bet. You think that's sexy, whore. I hate red, but I love a pink pussy." The man in the back seat says to no one in particular.

"Hey man I'm fucking her first I won the bet. This is the one I wanted in the first place."

"I don't give a damn. We're gonna have fun with this bitch for a few days anyway." Elliot says to the man in the back seat.

Jessica screams when she hears this, and begs for the men to let her go.

She feels a sharp numbing pain against the left side of her face, and she realizes Elliott hit her with the butt of the gun. Before Jessica can bring her hands to her bruised face, the man sitting behind her Grabs her left wrist, and forces it behind her seat. Jessica feels a cold metal object close around her wrist, and an accompanying clicking sound.

Before she can react, she feels her other hand being violently yanked behind the seat and both hands are quickly cuffed behind the seat. The man in the back seat then continues to violate her body with his hands and fingers.

"You see bitch, you wouldn't be here, if we could have gotten to your gook friend first. We've been following you two whores all day. I wanted that slant-eyed bitch the minute I saw her in the mall. I have a thing for gooks, but when we watched her faggot boyfriend pick her up at the curb. We had to change plans, so you're the lucky whore. We get to fuck you instead of your friend. It is going to last for a long time. It's a good thing you hate niggers the way you do. If that cop had walked you to your car, I would've just walked away." Elliot says laughing ominously.

All Jessica can do is cry as the car heads further, and further into the darkness. As they drive her to an unknown destination, and an unknown fate, she hears the same five words in her mind repeatedly. That man was a cop. Her tears won't stop falling.

Is it man's fear that has stopped him from making his world a paradise, or something else?

MAN CHOOSES

Friday August 27, 2011
MLK Avenue S.E. Washington D.C.
11:30 p.m.

Seventeen year old Chris is on his way home. He works the evening shift at a local neighborhood liquor store. He doesn't like walking these streets so late at night, but he can be home before the bus arrives, and there never on time anyway; at least not in this neighborhood. Chris walks the six blocks to his home, and thinks how nice it would be, if his mother could afford to move out of this horrible ghetto. He knows in his heart that she would if she could afford to. Years before graduating high school Chris had become sick of the violence which plagues the streets he now walks. He has grown to hate the people who make his neighborhood a place to be feared, and avoided. He hates the sound of gunshots, and police sirens at all hours of the night. He doesn't want to leave his family behind, when he goes off to college in the fall, but he has little choice. College gets him out of this hell hole, of a neighborhood, but he worries for the safety of his mother, and younger sister. Chris hates where he works, but the job at the liquor store was all he could find this summer. Even though he hates working there, seeing the people that come in to the store give him the motivation, to succeed in college, to help to get his family out of Southeast D.C. Seeing black men of all ages spend what money they have, buying liquor and beer to quench their alcoholic addictions; instead of trying to help themselves sickens Chris. Every day watching drunk, filthy, men beg for change on the sidewalks, in front of the store, and fighting his way past them, to get to work makes him even angrier. There isn't anything he can do about it, so he ignores them, and does his job. The money he earns there is good, he thinks to himself, as he walks home. It lets me help mom, with household expenses, and she is proud of her son, for wanting to make her life a little easier. Many times his mother doesn't want to take his money, but he insists, because he feels it's his job to help when, and where he can. Chris loves his mother, and feels it's his responsibility to help her. Chris's father does nothing to help them, and never has. All these thoughts, and more play in Chris's mind, as he walks the quiet, and dimly lit streets of his neighborhood. Chris wants to reach the safety of his home.

Engrossed in his own thoughts, Chris fails to take notice, of the three men now walking behind him. The men pick up their pace, just enough to close some distance between them, and Chris. The men do not over take him, but closing the gap between them. As Chris turns a corner, one of the three men following him speaks out, and all three quicken their pace.

"Yo, my man, we wanna talk to you."

Chris turns to see the three men closing in on him, and immediately he knows this is trouble. He starts to walk faster, but knows that if he runs, they will run after him. He knows he can handle himself in a fight, but there are three of them. He tells himself that maybe, they don't mean him any harm, but then quickly dismisses that thought.

He decides to pick up his pace, and maybe they'll just leave him alone, when they realize he doesn't want to talk to them. As Chris quickens his pace, another of the three shouts out to him.

"Yo homes, didn't you hear motherfucker, we wanna talk to you."

At that moment the three men break into a run, and quickly catch up to Chris. Chris starts to run away, but he is close enough to hear what he thinks is a metallic sound, like metal sliding against metal; the slide of a handgun being pulled to the rear, and released.

"Stop muthafucker! You try to run away from me, and I'll put a bullet in your ass." One of the men shouts holding a gun. The three men surround Chris, and the man holding the gun points it in Chris's face.

"Didn't you hear my boy muthafucker; we want to talk to your punk ass."

"The nigga heard us Juan, that's why his bitch ass tried to run."

Chris knows he is in deep trouble, as he looks at the three men now surrounding him, and specifically the one holding the gun. He prays in his mind for a car to drive by, or better still a police vehicle.

It's late the streets are dark, and almost deadly silent. Chris thinks to himself that his neighborhoods violence has finally touched him.

"Why the fuck you make us chase you homes." Asks Juan.

"Hey fella's I just wanna go home, I'm not looking for trouble." Chris says.

"Motherfucker who the fuck asked you what you looking for." Responds Juan. Juan moves closer to Chris, until they are almost nose to nose, Juan's gun now against his temple.

"Hey don't I know you bitch, you that motherfucker that work at Bowman's Liquor Store. Don't you know these streets belong to us motherfucker, if you wanna walk here you have to pay bitch. You got our money homes?"

Chris starts to reach into his pocket, and speak when he feels a sharp pain between his legs. Juan knees him full force in the groin. Chris falls to his knees, and tries to speak, but his pain won't let him.

"Dwayne, Pablo pick this motherfucker up, drag his ass across the street in the woods over there. I'm gonna teach his punk ass a lesson."

As Chris is pulled to his feet Dwayne pulls back his right fist, and hits Chris full force in the face. He goes down again, the left side of his face goes numb, and he tastes blood in his mouth. In his mind Chris calls out for his mother, and for someone, anyone to help him. He does not want these men to hurt him any further, but he realizes even through his pain, that if he doesn't fight back, he is going to be seriously fucked up, or killed. Dwayne and Pablo drag Chris across the street into the woods. All four are just a few feet off the main road; they throw him to the ground. The pain in his groin is still intense, and the blood running from his mouth, seems to be flowing faster. Chris spits out a mouth full of the red liquid. He turns from his side, and raises himself to his knees. His hands against the ground Chris tries to catch his breath. He mentally prepares himself for the assault which is sure to come. He plans to jump to his feet, and fight back no matter what. Chris can see the legs and feet of two of the men as he looks straight ahead. He knows the third man is behind him. At this point, he tells himself it doesn't matter who has a gun pointed at him. He only knows that he will not; go out like this, on his knees, begging. His anger and resolve strengthening inside him.

"Ok Juan, we got this little motherfucker here, so let's kick his ass, do our thing, and get the fuck out of here." Says Dwayne.

Juan looks from Dwayne and down on Chris, and then he begins to smile. Juan raises his gun, and points it at Chris's head, at the same time Chris looks up at Juan, and what Juan see's in Chris's eyes is a defiance that pisses him off.

"What, you eye-ballin me motherfucker like you want to do something to me, that what you doing nigga. I'm gonna blow your fuckin' brains out now."

Chris tells himself now is the time to strike back, while Juan is furious, and shouting at him. Chris tenses his muscles to make his move then he hears a man's voice coming from behind Juan.

"My son, why do you want to hurt this child, your brother? What harm has he done you?"

The man says as he moves toward Juan. Dwayne and Pablo both point there weapons at the man, but he continues to walk toward them as if he doesn't see the weapons, or is not afraid of them. Juan turns to face the man walking toward him.

"My sons please put away your weapons, you do not need them." Asks the strange man.

"Motherfucker do I look like your fuckin son." Juan says as he raises his gun, and points it in the strangers face.

"I wish you no harm; I only want to put an end to this senseless violence. Look at the pain you have caused this young man, your brother." The stranger says as he stops right in front of Juan. Juan points the barrel of his gun between the eyes of the stranger.

"This motherfucker is not my damn brother nigga, ok asshole, you want to help this motherfucker, how bout I blow your goddamned brains out right now." Says Juan as he moves his finger to the weapons trigger.

"My son, you don't want to harm me, you are really a gentle soul at heart. All of you are. I can help you see that violence against your brothers is not the path."

"Call me your goddamn son again, and your dead asshole." Shouts Juan.

"Look at me, all of you, this is not the way, there is within you a great emptiness that violence cannot fill. Let me help you discover the greatness that exists within you all, look at me."

Dwayne and Pablo look first at each other, than at this strange man who came out of nowhere, to help the boy they'd chosen to assault, rob, and kill. As they look into the eyes of the stranger, something neither of them can explain comes over them. Both men find themselves experiencing a feeling of shame, at the thought of harming the young man they have pinned to the ground. Dwayne and Pablo both drop their weapons, and bend down to help Chris slowly rise to his feet. Juan also drops his gun to the ground. He looks from the stranger to Chris, and as he does so he feels the terror, and fear Chris experienced at their hands. Juan is shamed to tears. In that same instant Chris experiences forgiveness for these men who he knows were going to kill him. His body still feeling the pain that was inflicted on it. Chris starts to walk away until the stranger stops him.

"Take my hand child; I can help to ease the pain of your body and mind."

In the instant both men clasp hands, Chris feels the pain of his body fade away, and a euphoric feeling of peace takes over him.

"You three apologize to your brother." All three men tell Chris how sorry they are for the pain, they have caused him, and that they will do the right thing by him, and for everyone they've harmed.

"Go home to your family my son; all is as it should be now. Your life and that of your families will be filled with happiness and success."

"Who are you? Chris asks this strange man.

"I am no one my son, my only concern is to help others."

Chris smiles as he looks at the man, shakes his hand once again, and then turns away. All the pain and fear he experienced only seconds ago is gone. Chris walks out of the wooded area with new found hope, and a confidence he has never known before. He turns toward his apartment building, and jogs the rest of the way home; he is filled with energy and peace of mind. A few minutes later, his three assailants emerge from the wooded area. All three man holding handguns at their side, just as a police cruiser pulls up to the corner. The officers in the vehicle spot the men, and the weapons they are holding, and the cruiser comes to an immediate stop, with lights flashing. One officer radios in their position, and quick descriptions of the men, while the other officer gets out of the cruiser with his weapon drawn, and aimed at the men. Without warning or directions, the three men toss their weapons toward the front of the cruiser. They turn away from the officers, put their hands on top of their heads, and immediately they drop to their knees. Both officers are out of the cruiser with weapons drawn, and covering the kneeling men while they wait for back up. In a matter of minutes the night is filled with the sound of sirens, as several police vehicles arrive on the scene. When asked by the officers what they were doing, and why they all had weapons, the men tell the officers that they were out committing crimes, and assaulting people. They also tell the officers, that a strange man stopped them from killing a young man only minutes ago; and that the young man left just before the officers arrived. At first the officers on the scene can't believe what these men are telling them. The three thugs confess, to the police about having committed multiple crimes, against numerous people. The officers listen to the cuffed and co-operative criminals. Information comes in over their computers, that each man does indeed have multiple outstanding arrest warrants. The arresting officers ask the three thugs about this man, who supposedly stopped them from killing someone tonight. Each man gives a different description of the man, and what he was wearing. The officers look at each other with puzzled looks. These thugs have been open so far, about the crimes they have individually committed, and as a group, but they can't seem to agree on what this man looks like, or where he came from. The officers suspect that the men maybe high of drugs or something, as they listen to the criminals calmly debate the man's appearance. Both Hispanic suspects describe him as Hispanic with different color hair, one suspect swears the man's hair is curly, and the other swears it's straight. While the black suspect tells the officers the man was black, bald, and no facial hair. The officers find the stories curious, but irrelevant since these three, where the only ones out on the streets with weapons. For now they discard the story of this mysterious man, and each suspect is put in a different cruiser and taken away.

Friday August 27, 2011
14th. & Euclid Street N.W. Washington D.C.
11:00 p.m.

A woman riding in a car is brutally beat in the face, by the man driving, and thrown from the vehicle at a stop sign. The car she was in speeds off. The woman is severely injured, and in terrible pain, she is totally alone in the world, but it wasn't always this way. She works the streets selling sex cheaply, to anyone who can offer her a little money, and sometimes when she's hungry enough, food. She doesn't care who her customers are as long as they can pay, because she always gives her best, and all she has ever hoped for was to be treated with fairness, if not respect. For months now she has lived on the streets sleeping where she can, abandoned buildings, cars, and outside on park benches. The woman wanders from shelter to shelter desperately trying to find some place warm to sleep for a night, if she can find it. She cleans herself as well as she can with whatever she can, given her circumstances.

Sometimes at the shelters, she's lucky enough to get into for a night. She savors a warm shower when one is available. Sometimes she washes her body on the streets, in alleyways with bottled water. Sometimes with water she collects off the streets, and always with rainwater when it does rain. She knows that if she is going to make her money selling sex, she has to at least look as if she's clean. Being homeless makes that task almost impossible for her, but for the last year she has managed to survive. Along the way though her addiction to crack, and other drugs have taken their toll.

She has been raped more times than she can count. She has sucked countless dicks for free, when the men refused to pay her for her services, usually after they came in her mouth, and on her face. She has been beaten for absolutely no reason by her customers, and forced to endure every sexual assault to which a woman's body can be subjected. For no other reason than, men and women see her as something sub-human, a thing that they can abuse, and take their frustrations out on because, of the way she is forced to survive. The only pleasure she is capable of even remotely enjoying now, are the drugs she pumps into her system. The drugs temporarily make all her pain, and fear, go away.

She walks away from the corner where she was just abandoned, wanting to cry, and feeling the pain of being hurt over and over again but the tears won't come. Once again she was forced to suck dick she wasn't paid for, and beaten for it. Her body and mind can no longer suffer this abuse. As these thoughts course through what mind she has left, her loneliness starts to drive her to the brink of insanity. She simply falls to the ground in a lonely and dirty section, of an abandoned city park, and the tears she needs to cry come in torrents.

She makes no sound, as the long felt emotions she has suppressed, find their way to the surface, she wishes for her mother, the way a child would when they feel pain. Unfortunately, she knows her mother would never come to her rescue. The tears falling from her tired eyes just won't stop falling, so she lays there in the dirt totally alone, abandoned, and hopeless. Long ago forgotten by her family, and any friends she once had, she thinks to herself she is so all alone, and so tired. Tired of the pain she is forced to endure daily, of not being able to defend herself, of selling her now worn out body on the streets. She is tired of the beatings, of living in fear, of living in pain, of the uncertainty that comes with every minute of every day. She knows now she is tired of living period.

Lying in the dirt on her left side she takes her right hand, and reaches into her jeans. She finds the string coming out of her ass, and pulls on it slowly. She learned long ago that men didn't want to fuck crack whores in the ass, and since she has been robbed more times than she can count, she learned to carry her drugs in vials in her ass. She now recalls with great sadness, that gay women were the worse when it came to robbing and abusing her. Those memories only bring her more pain, as she relives some of those encounters. They would find me after just having left a club or party, they'd pick me up, and then make me eat pussy kneeling on the driver's side of the car. Kneeling on the floor of a car under the steering column was painful, but they didn't care about my pain. As long as I sucked and licked their pussies the way they wanted me to. They would talk on the phone sometimes arguing with lovers, smoke, pretend to be alone when cops would drive by the car. They would become angry with me for no reason, and when they knew I wouldn't fight back, or try to get out the car they would bury my face in their pussy, and force me to eat them until they were satisfied multiple times. Pulling my hair and slapping me until they got what they wanted. Sometimes pissing in my mouth, more painful memories to run away from she thinks. Through all this she thinks her drugs never got taken from her, and now that's a good thing. Heroine, the only real thing she has to look forward to in her life, that's been good to her, her only real friend. The medicine she needs to make all the pains go away. Heroine, her one true real friend in the entire world, stashed safely away in her ass. She pulls the vials out of her body, and opens a hidden compartment in the handbag she carries. She pulls out the materials she needs to prepare the drugs, through teary eyes while still laying on her side. She knows exactly how much of the drug to take, to end her loneliness for good, and she has decided to do exactly that.

"My child what you are about to do is not necessary. You don't want to end your life this way."

She is startled when she hears a man's voice coming from behind her, but she is too weak and tired to turn over. At first she thinks that maybe it was her imagination playing tricks on her, until a man comes from behind her, kneels down, and sits in the dirt in front of her. She quickly moves away and holds on to her drugs tightly.

"Please don't hurt me I haven't done anything to you, I'm so tired." She pleads as tears fall from her tired eyes.

"You don't have to be afraid of me child. I will not harm you in anyway. I only wish to talk with you, nothing more."

Still holding her drugs to her chest, and laying on her side she looks up at the man sitting in the dirt with her, and for an instant he seems familiar somehow. She feels a strange sensation when she looks at him, and something tells her on a sub-conscience level that she knows this person somehow.

"Can you sit up child, please let me help you. I will not steal from you, as so many have in the past." He says.

She is frightened of this man who for some strange reason seems familiar to her, but she allows him to help her sit up.

"Mister I'll suck your dick for you, I'll do it right please just don't hit me. I'm so hungry I just want to buy something to eat, just give me a few dollars, some change anything, I don't care and I'll take care of you good." She says in a low voice filled with pain, her body trembling, tears falling from her eyes, and blood from her mouth.

"No my beautiful child, I am not here to judge you, I want nothing from you. My only desire is to help you." He raises his hands to her face, and she flinches thinking he is going to strike her or take her drugs. "Do not be frightened, let me help you, you will see everything will be fine." He touches her face with both hands, whipping away her tears and blood with his fingers, and the palms of his hands. Their eyes meet and for an instant, she feels a serenity she has never known, somehow she knows this man means her no harm. He pulls her to him and cradles her head in his arms and holds her there.

She drops the drugs to the ground, and puts her arms around him, and she feels as if the weight of the world has just been lifted off her shoulders.

"You need not be afraid anymore my child, nothing can harm you now. Tell me, why do you want to end your life?"

"I'm just so lonely, I don't want to live like this anymore, I can't do this anymore, no one cares about me, and everybody who looks at me looks at me like I'm dead anyway." She says crying as she holds on to him even more tightly, feeling the comforting warmth of his body.

"What is your name, I would like to know it."

"Nobody cares what my name is, no one has asked me my name in a long time, sometimes I don't even remember what it is, nobody cares." She says and starts crying.

"I want to know your name, and I care."

"Why?" She asks.

"Because my child caring is what I do?" He responds.

"My name is Carolyn."

"Beautiful name Carolyn, a gentle name, just as you are both those things."

"Let me say to you Carolyn that you are not alone, you will never feel that way again. You have simply been lost, I will show you that your life is indeed worth living. There are people in this world that do care for you. You are young and can go on to accomplish great things my child, you don't want to die Carolyn, I can tell you, it is not yet your time to die." Carolyn looks up slightly, her head still cradled in his arms.

"How do you know, are you God?"

"Who I am is not important, you and your needs are what matters, I am here to help you."

"How? I don't have anything or anybody, people only want to hurt me, and take advantage of me. I don't know how to turn my life around, it's nothing but a mess. It's just easier for me to be dead, I'm just so tired." A tear falling as Carolyn speaks.

"Oblivion my child is not the easy thing you may think now. That darkness is not for one such as you. There is always disappointment in life Carolyn, sometimes we don't accomplish our goals when we think we should, life my child, is sometimes both hard and unfair, but it is always worth living. It is within you to overcome the challenges life presents you with Carolyn, you have just forgotten how." He tells her.

"I don't know if I can, I don't know if I want to. I would love to have my family back in my life, but growing up for me was so painful, every day of my life growing up was nothing but hurt."

"Carolyn, my child you have to trust me, you can and will turn your life around, and it will be beautiful. The life you knew on the streets is over, the pain of these last years will be forgotten. All the wrongs committed against you will be forgiven, you need to trust me. Look at me Carolyn, do you trust me?" He asks her again.

Carolyn pulls away from him just far enough to look into his eyes before she answers. When she does look at him, it's as if the answers she's searched for all her short life, instantly come to her mind. For a second these new revelations overwhelm both her mind and body. Carolyn feels herself become so weak that she needs to hold on to him for support. In an instant the sensation passes, and she realizes how different she now feels, how strong her body feels, how unclouded her mind now is.

"Yes, I do trust you, what do I need to do." She says with a much stronger voice.

He helps Carolyn to her feet, and they stand facing each other, with his hands on her shoulders. He tells Carolyn to close her eyes, and she does so, her arms at her side. She feels a slight tingling sensation all over her body, and she feels him put something in her shirt pocket.

"My child you have done all you need to, I want you to go now, cross the street, and walk two blocks to the hotel on the corner of 11th and Main Ave. go to room 601. You will find everything you need there, but first you need to rest. When you wake in the morning you will be as one newly born, and you will have everything to look forward to. Do you understand child." He asks her. With her eyes, still closed Carolyn tells him she understands what he wants her to do.

"Can I ask you something, I need to know something? Will you please tell me who you are?" He leans forward and touches his lips to her forehead.

"I am who you needed me to be Carolyn."

When Carolyn opens her eyes she is stunned to see that the man she was just talking to, and holding for the last couple of hours is gone. She finds it impossible to believe, because she knows she didn't imagine anything that just happened as she looks in all directions to find him. Especially now that she see's everything with clarity she's never known. She also realizes that she feels strength, coursing through her body that wasn't there before. A single tear falls down the right side of her face, this time it is a tear of joy. Carolyn drops to her knees, and says a prayer, something she hasn't done in a long time. She thinks that she will never see the man again, and that saddens her so she thanks him again in her prayers. Carolyn stands and looks up at the night sky. Taking in the celestial beauty above her, she pauses for and instant, and sets her sight on one star in particular. Carolyn doesn't know how she knows the name of that star, but she does, its name is Orion, and for some reason that thought gives her great comfort. She thinks to herself *I guess sometimes we do get second chances.*

As Carolyn walks out of the darkness of the park, and toward the hotel she wonders if she will ever again meet the stranger who saved her life, or is all that's happened to her a cruel dream, and she's still asleep or dying from a heroin overdose. If this is a dream she doesn't want to wake up she tells herself, as she pulls a room key from her pocket and approaches The Hotel Indigo.

Friday August 27, 2011
The Views Condo's, Downtown Washington D.C.
12:00 p.m. Midnight

An angry drunk man pulls his car up to the complex entrance, and is buzzed in the parking garage by a woman who he thought he'd gotten rid of for good; A woman who he had absolutely no intentions of ever seeing, talking to, or fucking ever again. A woman who today out of nowhere has threatened him concerning the affair they had going for a while. An affair he thought was over. An affair he thought he'd broken off months ago, to work things out with his wife. The news she gave him which she thinks is so good has filled him with rage. He pulls into a parking spot, turns his car off, and sits there for several minutes as he finishes off a bottle of Patron and lights a cigarette. Every time he thinks about their conversation earlier today when she called his office, and what she said to him, he gets angrier and more filled with rage.

"Hey babe we need to talk, do you think we can meet someplace this week." Ashley asks.

"What is it you want Ashley, I haven't spoken to you in months. I thought I was clear, it's over between us." Brendon angrily replies.

"It's been barely eight weeks since the last time we spoke, you make it sound like years."

"Ashley look, I really need to get on with my life, and so should you. I'm not interested in meeting for any reason. Our relationship is over Ashley."

"Just like that, it was my understanding, that you needed time to take care of things with your wife, so that we could be together. I missed the part about us being over."

"That's because Ashley, you hear what you want to hear. I specifically told you that I was tired of the sneaking around with you, and that I could never work things out at home as long as that was going on."

"I hear what I want? I don't think I heard wrong when you were fucking me. I didn't hear you say anything about leaving me permanently when you had your dick in my ass. I heard you telling me you were tired of being married to that bitch."

"Ashley I have work to do, and I don't want to deal with you any longer, so could you please tell me what you want, and get it over with so that I can go on with my life."

"I tell you what Brendon, how about I tell your wife about us, and that I'm pregnant with your baby. How about we do that? Since you want to act stupid, I can be that way too."

"Did you say you're pregnant with my baby?"

"Yes I did, and don't play stupid because you know we never used protection."

"How the hell do you know it's mine. I haven't been with you in a long time. What do you want me to do? You know damn well I'm married." Brendon's heart beats faster after he hears she is pregnant.

"Your being married has nothing to do with it. I know it's yours, because I haven't been with anyone since you. You need to come see me, so that we can discuss this."

"Discuss, there's nothing to discuss. If it's true you're having a goddamn abortion!"

"Don't tell me what I'm going to do. But since I know you're not serious about this I'll just call your fucking wife, and see what she thinks."

"No! Where the hell do you want to meet today?"

"Come by my place later this even, about 10:00 p.m. I'm off tomorrow, so we can discuss this situation like goddamn adults."

Brendon sits in his car going over their conversation, and finishing his bottle of liquor. After telling Ashley he'd be at her place later to discuss the situation, he needed time to think. So after work he didn't go home he went drinking, trying to figure a way out of this mess with Ashley. He called her after each missed hour to tell her he was still coming. Brendon sits in his car, as the alcohol in his system takes hold of his thoughts. Everything was going so smoothly between my wife and me, he thinks, and now this bitch comes back into the picture telling me she's gonna have my fuckin' kid. The bitch knows full well that I don't want to have anything to do with her. I'm so mad I could kill this bitch. As soon as that thought crosses his mind an idea comes to him. *Why not just kill the bitch for trying to ruin my life. I know exactly how to do it too. I'll just push her pregnant ass down that long flight of stairs in her condo. Even if I have to carry her ass to the top, and through her down a few times, that should kill her, and settle all my problems. It'll look like an accident. People fall down stairs all the time. After she's dead, I'll set her fucking Condo on fire. Yeah that's exactly what I'm going to do, the hell with this bitch. Why couldn't she just stay out of my life, now she shows up out of the blue telling me she's knocked-up. I'm not letting her pin this shit on me, and ruin my life, fuck her. Push her ass down the steps, that's exactly what I'm going to do when she tells me she's pregnant.* The alcohol in his system and his anger assure him he can do this and get away with it. Brendon throws the empty liquor bottle in the back seat of his car, takes his keys out of the ignition, and lights another cigarette. He gets out of his car, and slams the door shut. The sound of the slamming door echoes across the silent parking garage. He is so angry and intoxicated he can't focus clearly, when he tries to put his car keys in his jacket pocket. He drops, and then accidentally kicks them as he walks forward. The keys go sliding many feet in front of him, and he curses his own clumsiness. Brendon quickens his pace to get his keys, and as he does so he takes one last drag of his cigarette, and plucks it away turning his head for an instant. Brendon is momentarily startled to see a man he could have sworn wasn't there a second ago walking toward him. The man looks down and picks up the keys as Brendon walks up to him. The man hands Brendon his keys, Brendon thanks him, then walks away, is anger growing by the second.

"My son, is your anger so great that you would kill a mother, and her unborn son?" asks the man as Brendon walks away.

Brendon freezes as the question is asked. He turns to face the man who asked the question, and for a split second his heart beats just a little faster.

"Excuse me, what did you just say?" Asks Brendon.

"I asked you a question that I would very much like an answer to my son." The man replies.

"What the hell makes you think I'm gonna kill anybody? And just who the hell are you anyway?" Brendon asks in a slightly slurred voice as he nervously approaches the man.

"I am no one of importance, I just want to help you if I can. Would you like to talk."

"Look whoever you are, I don't know you and I don't know what you're talking about. I came here to see a friend about an urgent matter, so no I don't have time to talk with you. I need to be on my way, and you need to mind your business."

"Before you go, let me ask one final thing." Brendon stops, sighs out loud and thinks he should punch this guy in the face.

"Have you ever in your life done something, and regretted the decision to the point you wished you could turn back time?"

Brendon stands silent for a few seconds, and thinks about the question, although he's not sure why. He wants to walk away but for some reason he feels almost compelled to give this stranger an answer. He looks the other man in the eyes, and prepares to answer him, and then he realizes that the rage he felt minutes ago is starting to fade.

"I guess we've all done shit we wish we could take back. So yes, I've made a few bad decisions in my life."

"What of the friend you are going to visit tonight? Do you think you wouldn't regret what you are planning to do for the rest of your life. Do you actually want to destroy two lives, one being an innocent." The man asks.

Brendon finds himself not knowing what to say, he is still angry, but now the anger has faded and been replaced with another emotion, Shame.

"Let us sit down so that we may talk my son."

The man puts his hand on Brendon's shoulder, and guides him to a sitting area near the garage elevators. Brendon walks quietly with him saying nothing. As they approach the bench Brendon lights a cigarette, and offers one to the stranger. He accepts the cigarette, and they both sit down.

"Now please tell me what is troubling you so, maybe we can work this out." Asks the man.

"Why are you referring to me as 'my son', are you a Priest or something.

"In a manner of speaking, I could be called by that title. It's just that I see everyone as a child of mine, every man, woman, boy and girl, it makes no difference to me. I see us all as family, after all we do share a common origin. If my referring to you in that manner disturbs you I will stop. Would you tell me your name that I might know you better."

"Sure, my name is Brendon and you are?" Brendon asks.

"My name is not important, what is important is you Brendon, and why you would contemplate murder as a solution to any problem. An act as heinous as what you are planning would solve absolutely nothing, why would you ever believe any problem could be solved in such a manner?" He asks as he touches Brendon's shoulder.

With his cigarette between his fingers Brendon brings both his hands to his face, he feels a whole range of emotions at this point. He feels his mind start to clear, and he no longer feels the effects of the Patron. He takes a deep breath, and answers the question.

"I'm married and I've gotten myself into a terrible mess, my wife and I have had problems lately, but nothing major, at least not on her part. I love my wife, but for a while our relationship was less than fulfilling for me. It became more so after I met someone I should have stayed away from. We started an affair and things got worse between my wife and me. After the affair had been going for a while I started to distance myself from my wife, which I knew was wrong, but I thought my feelings were changing. I thought that if I had someone on the side it would make my marriage better, you know take some of the pressure off, and I'd get the excitement I wasn't getting at home. I thought I could have my wife and a playmate on the side, someone I could be with when I wanted, and could discard when I wanted. I thought that it would be easy to walk away from the other woman, but it hasn't been. After all she knew I was married when we met so she knew what she was getting herself into, she knew there wasn't gonna be any long term commitment with me. I thought I had broken it off weeks ago, that she was fine with it. I was really working hard on my relationship with my wife. Then she calls me today, and tells me she's pregnant with my kid. I got angry and thought that if I could get rid of her and the ba... Brendon stops before he can finish the sentence, and discards his cigarette butt and drops his head down, the shame he feels is devastating.

"I understand what you are saying Brendon, you know it is wrong to kill, and that even if you had carried out your plan it would have solved absolutely nothing."

" I don't want to lose my wife, my marriage or my home. I fucked up! And I don't know what to do!"

"Brendon you are not a violent man, you certainly are no murderer. All men, even the best of men make mistakes. It is part of the human condition, but you have the capacity to reason, to solve problems. Use those abilities now to come up with a workable non-violent solution to your dilemma." The man states.

"I don't know if that is even possible. Ashley, she's the other woman, and she wants me to leave my wife for her. If my wife finds out about this my marriage, and my life to this point is over. I don't want to spend the rest of my life with someone like Ashley. It was never meant to be that way; she was not supposed to let herself get pregnant. She was just someone to screw on the side, and have fun with; this was supposed to be no strings, no complications."

"Nothing is as easy as it appears on the surface Brendon, every action we take every second of our lives carries with it consequences, both good and bad that we cannot anticipate." The man responds.

As the men speak Brendon's feelings of anger are gone as are his plans for homicide, but he does feel the frustration of his situation creeping back into his mind, and a question comes to him he needs to ask.

"Hey, how the hell did you know what I was planning to do, I was so angry earlier today, the thought of hurting Ashley didn't even occur to me until I got fucked up. I mean I've never seen you before in my life. I do appreciate your talking with me now, but how did you know? You also said something about a mother, and her unborn son. Dude who the fuck are you?" Brendon asks calmly.

"It was easy for me to read what was in your heart, the second I looked into your eyes Brendon. The pain you are carrying is obvious; the uncertainty of your future weighs heavily upon you, and with good reason. And while you will not carry out your plan today; you may at some future point. It is for that reason; I would like to show you something."

He lightly touches Brendon's temple and Brendon freezes still for a second. His eyes are wide open, but he feels as if he is being transported to some distant place, to a place that is familiar yet not familiar, he feels as if he's dreaming, but conscientiously traveling outside his body.

The next thing Brendon is aware of is seeing himself picking up his keys and going to the elevator. Brendon looks at himself, and he can see the alcohol induced anger on his face and rage in his eyes. He takes the elevator to Ashley's floor, Brendon tries to shout at himself not to do what he is planning, but his physical form doesn't seem to be able to hear him. Brendon stands in front of himself in an attempt to bar his way, but again his physical self seems to pass right through him as if he's a ghost. Brendon watches as he knocks on Ashley's door, and she is there in seconds, a big smile on her face. Brendon watches as Ashley lets him in her condo. Brendon's disembodied consciousness follows him in, he sees Ashley try to hug Brendon, but he pushes her away. He is angry and soon whatever they are talking about appears to turn into a heated argument. Brendon's astral form can only view what is happening. He cannot hear anything that is being said, nor can he physically affect the things he is seeing. He watches himself light a cigarette, and go to the refrigerator and take out a beer. Ashley is visibly upset as she sits on a chair with her arms folded across her chest; watching Brendon drink his beer in seconds, then he gets another one. The two start to talk again, for a while it appears this time it's calmer. After a while Ashley starts to shout at Brendon. Brendon is visibly angry, and says something to Ashley that makes her turn away and walk toward the door. She points at it, as if to show Brendon the way out.

He looks at her and throws the half-finished bottle of beer at the door, the bottle shatters on impact. Ashley runs to the steps shouting at him as she climbs, frantically trying to hold onto the railing. Brendon watches Ashley go to the top of the stairs, still shouting while pointing at the front door as if she is now demanding that he leave. Brendon's astral form watches his physical self-go after Ashley to the top of the stairs. What happens in the next fifteen minutes is horrifying to watch, and Brendon's astral form is totally powerless to stop it. Brendon quickly goes after Ashley; he takes the thirty odd stairs two at a time. The fury on his face is unmistakable. He reaches out to Ashley with both hands; he grabs her by her shoulders, and shakes her violently. She is shouting, and trying to pull away from him, but he's too strong. Brendon being much larger than her pulls her to him, and then moves to the middle of the staircase. Without warning he throws her as hard as he can down the staircase. The look of horror on her face is indescribable; Brendon cannot believe that he is watching himself do something like this. As Ashley falls sideways down the stairs, her head is the first part of her body to make contact with the steps. On impact blood shoots from her nose and mouth, when her full body weight crashes into the stairs the jolt to her system is bone shattering. She quickly tumbles and slides to the bottom of the stairs, her body contorted at vicious angles. Brendon stands at the top of the stairs looking down on her, trying to decide if she is dead.

He quickly runs down the stairs, grabs Ashley's barely moving body by her feet, and drags her to the top of the staircase. Her head banging onto each step as she is pulled up, a trail of blood marking each step. When they get to the top of the stairs, Brendon's astral form watches in utter disbelief, as he stands her limp body up at the top of the staircase, and pushes her down back first. Her body again slams against the stairs, blood splattering in all directions, her weight and gravity pull her down the stairs. Brendon is almost pleased his astral form can't hear the sound her body makes on impact.

He can however see her bloodied face as her body tumbles down the staircase. Ashley's body comes to a halt head first at the bottom of the stairs. Blood running from Ashley's mouth, and nose in torrents. After staring at her unmoving body, at the bottom of the staircase for a few seconds, Brendon goes into two of the upstairs bedrooms. Seconds later, he calmly comes down the stairs stepping over Ashley's unmoving body. He looks around the Condo, and takes out his cigarette lighter, and starts to set fire to the furnishings and drapes. He goes into the kitchen and turns on every burner of her gas stove. He sets the oven to its highest temperature, and opens the door. He then quickly dashes to the front door of the Condo, making sure the locks set, as he closes the door.

As Brendon's astral form watches the condo go up in flames, he looks at Ashley and it's as if he zooms in on her face. She is breathing, and starts to cough as smoke fills the room. When she opens her eyes the panic she feels is horrendous, as the smoke gets thicker. The only thought screaming in her mind as she looks at her front door is get out of here. Her broken body trapped in an oven, and she is unable to crawl away, she feels the heat of the flames on her crippled body. Brendon's astral form screams she's alive!, Goddamnit she's alive! Somebody help her! But no one can hear him. Then he remembers she's also pregnant with his son.

Brendon quickly opens his eyes and stands, he lets out a shout of agony and relief, he frantically pats his body as if something is wrong, as if he's trying to make sure, his body is his own. His breathing is heavy, and he is terrified to the core of his being. After a few seconds he realizes, that what he just saw wasn't real. He looks around the silent parking garage, and realizes he is alone. He sits back down on the bench, and starts to cry, he cries for himself, that he could even contemplate doing something so brutal to another person, he cries for having to witness something like that, knowing he himself could have set those events in motion, and he cries for the chance to make things right in his life.

Saturday August 28th 2011
Los Angeles, California
9:00 a.m.

Chase, a very lonely and disturbed young man walks out of the apartment he calls home on his way to work. He is angry and full of resentment for everyone and everything. He feels his whole life he has been ignored by everyone. His father, relatives on both sides of his family, he has no siblings, and no one in his life he calls friend.

He is in his late twenties, and has never had a girlfriend, or even a female buddy he could just talk to. He has owned a cell phone for years, but has only used it to call his job, no one ever calls him. He has felt empty his entire life, he walks down the boulevard, and no one takes notice of him. Men don't see him and he is invisible to women.

Small children though, especially infants and toddlers always make him smile when he sees them. He feels that they are the only truly innocent people on the planet. At least when he smiles at them they smile back. Sometimes he wishes he could be a baby again, so that he could feel his mother's embrace. To fall asleep in the protection of her arms again. He knows that she was the only person who ever truly cared about him, and how he felt. He remembers the day she was taken away from him. She died in child birth when he was eight years old, that day he lost his mother, a little sister, and a father who emotionally abandoned him. Over time he has tried to get his life together, but things never worked out for him. The military didn't do much for him, nor did going to college, and because of poor grades he dropped out. He sees no future for himself where he is currently working. His job at Five Guys Burgers barely pays the rent in the rundown apartment he lives in. Even the managers and employees barely acknowledge his presence at the restaurant. His job there however is perfectly suited to the way he has always felt, and fits his mood and personality. He works alone in the backroom off the food prep area; mixing, spicing and shaping hamburger patties, day in day out. Unwrapping and prepping hamburger for eight hours a day. Since no one ever comes in the room, what he plans to do today will be that much easier. He plans to add a very special spice of Arsenic, to all three hundred pounds of the meat today. He bought the chemical in powdered form in small amounts on-line, until he had enough to carry out his plan. He also mixed in large quantities of ground rat poison hoping this would help to increase its toxicity. Since he is invisible at work, no one will know what he's done. The meat will not be used until the following day, by which time he will be long gone. He has planned to quit this dead end job, and move on once he is paid this afternoon. He knows that no one cares about him, so why should he care if dozens, or even hundreds of thoughtless cruel people get sick or killed by what he is going to do. He continues his walk to the bus stop lost in his own thoughts, and then he hears an unfamiliar sound. As he walks he slowly realizes it's his cell phone that is ringing. He assumed it was one of the dozens of phones belonging to one of the people he passed on the street. He wonders who could be calling him, and why. He's not due at work for another forty-five minutes, so it couldn't be the job calling. He figures it's probably telemarketers trying to sell him something he doesn't want. His father is the only other person with the number, and he never calls. He is curious, so he momentarily stops walking to answer his ringing cell phone.

"Hello."

"My son, why would you want to do something so inhumanly cruel?" The caller asks.

"What? You have the wrong number."

"No my son I have the right number, we need to talk about what you plan to do."

"Look I don't know who you are, or what you're talking about. Please don't call this number again." Chase says with fear in his voice.

"Chase will you at least talk to me for a few minutes?"

"Look, I don't want to talk to you. I don't know you or what you're talking about."

"Yes you do, the poison you are carrying in your backpack, is capable of destroying many lives my child. This is not really what you want."

"You don't know anything about what I want, and I don't care who you are. I'm hanging up."

"Then what would be the harm in talking to me for a while, you have plenty of time before you have to report to work. Why don't you sit down, and let us talk for a while."

Chase looks around and sees an empty bench, he doesn't want to talk to this person, but now he is curious, frightened, and for reasons he can't explain he wants to tell someone how he feels. As he goes to the bench he tells himself, that whoever this person is he's not a cop, or he'd probably find himself under arrest now. Chase tells himself that he will humor whoever this is for a few more minutes, then he's going to work.

"Are you still there?" He asks with trepidation.

"Yes my son, I am here."

"Who are you man? And how the hell do you know my name, and how'd you get my number."

"Who I am is not important, what is important Chase is that I want to help you. I want to help you see that you don't need to poison anyone, and that you are not alone in the world."

"You don't know anything about me."

"I know that you need a friend, I know that what you're planning to do is wrong, that is all I need to know, for now."

"If you know so much why not just call the cops, and tell them what you think you know." Chase responds with fear in his voice.

"I don't think that is necessary, I believe that you and I can work this out before you do something you'll regret forever."

"You still haven't answered my question. Who are you, and how'd you get my cellphone number, nobody calls me, and nobody has this number."

"My son the more immediate question you should be asking, is why you want to poison hundreds of innocent people, and destroy the lives of untold more people indirectly. Many of those whom you would harm will be children. Those innocents you care most for in the world. Is that what you really want to do my son?"

"What are you talking about, who said I was gonna poison anybody, your crazy man?"

"Then tell me why you are carrying enough arsenic to kill untold hundreds in your backpack. For what purpose do you need that substance, and why carry it with you to work.

For the next few minutes Chase sits on a bench, and lets that question sink into his consciousness. He looks around his immediate area, and watches more intently than he ever has before at the activity that's going on around him. People in their cars going places, people walking all around him involved in conversations, and appearing happy and untroubled, guys walking hand in hand with their girlfriends. Mothers and fathers holding the hands of their children, as they walk to where ever their going. With more intense concentration Chase notices the smiles on all the children's faces. The children look up at their parents pointing in all directions, and asking questions about the world around them, those innocent little faces. Chase thinks to himself.

"Are you still there?"

"I will not leave you my child, I am here."

"I need to know where you are."

"Would knowing where I am make it easier for us to talk? I am closer than you think."

"I don't know, maybe?"

"Would you like to just talk for now, and maybe after a while we can meet face to face?" The caller asks?

"Sure why not?"

"Tell me my son, why do you want to commit such an evil act against your brothers?"

"I don't know, it's just that I get so tired of being ignored all the time by everyone. It's like no one even knows I'm alive, I've never even had a girlfriend. I've grown to the point that I hate everybody. Since no one cares about me, why should I care about what happens to them? I thought that maybe if I do this, it would make me feel better knowing that I made them suffer for the way I've been treated."

"No my son, causing death and sickness to others will not help you to find what you're missing. What you seek is within you, I can help you find the strength to overcome these feelings, if you let me help you."

"How can you do that, when I've tried all my life, and haven't been able to help myself, the only thought that makes me feel good anymore is the thought of killing people."

"You know in your heart that is wrong. For years you have let these feelings, and thoughts fester in your mind."

"You didn't know how to find the help you needed, so your thoughts just grew darker with each passing year, yet until today you haven't acted on them. You don't need to feel this way anymore my son, I will help you if you let me."

"How can you help someone you don't know?"

"I know your heart my son; will you allow me to help you?"

"Yes, what do I need to do?"

"I think it is time for us to meet. Stand up and turn around, walk down the street a little ways, and I'll be the man sitting under the tree wearing a white ball cap."

Chase hangs up, and does what the caller instructs him to do; he stands and walks down the street. He doesn't feel nervous or apprehensive about meeting this person, who called him out of the blue, and knew exactly what he was planning to do today. Instead he feels almost relieved, and for reasons he can't explain he wants to meet this person. He soon spots a man sitting on a bench under a tree wearing a white ball cap. When their eyes meet Chase knows that somehow this person can help him. Chase thinks to himself as he approaches this man, he isn't what he expected. He appears to be a lot younger than he would have thought. As Chase gets within range of his voice, the man speaks to him.

"Hello Chase let us sit for a while and talk. We have much to discuss." Says the man. Chase responds by sitting down.

"Chase give me the container of poison you are carrying in your backpack, I will dispose of it for you." Chase takes off his backpack reaches inside and gives him the container of poison. The look on his face as he hands over the container is one of both embarrassment and relief.

"What do we do from here, are you gonna turn me in to the police. I'm sorry for what I was gonna do." "You still haven't told me how you knew." Chase asks.

"We are simply going to talk, nothing more. I don't need to tell anyone of what you were planning, including the police. How I knew is unimportant, helping you see the seriousness of what you were going to do is what matters. Who I am is a friend, that doesn't want to see you make a horrible mistake." As Chase listens to the man the feelings of loneliness, abandonment, and hatred he's felt for years are gone as if they never existed.

"They are beautiful aren't they."

"Who are you talking about?" responds Chase.

"The children Chase look around you."

As he speaks Chase looks in every direction and observes with new wonder, all the children on the streets with their parents and guardians. He sees a group of children walking hand in hand behind adult chaperones. He figures they must be a school group. All the little ones are smiling.

"The children are so little and so innocent, their love and trust is unconditional. They give so much joy to their parents yet they themselves are so vulnerable and fragile. It would not take much to destroy one so young. The loss of parents for instance can cripple the growth, and development of children. The young ones are the most susceptible to the horrors of the world around them, since they are the most defenseless. Wouldn't you agree Chase, having lost your own beloved mother at an early age."

For an instant Chase holds his head down, and feels as a man does, not a child. A powerful and un-controllable rush of emotion. Similar feelings he had as a child magnified tenfold now, of when his mother died all those years ago. So painful are the emotions that they cause him to cry out in agony, just for an instant in time. When he

229

recovers his body is physically drained, mentally he feels paralyzed. For long seconds it is as if he is incapable of functioning in the world around him. He wants to retreat to somewhere in his subconscious, someplace no one can touch him. It is the sound of the man's voice that brings him back to reality.

"You understand now my child, what you just experienced in your mind is what hundreds of people would have felt, had you carried out your plan to kill. What you felt deeper in your being was the emotional destruction you would have cause dozens upon dozens of helpless, innocent children. That same inner fear and abandonment that you yourself experienced when your own precious mother died."

Chase says nothing at first, he cannot find the words to adequately express what he feels so he doesn't try. The tears falling from his eyes and the trembling of his body speak volumes for him. It is not until he is touched on the shoulder, by the man he sits with that he finds himself starting to calm down both mentally and physically.

"Do you understand now my son?" Chase looks at the man and nods his head as he wipes away the tears.

"I didn't realize the depth, or the consequences my actions would have had on so many innocent people. The pain I just felt, I would never want a child to feel, and I am sorry. Is it possible to forgive something like this." Chase says.

"Yes my son you are already forgiven, and I know that now the pain you've carried for so long is no longer a part of you, the happiness and fulfillment you seek will be yours."

Chase smiles and looks away from the man he's sitting with, and focuses his attention on the people around him. For the first time in a long time he doesn't see them as objects to focus his hatred. He sees fellow human beings just like himself, and he smiles. He turns to thank the man he sits with, and he is gone. Chase frantically looks around to try and spot him but he is nowhere to be found, Chase thinks to himself how the hell could he be gone just like that, he was just here. As he looks around a young woman passes Chase, and smiles at him as she walks by. He notices the uniform she is wearing under her open jacket, and it's the restaurant where he works. He finds the courage to walk up to her, and say hello. As he catches up to her he looks at his watch, and is relieved to see that he has plenty of time to get to work. Despite the fact that it seemed like he'd been with that man he was talking to for hours. Chase dismisses the thought, catches up with the young woman, and is pleasantly surprised that he has the confidence to introduce himself.

Saturday August 28th 2011
Dale City, VA.
1:00 p.m.

Alfreda removes the handset of her cordless phone from her ear, pushes the off button, and puts the phone down on the counter. She stands over the sink in her kitchen, and stares at the vial she is holding in her left hand. She knows the vials liquid contents are extremely lethal. What she was planning to do with it would have been a horrible mistake. She takes the top off the vial, turns on the hot water, and pours the contents down the drain. She is now grateful for the phone call she received over an hour ago. A Mystery caller, who talked her out of poisoning her violent on-again off-again boyfriend Eddie, She does wonder though for a second, how that stranger knew what it was she was planning to do, and how he got her home phone number. The thought quickly fades, and the question is forgotten. Alfreda had made up her mind that she was never going to let him ever hit her again. Even if she had to kill him to do it, she refuses to ever be a victim of his violence again. Thanks to the strange phone call she just received she now has the courage to handle things differently, and to change the way things have been. She throws the vial in the trash, and the beer she bought for Eddie. She picks up the phone, and dials the police non-emergency number. Alfreda tells herself when she's done with them she's calling Eddie to let him know he is out of her life forever. The pain of the black eye he gave her last night is gone, and as she rubs her face she finds that the swelling is almost completely gone as well.

Saturday August 28th 2011
Seattle, WA.
2:15 p.m.

Jesus Lopez walks down Washington Ave in the town of Renton, Seattle on a cold and wet afternoon. The day's weather mirrors how he feels perfectly, gloomy and depressed which makes him feel even more hopeless. Jesus is a very hard working but troubled man. He has been in the states for some time now, he came into the country illegally from Mexico over eight years ago looking for work. Over the years he has been here, Jesus has been able to earn enough money to bring his wife, and children to Seattle. And even though times have been hard, he has been able to make Seattle their home, but it has been a constant struggle, and came at a terrible cost to him. For years it has been an uphill battle, every day for Jesus to make ends meet, as much as he loves his family, providing for them has been a fight every day, and one he is losing. Since he is in the country illegally, he cannot get the proper state identification he needs to find what he considers decent employment. Jesus is a skilled carpenter, and any job that would carry with it benefits, that would help him and the family would be welcomed. Because of his legal status those kinds of jobs are out of his reach. On most days, he has to take whatever work comes his way, for whatever is offered for his labors. He and his wife have been able to get their two oldest children enrolled in school, and they are doing well, which he is very proud of. The only health care any of them receive is provided via free clinics in his area, which supports the needs of the immigrant community in his part of town. Jesus is grateful for what he has been able to accomplish for his family. He was dead set against having any more children, until his financial situation had become more stable. His wife however, wanted to keep the baby she was carrying a year ago, and convinced him that they would be ok. She would help him by getting a job to supplement his income. Since it made her so happy to give birth to their youngest son in the U.S., he decided that he would simply work harder to support them all. Jesus knew she would have to quit her job at the Dollar-Mart, after the baby was born, and with the loss of her income the pressures on him increased quickly, and drastically. Many times he wouldn't eat so that his family could. He found that the baby's needs were almost overwhelming. Friends had tried to convince him to seek some form of state aid, but he is fearful of being deported back to Mexico when they find out he's here illegally. His older two children love being in the states, and can barely remember having lived in Mexico as neither one speaks the Spanish they were taught early in life. His youngest son is a U.S. citizen by birth, and Jesus will not see his family sent back to Mexico under any circumstances, to face the horrors of drug wars, gang violence, and the poverty he knew growing up as a child. Jesus is determined that he will not let that happen under any circumstances. He decides to sit down for a while, and think about what he's going to tell his wife, about his not getting paid today. He just completed laying a kitchen floor for a client that was recommended to him. He worked on the job laying ceramic tiles in that damn kitchen for two weeks. He was proud of the job he had done when the work was complete. When he went over everything he had done for the client, she told him that it would be at least two weeks before she could pay him. She gave him a sob story about some relative who had taken ill, and that she needed to help her family before she could pay him for his work. Jesus was counting on the two-thousand dollars he would have earned for that job. So was his wife and family, he tried his best to explain his situation, but his explanation and his needs fell on deaf ears. That much money would have carried him for a while, he could have provided for his family for a month, on that money alone. And he is certain it would have brought him other work, now that's not going to happen. He was taken advantage of again, and done wrong in the worst way. The client didn't give a damn about his family. He left the work site pissed off, but there was nothing he could do. He couldn't make the client pay him as they had agreed, so he simply walked away. Jesus swore to himself, that he would not return to the only other source of income he knew. The one that his wife didn't know about, and one that sickens him even thinking about, but it provided the extra money he needed when he needed it. He tells himself that what he did, he had to do, to support his family. Even though it disgusted him to no end he did what was necessary. The thought of performing oral sex on men for money, turns his stomach now, as it did then. The fact that he's not gay only compounded the situation, and the problems it caused him internally. Especially during intimacy with his wife, what he did makes him feel beyond ashamed. Jesus swore to God that after his baby was born he would never stoop so low again. The mere thought that he may have to resort to something like that sickens him, and he swears to himself that he will die first.

So he finds himself sitting in front of the Holiday Inn hotel where he sometimes brings his wife for dinner when he has a little extra money. He is totally broke, and the rent on his apartment is already two days late, his utilities are coming due, and his daughter needs reading glasses he cannot afford. He doesn't know what to do, or where to turn for help, but he will not see his family suffer because he cannot provide for them. Jesus puts his hands in his jacket pocket, and feels the butt of the .38 in his left hand. He tells himself that he could sell the gun, but he knows at best he'd only get a few dollars for it, and that's not going to help his situation. Jesus tells himself that he can't support his family, and he loves them too much to see them suffer, because he's not man enough to do the job himself. He holds the pistol grip in his hand, and decides that it is for the best. If he takes their lives, then his own, they will be together forever. They will find the happiness in death that he could not provide for them in life. He decides he will wait until the family is asleep, and starting with his beautiful wife, he will kiss her body goodbye, and shoot her in the head, muffling the sound of the gun with a pillow. Then he will shoot each of his children in the head; the same way after telling them he loves them. He tells himself he will then get in bed with his dead wife, holding her as tightly as he can, kiss her dead body goodbye, put the gun to his own temple, and pull the trigger. Jesus convinces himself, that this is the only way he can take care of, and protect his family, that after tonight they will all be in heaven together. So deep in his own thoughts Jesus doesn't notice when a man walks up, and sits next to him on the bench.

Translated from Spanish

"Hello my friend how are you doing today?' Asks the man. Jesus looks up and realizes that someone asked him a question in Spanish.

"Oh, hi, I'm sorry what did you say, I was lost in my own problems."

"I understand, I just asked how you were doing today."

"Not too good today, I have a lot on my mind." Jesus responds.

"Would it help if you talked about what's troubling you? I find that sometimes talking about our problems can be the first step in solving them."

"I wish things could be solved so easy, just by talking about it."

"Well if you like, why not give it a try, you never know what solutions a stranger could come up with, I might have just the answer you need." The man responds.

"I'm really not good at expressing my problems; I like to try to find my own solutions. But I do appreciate your wanting to listen, but right now that's not what I need."

"I completely understand, but what is it you need right now, maybe at the very least I can help you with that, if it will solve your problem at least temporarily."

Jesus looks at the man sitting next to him and doesn't know what to think. His first instinct is that this motherfucker is trying to pick him up; that this gay bastard is hitting on him, and he feels anger grow inside of him that he wants to release. Jesus grips the pistol in his hand a little harder, his next thought is to take the gun out of his pocket, and blow this faggots brains all over the street.

"Look man, I don't know what you want, and I don't care, now why don't you move on before you get yourself hurt."

"My friend I intend you no harm, and I don't want anything from you. I can assure you all I want to do is talk nothing more."

"Well why don't you go talk to someone else, I have my own problems, and I don't wanna hear about yours." Jesus says angrily.

"I merely thought that you looked like a man who could use a friend." He responds.

Jesus grows angrier and angrier he has asked this intruder nicely to leave him alone, and he refuses to leave. Jesus thinks that maybe he should just get up, and leave himself without saying another word. But he is so angry now he tells himself why should he be the one to leave, when he was here first, and was bothering no one. Then he thinks to himself fuck it, I'll take my anger out on him. I'm gonna blow this faggots brains out right now, He starts to pull the .38 out of his pocket.

"You don't need to pull your weapon out Jesus, I will leave you if that is really what you want."

"What are you talking about, and how do you know my name."

"The weapon that you have in your left jacket pocket, it is not necessary for you to shoot me friend." Jesus stands, pulls the gun from his pocket, and points it at the man sitting with him.

"I asked you to leave me the fuck alone, since you won't I'm gonna take care of whatever fuckin' problems you have right now, by blowing your goddamn brains out."

"If that is what you feel you must do, and if killing me spares the lives of your wife and children then do what you must Jesus I will not stop you." For an instant, Jesus is stunned when the man mentions killing him may spare the lives of his family. Jesus hesitates long enough to think hard about what this man just said.

"What the fuck! do you know about my family man?, you don't know anything about me." Jesus shouts still pointing the gun at the man's face.

"I know that you really don't want to harm them, and that you do love your wife, and children with every fiber of your being. Why then Jesus would you contemplate destroying them and yourself? Doing such a thing is never the answer?"

Jesus doesn't want to answer the question, so he simply looks at the man in stunned silence. After a few seconds he lowers the weapon, and stares at it. Unable to say a word he returns the .38 caliber pistol to his pocket, and sits down. He can't find the words to express what he is feeling now. The man puts his hand on Jesus's shoulder and talks to him.

"Let us talk my friend, I'm sure things are not as bad as you think they are. You'd be surprised how really talking about what's bothering you, can help you see things from a different perspective." As Jesus speaks he holds his head down, and the words come slowly.

"I was actually mad enough to pull the trigger, I was really going to shoot you, and you weren't afraid. I have never seen that kind of courage before, why weren't you afraid." Jesus asks.

"My friend, fear exists where there is no understanding, and I understand the human condition well. What drives us to do the things we do, for good or ill"

"You are not that kind of man my friend, you have much on your mind, and the weight of your circumstances is a heavy burden to carry, but carry it you have. That is why I thought you could use a friend to talk to."

Jesus looks at the man, and questions start to come together in his head. The most puzzling of which is, who is this person.

"Who are you man, how do you know so much about me?"

"I am no one my friend, that is to say, I am no one of importance. I believe that we all have a purpose in life, and I have come to know that my purpose is to help others anyway I can. It is what I have done my whole life."

"Why, nobody helps nobody unless it's something in it for them."

"No my friend that's not always the case, some are better able to help, and to share what they have. While some are hesitant due to personal circumstances, but would never the less come to the aid of perfect strangers in need, just as you have in the past."

Since you are carrying a weapon, and thought about using it against me, I quickly realized that there is more going on inside you, than is apparent from the outside."

"How did you know about my family, and what I was thinking of doing? Do you have some kind of power that lets you see inside people? You are not God that you can read people's minds."

"No my friend I am not, but I can however recognize depression, and sadness in others. I do have a sense of when people are deeply troubled, it is what I'm trained to do."

"Oh then you're some kind of doctor, the kind that talks to people to find out if they are crazy or something?"

The man talking to Jesus smiles before he answers.

"In a manner of speaking you could say that, talking to people to help them figure out how best to deal with their problems is what I do."

"But how did you know my name?" Jesus asks.

"Well my friend you are wearing a monogramed jacket." He says laughing.

Jesus looks at the left front side of his jacket and starts laughing. He had forgotten that his wife had put his first name on all his work jackets, and a few of his shirts. When his laughter fades he remembers what he was going to do with the gun in his pocket; tonight after his family went to sleep. Now the good feeling of his laughter is replaced with sorrow as he hangs his head down.

"What is it my friend? Let us talk about what troubles you."

Jesus looks at the man sitting with him, and decides that he needs to get what he is feeling out of his system. Jesus looks at the man he sits with and begins talking.

"I don't know where to begin; I was supposed to get paid today for putting in a floor for a client. I'm a carpenter by trade, but she told me she couldn't pay me today, and I was counting on that money. I got so angry I wanted to kill that white bitch, but there was nothing I could do except walk away. And wait for her to pay me when she can, if she ever does. All my utilities are coming due, and I'm late on my rent as it is.

My daughter needs glasses, and I don't have any money at all, we have just enough food in the house to last a few days. I was counting on the money from that job. I earned it for all the work I did, and now I have nothing. I don't know what to do, it's been so hard since my youngest was born. I can't ask the city for help because I'm in this country illegal. I feel like I've let my family down, because I can't support them the way I need to. I want so much more for my family than I had growing up in Mexico. I feel like a failure because the man of the house is supposed to take care of his family. But for me it's been getting harder every day. I'm ashamed to admit this to anyone, but I've done things to earn money that sicken me to my stomach, but I had nowhere else to turn."

Jesus looks at the man sitting next to him, and slowly turns his gaze toward the streets.

"My friend you do not need to be ashamed to tell me anything. I'm not here to judge you or your motivations, in life we are sometimes forced to make hard choices. Making choices that we don't always like, and that put us at odds with who, and what we are, but we try to balance what we are forced to do against taking no action at all. Many times circumstances force our choice, then we live with the consequences."

Jesus puts his face in his hands, and tells the man he is sitting with how he found himself having to perform oral sex on men to pay his bills for many months. He tells him how having to do something like that has destroyed his sense of self-worth, and his manhood. That he is so shattered internally that he can barely stand to look his son's in their eyes, or look at himself in the mirror. That the only reason he found himself in that situation, was because he needed to support his family, and he wasn't going to see them living in the streets, as he once had to do growing up. He talks of his inner humiliation because he wasn't strong enough to find another way. As Jesus speaks his tears fall to the ground, but they do not lessen his pain. He tells the man how his final solution to his struggle, is to murder his family then kill himself, so that they will not have to suffer, because of his failures as a man. After he finishes speaking Jesus keeps his face in his hands. The shame of his words is powerful and overwhelming, so much so he feels his hand move from his face to the pocket containing his pistol. He doesn't want to kill his family anymore, now he wants to end his own weak pathetic life.

"Jesus my son, just as you didn't really want to kill me; I will not let you kill yourself now."

The man stops Jesus's hand from reaching into his jacket, and he takes the weapon himself. Jesus lets him take the weapon and says nothing.

"I understand that the choices you had to make to support your family were devastating to you on many levels. Believe me when I say that I know how hard that must have been for you. Jesus you are a good man who only wants to give his family a good life, and your children the best opportunities you can, opportunities you didn't have growing up in the slums of Mexico. Understand this Jesus, your wife and children love you, you see it every day in their eyes and on their faces when you go home to them. Your children would live with you, and their mother in a tree house if that were the case. As long as children know their parents love them, they would be completely happy no matter what your financial circumstances are. My son I'm not saying this to you to further hurt you, but taking the lives of your family is not the answer to your problems. The shame and humiliation you feel for having to engage in the sex acts you did will in time pass and be forgotten. What you did you did out of a necessity to feed your family. You feel violated and used but that too will pass in time."

"How do I live with what I've done? How do I forget sucking the dicks of other men to pay my bills? How do I live with maybe catching aids, and giving that shit to my wife? I can't even afford to get a aids test. How do I get rid of the shame I feel inside, or forget that I betrayed my wife and children? How do I live with what I was going to do to them, my own family, can you tell me that?" Jesus asks as the tears fall from his eyes.

"You spoke of what you perceived as courage earlier my son, let me tell you what I think true courage is. You leave home every day to work to support your family, sometimes not knowing what, if anything will come from the work you do, or if you'll be paid for your labors. You put all your heart and soul into the work you do for others on a daily basis, with no guarantees of payment. You have done this every day for years and your motivations have been pure and singular. The wellbeing of your family has always been paramount for you, with you never stopping to consider yourself. You do this for years and bring home the money you earn for its intended purpose; regardless of the perils you might face both emotionally and physically. My son every man has his breaking point, and you have been the backbone of your family for years, and you have been able to achieve what you have with extremely limited resources. In my opinion what you do and what you have been able to do, in the face of the terrible adversity you endure, speaks to a courage not many men possess. I want you to remember this no matter what happens for the rest of your life, on this day you did not murder your family, nor take your own life. Unfortunately my son sex for money is a reality of the world in which we live. It has always been that way; the exploitation of our fellow man too, is a sad reality of our world. But I believe in time that too will change. Jesus you are a kind decent man now, and you always have been. Trust me when I tell you that your life, and that of your families will be good and fulfilling. But they will not reach their true potential without you, nor will you know the satisfaction, and joy that comes with a harmonious family without them. No my son it is not yet time for death to take away you and yours."

Jesus listens carefully as this man speaks to him, and his words make sense. Jesus doesn't feel ashamed of what he told this man about himself, nor of the things he had done. That is all in the past now, and it's time to look toward the future even an uncertain future. Jesus also finds that this man was right about his burden being lifted, by doing something as simple as really talking about what was on his mind, and in his heart.

"Do you understand now my son? Do you see that the pain you have been carrying with you all these months, has been like the weight of a mountain on your back. Your devotion to your family is what has kept you strong, it is your doubt and fear that has worn away your resolve, and temporarily weakened you. Jesus I want you to look at me, and answer a question I would like to pose." Jesus looks up and stares deeply into the brown eyes of the man he is sitting with.

"My son can you imagine your life without your cherished family?"

Jesus hears the question and immediately his mind processes the scenario of him living alone, and never having had a family. He tries to imagine himself never having met his wife those many years ago, and living without the happiness they have shared. Jesus tries to imagine never fathering his three children. He tries to imagine not being in their lives watching them grow to their current ages; and missing out on the adults they would have become. He thinks about all the missed games they've played, and not playing baseball with his oldest son. He tries to imagine not being in the hospital, and experiencing the birth of his youngest son, and of not holding him seconds later. Jesus runs scenario after scenario through his mind, of him living without the family he loves with all that he is. He finds that he can imagine no scenario where he doesn't experience an endless void due to their absence. Jesus realizes that nothing in his life matters more to him, than taking care of his family. Not the life of gay sex he temporarily found himself lured into. Not the uncertainty of his work and finances; and not his legal status in the states. As a multitude of thoughts course through his mind now with vivid clarity, he finds it is increasingly easy to see a few workable solutions; to what has been troubling him lately. It's as if a veil has been removed from his eyes, and he now sees clearly for the first time in a long while. Jesus is troubled by something though and he doesn't quite know why. There are things he can't remember, that he should know, things about himself that are quickly fading. As if the memories are running away from him, and he can't hold on to them. Jesus decides in an instant that it was probably nothing of importance anyway. Before Jesus opens his eyes his first thought, is to thank his new friend he met today, who really did have the answers he needed. When Jesus turns toward the man who is sitting next to him he is puzzled, and a little shocked to find that there is no one sitting with him. He stands quickly, looks around his immediate area, but there is no one around. He walks down to the sidewalk, but again he can't find his new friend.

Jesus is confused, and a little sad, where could that guy have gone that quickly. As he ponders that question he feels his cell phone vibrate, he answers the call.

"Hello this is Jesus."

"Jesus hi, this is Amy, I just wanted to know if you could meet me at my bank at 3:30 p.m. this evening. I know it's short notice, and I hope I didn't catch you at a bad time, but I have good news. My husband just transferred funds into my account, so I will be able to pay you today. A friend of mine just looked at your work, and she wants to hire you."

"Sure Amy what bank should I meet you at?"

"The Bank of America at the Renton Mall." Jesus feels as if he just hit the lottery. He is so overwhelmed with joy, he smiles all the way to the bank.

Sunday August 28th 2011
New Orleans, La. The French Quarter
11:30 a.m.

Angelica Roberts is a very young and dysfunctional girl who was recently put out of her parents' home, and cut off from their support both emotional and financial. She had gotten herself knocked up the summer before her last year of high school, and is now paying the price. She sits on a broken bed in a dirty one bedroom apartment in one of filthiest districts in New Orleans. Crying and screaming her frustrations at her new born baby. She loathes the thing in her mind, and her indifference toward it grows by the hour. She feels abandoned by everyone she has ever known, and blames the little shit in the crib for her life being ruined. She was once a very popular girl who had her whole life ahead of her, and wealthy parents behind her. She was on the cheerleading squad, fucking the most popular player on the basketball team, and she counted herself among the most beautiful girls in her school, and everybody knew it. Like most of her peers she was narcissistic, vain, and had the attitude to go with it. Like many teenage girls she was rebellious and head strong, she had to have everything her way, and she was determined to do whatever she wanted, when she wanted, and fuck the consequences. Her parents who were always too busy with their own lives to pay much attention to her only saw what they wanted to see. They had a beautiful, blonde, blue eyed little, angel who could do no wrong. So she was showered with whatever she wanted, and was rarely if ever corrected, or disciplined for misbehaving or anything else. Now she sits feeling sorry for herself and angry, wishing she never had this fucking little thing that has totally ruined her life, and won't stop it's fucking crying. Angelica feels as if she's about to go mad. None of her inner circle of friends come around, or call her anymore, her one time boyfriend is on a fast track to a major university, on a full ride basketball scholarship, and denies he's the father. He is already fucking her best friend. Angelica sits on the bed, and covers her ears, trying to silence the noise. She is trying to summon the strength to put up with its crying another day. But it won't stop crying, it cries, and cries all goddamn day, and night and it's driving her crazy. Her heart is beating faster now and her breath is short. She feels as if her head is going to explode. Angelica has reached her breaking point, in a fury induced rage she bolts to the things crib, and begins to shout at it.

"Goddamnit! Why won't you just go to sleep, and stop that damn noise! She says as she shakes the crib violently. My whole life is ruined because of you, I've lost everything I had because of you! I don't have any friends anymore, my boyfriend is gone, white shit runs out of my tits, and my parents kicked me out of the goddamn house because of you! I don't have my car, and they took all my money, I don't have anything because of your shitty little ass!"

Angelica's screaming at the baby only makes him cry louder. The baby looks in her direction, and reaches up to her still crying, as if he is asking to be picked up, but quickly pulls his little arms away, because the volume of her voice is frightening, and the more she rocks his crib the louder he cries.

"I fucking hate you! Do you hear me you little shit, I fucking hate you! Your dirty and smell like shit, and I'm sick of you, why don't you just go to sleep, and leave me the fuck alone!"

The baby just cries louder as she rants and raves at him. Shaking his crib almost to the point it falls apart. The baby doesn't understand her rage nor does he care, but Angelica see's it's crying as an act of defiance so she stops shaking the crib just before it falls apart, and snatches the crying thing out of the crib. She doesn't see a baby in her hands, her unbalanced mind tells her it's a thing to be silenced. Crying and screaming at it she starts to throw it against a wall to silence it, and just as suddenly as she snatched it up, she drops it down into the crib. It bounces on the thin mattress and continues to cry. Angelica screams at the baby again before she bolts out of the bedroom, and closes the door. She sits on a lounge chair that used to be in her room, when she lived with her parents in their large home in The Garden District. It reminds her now of all the comforts their money provided for her. When she was put out they allowed her to take some of her bedroom furniture with her, but not much else. She had only a little time to find somewhere to live, and the hole in wall she finds herself in now is all she could find.

She thought everything in her room, and in the house she use to occupy was hers, they showed her otherwise. This too she blames on that thing in the bedroom, that she can't make stop crying. She misses what she had at home, and the life she could have had if not for that little shit that won't stop making that damn noise. Angelica thinks of all this and everything that could have been hers, and it only serves to make her angrier. Covering her ears with her hands isn't blocking the noise, so she grabs two pillows, and puts them against her ears, and for a few short seconds it gives her some relief. Then the noise of its crying comes through clearly, She throws one pillow across the room, puts the other one on her lap and presses her face onto it as hard as she can. Angelica starts to cry her frustrations into the pillow, until she realizes that it's hard to breath with her face pressed into it. She raises her head up, wipes away her tears, looks at the bedroom door, and something occurs to her. A way to shut that little shits mouth forever, she looks at the pillow in her hand as if she's studying it, and she tells herself it should be over quickly. She gets up and walks toward the bedroom door. Opens it and moves straight to the crib, and the crying little shit in it. The crying infant looks up, and his little eyes focus on the pillow as it is lowered to his face. Angelica hears a loud knock on her front door just as she puts the pillow against the babies face. In fact the knocking is so loud it startles her. She looks up, pulls the pillow away from the babies face, and throws it against the wall. She momentarily stares at it crying in the crib, contempt for it all over her face.

"When I get back you little fucker your dead."

She hurries to the door, her rage only temporarily abated. She open the door to see a delivery guy of some sort. He looks like he's in his early twenties not much older than her, his looks are un-remarkable, and he's short, but his brilliant hazel eyes catch her attention. She thinks to herself a year ago she wouldn't even give someone like him a second thought, let alone find attractive in the least. For a second, even though she's angry, Angelica finds herself strangely attracted to this little guy. His clothes are very ordinary, and the large brown bag he's holding makes him look like even more of a dork, she thinks to herself.

"What do you want?" she says to the man.

"This is 404 Terrace Drive, apt. 5. I'm delivering the food someone ordered." He responds.

"You must have the wrong apartment I didn't order any food so please go away."

"Ma'am I'm certain that this is the correct address, are you sure you didn't order anything to eat." He asks.

Angelica looks at the brown paper bag the man is holding, and she realizes that she hasn't eaten in a while. The aroma coming from the bag has her empty stomach making noises of hunger, so she decides to ask him what is in the bag.

"Look I didn't order anything, but what's in the bag, I might buy it from you anyway." She says.

The delivery man tells her four mini cheeseburgers, fries, a strawberry shake, and an apple pie. Angelica's mouth starts to water and the pain of her empty stomach increase.

"How much for the food?" She asks. The young man lifts the bag so he can read the receipt.

"It'll be eleven dollars and seventy-five cents. But since you didn't order the food let's make it an even eight bucks ok." He responds.

She tells the delivery guy to wait in the hall. She closes her front door, and goes into her bedroom to get the money. Walking into her bedroom and hearing the baby cry brings back the anger that had subsided, but her stomach is screaming for the food so she ignores the baby. She gets the money, and heads back to the front door leaving the door to her bedroom open. When she opens the door the delivery guy is waiting.

"Here's twenty dollars." She says as she hands him the money, and reaches for the bag of food.

"OK just give me a few seconds to count out your change."

As the delivery guy counts her change the babies crying can be heard clearly at the door.

"That little guy sounds like he's hungry too." He says to Angelica. She flashes a weak smile, and tells him she's gonna take care of that after she eats.

"I'm a wiz when it comes to handling babies." He says.

"Is that a fact."

"Yeah I've always been good with babies, never met one yet that I couldn't handle." He tells her.

He gives Angelica her change, thanks her and starts to walk away. Angelica stands in the door for just a second longer, contemplating if he could get the little shit to shut up, long enough for her to eat her food.

"Can I ask you something? I'm feeling a little stressed right now, if you have a few minutes could you do me a really big favor. I mean since you're so good with babies would you mind helping me out with mine for just a few minutes, while I eat this." She says as she holds up the bag, again flashing a weak smile.

"Sure I've got a few minutes, I'd like to meet the baby, is it a boy or girl." He asks.

"It's a boy, and he just won't stop crying, I don't know what to do. This mother thing is new to me, and to be honest it really creeps me out."

"Oh I think I can help you with this." He responds.

Angelica steps aside and allows the delivery guy to come into her apartment. At first she feels embarrassed about the condition of her place, then her hunger gets the best of her, and she decides she doesn't care. She points to her bedroom and tells him the baby is in his crib, to just follow the noise.

"Hey what's your name?" she asks as he walks past her.

He doesn't answer her, and continues to the bedroom. Angelica sits at her table, takes the food out of the bag, and eats as if she's starving. The delivery guy walks into the bedroom and walks over to the crib. He stands above the baby and looks down on him, the crying of the child is a horrible sound to his ears. He lowers his left index finger toward the crying baby so that he can grab it. The baby takes hold of the offered finger, and gives it that gentle infant squeeze all parents know, and his crying stops. The man standing above the helpless child looks down on him, and a single tear falls down his cheek.

"You have a good grip my child, I am here little one, no harm shall come to you."

He says to the baby. The baby looks at him, and tries to smile still holding on to his finger, and reacting to the sound of the man's soothing voice. The man takes his free hand and gently rubs the babies little stomach with his finger, and the baby smiles.

"Hey! Do you mind if I change his diaper, the one he's wearing his soaked." He asks Angelica loudly.

"I don't care, there under the crib. She shouts from the other room.

"I will be right back little one." Says the man smiling as he walks away.

He goes to the table where Angelica is still eating.

"Excuse me the baby is going to need a bath, his little body is soaked in pee, and his diaper is full of poop. If you want I'll give him a bath too." He tells her.

"Go ahead I don't care, all his crap is in the bathroom." She responds.

"OK, this may take a while, but don't worry I have plenty of time, I'll have the little guy fixed up in no time."

Angelica looks at the delivery guy, and thanks him as she eats her apple pie, and finishes her milk shake. She stops long enough to ask him his name again as he walks away.

"Hey, you never did tell me your name." He stops and without turning to face her, answers her question.

"My name isn't important to you, only the wellbeing of the baby matters."

He then continues to the bedroom. Angelica looks at him walk away and thinks to herself *whatever dork, as long as you can keep that little shit quite I really could care less about your fucking name. Because as soon as you leave I'm gonna permanently shut that little shits mouth.* He goes into the bathroom and runs warm water, he looks around until he finds the towels he's going to need, and places them on top of the sink. He stands over the baby lying in the crib and smiles.

"Just a second little one and I will get you out of that diaper, and out of that soiled crib."

The baby's only response to the sound of his voice is to smile and move his little arms, and legs excitedly as he follows the man with his eyes. He looks under the crib, and finds what he needs, an infant washing tub, soap, diapers and powder. He lays out all the materials he needs for the baby on the bed. Then with the baby in the crib he unfastens the tape holding on the diaper, and lifts the smiling baby out of the crib, and lays him on a blanket on the bed. He then takes the feces filled diaper, the babies mattress cover, and sheets out of the crib, and puts them all in the garbage can next to the bed. He takes the infant bath tub, and fills it with warm water then brings it back into the bedroom, and places it on a table.

"Come little one lets rinse your tender skin under the warm running water."

He takes the baby into the bathroom, and puts him under the faucet allowing the warm water to run over his skin, the baby happily chews on his closed hand. The urine and feces stains quickly rinse away from the baby's body.

"Does the water feel good little one." He says to the now cooing and smiling baby as he turns his little body under the water several times. He lets the water run on the baby's head and neck, and his little arms and legs flex with joy at the feel of the warm water.

"Ah, you like this don't you little one, the water feels good?" He says to the baby.

Even as he enjoys the water the baby's eyes are locked on the man bathing him.

"That's enough running water little one, it's now time for us to cleanse your skin with soap."

He holds the baby with one arm, and turns off the running water. He then takes the baby, and gently places him in the bath water. The baby bath is made so that the infant can be placed in the water on his back, the babies bottom rests on a built-in seat so the water doesn't rise above the baby's nipple line. Everywhere the man moves in the room the babies eyes follow him. The baby splashes his arms in the water with joy, and smiles when the man sits in front of him. What is reflected in the baby's eyes is wondrous.

"Yes little one, you can see me as I truly am, all infants can. It is the reason why all babies smile as they do, and are at peace. You also see a spark of what I am in your parents as well. Just as I am here with you now my son, I am with every child everywhere. When you dream I am with you, and when you wake I am always close. He communicates with the baby wordlessly as he washes his little body.

"Yes, I can hear your thoughts my child as well as feel the joy you feel now. Even though you cannot verbally speak to me now, I know what is in your heart. No little one words are un-necessary

between us, I understand you perfectly, and you hear my voice in your mind. As with all my innocents, you know the joy of life and of love, which is as I intended it to be. No my son I cannot allow your mother to see me as you do. There is a reason why I do not allow myself to be seen by adults as you see me. Adults see what they want to see, and I do not interfere with their perceptions. After a certain age, and level of maturity has been reached people's views are molded by their experiences, and what they are taught. In other words my son adult pride and arrogance blinds them to me, it will one day happen with you as well. But your attachment to me is never truly broken. But you must bond with your parents and each other, it pains me to allow this little one but it is necessary. For me to do otherwise would be arrogant of me, justified or not, and it would hinder man's growth with knowledge he will never be ready for. Even your memory of me little one will fade in time, which is as it should be. As much as I love you, even I have to let you go, but I will always exists in your heart in ways you do not understand, just know I will still be there." He tells the baby and touches his little chest with a finger. *Yes my child, as much as it pains me you must be allowed to walk your own path, just as all men must but we will meet again in the distant future. Your mother also knew me at your age, but there comes a time when even I have to let my children go. She is sleeping now, but your mother is herself very young, and like most young people she has not yet discovered her reason for being or her place in life."*

"No my child, right and wrong do not apply to you. You have done absolutely nothing wrong little one. Do not think that she doesn't love you, she doesn't know how yet, but that is why I am here. I want you to know that your mother does indeed love you. She is just lost and frightened now. Yes I know you understand little one, you will see all will be as it should be. Do not worry about your mother she is alright my child, she is resting now, locked in the calming embrace of sleep. I will help her come to know how special the bond between a mother, and her child is, and what it means to truly love herself and you my son, the life that grew inside her body. I will see to it that one so young never knows fear again. I have much to do in your world my son, I want the world that you and your brothers inherit to be far different from that of your parents, and their parents before them, it is your birthright to live in a world free of violence, and hate, but it will not be easy. If I am

successful, your world will be a true paradise my child, but the choice rests with man, and I hope I never have to call upon you to fulfill your intended purpose. Now it is time to get you out of the water little one, I will dry you off, and put you in something comfortable."

The baby responds to his voice by shaking his hands and making sounds as if he is trying to talk. When he is laid on the bed the baby's eyes lock on his, and then he reaches upward to be held by him still smiling that big baby smile, as if knowing his time with this person is coming to an end. He gives the baby his finger as he speaks.

"I am not leaving you little one I have to get your clothes on." The man says smiling back at the baby. The baby smiles, and his little body moves excitedly on the bed, his eyes follow the man as he moves around the room. He places a pacifier in the baby's mouth, pours a little baby oil in his hands, and gently rubs it on the baby's skin. Every touch of the baby's skin brings an excited reaction from the child. He sprinkles a little powder on the baby, puts on a fresh diaper then dresses him in a little T-shirt and socks. After that is done he goes about straightening up Angelica's messy bedroom, and fixing all the broken furniture. He quickly finishes Angelica's room, and sits on the bed with the baby. He picks the baby up and lays him on top of his thighs.

"Now I have a question for you little one, can you tell me your name? That is very good my son, yours is a very old and honorable name and it happens to be one of my favorites. No little one it is not possible for your mother to speak to you as I do. People are not even aware that infants are capable of this level of communication. You are all born with this capacity, but long ago your ancestors chose oral speech. A form of communication that was meant to be used with the other animals of this world. This was another gift man rejected, and now infants loose this ability as they begin to speak their first words. It is part of the reason why infants must bond with their parents, especially their mothers." He says to the baby and smiles.

"Are you ready to meet your mother my child?" He asks the baby, the babies eyes never leave his. *"You don't need to be afraid of her, I will be with you. I promise no harm will come to you, but you are hungry little one, and you need to be fed. Yes I could feed you myself,but it is time that your mother learns to do it correctly while she can, it is very important for both of you, I will show her how."*

The baby's eyes never leave his and the child feels such joy that his smile seems a permanent part of his face.

"The joy you feel now little one you will feel with your mother, and just as you trust me you will trust her, she will be your biggest fan, and greatest protector and I will still be watching over you as well. Now my son let's go wake your mother and get you fed."

He puts the baby against his chest and holds him there with both hands, and walks into the living room of the apartment. Angelica is at the table with her head on top of her arms sitting in the same chair she was in earlier sound asleep.

"You see Michael your mother is alright she is just tired, when she wakes from her peaceful slumber things will be different, now let's wake her up."

He tells the baby this without saying a word. Holding the baby with one arm he walks over to Angelica, and gently rubs her shoulder until she wakes up. Slowly she comes to her senses, and looks at the man holding her baby.

"Oh your still here, how long was I asleep?" Angelica asks him and looks over at the clock, she can't remember when she went to sleep.

"A little while now, I didn't want to wake you. I didn't mind staying with the baby. I think he's hungry though, you need to feed him."

"Since you're still here can you do that for me, I'm not good at that, and every time I do feed him he goes right back to crying. Come to think of it he must really like you because he's not crying now."

"I told you I have a way with babies, haven't met one yet that didn't like me. And me and Michael have been getting along just fine since you've been sleep Angelica."

"How do you know his name, I don't remember telling you that? Or my name for that matter." She says.

"Michael here told me when I asked him." He says and laughs.

Angelica looks at the little man holding her baby, and laughs out loud, she doesn't know why, but the thought of a baby talking she finds hilarious considering that all hers does is cry.

"Ok a baby who can only make noise and cry told you our names, ok I'll buy it. He really likes you though he is so quite." She says in amazement.

"He won't be for long unless you feed him."

"Can you do it for me please he seems to really like you?" asks Angelica.

"I'll tell you what, you take him, and I'll get a bottle ready." He tells Angelica. He moves toward her to give her the baby and Angelica hesitates for a second.

"What if he starts to cry, what do I do?" she asks.

"I'm here don't worry I'll show you what to do." He says as he gives Angelica the baby.

As the baby's head is lifted off his shoulders he looks right at the man, and his wide smile instantly turns to a frown, and he starts to cry as he is handed to his mother.

"Do not worry little one I am here, I'm going to show your mother the proper way to hold and feed you, everything will be alright."

He hands the baby to his mother, and asks where she keeps his bottles and formula. Angelica tells him and he goes about preparing a bottle. He looks at how Angelica is holding the baby, and asks her a question.

"Why do you look so uncomfortable when you hold him?" He asks her.

"Like I told you I'm not very good at this, and I don't think he likes me." She replies.

"No that's not true you are his mother he knows nothing but love for you. Hear let me help you, there are a few tricks to holding a baby, and you need to learn them all." He tells her. He walks over to Angelica and takes the baby from her. She notices the baby's reaction instantly.

"You see you have to cradle the little guy in your arms like this, and at the same time you must support his head, that's very important because one so young cannot hold his head straight."

"You see how I'm holding him against my chest, now when you feed him you want to use one arm to support his whole body, and his head like this. And when you hold him in both hands to play with him while standing him up, you support him like this, remembering that he cannot stand on his own now."

"Wow, you really know what you're doing, but you look way too young to have kids of your own." She says.

"I come from a large family we learned to handle babies early; we all had to help out." He responds.

He demonstrates numerous ways to hold the baby. In addition, how to support his head with each position. He watches Angelica practice each hold until he is sure she has the technique correct.

"He smells so good, what did you clean him with?"

"You only need to use mild soap, and warm, not hot water to cleanse his skin, then you can apply a little baby oil or powder." He tells her.

As Angelica holds her baby she feels the weight and warmth of his little body and his slight movements against her chest. She also realizes something else she never noticed before, there is a very pleasant smell coming from his little body that is not the perfumed smell of soap and baby oil. She doesn't know what it is, and she wonders why she never noticed it before, but it is relaxing. The baby squirms under her hands and she pulls him back just enough until his hands touch her face, and as he does he smiles at her, and their eyes lock. As Angelica looks into her babies eyes she notices something else that she hadn't before. There is an innate link this little person has for her, and the smile on his face is one of pure uncontaminated affection. There are no strings attached, ulterior motives, nor hidden agendas, she knows that what he feels for her is a pure love, the kind only a child can give, and a love that is precious beyond anything she has ever felt. She pulls her baby back to her chest, and gently holds him there and closes her eyes.

"Angelica the bottle is almost ready I'll go into the bedroom and get a blanket, and a small towel. I'll be right back." He tells her but Angelica doesn't respond. He returns to the living room, and sits in a chair next to Angelica.

"Angelica is formula the only thing you feed him? it's ok, and it will do the trick because he's only a few months old, but you might want to consider breast feeding him too." He tells her.

"I've never thought about that before what's the big deal? Isn't the formula the same thing." She asks as she holds the baby, not realizing at first that she is holding him against her breast.

"It's not that Angelica a mother's breast milk contains antibodies, and other things that are good for your baby. Store bought formula doesn't compare to a mother's milk. You can do both if you like, but breast feeding is very healthy for him." He tells her.

"I wouldn't know what to do, I didn't really know how to hold him until you showed me." She replies.

"I'll tell you what, I have to leave in a minute anyway, I'll tell you what you need to do, and the rest will come natural to you. You really should try breast feeding him, according to my mother it is a natural intimate experience between a mother, and child that brings them closer like nothing else can." Angelica brings the baby down and cradles him in her arms looking at his face and she smiles.

"Ok what do I have to do?" She says looking at her baby.

"I'll take the little guy for a minute while you go get yourself ready. You need to wash your breasts with warm water, and if you like put on a button down shirt or anything you can pull up to give him your breast." Angelica gives him the baby and goes into the bedroom. When she hands the baby to him he once again squirms with excitement and smiles widely.

"See little one, I told you everything would be fine, your mother is starting to feel the emotions of motherhood, and her connection with you has been awakened. Remember little one I will be with you even when your mother cannot see me. So it is not as if I'm leaving you, you have not yet reached that time."

Angelica turns the water off, dry's herself and puts on her bathrobe. She looks at herself in the mirror, and wonders how her baby sees her. She wonders does he see her as a giant, someone he knows, does he see her as his mother, or what. She ties her robe shut and goes into the living room.

"Will this do?" she asks.

"Yes that will do nicely, now when you do this you need to be comfortable, and if possible in a quiet place, that's not always possible, but you'll work it out. Now you sit down, place this towel in your lap, and take the baby. Remember how I showed you, when you hold him support his head. You can cradle him in your arms, and feed him at the same time." He explains to her.

"Ok I'm ready what do I do now?"

"I'll stand behind you, since you have him on your left side start with your left breast. All you have to do is put the nipple in his mouth and he'll do the rest." He tells her.

Angelica is hesitant at first, she thinks about the man standing behind her instructing her on how to breast-feed her baby. A complete stranger to her, then she thinks to herself he has been nothing, but kind to her, and her baby. He even watched Michael when she went to sleep. She realizes that he is no threat to her or the baby. In fact she feels totally comfortable with him, as if she's known him all her life. Angelica brings her baby to her breast and gives him the nipple, he starts to suckle immediately. Angelica smiles as she looks down on her baby feeding from her body.

"He's doing it, he's actually drinking from me." She says.

"Yes he is and you should try to feed him this way at least twice a day. You can mix in the formula with breast feeding that's not a problem." He explains.

"Angelica it's getting a little late and I think you have things here under control, so I'm gonna leave you two alone now." He tells her.

She quickly turns her head as far as she can without disturbing the baby.

"No, please don't leave yet, I have so many questions to ask you. You've been so kind to us can't you stay a little while longer." She pleads.

He stands and walks to her bathroom, when he comes back he stands behind Angelica and lightly places a towel over her exposed breast and the baby's head. Then he sits down in front of her.

"Remember if you find yourself having to feed him in public this is how you should do it. Breast feeding still makes some people uncomfortable in public."

"How will I know when he's had enough? How will I know if I run out of breast milk to feed him? I don't know, will feeding him like this ruin my body? What do I do when he's finished drinking? I have a thousand question I need you to answer for me." She says. He laughs in a very pleasant manner before answering her question.

"Hold on Angelica let's take it one at a time, I may be good at handling babies, but you should be talking to my mother, I only know what she's told me about this kind of thing, but I'll do my best. As you two grow together there are ways to tell when he's hungry, crying is one indication, but you have to put him on a feeding schedule. You can tell when he's full by watching his reactions, he may spit the milk out, not take your nipple or try to turn away. Remember all that means is he's full. After he has eaten you have to burp him, you hold him on your shoulder with his stomach against your body, and gently pat his back, you'll hear him make a sound and that's it. Chances are he'll go right to sleep, you have to do that for about six months then he can burp himself. Angelica you can breast feed him for a couple years, how long you do it is up to you. It will not ruin your breasts or your shape, in fact you're gonna be surprised how soon you get your figure back. If you don't mind my saying you look good now. There is no need to be afraid Angelica you will learn all these things, my mother says with a little patience it'll all come to you naturally." He tells her.

"That's the problem I don't have anybody to teach me, you've shown me more in a few hours, than I've learned in a month and I appreciate it, I really do." She tells him.

"I think he's finished I feel milk running down my stomach."

"He probably is, wipe his mouth and I'll stay until you burp him just so that I'm sure you know what you're doing."

After Angelica burps the baby she cradles him in her arms, and watches as he quickly fades to sleep.

"You see that wasn't so difficult now was it." He says.

"No actually it was nice, it made me feel, I don't know special I guess. To know that he depends on me, and that he needs me to take care of him, and that he loves me with all my faults, he loves me." She tells him.

She looks at the man sitting across from her and she feels as if she can tell him anything. That he would gladly listen to what she had to say, and would understand her feelings. She feels as if he's the friend she never had, but always needed.

"Angelica I have to leave now I think you, and the little guy will be ok from here on out." He tells her.

"Before you leave can you please tell me your name, I'd like for you to come over again when you have some time. Maybe tomorrow you can bring me lunch, and you can see Michael too."

Her eyes move to the sleeping baby in her arms, and as she wonders at his little features tears start to fall from her eyes. She makes no outward sounds to express the sadness that has come over her. She watches her baby sleep, and a steady stream of tears fall down her face.

"Angelica what's wrong, why are you crying, do you want me to take the baby?" He asks her. Angelica responds by shaking her head, she has to give voice to the overwhelming rush of emotion she now feels.

"I feel so guilty and ashamed now for something I was gonna do, I can't believe now that I even thought about hurting him. Before you knocked on my door I was so frustrated, and couldn't make him stop crying, that I thought I was losing my mind. I was gonna take a pillow and smother him to make him stop crying." She looks at her sleeping son in her arms and says to herself over and over that she is so sorry for what she was thinking.

"Angelica please look at me, you do not need to torture yourself with guilt over your earlier thoughts and feelings, over what might have been. It is understandable that at the time you felt truly overwhelmed physically and emotionally. Believe it or not sometimes it takes an extreme emotional event to help us change who we are." He tells her and then wipes away her tears.

"What would I have done to him though if you hadn't knocked on my door? I can't imagine him not in my life now, I have never loved anything, or anyone like this before I know that now. He is so innocent and precious, and I know he loves me too."

"Yes, Angelica he does love you unconditionally and without reservation, it is up to you to nurture him and to guide him until he is capable of taking care of himself." He tells her.

"I don't know what to say except thank you, so much for helping me understand what being a mother really is. I don't know what I'd have done if it wasn't for you."

"How do I pay you for what you've shown me? Please tell me your name, will I ever see you again?" She asks.

"Angelica the only thing of importance here now is the child you are holding, and the love you both have for each other. The feelings that have been awakened in you for Michael are what matters. I heard a baby cry when you opened your door, you let me help you with him. I am no one of importance, and the only payment you can offer me is for you to love your son."

Angelica wakes up on her chair with Michael still sleeping in her arms. She looks down on him and smiles. She whispers in his ear that she loves him, and kisses him on the cheek.

"Come on Michael mama's gonna put her baby to bed then she's gonna turn in too."

She puts him in his crib, and kisses him once more then leaves the room when she hears her cell phone ring. She looks at the phone and sees the number is her mothers. Michael sleeps peacefully and hears a very comforting voice in his mind.

"Rest well little one, all is as it should be."

Monday August 29th 2011.
Tempe, Arizona
12:30 a.m.

Dr. Fillip Gooding is a brilliant criminal psychiatrist and chemist who has practiced his particular craft at the same facility for the past twenty years. Some in his field would say that he is privileged beyond belief, to work with the particular subjects he does. Others though would condemn him, and the agency he works for concerning that very same work. Few in the government know the nature of the work he's involved in, and fewer still would want to acknowledge they even exist. The work he's involved in is highly dangerous, and highly classified. Very few outside his facility even know what he does. Even the location of his facility is classified. In recent days however Dr. Gooding has experienced something he has not encountered in all the years he's practiced psychiatry, and it has him puzzled. Rarely has he encountered a situation in his field of study that he cannot solve or explain. So on this night, as he's driving home he decides to stop at the only diner along his route, to get something to eat, and to give serious thought to what he's recently encountered, and what the world is experiencing. He likes the food at this particular place, and at this hour it should be nice and quiet. Which is the way he likes it, when he needs to study a problem? Dr. Gooding parks his car and walks into the Diner, and just as he knew it would be, the place is quite with few customers. The first person he sees is the owner at the counter.

"Hey Max how's it going tonight."

"Hey doc how you doin'? Cup of tea to get you started."

"That's fine, I'll sit at the counter" He tells Max.

"One cup of tea coming up, you want to see a menu Doc, or will it be the usual."

"I'll have my usual in about thirty minutes; I need to go over some notes first. I've encounter some very unusual shit the last couple days that has me puzzled." He tells Max.

"Finally run into something you can't solve ha doc?"

"I didn't say I couldn't, it may take a little time, but I'll figure it out." He says laughing. Dr. Gooding takes a seat at the end of the counter, and opens the folder he is carrying. He opens the folder, and flips the pages inside, until he comes to a small binder containing his day's notes. He turns to where he stopped earlier, takes out his pen, and continues writing where he left off at his lab.

I must admit to being faced with an enigma, today patient's one thru seven all showed remarkable improvement in both conduct and demeanor. In fact I'd say that if I didn't know them, I'd think they were completely sane individuals, were I to meet any of them on the street. There is no known phenomenon that explains sudden complete personality reversal from the psychotic to what society considers the norm. I have worked with these patients for years now, studying their behaviors, and idiosyncrasies, both on and off behavior modification drugs. While chemical modification does work for these particular patients, it has proven to be only a temporary solution in the past.

The current experimental drugs I've developed and administered to these patients for years would no doubt, cure thousands of less mentally disturbed patients permanently, of all aberrant traits, and behaviors. I've proven that in other human experiments, my drug's effectiveness was verified shortly after I developed, and tested the first compound.

My current drug however, still needs further tests, refinement, and verification; although it is potentially much more promising than my first drug. The time is almost right to release my findings, but I won't until I can cash in on my work, and complete my current study. The fact that my new drug has no side effects that I've been able to detect thus far might explain this new behavior in my patients. Further research is needed; scans of the brains for each of these patients show nothing anomalous in their chemical make-up, which was not the case only a week ago. Still, for years my drugs effects have only been temporary on these particular patients. I need to find out what has caused this change to occur; now though, their tests results say they are cured, and perfectly normal. They show no signs of their former deviant traits, but cured or not, these abominations will never be allowed to go free.

"Here you go Doc, you want me to wait a bit before I fix your food?" Max asks. The doctor looks up from his notes before he answers.

"Thanks Max, give me ten more minutes before you fix the food, I'm almost done here, I just need to finish a few more thoughts, and I'm gonna give this shit a rest."

"Sure doc whatever you want, no problem." Max responds.

After a few more minutes the doctor puts away his notes, and tells Max he'll be right back, after he puts his notebook in his car, and takes a smoke. The doctor hadn't noticed that since he's been in the diner, a few other customers have come in, one sits at the counter while others sit at the tables.

"Hey doc you forget, at this hour I allow my customers to smoke at the counter, I know it's early in the morning, but it's still hot as hell out there."

"That's right I forgot, in that case I'll be back in a second." As the doctor leaves the diner another man walks in, and takes a seat at the counter.

"What can I get you for?" Max asks the new customer.

"I'll have a coke please."

"Would you like a menu?" Max asks.

"No the soda will do for now." The man responds.

The doctor comes back in, and takes his seat at the counter, he says hello to the other man sitting at the counter, and lights a cigarette as Max comes over and joins him.

"So Max how was your day, business running at full steam?" The doctor asks him.

"Yeah Doc I can't complain, we did pretty good today, hell if it keeps up, I might sell the joint, and retire back to New York."

"Max how long have you been saying that same shit, I've known you for a few years now, and we both know you're too attached to this place to sell. Besides if you leave who am I going to talk to in the wee hours of the morning, shit this is part of my routine don't fuck that up now Max." Says the doctors as both men laugh.

"I don't know doc I miss New York, the grime, the crime, all that crap. As fucked up as it can be, its still home. But I have gotten use to the quite of Arizona too. I gotta admit it's not a bad trade off, and working the night shift gets me outta the house when I don't wanna be bothered with the old lady." Says Max.

"How's she doing by the way, I don't see her as much when she's running the place in the mornings."

"She's doing fine; her sister is coming down for a few weeks, so she's looking forward to that but I'm not. I tried to talk her into taking her ass to Detroit, but she hates it up there. Thinks a change in scenery will do her sister some good after an ugly divorce from that asshole she was married to." Both men laugh.

"Hey Max! delivery is here out back." A voice in the kitchen yells.

"Hey Doc I gotta go take care of this. It'll be a while so when you're ready to eat let Kenny know, and he'll hook you right up." Says Max.

"Go ahead and tell him to place the order for me now."

"Sure doc I'll be back before you leave." Max tells him, and walks away to handle his delivery.

The doctor turns his attention to the TV. He hears a breaking news report, of a suspected serial rapist in the Tempe area who turned himself in to police just a short time ago. The report goes on to say, that this individual could be the long sought after suspect the media dubbed The Tempe Terror. This man is suspected of committing over thirty brutal sexual attacks on woman, in the Tempe area; attacks over a period of four years, leaving nine of the women dead, and the city living in fear. He has eluded capture by the police for years, and law enforcement officials are baffled as to why he turned himself in. In fact, law enforcement officials all over the country, from the FBI, to State, and local officials have been inundated by criminals of all types turning themselves in to the authorities. The local news report goes on to say, that at the 9:00 a.m. hour, there will be a full report on these breaking stories. The news goes to commercial, and the doctor takes out his phone, types a lengthy message and hits send.

"That is most interesting wouldn't you say friend." Says the man sitting next to the doctor. The doctor turns and faces the man who just spoke to him.

"Are you referring to the news story on the serial rapist?" He replies.

"Yes, I wonder why after so many years such a man would voluntarily turn himself in to the police." Says the man.

"There are a number of factors involved that could lead to someone like him, or other categories of criminals turning themselves in to the authorities. I for one am just happy to know that, if this is the serial rapist the report claims, that he is finally behind bars where he belongs. In my opinion people like him should never be allowed to walk the streets, they should be caught, thoroughly studied, and put to death."

"You don't believe that these people could be helped in any way to change their criminal behaviors." Asks the man.

"There are those that could be helped, but whether or not counseling, and drug therapy would be effective depends on several factors; the two most important being the individual, and his or her psychological make-up. Today's therapies are not always effective on some of the more extreme types of individual personality disorders."

"You sound as if you know a great deal about this subject." Responds the man.

"Actually I do, Criminal Psychiatry is my field of study, but even todays best known treatments simply will not cure most hardened criminals. I am all for treating those that respond to therapy, those that don't are a burden on our society, resources, and should be put down like the feral animals they have become, because those are societies nightmares like this serial rapist."

"It's interesting to hear a doctor say that, as a clinician I always thought it was the job of men such as yourself, and your colleagues' to help even those individuals who are afflicted with difficult, even impossible conditions. To condone killing, simply because science can't cure their behavior sounds a bit draconian. I only say this because, I believe that there is good in everyone, even the most harden criminal."

"Well my friend, I'm more on the research end of medicine, and I study society's worst sociopaths. Please don't take offense to what I'm about to say, but you sound like a clergyman, or someone who is simply out of touch with the real world. Believe me, I wish it were that simple to cure the anti-social behavior we see in our society, and around the world. But people are complicated beings, with complex mental issues, and when they go anti-social it takes time, money, resources, and knowledge to address their issues. Our governments simply don't want to make the necessary sacrifices, to address the problems of crime, and anti-social behavior in today's societies."

"I am not in the clergy, but like you, I am an intelligent individual who simply doesn't condone killing for any reason, and I believe that one day society will be able to deal with this problem, without resorting to death penalties, or extreme solitary confinement. Doctor how do you explain reports of criminals suddenly, and unexpectedly turning themselves in for their crimes."

"I don't have an answer for that, but it is something that needs to be looked at. Nothing like this has ever happened on the scale the news is reporting, so it's an interesting phenomenon."

The doctor feels his phone vibrate, and excuses himself to read an incoming message.

Once we verify that the locals have The Tempe Terror in custody, we will arrange to have him moved to your facility for study. The message ends.

"Doctor I'd like to ask you a question, since you approach this issue from a research stand point. When do you think human drug trials cross the line, from being medically necessary to immoral?" He asks the doctor.

"Well before any drug is allowed to be used in this country, it has to have the approval of the Food and Drug Administration, and it undergoes rigorous testing for safety. The process of drug approval for human use can takes years, and from the research end studies can take decades. Eventually human trials become necessary to study a drug's effects, and negative side effects on the body. In medicine, there is no way around human trials, when developing medications to be used by people. Without them we can't advance our understanding, and knowledge in medicine. Many do believe that human trials are immoral, and unethical, as a man of science I don't share those beliefs. If they help us to find cures, and advance our knowledge I'm all for them, I'm a scientist not an ethicist, so I don't have a problem with those issues."

"Well doctor I guess when it comes to your own medical research, no matter how well intentioned your motives, for you, the ends justify the means; in your mind, and those of the men you work for, at The Institute for Criminal Studies. What about the men that you, yourself use, in your own experiments. Do they deserve to be treated as nothing more than laboratory subjects?" Asks the man.

The doctor looks at the man, and focuses on his eyes. The doctor's facial response to the questions does not betray his reaction to the question, but he feels anger, then his own curiosity takes over.

"Just who the hell are you friend, and how do you come by your information?" asks the doctor.

"I am no one of consequence; I just want to know how a man such as you, cannot see that what you are doing is wrong. No matter how noble your motive, what you do is barbaric in a civilized society."

"I'll tell you what's barbarous, barbarous is a man who captures, tortures, and consumes his victims organ by organ. Barbarous is a man who lures young boys to his home, sexually tortures, kills, and buries them in his basement. Barbarous is a man who charms his way into women's lives, then brutally rapes them, cuts off their breasts while they are still alive, and watches them bleed to death. Barbarous is a man who convinces himself he's not a homosexual by capturing, drugging, and cutting off the penises of gay men then eating them. Barbarous is a female nurse, and her husband who kept captured young woman in a sub-basement in their home. Used her own husband's sperm to impregnate the young women. Sells the babies to desperate childless couple on the black market; and when the malnourished young woman can't become pregnant anymore, their throats are slit, and their bodies dismembered. Would you like me to go on?"

As the doctor speaks about these acts of horror, the man's expression never changes. He appears as serene after the doctor finishes, as when he started. The doctor continues.

"This world is filled with psychopaths, who commit all manner of horrendous crimes. The general public doesn't have a clue what's loose on the streets of America. Do you know that there are hundreds of sociopaths, serial killers, rapist, and mass murderers roaming the streets of this country? There is no way to know who they all are, until they carry out their crimes. Or are caught for the gruesome crimes they commit against their fellow citizens." The doctor says with emphasis to make a point as he continues.

"Law Enforcement can't stop them before they kill, and slaughter their victims, which they see as sheep. Unlike your run-of-the-mill mass murderer, who carries out his or her agenda of slaughtering as many innocent people as they can; in one quick act of violence, and then blows their own fucking brains out. Serial killers are almost never caught alive,

264

on rare occasions though the police get lucky, and a few are caught. What's interesting is they are caught, because they want to be. They allow themselves to get sloppy, they can't stop themselves, and it's like a call for help, and they happily surrender to police. When these vicious psychopaths are captured, it does society no good to execute them, their crimes are history, and they are far too valuable from a research perspective. There is a wealth of data that can be gathered, studied, and used to help us to identify those individuals who are likely to kill. We can use that data to prevent these horrors in the future, and to develop treatments if possible for whatever illness causes these behaviors. Our government has come to realize the necessity of this kind of research. So among my patients are Jeffrey Dahmer, John Wayne Gacy, Ted Bundy, Richard Ramirez the Night Stalker, David Berkowitz the Son of Sam, The Zodiac Killer, and Rodney Alcala. The government allowed the public to believe, some of these fucking monsters have been executed. It gave the people, and the victim's families closure believing their babies killers were put to death for their crimes."

"I understand that the men in your custody, have committed terrible crimes against their fellow man, but how is what's being done to them anymore humane then the crimes they committed against others. Does any man deserve to be held in captivity in secret, and experimented on against their will?"

Before the doctor can answer the question his order is brought to the counter. He looks at the man he's talking to, and asks him would he like to continue their conversation at one of the booths. The doctor takes out his cell phone, keys in a code and presses send. Then picks up his food, and the men move to a table at the farthest corner from the counter; the doctor faces the door, and the men continue their conversation.

"Now let me answer an earlier question you asked concerning my subjects. Our government sanctions what I do. My work is necessary scientific research that will have long lasting benefits for society. My subjects on the other hand should consider themselves lucky they aren't dead. They live so that I can complete research that furthers our knowledge of criminal psychotic behavior. If I could turn their asses over to the families of their victims when I'm done with them, I would without hesitation or remorse. As far as I am concerned they no longer deserve to be considered human. But they will live out their lives away from anyone, that could be harmed by them, or who would kill them. I don't know you, and I don't know how you know about the nature of my research. We will discuss that in length, but let me pose a question to you, before we continue this most interesting, and forbidden conversation. Having had this conversation with you, do you think I'm going to allow you to leave here, with what you know, without you telling me how you know these things?" The doctor says with a slight smile.

"I am aware of a great many things that occur in this country, and around the world. I do not agree with the wars that are fought around the world, or for the reasons man wages such conflicts. I am aware of the great amount of needless suffering that occurs everywhere, and of the need to help put an end to it. I am aware of man's violence against his brother that goes unchecked everywhere. It doesn't take much to see what is happening in the world for one whose eyes are opened. It just disturbs me that a man of your genius would not see beyond personal profit, when your work at its current stage could help thousands, and I know you, because I've followed your work. I told you earlier that I am not in the clergy, and that is true. But I'd like to know, do you believe in God doctor? Do you think that God would want the world to be as it is today? Do you believe that your talents and skills are solely a product of your own hard work and study? Do you believe that sometimes an individual's intellect can be so far above the norm that it can't be explained?" Asks the man.

"I don't believe in God now, nor have I ever held any such beliefs. I can't speak for what such a being if it exists, would want from any of us, nor would I waste any energy contemplating that question. As far as my intellect goes, that was indeed cultivated through hard work and hard study. I know many brilliant men in various fields of study from medicine to particle physics. The world is full of intelligent people from the average to the extraordinary. I do suspect it's been that way throughout recorded history, and I attribute none of that to any higher power than man himself."

Before the doctor finished his last statement he felt his phone vibrate as a car pulled into the diner's parking lot. Shortly afterward two men come in, and sit at the counter. The doctor is facing the entrance to the diner, so he sees the two men come inside, and look in his direction.

"Doctor Gooding what would you say, if I told you I know why that serial rapist turned himself in today to the authorities, and so many others who have committed crimes have also turned themselves in. Would you be interested in knowing the answer to that question?"

"Actually my friend, I would be interested in hearing your perspective concerning today's events. However, I doubt very seriously anything you say would be based on any scientific facts that could be verified. So while I'd love to hear the shit you have to say, I'll find my own answers." The doctor says as he smiles.

"Alright Dr. Gooding I understand, and I am truly disappointed you feel that way, if you'll excuse me I need to go to the rest room." The man says as he gets up to leave the table. The doctor tells him the restroom is straight down the hall on his left.

"Hey, you never did tell me your name, or how you knew mine without me telling you."

The man stops half way to the bathroom door, and responds to the doctor's question without turning around.

"I told you earlier I am no one you need worry about. I've always known you, it is simply sad that your great intellect has not enlightened you, and all men like you. But unlike so many recently, you doctor, will remember every word, and every second of our conversation this morning." He goes in the bathroom, and the door closes behind him.

The doctor quickly waves to the two men who are sitting at the counter. When they get to him the doctor gives them a quick description. He tells the agents he's a Native American male, with thick black straight hair. They are told to go into the bathroom, and bring the man inside to the institute for questioning. The doctor tells them he will meet them there. The doctor quickly gets up from his table, and walks to the counter. He pays his tab, and prepares to leave the diner when the agents turn the corner, and tell him there is no one in the men's room.

Tuesday August 29th 2011
Parrish County, Alabama
4:00 p.m.

Seth Carpenter lives in a small backwater town miles away from everything, and all but forgotten by the world at large. Even when the town was thriving in the 40's and 50's its population stayed small. This was the kind of small rural community where everybody knew everybody else, and the people who lived here were lifelong residents who normally died here. This was not a town where outsiders were welcomed. Visitors who stopped in town, on their way to the larger cities surrounding his town, did so because this was the last stop for miles if a traveler found himself in need of gasoline, food or water. The small general store and the gas station use to do good business. Many travelers that drove down the highway would see the stores advertisements along the way, and would come into town, buy what they needed and move on.

But many rural towns of that day had a dark side, unknown to the world at large. And like every rural town of its kind in America, this one's secrets live until its last resident dies. In this town there were always those who were not wanted.

The people who lived here were not shy about letting outsiders know, who was, and was not welcomed. They kept things simple, if you weren't white you were not wanted period, and even some whites were met with suspicion. Seth remembers growing up, that when black travelers pulled up to his father's gas station, they were told to move on. Many times he heard his father tell them that he didn't serve niggers at his station and that if they wanted to live to see another day, to not go into town either. It was almost like he was the towns look out for the unwanted, because you had to pass the station before reaching town. He would screen the drivers as they pulled up, welcoming those that were permitted, and turning away the undesirables. Seth recalls with perfect clarity.

Many niggers back then did what they were told, and moved on, but a few found the balls to go into town anyway, where they'd run into signs everywhere that read we don't serve niggers in this town. They'd soon get the picture, and haul their black asses away as fast as they could. Seth thinks to himself and smiles. Seth remembers the first time his father took him hunting. He was ten years old, and even then he had his own .22 caliber rifle. His father and some of his friends, including the Sheriff would go hunting together on many occasions. On one trip he was told by his father, that they were going on a coon hunt, and it was time he learned how to shoot a coon. Being a child he assumed at first that they were going to hunt raccoons.

He recalls that first hunt, and how shocked he was when he learned it was people, not animals they hunted. He also recalls that during that first coon hunt, when they had the nigger cornered in the woods. It was his father that ordered him to "shoot that nigger in the head boy, be a man son, and make me proud." Seth remembers it took two shots to the niggers head to kill him. That wasn't his last experience with murder, or other crimes, to which his father introduced him. Seth recalls soon after he killed his first nigger, he had come home from school one day, to his father beating his mother to a bloody pulp. The next morning she was dead. Seth always knew it was his father that killed her, but they never talked about her death, even up to the day he died. Years later, at the age of sixteen his first sexual experience was the rape of a black woman; who found herself in the wrong place, at the wrong time. Again it was his father that introduced him to sex, in the most violent way possible. A young black woman stopped at the gas station to ask for directions, and to use the restroom. He recalls how his father just walked in behind her, fucked her in the bathroom, and after he was done he called me in, and told me to fuck her as he held her down. We let that black bitch go, because we knew she wasn't going to say anything, and even if she did, back then we knew no one would believe her, or care.

Seth sits in the rundown living room, of the home he grew up in, and wonders why memories he hasn't thought of; or cared about in years are coming back to him now. He tells himself that he doesn't give a damn about all the niggers he's killed, and raped over the years. It was fun killing the men, and fucking the women when he could, he tells himself black whores have good juicy pussy. He thinks to himself he never killed any white people, so in his mind he's done nothing wrong. Who cares about dead niggers anyway, they do a fine job of killing each other. The only regret he has is that after a while his killing and raping had to stop, because he would have gotten caught. Seth thinks to himself he didn't want to go to prison. Especially, after the law gave those niggers the same rights as whites. Besides his father had taught him how to kill, without being caught, and as much fun as it was there would come a time when he had to quit.

Seth stopped killing for many years after his father died, but the hate that was instilled in him for niggers still burns to this day. He blames them for his home being in a ghost town, and for everything bad that's ever happened in his life. He misses his father, and promised himself that after his father passed away, that he would keep the station opened in town. And take care of the family house that passed on to him. Eventually Seth had to sell the gas station, and all the property that his father owned in the 80's. Times had changed, and he didn't want to try to keep up with the rest of the world. He had considered moving away since many of the town's people he grew up knowing, either died or moved themselves. The sale of his property left him with more than enough money to survive, or to do whatever he wanted. After so many more years of living in his rundown house, and in his dying town, he grew more bitter with each year, and his self-imposed isolation took its toll. He came to know that he didn't want to be bothered with people at all; especially after his father died. The one thing that really gave him pleasure was killing niggers, and when he still could, raping one was icing on the cake. But because of the way things are today he found himself changing how he went about satisfying his needs. His father always told him to stay informed about the law, and taught him how to cover his tracks so the police couldn't catch him.

To satisfy his need to kill. Seth would drive a few miles from his house on back roads, park his truck, and hike to a nearby highway with his rifles, and binoculars. There he would watch out for niggers driving down the freeway, and would try shooting out a tire on a car to either crash it, or he'd try shooting one in a moving car. It was hard shooting a speeding vehicle, but he learned to get good at it. He would do this once every few months, when the urge to kill became too strong to resist. Sometimes he'd get a vehicle to crash, or the driver would be able to control the car enough to pull over; and he'd shoot the driver in the head. It was always a rush to get a kill. Sometimes, he'd even see on the news reports of his shootings. This is why he'd constantly change locations, and kill less frequently, because it threw the police off. Sometimes years would go by without a kill. Seth thinks to himself, as he drinks a beer that he's getting too old for all the hiking through the woods, and carrying all his gear. I'm not a young man anymore. He tells himself. He looks at his gun case, he tells himself that he would love to go out one more time, and get one. He decides that maybe a little close in target practice, will satisfy his urge to kill. He walks over to the gun case, takes two semi-automatic handguns, and four boxes of ammunition, and places them in a back pack.

He opens a drawer and takes out a holster with a revolver inside, and clips it to his belt. He leaves his house through the back door, and walks to the creek behind his property.

It's a warm summer day and the sky is clear for miles. This is the perfect day for a killing he thinks to himself; too bad I can't get one today. It takes about twenty minutes to get down to the creek from his house these days. Since he's not in any hurry he smokes a cigarette while he walks, coughing all the way down the hill. He looks at the pack of smokes while he walks, and thinks about his father who he loved so much. Camels were his brand of cigarettes as well, smoking is something else his father turned him onto at an early age. As Seth nears the creek he sees a sight that freezes him in his tracks. He throws away the cigarette he's smoking, and takes out his binoculars. He brings them to his face and focuses on the sight before him. He sees five deer at the edge of the creek in a circle, and something appears to be in the middle of the group of animals. Seth zooms in with his binoculars, and sees what looks like a man, sitting in the middle of the animals at the edge of the creek. One large deer actually looks in his direction, as if it knows he's watching them. The animals all quickly take off running in different directions, and the man is left sitting by the water. When Seth gets a clear look at the man he becomes infuriated. Quickly Seth makes his way to the edge of the creek, with his revolver in his hand. He doesn't make any effort to quietly approach the man; he walks as fast as his aging legs can take him. When he reaches the man he stops about ten feet away from him. Drops his back pack, and levels the revolver at the back of his head. Seth feels that familiar sensation of a rush starting to build.

"Hey boy, you mind telling me just what the fuck you doing' on my goddamn property." Seth says to the man sitting by the water.

"I'm sorry friend I didn't mean to trespass I'll be on my way." The man responds as he starts to stand up.

"Stop where you are motherfucker." Seth fires a shot from his .38 off to the side at the man's feet, dirt from the bullets impact shoots in the air.

"Now since you want to be by my creek, get on your knees nigger facing the water, and stay your black ass right there. Seth orders the man. I didn't tell you to stand up nigger, you think I'm gonna give your black ass a chance to attack me. Trespass you did boy, and I have every right to blow your goddamned head off for being where you ain't wanted."

"Friend I mean you no harm, I was simply taking a walk in the forest, when I came upon the creek. I only wanted to sit for a while, and enjoy the sound of moving waters." The man says.

"Let's get a few things straight boy, I'm not your goddamn friend, I've never had a nigger friend, and I never will. I've killed niggers and fucked black whores my whole life. I hate you fuckers with everything in me, and I will till the day I die. I was just gonna come down here, and do a little target shootin' but now I guess I'll practice on your black ass."

"Have I committed such a great sin against you, that it warrants my death? Can you find it in your heart to forgive me, and allow me to leave your property?"

"Oh you'll get to leave nigger, just not the way you came, I'm gonna blow your fuckin' head off. It's been so long since I shot one of you. This is gonna feel almost as good as fuckin one of your black whores. The lord heard my prayers; he gave me a nigger to kill today, so you must be one sorry piece of shit."

"Our father in heaven doesn't grant such wishes my friend, you do not have to do this to me, please let me go, show that you can be compassionate." The man asks.

Seth aims his .38 at the man's left shoulder, and fires his weapon. The bullet hits him in the shoulder, and Seth sees a slash in the water; telling him the round passed through his shoulder. He makes no outcry of pain, but the man immediately grabs his injured shoulder with his right hand.

"That's about as much compassion as you gonna get boy. I thought I told you not to move nigger."

Seth shoots the man in his right shoulder. Again he makes no outward cry of pain. The bullet passes through his right shoulder, and splashes in the water.

"The next one's going in your head nigger. There ain't no one around here for miles to help your black ass, and nobody cares if you die today or tomorrow. Is there anything you wanna say before you die motherfucker?"

"Why must you do this?" I will not hurt you, and I will forgive you for wounding me. I beg you; find it in your heart to spare my life." The man pleads.

"Nigger I don't give a flying fuck if you forgive me or not. I'm sending your black ass straight to hell." Seth responds, and fires another shot into the man's left thigh. Again the man makes no outward cry of pain.

"I only wanted to enjoy the running waters, and for that I must die. Have you no mercy in your heart for a fellow human being?"

"Niggers ain't human beings boy, yall nothing but filthy fuckin animals, didn't you learn that in school boy."

Seth laughs, takes out his cigarettes with his free right hand, shakes one out of the pack and lights it. It is then that he notices something strange about the water in the creek. Something seems out of place then he realizes that the waters are still. The creek runs downhill, but the waters are no longer moving. He drops his cigarette then looks up, and down the length of the wide creek, and as far as he can see the waters are still, unmoving and silent. He looks at the kneeling man in front of him, and he becomes infuriated.

"Nigger what the fuck have you done to my goddamn creek?"

Seth shoots the man in his right thigh. This time there is no slash in the waters when the bullet strikes his leg.

"Oh, you're one of those tough niggers. why won't you scream boy! Why won't you beg for your worthless life nigger, I done put four holes in your sorry black ass!" Seth demands.

"Your father has filled your heart with so much hate, that you cannot see that the things you have done in your life, are beyond evil. Still I would forgive your sins, if you would take mercy on me." The man tells Seth.

"Nigger you don't know jack-shit about my father, now you done pissed me off now boy! I was gonna kill you quick, now I'm gonna make this last all day you filthy motherfucker!" Seth screams.

"You were not always this way, nor was your father before you, but you both chose to walk this path. Would you condemn the people of the world, and the children, what of the innocent children?"

"What about the fuckin' children, nigger I don't give a fuck about nobody but me, and I done shot little niggers in the head too; none of you mean shit to me. The rest of the fuckin world can go straight to hell for all I care." Seth angrily responds."

"I could stop you from killing me, but I will not interfere with your will. I implore you please choose to break this cycle of evil, before it is too late. Show me that man can change. By your willingness to spare my life, you save all humankind. The best of you are the newly born, and they are corrupted before they have a chance to succeed. They enter the world knowing only joy and peace, they carry within them seeds of greatness, but hate such as you were exposed to destroy that potential. The little ones have always been born with latent abilities that could turn your world into a paradise; it is adults like you who choose purgatory. You do not have to do this, there are so many millions like you in the world; it didn't have to be so."

The kneeling man raises his arms to shoulder level. With his palms out, and fingers pointing upward, and holds them there.

"I will give you a choice to not kill me Seth Carpenter, and purge the evil from the souls of all men, or kill me and you seal the fate of all mankind." He tells Seth.

"Boy I don't know what the fuck kind of religious shit you talkin about and I don't care. I told your black ass not to move, now you're just one more dead nigger."

Seth takes aim at the man's head, and smiles wide as he pulls the trigger. He sees the bullet impact the man's head. He expected that the body would fall forward into the water, but it doesn't. It's as still as a statue. Seth stands there looking at the back of the man's head. Then he looks at each of the places on the man's body, where he shot him.

Seth doesn't see any blood coming from any of the wounds. In fact Seth looks harder, and he doesn't see any wounds on the body at all. His mind tries to make sense of that, when he realizes that before he shot him in the head; he was called by his name. Seth thinks how the fuck could that nigger have known my name. Seth looks at the creek, and still the water is unmoving. It's as smooth and reflective as glass. He wants to walk to the water's edge, but now he's afraid to. He feels something is very wrong and a sense of dread comes over him. Seth looks at the man still on his knees, and his body slowly rises off the ground. Seth's heart starts to beat in his chest like a jackhammer. He wants to reach into his back pack to get another gun, but his body is frozen in place. He can't move a muscle as the man's legs straighten, and his body slowly rises higher off the ground. Then the suspended body rotates until Seth can see the man's face. Seth watches horrified as the eyes snap open, and they are pure white light. He watches frozen in sheer horror, as the head lowers slightly, and he feels the stare of those white eyes on his.

Seth wants to run, but he can't. He stares into the pure white eyes of the man he thought he killed, in his mind he sees certain events unfold. His body feels the pain of death, for everyone he's killed. Every adult killed, every child murdered. He feels the pain, and anguish of every woman he's raped and sodomized. He feels the anguish of every child whose parent was taken away by his actions. He experiences the agony of every vile act committed by his father. He witnesses every second of the death of his own mother; by his father's hands in vivid clarity. He watches as her head is continuously pounded against the floor. His father sits on her chest as he pounds her in the face with his fists, and he hears her plead for mercy, for him not to kill her. He watches as her face is turned into a bloody pulp and he screams. His body experiences instantly all the pain he has caused others, in his life time. He feels agonizing pain in his face and his screams continue. He feels something happening to his face, and the pain he feels amplifies. He reaches up to touch his eyes and his screams get impossibly louder. Seth is suffering pain no human could imagine. He touches his face and knows is eyes are what exploded out of his head, and still his screams continue.

It is I, who am keeping you alive, and your brain functioning Seth Carpenter. The voice you now hear in your tortured mind is that of the man you tortured, by shooting over and over with bullets. The man you refused to show the slightest bit of mercy. The pain and the agony you now see and feel is that which you have caused. By choosing to destroy my physical form you have condemned yourself to this fate. You and all men like you have abused your given right to choose. You no longer have that option, you and those like you are flawed creations Seth Carpenter, and thus you all forfeit your existence. There is no Heaven or Hell; those are the creations of man, to justify his actions in life. I am allowing your mind Seth Carpenter to create that which you are experiencing now. This is your own depiction, of the hell that you have believed in all your life. Now you know the true potential of the mind you were given, and have wasted. This is the purgatory to which you wanted to condemn me. The excruciating fires you feel now consuming your physical form will burn for as long as I allow it. Before I allow your energy to dissipate to nothingness, I will also allow you to see all that man has rejected. For I am the being who created humankind, and it was I who created all life as you know it in the beginning. I have accepted a measure of responsibility for man's evil ways, but no longer. With man's final rejection of me, and my physical death by his hands in your world, it heralds the coming of The Arrivals.

In a brilliantly blinding flash of light, the floating body blinks out of existence leaving what is left of Seth Carpenters body to burn to nothingness. After many minutes, it too fades away in fires that burn nothing but his body until the fire too is gone.

For a fraction of a second, conscious or asleep, everywhere around the world, every person on the planet hears, or thinks they hear a tiny voice in their mind that whispers, beware the coming of The Arrivals.

EPILOGUE

New Orleans, La

Angelica puts her sleeping baby boy Michael in his crib, and kisses his little face. As she turns to walk away Michael's eyes snap open, and they shine a pure white light. In his mind he hears a familiar voice. *"Wake up little one, it is now the time of The Arrivals."* Michael closes his eyes, and a smile forms on his face.